Dancing on the Ledge

DANCING ON THE LEDGE

Based on a true story

Carol Lynn Jones, MSW

Van Fossen Publishing   Martinsburg, WV

Printed in the United States of America

First Printing, 2021

ISBN: 978-1-7365514-0-0

Van Fossen Publishing
68 Ora Lee Court
Martinsburg WV 25404

This book is dedicated to the workers, especially single women with children, who are struggling to survive within this constrictive, inequitable, and exploitative Capitalist economic system.

Contents

Prelude

My childhood was a vacuous, lonely one. After I escaped the folds of my oppressively stern parents, the journey was fraught with blind wanderings, and reckless escapades. Consequently, I fell into all sorts of sordid scenes. Oh, I tried at first to hang on to the conservative middle-class expectations imprinted by my upbringing, but since most of those values were superimposed on me by an abusive mother, I didn't adopt them, and so, I really had no standards at all. I tried to hold on to a job, but before long unfamiliar, undeniable rumblings in my soul shattered my superficial identity, and I felt compelled toward experiences which would perhaps help determine just who in the world I was.

(Jesse, 1974)

Part One

The Mother's Story

t was a day in early spring when Louise arrived home from school, creaked-open the screen door and walked in to an unusually dark and quiet house. She waited. The sun was down by the time Herald, her father, brought her mother home. As was her father's taciturn way, he spoke few words, "Your mother is sick, Louise. You'll have to take care of her until she gets better."

Louise was eleven. She watched as her father left the room, and then she quietly made her way into the guest room. There lay her mother, Elizabeth, pale and still under the covers.

For the next few days, she washed pools of blood from the sheets. It seemed to Louise that her dear mother, who cooked, sewed, loved, and cared for her and her brother, was bleeding to death. Louise, who had never seen blood flow from her own private parts, was trying to soak up the stream gushing from between her mother's legs, trying to keep the blood from ruining the mattress. Hidden from the little girl's understanding was her mother's mind, splintered with silent screams, outraged at the atrocity committed against her by the husband she had honored, and the doctor, his conspirator in murder. Her mother lay in bed, struggling to stay alive, remaining as still as she could in hopes that the flood would finally stop.

In the year 1936, an anonymous man in a white coat (he may or may not have been a licensed physician) performed an abortion on an unsuspecting woman against her will and without her knowledge. She had hemorrhaged and almost died.

The blood did stop. Elizabeth did not die, but Louise sensed a change in her mother. Although she seemed to be recovering physically and gaining strength every day, it was as if something else had died. The anxiety and trauma had begun its insidious destruction of a human mind. The abortion of her unborn child, the humiliation, the realization that people could be so grotesque and unfair, and these thoughts left her no peace. Slowly at first, and then with alarming speed her perceptions of reality degenerated into an inescapable nightmare.

Louise had pieced together the horrible story from bits of conversation she had squeezed from the visits with her mother.

"Your father came into the kitchen where I was preparing green beans, handed me my coat and Sunday hat, and ushered me into the car, just saying that we had an appointment with the doctor for a checkup. Now I knew I was with child again for a third time, but I hadn't any reason to see a doctor yet, so I thought it was unusual for your father to act this way."

Within months of the abortion, Elizabeth was responding less and less to her environment, and still less, to her husband Herald. She had lapses of memory, and could be found sitting silently on a chair, or on the edge of the bed.

Herald, fabricating a story that his wife had tried to kill herself with Phenobarbital, was able to have her committed to Camarillo, a state mental institution. Elizabeth had always argued that she had done "no such thing," and Louise tended to believe her, since her mother's devout Christian faith, and eighth grade education imparted wariness about swallowing anything "foreign to the body." She had never seen her take anything, not even an aspirin.

The day Elizabeth was committed and transported by the state, Louise and Charles were unceremoniously taken away from their home and placed in foster care. At this time, it was commonly accepted that a single man could not possibly take care of two children, so it was relatively easy for Herald to accomplish this. After that Louise rarely heard from her father, not on her birthday nor holidays. She recalled how her mother had once said that he was "a cold man who should never have had children." Now, she truly understood what her mother had meant.

Brother and sister were separated and housed in wings on opposite sides of the institution for orphans. Charles, who was 2 years older than Louise and almost as timid, suffered as well. However, it was customary in those years to ignore or minimize the trauma caused to children by severing family ties. Orphanages festered with alienation, and problems with social adjustment always followed internment.

Louise was alone for her twelfth birthday, the first time away from her family and home. She thought about her mother often. During her stay at the orphanage, she wrote to her, but never received replies. Legally she was not allowed to visit until she turned twenty-one, nine years in the future. She took in ironing in order to earn money for shoes and other necessities.

One rare occasion nearly a year after her mother's commitment, the Director called for the little girl to get cleaned up for a visit from her father.

When he arrived, he did not speak much. He simply took Louise's hand, and led her to an open car door. There, sitting in the back seat, was her brother who had recently been staying with a foster family in town. Of course, Louise had not been told. Silently she endured a terrible pain and wondered why she was treated as if she didn't exist and didn't matter.

The three of them drove to the ice cream parlor for cones. Louise remembered that the ice cream, usually so sweetly coating her taste buds, had no flavor at all. Afterwards she was dropped off at the orphanage just as unceremoniously. It was the only visit she would get. Her father did not have time to attend to her needs. He was busy getting a divorce so he could marry his assistant, a pretty young nurse he had met while working as a pharmaceutical research chemist. It was a position that didn't require a college degree, only time as an apprentice under a professional.

To a child, love is laughter. But Louise had been born with a cleft palate, a big hideous gash running from her nostril down through her lip, and she knew that her smile was ugly. She was flawed, and her worth was suspect. She just did not have many reasons to be happy.

At sixteen, Louise legally left the institution to live on her own. She gave up the ironing board for the checkered floor of the local diner. Small of stature, and quick on her feet, she found that waiting tables gave her fast money, and a chance to meet people. A year later she met a guy running a cash register at a booth on the Santa Monica pier. He was sixteen, living at home with his mom and seven brothers. Bami, as everyone referred to the old matriarch, took Louise in when she became pregnant with her son's child. During Louise's eighth month of pregnancy, the man she had given her virginity to, the father of her baby, walked out of her life. "Devastated..." Louise once had remarked to her daughter, Jesse, that she couldn't handle it, being pregnant, and abandoned, "first by my father, and then by your father."

Being a constant reminder to her mother of the wrong that had been committed against her, Jesse became the receptacle for her mother's bitterness against her father, a man she had never met.

When Louise turned twenty-one, she signed her mother out of Camarillo State Hospital. Finally, she was able to legally take responsibility for her mentally ill mother. By then Elizabeth had been interned for ten long years full of shock treatments and experimental drugs for schizophrenia. Louise always believed that her mother had been railroaded. She thought it was quite possible that she wasn't even sick. The inexperienced but well-meaning Louise could not cope the first time that neighbors called to tell her that Elizabeth was walking in the hallway cursing, gesturing and threatening... no one in particular. She felt she had no choice except to call the state hospital. But after a short stay, shock treatments, and a new run of psychotropic drugs, the psychiatrists assured Louise that her mother was much improved and would be easier to manage in the community if she wanted to sign her out again.

Louise rented a wood-sided beach efficiency for her mother. It was painted white and sat along a sheltered walkway about a block from the sand in Ocean Park. Elizabeth seemed happy and able to live independently. She took to the task of watching the three-year-old Jesse whenever her daughter waitressed. It was something to do. Those long years behind the locked doors of the institution had drained Elizabeth, but she promptly developed a dependable attentiveness towards the child, having had her own maternal years cut short. Unfortunately, the schizophrenia had noticeable effects on the woman. Odd preoccupations, weird gestures, and at times nonsensical mumblings, left Jesse wondering.

"Why do you do that with your hands," she would ask.

"You wouldn't understand," was the only answer she ever got.

One afternoon toward the end of summer Elizabeth grabbed the little girl's hand so that they could go down to the beach to jump the waves. It was one of their favorite pastimes. The late afternoon sun dipped behind the gray clouds of the storm coming in from the Pacific. The wind whipped the waves, and the two of them jumped and laughed with abandon. Then they jumped right in the middle of a huge jellyfish. Jesse felt its slippery substance all the way up her legs. Her grandma reacted quickly, backed up and away from the blob in the surf, and ran the sandy block to their house. Jesse cried all the way there from the stinging.

Another accident left Louise skeptical about her mother's competence. Jesse was in the garden at the side of the house when she decided that she wanted her wagon that hung high above her on a nail in the wooden fence that separated the closely spaced houses. Being impatient she tugged, succeeded in bending the nail, and the wagon came down on her, metal piercing the tender skin of her forehead. A stream of red flowed.

Elizabeth came running. To stop the bleeding, she pressed a clean hanky against the gash. They traveled by bus to a clinic where the doctor gave the injury two stitches that would melt, with time, into Jesse's growing body.

When Louise had the opportunity to move her mother into the same apartment building where she and Jesse lived, she took it. A basement apartment, one big room, modestly furnished with an icebox near the door (to save the iceman additional steps). It would be convenient to have Elizabeth close by to babysit, and it would be easier for Louise to supervise her activities.

Jesse spent more time with her grandma than with her mother, days learning to knit and how to time hard-boiled eggs. Jesse felt sheltered and nurtured until the day her grandmother ran out through the front door into the hallway shouting, "You sons of bitches. I hear you talking about me. You better shut up or I'll shut you up!"

She didn't stop, and she couldn't be quieted. Jesse had never seen her grandma act that way.

Shortly after that, Louise checked her mother back into the sanitarium permanently.

Part Two

The Child's Story

Dance is an elusive art, and its sister, Music. They are not like paint and canvass—solid, tangible, able to be revisited, reviewed, scrutinized and held up for a consensus judgment. Of all the arts, dance is the most fleeting; it moves. It dares the viewer to catch the ever-changing vision and its trace nuances. (Jesse, 1974)

esse had always danced, well at least from that fortuitous moment when the babysitter taught her how to do The Bop. The minute Marsha grabbed Jesse's hand and showed her how to use her weight to counterbalance her partner's, the little girl was hooked. The next day when Jesse attended kindergarten, during lunchtime she showed her classmates, any who would watch, the little swing step she and Marsha had practiced. It was the beginning of a love affair with her muse, The Dance.

The year was 1952. Jesse's newly married parents liked to attend 'the movies' one night a week. Hiring Marsha to watch the little girl was convenient since she lived less than a block away, and additionally she was mature for her sixteen years. Jesse was sensitive, smart and alert, but abused and neglected. The bit of attention given to her by the babysitter perhaps made a difference, an elusive difference that cannot always be traced. The kindness given in those two hours was perhaps the discounted or missed gesture that weighs significantly in a person's development, where the forces of life and death are stacked unfairly, and one cherished child is brought up in a nurturing home environment, while another is not.

But before Clayton married Louise the abuse had been worse. Louise would erupt for any unpredictable reason, and Jesse was always the target. When her mother set angry eyes upon her, Jesse genuinely believed that she wanted her dead.

Like any four-year old, Jesse liked to run and jump. But since they had lived on the second floor of the apartment building, Louise had been overly concerned that the noise might bother the neighbors downstairs directly underneath their living room. After warning Jesse about the noise, she came home one afternoon and, mistaking the child's jubilance for rebellion (Jesse was routinely locked in the apartment for the four hours that her mother was waitressing at the diner), marched her down the outside stairs to the backyard of the building, and ordered her to pick a switch from under the ancient and unmanaged tree that stood there.

The little girl screamed as her mother swiped at her bare legs once or twice before commencing in full when they were away from eyes and ears behind the closed apartment door.

That evening she crept quietly down the hallway of the apartment building, stepped inside the bathroom shared by the residents of that floor, and turned the latch. While sitting in the soothing warm water of the community bathtub, she inspected the stripes on her legs, especially the skin where the tip of the switch had completed its arc. Blood blisters were forming; tears and snot mixed with the bath water. No one heard her crying.

Being an intelligent child, she quickly adapted to her mother's demands. She could be seen oddly walking around the apartment, and in the hallway on her way to the bathroom, in a hunched up and over position. On closer inspection, one could see that the little girl was learning to walk silently on the balls of her feet. Her habit became crystallized and so obvious that her new stepfather asked why she was walking so weird. He coached her in attaining proper posture, and probably saved her from years of ridicule.

Once Louise started dating her husband-to-be, she seemed to forget Jesse was there. This break in her mother's reproach gave rise to her wandering. Sometimes she walked as far as she could go in her neighborhood, so far that she could barely hear Louise screaming for her.

Taking her rubber beach ball, which was almost as large as her, she bounced it down the stairway of the old apartment building out onto the paved sidewalk. Being only four years of age, Jesse lost control and it shot across the residential street. Without hesitating she darted from behind a parked car only to put herself directly in front of a shiny car with lots of chrome bumpers. Jesse turned toward the car and as if to stop it, she put out her tiny

11

hand in cross-guard defiance. The car stopped where the chrome touched her fingers. It was years before she understood that it was fortune and the driver's keen eyes that had saved her from being hit, not her own power.

A day at the beach was inexpensive entertainment for the working classes, and Louise was a sun worshipper who slathered on olive oil and baked on her towel in the salty white Santa Monica sand. It was just such a day when the little girl and her mother were out. Jesse nudged her mother and, pointing her finger, said a little too loudly, "Look at that girl over there." The girl was on crutches dragging her useless legs along, probably a victim of Cerebral Palsy. This was the first time in Jesse's short life that she had ever seen such a thing.

Smack! Jesse's tiny hand stung with the slap. Startled and hurt, she tried to figure out what she had done wrong.

"Don't you ever stare or point at someone who has a handicap," Louise spit out the rebuke as if in answer to Jesse's bewilderment.

That day Jesse learned another valuable lesson from her mother. *Keep your eyes closed to the world. Your curiosity and awareness are bad and without value.*

Scolded if she spoke and banished to her room, it became a refuge from the daily rejection. She learned to be quiet, her ideas and thoughts equally without merit or consideration. She stayed in her bedroom reading, or she could sit outside in a screened porch area and mold with her play dough. Alone in her room, she assembled a jig-saw puzzle, the still-life finished picture, an empty and frozen dark room where slivers of sunlight shine through the blinds upon a sleeping terrier dog, a metaphor of her own young life.

School gave her a needed reprieve from the isolation and solitude of her life at home. But social skills, like communication and empathy, did not come easily for Jesse because once the school bell rang, she went back home to the oppressive atmosphere of silence and austerity.

As Jesse continued to be victimized by her mother's routine outbursts of rage, she was made to believe that she was the reason for her mother's unhappiness. As much as Jesse might try, she was unable to please her. Most of the time, she was unable to get any acknowledgment at all, unless it was criticism. Jesse's hair, her teeth, and her breath, all were below standard to unacceptable. Subtle physical abuse began almost unnoticeably when she was young. Louise grabbed Jesse's upper arm, digging her fingernails into her daughter's tender flesh, and lifting her off the ground at a street corner if Jesse wasn't quick enough by her mother's judgment. Looking at the half-moons swelling on her tender pale underarm, she felt hated. Childhood with its innocence and laughter did not exist in this household. Jesse knew she was defective, as well as guilty, for her inability to meet her mother's expectations. Attempts to be silly or funny were met with disapproving sternness; no spontaneous outbursts were tolerated. It was robbery, a stolen childhood.

Even so, Jesse managed to have a friend from her class at school who lived across the street. One day she followed Kathy, along with two visiting cousins. The girls decided to walk around the neighborhood and were called over by an old man sitting on his porch. He had a plate of cookies, and since it was mid-morning, we were all ready for a snack. As the others took cookies and followed him into the kitchen to get glasses of milk, Jesse stayed back on the threshold of the front door. Coming back through into the living room, the man sat down on a big chair and called Jesse over.

"Come here," he coaxed the little girl. "I bet you'd like a horsey ride," crossing his legs so he could provide a saddle on the crook of his ankle. Jesse's seven-year-old sensibility told her to leave. She turned and ran out of the house, down the porch steps, back home two blocks away.

DNA and Dance

*D*ancing enchanted Jesse from the first time she saw Gene Kelly gliding across a stage on the black and white TV screen in front of her. The connection was instantaneous, energy vibrating from somewhere deep within herself and unavoidable. For the duration of minutes that those images danced on Jesse's retina, she was transformed, altered, and transported to this joyous musical play land where adults sang and gazed with love. Children danced and peals of laughter encircled them like doves.

DNA from both sides of Jesse's family predisposed her to being a dancer. Her paternal grandfather Eno Seaton and his wife emigrated from Europe and then as a vaudeville husband and wife dance team, they added Mc to their name ostensibly to add selling power to their act. At the time, the Irish were popular on the vaudeville circuit. Changing one's name in order to enhance the audience's appreciation, and perception of your act and to increase marketability was, and still is, employed in the entertainment business. However, there were other family stories. One that said as German Jews, altering one's name was the quickest, most expedient way to integrate into the existing social scene, here in America. They danced until, saddled with seven sons, the McSeaton's landed in California.

On her mother's side the Wyandot ancestors could be traced many generations back through birth and death certificates. The centuries-long dancing culture of the Hurons and then Wyandots, the impulse and need to dance, the desire of indigenous humans to punctuate every life experience with dance, this gene had been passed on to Jesse.

Watching tap dancers and baseball was American. Dictated by Hollywood and the persuasive media, they became national pastimes. Like so many southern California residents, Jesse's mom was smitten by movies and their illustrious representatives, the actors and actresses who lived in styles of nobility just a few miles inland from her beach town. Possibly intent on molding her child into another Shirley Temple, she enrolled Jesse in a combination tap and acrobatics class at Brownie Brown's School of Dance. Whatever the reason, she did not discuss it with Jesse. Like every other part of her existence, she was not consulted. She was not a person, but rather an extension of her mother, a puppet. She was expected to do exactly as she was told, and not to talk back.

Frightened at first, then class by class Jesse began to experience a sense of happiness not present anywhere else in her empty life, not in school and certainly not at home. Learning to dance was fun. She had to remember the steps, the beats, the counts, and how to hold her head, arms and hands; and where to look when she turned. Her tap teacher saw that she had a natural aptitude for dancing. Jesse was asked to help some of the slower students, and other times asked to demonstrate a dance phrase for the entire class. It was the only place during those two formative years that Jesse received attention and positive feedback—the dance studio, with its promise of the recital stage and then beyond since many of Brownie's students had made the jump to Hollywood.

The television became a window into life's possibilities; it was her companion for two hours after school every day. Between the time she got home and her mother's arrival from work, Jesse felt free.

One channel aired the same movie every day after school for a week at a time. For a month, the many musicals of the forties starring Jesse's favorite's, Fred Astaire and Ginger Rogers, were being shown. She knew she had a list of after-school chores that were supposed to be completed before her mother arrived home each day. Emptying the trash could be a disgusting and eye-opening experience, especially since she discovered a moving mass of maggots under the lid. Her awareness grew quickly.

On this weekday, Jesse ran straight for the television and excitedly turned the knob until it clicked on. *Carefree* was on, a romantic musical that drew her in with its dancing, songs, and magic. She was vigilant, jumping up to work on her chores during the commercials. But the sink was filled to the brim with dishes and pans, and she had underestimated the amount of time it would take for her to finish. Jesse panicked when she heard the key in the door.

"Jesse, where are you?" The accusing voice rang out.

"Right here, mother. I'm just finishing the dishes," she offered weakly.

"What do you mean? You're still working on them?"

Jesse's voice faltered sensing this was not going to be considered a small infraction. "I didn't get them done yet."

Her mother's shift from regular person into a screaming banshee happened lightning fast.

"So, you think you don't have to mind me anymore?" She came through the kitchen door menacingly.

"No, I don't think that." Jesse's heart was beating wildly like a cornered animal.

"Then why aren't your chores done?" Louise's stare was piercing.

She didn't have an answer, she was paralyzed with fear. Her mother took this silence for insolence and stepped forward. Jesse flinched, expecting a blow.

"Jesse you are getting too old to spank. Do you know what happens to children who don't mind their parents? They go somewhere else where they learn to mind. They go to the orphanage." Her delivery was perfectly severe, perfectly clear. "Jesse, go pack your suitcase. I'm going to call for the welfare worker to come and pick you up."

Blindsided, as if struck, Jesse fell to her knees in front of her mother crying, "Please, no. I'll be good, I'll mind you."

She grabbed her mother's shoes in supplication. "Please, don't send me away," she begged hysterically.

Suddenly Jesse's small mistake had become a huge life-changing transgression. Her miscalculation of time had a horrible deeper meaning. To her mother it meant something more sinister. The appearance of this stubbornness was a threat to her mother's own precarious self-esteem. She required total compliance and submission in order for her to feel OK.

Jesse watched her mother go through the motions of calling and talking to someone on the telephone. Her throat constricted, and her sobs were unrelenting.

"Go to your room." Jesse jumped to do her mother's bidding like she had been shocked.

After twenty minutes in her room with the door closed, Louise walked in, and Jesse ran to throw her arms around her.

"Mommy!" She hadn't used the diminutive in years.

"I'm going to give you one more chance to straighten-up." With that she turned, and left the room, closing the door behind her.

The storm had passed. Jesse was exhausted and stayed in her bedroom listening to the muffled voices of Clayton her stepfather and her mother. Looking around at the walls of her bedroom and then laying back on her bed she tried to imagine what it would be like to live in an orphanage, remembering descriptions somewhere in her young head. She didn't have a clear picture, but drifting into a fitful sleep, she knew that she would rather live here. At least it was familiar.

The next day, Jesse began to speak to herself. The voice arose like a silent mantra to keep her from ever making another mistake that might result in her being sent away. *I'm a bad girl. I'm a bad girl. I'm a bad girl. I'm a bad girl.*

Now Jesse was clear, she understood that she had no value, and was expendable. It was then that she began to have a recurring dream. She never told anyone about it, though it disrupted her sleep frequently.

It is dusk; dark clouds are heavy in the sky. The air is wet with humidity. The fenced yard is rutted, wild and full of boulders, and patches of impassable briars. Little Jesse is running from a man with an ax. He looks like an old farmer with a straw hat. He is gaining on her; she can smell his body warmth and odor right before he lunges. He slices her in two straight through her skull. Then she wakes up.

Lacking any opportunity for self-rule, Jesse struggled to thrive, to forge an identity of her own apart from that of her iron-willed mother. Into her teens, her mother chose her clothes, and limited her access to social events. The excuse she used most often for isolating her daughter was her poor health; recurrent hypochondria that took the form of sudden overwhelming maladies, undiagnosed fibromyalgia, heart palpitations, arthritis flare-ups, and various other persistent or recurring complaints. These 'attacks' disrupted the family's routine and required everyone's complete attention to her needs no matter how insignificant they seemed. She had trained everyone including her husband to cater to her.

Jesse's weeks consisted of school, homework, dishes, and bed. Weekends she was mother's maid and housekeeper. Louise required that the house be thoroughly vacuumed and dusted, and without warning would extend the chores to washing the windows inside and out. Upon one occasion, it rained shortly after Jesse finished the task, and was informed that she would have to do the outsides again.

For two years Saturday dance class was the one place Jesse felt happy. Time for herself during the walk to and from the studio, and the two thirty-minute classes sustained her and gave her a sense that much was possible. Jesse trained for tap dancing and acrobatics. She participated in the processes of choreography, learning the routine, rehearsals, dress rehearsals, and then the recital.

She could see the stage in her future. It was where she belonged.

Then without warning her mother announced that she would not be attending dance classes any longer. The tears rushed to burn Jesse's eyes as she heard her mother's decree.

Louise spit out her criticism. "You don't appreciate the classes. I never see you practice."

She didn't dare defend herself, but it wasn't true. Jesse did practice every night and morning. While she was in bed, right before she drifted off to sleep, she would pretend that her fingers were her legs; she would repeat the steps; shuffle, ball, change, flap, hop, step. It was her way of making sure she remembered what she had learned. When she was outside playing, she would find a place on the huge grassy courtyard surrounding the apartments where they lived, and practice the handstands, backbends, and summersaults her teacher demonstrated each week. Her mother and stepdad were never around to see it.

Jesse didn't know how to fight for what she wanted. Repeated doses of her mother's rage had trained her to be passive and helpless. She accepted the verdict, the dancer in her retreated.

Jesse learned why the dance lessons stopped. Louise was determined to save enough money for a down payment on a house. She had just given birth to a son and told her husband that they needed a house of their own, and an extra bedroom.

Without her Saturday routine at the dance studio Jesse felt restless. On one such occasion, she wandered down the alley behind her apartment building. The neighborhood was quiet. No one was around. At the end of someone's dirt driveway, over at one side was a tall tree. As she approached it, she could see that someone had constructed a rickety ladder leading up the trunk to a platform high above the rooftops. Up she went, her thin body easily navigating the shaky structure. At the top she reached the makeshift landing. There she stood. The broken railing of two by twos hung crooked. She did not lean on it. From this height she felt above and beyond all recriminations and pain. The silence was broken only by the waves of wind whistling through the leaves. To the little girl, the tree house was a safe place. She visited this avian sanctuary a few more times before they moved from the neighborhood.

Jesse was used to spending time alone and not being noticed. One day on the school yard Jesse inadvertently discovered an orgasm at the top of a tether-ball pole. Somehow the ball and rope had wrapped itself in a knot at the top. So, the tomboy quickly shimmied up the pole using her inner thighs and pulling her petite body up arm over arm. Reaching the apex, Jesse unknowingly grabbed the pole even tighter as her young mound with its secret button rubbed the pole in her effort to retrieve the ball. She described it to herself as 'a nasty feeling' pulsing up from her prepubescent groin.

Her parent's new house was within walking distance of the Pen-Mar playground. It beckoned with its clubhouse, billiards, rings, and gymnastic equipment. By now she was eleven and loved to test her strength by shimmying up the tallest poles of the parallel rings.

Indiscretions and Betrayal

ourteen years old, Jesse's puberty came like a vengeance, her body suddenly strange to her.

Boys in the neighborhood wanted to get to know her. She exuded sex although she was innocent of experience. She liked to masturbate. Jesse found a way of simulating the pressure and motion of climbing the pole by straddling the corner of her dresser, holding her body with her taut arms and rocking until she achieved a climax. It was one of those times on a hot summer night that she heard a snapping sound outside of her open bedroom window. It didn't seem unusual; there were cats in the neighborhood.

Junior high school was demanding, and Jesse was getting familiar with the new surroundings and trying to make friends. It was early in the week and Jesse had been studying a chapter in human physiology when she called to her stepdad.

"Clayton, can you help me for a minute?"

Clayton came into her room where Jesse was standing, holding the textbook open to a diagram.

"Can you tell me where the floating rib is? I can see where it is in the picture, but I was wondering if I could feel it?"

With both of her hands occupied, Clayton reached up under her gray sweatshirt. "Let me see if I can find it," he said with no hint of his intent.

He stroked his hand across her belly, and then in one smooth move fondled and squeezed her breast and nipple.

"Whoops, that's not it," he chuckled to make light of the 'accident'.

For a moment Jesse could not register what her stepdad had just done. She moved to put down the book to free her hands. As she did, they both heard the front door open. Louise was home from shopping. Not a word was said as Clayton left Jesse's room to greet his wife.

Jesse's face burned with embarrassment. She quietly closed the door. From that time forth, she was on her guard. It disgusted her to think that he had touched her. Her repulsion grew when two weeks later, while she was vacuuming, Clayton jumped out from the hallway as if to kid with her. Scared, Jesse dropped to the floor as was her reaction when her mother beat her. Then he wrestled her over onto her back in horseplay. Lying on top of her, he made a buzzing sound in her ear. She could feel his penis dragging on her leg from the opening in his flannel bathrobe.

"Stop it, get off of me!" Jesse flipped her head and struggled to roll to the side to avoid his advances.

Clayton got up and pulled her up with him.

"Oh, don't be so sensitive. I was just kidding with you."

Although Jesse had not felt life-threatened, still the experience of having this grown man on top of her, against her will, had left her shaken. Apparently, it was all just clean fun to him.

Minimizing the offense of his indiscretions, he remarked with a smile on his face, "Jesse, your mom has been so mean to me lately. She is so angry all the time, and she won't let me touch her," and then jokingly added, "I thought about coming in and getting in bed with you."

"That's not funny," Jesse replied curtly.

He betrayed her. This man, who had won her heart at age six by taking her to the movies on Saturdays before he and her mother had wed, and had occasionally shown her some attention, now was stalking her.

Jesse became hyper-vigilant in protecting her privacy. She closed her windows regardless of the heat. She took notice of sounds outside her door and window when she was left alone in the house with him. In one instance she recognized the sound of her stepfather's creaking knees. To verify what she believed he was doing, she opened her door and searched the house. He was not there. He had been outside her window peeping in at her.

For the next year Jesse stayed clear of him. She talked to him only when it was necessary and avoided any kind of solicitous behavior. He couldn't be trusted. The person he pretended to be didn't exist.

Like toxic fumes that need venting to prevent explosions and damage, Jesse too needed to vent. The perfect opportunity came when her mother arranged a rare outing at the beach with the daughter of a friend. Fifteen-year-old Jesse was delirious, excited to spend time with a potential friend.

Somewhere between the hamburgers, and ice-cream cones, during the sandy trek to the stand, or lying close on beach towels, Jesse's long-denied desire for communication and companionship compelled her to relate the entire story of Clayton's pedophilic inclinations toward her. Her new friend was quiet during the discourse but lost no time in relating all that she had heard to Louise.

Jesse was accustomed to feeling the pressure mount in the household right before her mother's rampages. This time was different. She waited only long enough to see the girl drive off with her parents, and then she attacked.

"What is wrong with you?" Louise screamed. "How dare you make-up those horrible stories about Clayton. He has been the most wonderful father, and good to you. And this is how you repay him?"

Her mother's nastiness ripped through her. She felt guilty for betraying the code of silence that she had unconsciously followed. She had not meant for the disclosure to go any further than her friend. Now she faced the full fury of her mother's wrath as she accused Jesse of lying.

The turmoil eventually subsided, and in its place an uneasy homeostasis. There were no further discussions about the truth of the story, nor was Clayton confronted. Instead, he was protected by silence and routine. In time, it was as if it nothing ever happened.

Jesse shifted her attention away from the unfairness and dysfunction in her house to a boy who lived across the street; he was eighteen. Always the perfect gentleman around her parents, Han won their trust and was allowed to take Jesse on dates in his car. Not wanting to violate her virginity, it was with Han that Jesse was initiated into the delight of cunnilingus. They went to drive-in's but rarely watched the screen. Jesse learned to be evasive when her mother questioned her about the movie's content. Han planned to marry Jesse, but her family moved to another house, and they stopped seeing each other.

Don't Go Too Far

*D*uring the summer of Jesse's sixteenth birthday, she took a job as a maid at the Bel Air Hotel where her mother worked as a waitress. Louise thought that the summer work would be good for Jesse, and besides, she wanted help buying new curtains for Jesse's bedroom. The work was mundane, cleaning bathrooms and changing bed linens, however here she was in the bedrooms of the entertainment industry. She noticed that Carl Sandburg, who read the newspapers from front to back, left them scattered on the floor next to his bed.

She would knock with her master key and announce, "Housekeeping, May I come in?"

Most of the time there would be silence. However, on occasion, the silence meant the renters did not hear her. When she walked in on an entire family getting ready for the pool, naked family members of every age, because they did not bother to answer her knock, the father's response was, "Don't worry about her; she's used to it." Yet nothing could have been farther from the truth. She was a virgin in mind and body despite her late-night drive-in discoveries with Han.

Though extraordinarily pretty, Jesse's friendliness and lack of self-importance helped her fit right in with the other maids and the kitchen help with whom their department interacted hourly. The maids routinely telephoned the kitchen for clean-up, and a waiter was dispatched to whisk away the dishes on the rolling carts. One waiter caught Jesse's attention. He was short and muscular like a gymnast; with black hair and black eyes; eyes that also had not missed the young new housekeeping recruit.

They began eating lunch together. Ozzie was not a U.S. citizen and spoke English with a thick German accent, but he was easily understandable. Jesse was instantly attracted and soon they began stealing kisses in the hotel rooms when she called the kitchen for clean-up.

Since he was twenty-three, Jesse's mother was less-than-happy with their 'friendship', but after meeting with him and giving him a lecture about the privilege of dating her underage daughter, Ozzie was permitted to take Jesse for an all-day date horseback riding. What registered in her memory about that date was the grip of her hands violently holding on to the horn of the saddle so as not to fall among the bushes, bramble, rocks, and boulders, while her male horse galloped unrelentingly behind Ozzie's female horse. At the end of the day, she limped away with a bloody sore rubbed raw on the inside of her ankle the size of a silver dollar. Before taking her home, at Jesse's request Ozzie parked the car a few blocks from her house so that they could make-out. Ozzie's hands were all over Jesse's full teenage breasts. Jesse felt the heat, pleasure, bliss, and sense of being wanted, the same wonderful feelings she had had when she dated Han. Surely, this was love.

The two of them carried on while they worked at the hotel and planned to go on another date the upcoming weekend. Jesse's mother gave her stamp of approval, and they drove off to a near-by bowling alley. When they had bowled a game, Ozzie asked Jesse if she wanted to come over to see his place. It wasn't far from her parent's house. They snuggled and laughed hand-in-hand as they climbed the stairs to his one-bedroom apartment where they sat on his couch, kissing passionately, and listened to a Peter, Paul and Mary album. The record finished; Jesse knew she had better not be late arriving home. Ozzie reluctantly drove her home. Before opening the car door, Jesse cryptically mentioned that she would visit him later tonight.

She donned fire-engine red nylon baby doll nighties that her mother had given her at Christmas, slipped on her gray sweats over them, and true to her word set out into the night after the family had gone to sleep, carefully closing the screen door without a sound. Ozzie's place was at least a mile away, but this was no challenge to Jesse who often went out running at night in her neighborhood.

Ozzie opened the door rubbing sleep from his eyes.

"What... How did you get here?" He asked as he stepped back to allow her in.

"I ran... I told you I would see you later," she answered with lusty enthusiasm.

They resumed their place on the couch. Their passionate tongue-kissing, and Jesse's yielding nature led Ozzie to undress her, slipping the sweatshirt up and over her head. He saw what she was wearing and pulled her closer so he could lay her back. Jesse had never touched a penis. She had seen her stepfather's when he routinely exposed himself to her and had felt Han's erect penis through his pants when they kissed. She had seen her nine-year-old brother dragged out of bed by her mother and mocked and humiliated because of his erect penis. But she had no desire to touch one. She felt stupid and awkward when Ozzie directed her hand to feel his. It was stiff and smooth; it seemed huge, though she had no experience of others with which to compare.

As he continued the foreplay, he had discarded her pants, and was freely enjoying every crease, curve, and cavity.

"Come with me, Jesse." He led her willing tender virginal body to the sacrificial bed. She held on to Ozzie's hand like a little girl, trusting and spell bound. He was her knight; she loved him.

The sheets were cold and crisp, and Ozzie was quick to get his pants off and place himself on top of her.

"You are so beautiful. Please, let me lay between your legs. That's all I want." He pleaded with her.

Jesse did not see the harm and opened her legs. Ozzie intensified his kissing, her tongue and his dancing in and out of each other's wanting mouths, his cock swollen and rubbing against her tight stomach and pubic bone. Then he dropped down to suck her inflated nipples, the tip of his penis brushing her vaginal opening. He stopped moving and said to Jesse, "Let me put it in just a little bit."

"I'm a virgin, please, don't go too far," Jesse panted trying to slow him down, trying in vain to turn her assailant into an ally.

Ozzie answered, "I won't go too far, I won't go too far..." his voice encouraging as she relaxed her thigh muscles.

With one thrust his pole ripped through her hymen. Jesse screamed in pain like she had been stabbed with a knife. Ozzie jumped up and saw the blood on his penis.

"Oh crap! I didn't know you were a virgin."

"I told you I was."

"Yeah, but you don't kiss like you're a virgin."

Jesse headed for the bathroom to sit on the toilet. She was fairly sure she wasn't a virgin anymore.

Ozzie called through the door, "Are you alright in there?"

"Yes, can you drive me home?" Feeling sick and a bit dizzy, she hoped there wouldn't be any argument.

"Sure, I can do that."

When she emerged dressed, Ozzie was attentive.

"Do you want to go home now?"

"Yes."

In the car Ozzie assured Jesse that he loved her and did not in any way want to hurt her. He thought she was sexually experienced, "And then when you showed-up at my door at one in the morning in those red baby-doll pajamas, I thought you knew what you were doing, for sure."

"That's ok; I just don't want to see you again, right away." Jesse replied self-consciously.

"No problem, I understand. We'll see each other at work."

Ozzie dropped her off without ceremony a few blocks from her house and she walked the rest of the way. It was around three a.m. She snuck in the door and crawled in bed.

The following day was Sunday, but Clayton never allowed her to sleep-in. She stayed in her room, and pretended to read, all the while replaying the night experience not realizing that she had been raped. To her, he was her boyfriend and what happened last night was a result of miscommunication, her childish mind not able to encompass the mind of a predator. She was an innocent, believing in love, needing of attention, and vulnerable to those she encountered who could read her.

Jesse bathed early that evening, and then took a close look with a mirror at her vagina. There was some blood coagulated at the opening. She put on a sanitary napkin and went to sleep. Around two in the morning, Jesse awoke with the feelings of warm liquid between her thighs. Sitting on the toilet she watched a steady drip of blood until the toilet water was dark red. With a towel between her legs, she went to awaken her mother.

"Mom, I'm sorry to wake you up, but last week I slipped and straddled a tub I was cleaning, and I think I hurt myself. I'm bleeding and it won't stop."

"Well, you're not gushing, are you?" She asked sarcastically.

"No." Then as she stepped back out of the room, she could feel something let loose inside of her. She ran to sit and passed a big blood clot. Frightened she went back into the bedroom to tell her mom what had happened. The bleeding had subsided, and her mother agreed to take her to the doctor the next day.

Following the exam, Jesse told the entire story to the doctor.

"You can't tell my parents. If you do, I'll run away. We already don't get along." Perhaps Jesse emphatic tone convinced him. To her knowledge, he never broke that confidentiality.

The Muse Returns

*D*ance found its way back into Jesse's life when she reached high school. She had the opportunity to substitute modern dance for the regular gym class, so for the next three years she danced! Ms. Roberts, the dance teacher, was an old bull-dyke with short, trimmed hair, and a stocky build trained in stage dancing and vaudeville. She took Jesse under her wing nurturing, guiding, and training her. She advocated for her dancers, and found ways to collaborate with the school drama department and shop in re-creating classics like Brigadoon, and Shangri-La. When Jesse tried out for the dance parts, she was always chosen. Jesse loved the stage, the costumes, and the attention. Oddly, the attention she received dancing did not translate into popularity around school. Jesse was odd, shy, socially inept, and a mediocre student.

She graduated from Venice High school, and after taking the written entry exam for UCLA, she was accepted. This pleased her mother who demanded that she attend the more prestigious college, rather than Santa Monica city college, Jesse's first choice. Compounding the pressure, she found the campus culture distracting and its flow of students intoxicating to her senses.

First Taste of Autonomy

outhern California was having its Indian summer, and the temperatures remained warm, even at night. Just seventeen, she had enrolled in a grueling schedule with a class load and assignments that were exceedingly difficult for the undisciplined girl. Not yet realizing the intensity and amount of work to be accomplished, Jesse sat enjoying the sunlight and shadows under the eaves of a stone archway. She turned her attention to people-watching. Students filed along the open corridors and streamed quickly to their destinations while others stopped between the pillars to catch-up with news. She noticed two long-hair dudes talking to each other nearby on the grass 'quad'. Although Jesse had been extremely timid in high school, her new identity as an independent college student, boosted by a rush of teen hormones, motivated her to walk up to them. She started talking to the one with dark wavy locks and before long she was responding to a dare he made by agreeing to meet him in Ocean Park that evening at midnight. In order to pull it off, she would have to sneak out of the house, and take her parent's car without waking them.

That night Jesse went to bed with her clothes on. She told herself that she had walked the neighborhood many times well after curfew, so this was almost the same. She crept from her bedroom toward the dining room. There she quietly coaxed the keys out of her mother's purse that she

35

always left sitting on the table. With elation and fear pumping adrenaline, she eased her body outside of the squeaking screen door and tiptoed down the driveway to the curb where the Pontiac was parked. If she were caught, she would be skinned alive and strung up for all disobedient teenagers to see. But for the moment, her need to meet-up with this gorgeous long-haired guy outweighed her fear and eclipsed her ability to think rationally.

That morning at school he had given her the Ocean Park address, and now at 2 a.m. in the glow of the streetlights, Jesse cruised slowly looking for it. After driving around the block once, she found a corner spot, relieved that she didn't have to parallel park, having never done it in the dark. She turned the key in the ignition and sat in the quiet car looking toward the building with the apartment number she had committed to memory. The perfume of honeysuckle drifted in the open car window as she collected her composure, opened the heavy door and boldly walked up to the steep wooden stairway.

"Is Jim here?" she asked with anticipation, looking past the guy at the door to the candle lit room beyond.

"Yeah, come on in."

Jim rescued her at the door and immediately put his arm around her like she was the center of his universe. He possessed charisma, an ability to focus entirely on the energy of the moment.

"Hey, you made it!"

"I told you I would," she boasted. Then with less bluster, "I've never taken the car without my parents' permission before."

He laughed, obviously not worried about her terrible infraction.

"Jesse, that's your name, right? Me and the guys are going down to the canals. Do you want to come along?"

"Sure!" Jesse was a beach girl and knew her way around Venice, Ocean Park, and Santa Monica; they were her back yard stomping grounds.

After one stop on the way to invite his friend, Ray, they pulled into a carport. During the sixties, the houses on the canals were low-rent and with the comfort of the captured ocean lapping just a few feet from the house, they attracted hippies in droves.

This beach house was in need of repair, but with the drought, fixing a leaking roof wasn't a big priority. Although Jesse had never been in a flophouse, this seemed like it might fit the description. No heat, no curtains, no ambience, but the boys didn't seem to mind. They had electricity which meant they had music! There were no instruments lying around; this house was way too vulnerable for such trust. A stereo was mounted on a shelf, and on another wall were speakers pieced together with lots of spaghetti wires. Hundreds of albums lined the walls. The Stones were preferred over the Beatles, Leadbelly over Jerry Lee Lewis.

Jim drew Jesse close and talked about the group he was forming with his friend, Ray, who played the keyboard.

"Yeah, we're really doing it! I write lyrics and Ray plays keyboard. We have a manager, and we're scheduled to begin recording really soon."

"Wow, that's exciting. What do you call your group?"

"The Doors; it's taken from a book by Aldous Huxley called <u>The Doors of Perception</u>. He took mescaline and then wrote about it expanding his awareness."

"I'm taking Psych.101 and Steppenwolf is required reading. Do you know the book?"

"Yes, all the articles and books on psychedelic experiences are required reading for the group members," he replied laughing.

After their conversation, Jim disappeared. Jesse didn't bring a watch and had lost track of time. She sat outside on an old lawn chair while the canal water steadily slapping two feet in front of her. The music had been turned down when the joint was lit and passed around so as not to attract the law. Jesse declined saying, "I don't need that; I'm high on life." However, she wasn't feeling high, she was worried. She had never done such a bold act of defiance as sneak out and drive off. The dread began seeping into her.

She managed to pull Jim aside so she could ask for a ride back to her car.

"Hey, don't get uptight. We'll get you back to your car on time." She was not reassured. Then he offered her a drink from a blue enameled camping mug.

"Here, you want a sip of this coffee; it'll keep you awake." It was weird because the cup was less than half full, and when she stuck her nose in it, she found that it was stone cold. It seemed gross to her.

"No thanks, I don't like coffee."

"Suit yourself," he said flippantly as he disappeared back in the house. Jesse followed him in feeling very much out of place. The guys were listening to records and talking about the band. They were becoming animated, full of testosterone induced euphoria, enamored with their music and plans. Jesse was invisible, so she found a big floor pillow and sunk down into it, hoping someone would drive her to her parked car a couple of miles inland. It was close but not within walking distance. Before long, Jesse was startled by the streaks of dawn filtering through the dirty windows. Her heart responded like a cannon in her chest.

"Jim, my parents are going to kill me. Will you drive me now?

He acted annoyed, but at the same time he had a vacant look in his eyes and left the room. When he came back he said, "We're going to Mexico; come with us!"

Hearing this, Jesse nearly vomited. "No, I can't. I have got to get home. My parents are not hip. They'll probably call the police when they see that the car is gone."

Luckily for Jesse, Jim was able to motivate the others. They squeezed into a little Peugeot just as the edge of the sun's disk blasted over the horizon. When the driver started the car, Jesse breathed a little easier... until the guy next to her crawled over her and heaved himself out of the tiny back seat window, elbowing her and leaving bruises as he went. Once outside the car, he climbed on the hood and began jumping up and down madly as if in an ecstatic primitive morning ritual. Everyone else burst out laughing while her panic mounted. Within minutes, the reveler was back inside, and they were on their way. Relief flooded her but she knew she wasn't in the clear yet. Stepping out of the car, Jim kissed Jesse, and then vanished with his friends down the street, motoring toward the border.

Her parent's car felt cold and unfamiliar. It started right up, and Jesse stepped on the gas hoping that her luck would hold. As she approached the house, she had no idea what situation she might be walking into. She thought the birds were twittering as loudly as they possibly could. The morning's full light was everywhere. Quickly Jesse snuck back in the door she had escaped from hours earlier, replaced the keys, and ducked inside her bedroom.

Mission accomplished! She could hardly believe that she was safe in her bed. The exhilaration and memory of her experience blocked any sleep, and within the hour she could hear her dad shuffling around and could smell coffee brewing. She tried to stay in bed, but her Dad had this awful routine of coming in, grabbing her foot, and dragging her out of bed if she didn't get up of her own accord. This Saturday morning was no exception.

All during the week she could not stop herself from thinking about her escapade to the Venice canals. On Friday she decided to try her luck again, planning to cruise down to Ocean Park to see if she could locate Jim. She remembered the street and what the bungalow apartment looked like.

Emboldened by last week's success, she again waited until about twelve, quietly snuck out the door and started the car, her heart racing. The streets seemed unusually deserted. As she drove, she promised herself that she would not relinquish her control by getting into a car with Jim or any of his friends. The last visit she had gotten home at dawn; easily within sight of the neighbors. What reason could she have possibly invented to explain her borrowing the car and leaving in the middle of the night? No, if she got caught, she might as well drive the car off a Pacific Coast Highway cliff.

As she circled the block where she thought the apartment was, she spotted the Peugeot, the sardine can she had been stuck in. She parked the Pontiac and headed for the wooden stairway. As she approached the same doorway, she could hear voices rising and falling. She knocked.

"Is Jim here? She asked timidly. From the darkness came a welcoming voice.

"Hey, Fox, I was hoping you'd stop by. Come on in. You remember the guys, right?"

"Yes," she answered, even though the room was too dark to see them clearly. As her eyes adjusted, she could see the same faces that had piled in the car as the sun rose last week.

Jim took Jesse's hand and led her to the bedroom. Like the first time they met, he immediately put his hands on her as they kissed. She went along for only a moment, and then pulled back to slow him down.

"I'm sorry... you're really going too fast. I do like you though. You know, I vowed to an ex-boyfriend that I wouldn't have sex until I was married."

Not realizing her inexperience and taking offense at her reluctance, Jim drew back like Jesse had scalded him. "You're nothing but a prick tease!" Seeing that he was not going to get some quick sex, he turned back to the living room to rejoin the discussion that was in full swing.

Jesse's feelings were hurt. Silent, she slid into the comfort of a huge pillow on the floor, and listened to the voices, though she couldn't see their faces. Candles and a black light illuminated a poster on the wall of a person

41

meditating with rings of colored energy emanating from wheels located in a row along the spine.

"So as the acid came on, I became aware of this vast ocean of energy that I was swimming or bathing in. I could see through the people in front of me, a part of a great cosmic collage, intricate interplay of matter and light patterns. After a while, the intensity subsided, and people looked like cartoon characters. They were so predictable I thought I could see their thoughts and words in bubbles above their heads. It was freaky but fun. I was god and could read everybody I encountered, like an open book."

Another voice responded, "Wow, that's cool, but what I experienced was totally different. I went inside myself; like there was no outside, only inside. Instead of seeing changes in things around me, I became the outside world. All those things you saw, I became. I was a woman and life was growing inside me, and then I became the fetus, and I saw my own cells dividing and changing. Time didn't exist, only present moment. But still, this minute connected to every other event throughout centuries, and me, I was the ultimate 'eye', the conscious being of the whole universe. Wherever I focused, that is what became animated or energized, as if I was the cosmic artist."

Jesse sat around for an hour and then excused herself and left. She certainly didn't want a repeat of last week. Within three months Jesse was falling behind and wishing to escape both college and her parent's house. It took one confrontation with her mother for Jesse's wheel of fate to begin rolling.

"Did you finish the paper you're supposed to write?" Louise asked nastily.

"No, I didn't, not yet" Jesse answered defensively.

"Well, if you're not going to do the work, you might as well drop out of college." Thus, came the challenge.

"You're right Mom," was all she said.

The next day, to her parent's surprise, Jesse began the withdrawal process.

Within a week, she found a job in Santa Monica as a long-distance operator for the Bell Telephone Company and began to plan her getaway. First, she bought a toaster, kitchen utensils, and towels. She packed them in a box she hid on the floor of her closet. As she accumulated more house wares, her excitement grew. She wanted to share her plans with her mother, and impulsively went to her one afternoon.

"Mom, come see what I've been buying." Her voice piped excitedly.

Jesse's mom looked at her with irritation and replied impatiently, "What is it that is so important?"

Happiness got sucked out of the room, and Jesse's interest in sharing with her mother wavered.

"Never mind, I can show you some other time." But it was too late; her mother was standing beside her.

Jesse rolled back the closet door and reached for the two boxes.

"I just wanted to show you the things I'm accumulating, so when I get my own place, I'll be prepared." Jesse's mom was silent, as she glared at the symbols of revolution and freedom before her. She turned around to exit the crime scene.

Following her out into the living room she asked, "Mother, what's wrong? What is it I've done that is so terrible?"

Her mother obliged her with an answer. "Jesse, I can't believe you're showing me all of this stuff, or that you're even thinking about moving out."

Dumbfounded, Jesse still did not understand why her mother was angry, after all, she was simply doing what every child does eventually. She was leaving home.

"Why are you reacting like this? I thought you might be happy for me."

Still spitting anger, her mother screamed, "The only reason a girl wants to leave home is because she wants to do things that her parents won't allow!"

Jesse had no retort. She hadn't thought of it that way but could see that part of what her mother said was true. The more accurate explanation was that Jesse could not please her mother, and tired of the abuse, she wanted to be far away from her controlling and tiresome mannerisms.

Up until the day Jesse moved out, her mother was stone-cold and refused to talk. Jesse would have liked a positive sendoff, but the truth is, it made the entire process of separation easier and simpler. Her stepdad was more cooperative in facilitating Jesse's transition. He knew that there would be no peace until Jesse was completely removed. As an obstacle to Jesse's departure, her mother had announced that she could not take the car unless she took over the insurance that her parents had been paying. Jesse's job as a long-distance operator at the telephone company paid only minimum wage; she could not imagine any way to cover the car. Resolving herself to being without a car, she instead bought her first ten-speed bike which began Jesse's lifelong devotion to bicycling.

Shortly after the end of her probationary period at Ma' Bell's, she began having problems. Since Jesse had no idea how to keep the job she was precariously holding, it wasn't long before she was being written up for non-compliance.

Jesse liked to take long walks at night and then she would swallow a handful of No-Doze (later graduating to prescription amphetamines) so she could stay awake at the board, watching the tiny flickering lights tease her. It was no use; inevitably, her sleepy head would tip forward in repose while the supervisor took note.

She was asked to resign or be terminated. She opted to resign, moved from her efficiency apartment blocks from the Pacific Palisades Park, and found an inexpensive girl's boarding house in the heart of Hollywood, a few miles inland from her beach beginnings.

Inland Without a Compass

T he 'Sunset Strip', that was the place to be. The social revolution fired its first shots to be heard, to be understood, and to be reckoned with, there in the heat on the streets in '66.

Jesse had migrated to Hollywood for the music. The Whiskey A-Go-Go, The Trip, Pandora's Box, and The London Fog featured the best rock n roll, and she wanted to be where the musicians were. The boarding house on Flores Avenue was close to the strip. She managed to make friends with a girl her own age among the residents. Most of the women who lived there were pursuing careers in the movie industry and were unfriendly.

Jesse and Donna met in the hallway and promised to rendezvous later that night to share a joint. This, of course, turned into an all-nighter, until dawn broke through the window reminding Donna of her daytime job, and Jesse of her sudden need to crawl into her hibernation quilt where Donna found her that same afternoon at 4:30 when she dragged home from work.

"Jesse, how can you sleep all day?" Donna drawled in her most condescending tone. "I distinctly heard you tell me last night that you wanted to get motivated and look for a job."

"Oh, please! I was stoned. It's a lot easier to talk, than to do."

46

"You are so full of it, Jesse James!" Donna was especially irritated because she had not come up with some witty reason to stay home and had managed to work on zero hours of sleep.

Jesse, who was prone to melancholy, looked guilty as she pulled herself together and sat bleary eyed on the edge of the bed.

"It's just that every time I go out looking, nobody hires me, and I'm not qualified to do anything anyway, except shit jobs that I can't handle, like the last one at the collection agency. You know what I did all day? I watched the clock! Between filing cards and answering the phone. If they hadn't fired me for missing a day, I would have been found, bones behind filing cabinets, dead of boredom."

"Well, I'm going to crash, Jesse. I'll talk to you later."

Donna soon discovered that Jesse's idea of looking for a job was hitch-hiking out on the strip. Then she would ask the person who picked her up if he (the driver was usually a man) knew where she could find a job. "Yeah, a blow-job," was the usual response. And she had the nerve to get offended.

Once she came home and told Donna how this black dude had picked her up on the strip. "He started to drive off in the wrong direction, I tried the passenger door, but it wouldn't open. He drove to east L.A., probably Watts. We went down an alley behind what looked like condemned tenement buildings and stopped. He scooted over in the seat trying to initiate sex with me. I had no idea how to get back to Hollywood and I was scared. So, I told this guy that I had taken a couple tabs of acid. I started to cry and freak-out like I was having a psychotic breakdown. You know what he did? He took me right back to the exact corner where he had picked me up. He let me out of his car and then drove off. Can you believe that?"

Jesse was shook-up but it did not stop her from hitching. Though it was a careless way to treat oneself, if asked she would tell you she did it because she was always broke or didn't know anyone she could call for a ride. This is how one lives without connections.

Her parents still lived a few miles away. Jesse went to their house to do laundry because without money, she did not have clean clothes. No one was home, but they always left the door open, so Jesse helped herself to the washing machine. They came home before she had finished. Before a time of cell phones and instant communication, her mother flew into a fury of indignation. Screaming, she threw her wet clothes into a plastic bag. "Get out. You don't live here. And call before you come over the next time!"

Clayton drove Jesse to an intersection in Santa Monica and dropped her off. He watched as she got out of the car, took her stance on the side of the road, arm extended, thumb out.

Back at the boarding house, one night her aloneness took her to an all-night cafe frequented by hippies, old Beatniks and some unsavory characters as well. Unfortunately, The Blue Grotto was not the happening place, and with empty pockets Jesse couldn't stay long. After a few minutes she walked out of the door unaware that someone had followed her.

The boulevard was mostly deserted at three in the morning. Her footsteps clicked loudly while her thoughts echoed in the emptiness. At that moment, a car pulled to the curb, and a bearded man offered her company and a ride which she accepted trustingly. They exchange a few words as she rode beside him. He seemed nice enough, then he spread-open his hand to show her an array of yellow and red capsules.

"What are they?" Her curiosity was aroused.

"Downers," he answered with a smile as if they were Christmas presents.

She had no idea what they did or how many to take.

"What kind of high is it?"

"Oh, it's real mellow," he smiled holding the pills out to her like candy.

"Make sure you take enough so you can feel the effect."

With that, the guy dropped three capsules in her palm, two red ones, and one yellow. He wanted to make damn sure she gave up a piece of ass. On an empty stomach it wasn't long before the two Seconal and the one Nembutal hit Jesse like a fall from the tenth story.

"Where are we?" She mumbled through a veil of confused dizziness. Now the car was stopped, and he was helping her walk.

He answered with his rehearsed story, "some friends of mine moved out of this house yesterday. They told me to go ahead and stay here until the end of the month."

Jesse began to shiver as the night chill and the effects of the sedatives worked on her body. The bare walls of strange rooms moved-in on her, and she clung precariously to her abductor's neck while he turned on all the burners of the gas stove in order to generate some heat.

"How's that? Feel warmer?" He whispered with putrid breath on her pale neck. Then he led her like a complacent child to a cold stained mattress without sheets or blankets.

"Don't you worry none, I'm going to do some things to you honey that will fire you up. You won't be cold for long." He laid her back, took what he wanted from Jesse who was passed out, and then he left.

Jesse awoke eighteen hours later stupefied. Staggering, she walked out to the sidewalk where she managed to stop a couple who were sight-seeing. Jesse was crying and hardly able to form her words.

"Please, can you help me; I need to go home. Where am I?" She was still so drugged that she could not focus her eyes. Once they figured out where she lived, the couple offered a ride back to the boarding house. Probably not exactly the Hollywood tourist experience they had been seeking. Unfortunately, the close call did not curb Jesse's dangerous behaviors.

Weeks later Donna rapped at her door hoping to catch-up on news. Jesse opened the door slowly. Donna was surprised that the shades were pulled down, and the room was dark. As Jesse moved into the light of the open door, Donna could see bruises on her neck. Her face was distorted and swollen, the white of her left eye, blood red from broken veins.

"My God, what happened?" Jesse turned away as Donna followed her in and closed the door.

"I was at the Whiskey A Go-Go last night. A fantastic band was playing, and I was talking to this guy who seemed nice, even if he did have short hair. When the lights came on, I asked him if he would give me a ride home. We walked out of the club and his buddy, who was black, joined us. They were both friendly and didn't act nasty or try to come on to me, so I figured they were for-real people. We drove a few blocks up the strip and I got this crazy idea. You know how I like to walk at night, right? So, I thought it would be neat to check out the Hollywood Hills. You know, see the city lights and listen to the crickets. I asked the guy driving to let me off on a road I knew would take me to the top. He stopped. I didn't give them a second thought and walked off into the dark. After a few minutes walking I could hear footsteps behind me and then all of a sudden, the black guy was beside me. He said for me to cooperate with him. At first, I hardly understood what he was getting at, but then he got pushy, so I fought back. That's when he hit me in the eye. It was like sparks flying in my head. It felt like blood dripping from my eye. He forced me down to the gravel."

Donna's arms circled Jesse as she talked through the sobs.

"In my mind I could see the headline in the newspaper. Girl found raped and slain in the Hollywood Hills. I was afraid he wouldn't let me live after he had done this to me. I kept fighting him. He told me to stop or he'd smash my other eye. So, I quit struggling. He pulled my jeans and underpants down and stuck his penis in me. Then something strange happened. He stopped moving on me."

"What am I doing?" He said out loud. I was crying, snot was all over my face, my back was ground into the dirt, pebbles were lodged under my skin, and he just stopped. I was so scared; I didn't know what was coming next. Guess what he did? He helped me up, started talking fast, saying he didn't want to hurt me... and that he was sorry, and he would pay my doctor bills. He helped me get dressed, and then we walked back toward the main road. We hitched back here."

"Back here? You mean he knows where you live? You better report this to the police." Donna was livid.

"No, it wouldn't do any good; I can't identify him. He is just a face with no features. And everyone would say I asked for it because I was walking alone at night."

Jesse was another nameless victim. Her nocturnal wanderings did not always wind up in such a mess, but after more than one close call, Donna could not understand what drove her out into the night. So, she asked her.

Jesse spoke softly, as though she had suffered an imprisonment, "The night calls out to me like freedom. All the years I lived at home my mother never gave me an inch of space that was my own. She intimidated me into acting the way she wanted me to. I couldn't be alone or read a book. She wouldn't even let me close the door to my bedroom. When we shopped, she decided what clothes I would wear. She had a total disregard for the individual that I was. I was a doll to dress up. Now... I guess I just love the feeling I get when my hand touches the cold doorknob. I open the door, step outside after midnight, and nothing compares with the rush of air into my lungs, through my hair, and the sight of galaxies exploding in my vision. It feels like the universe is mine and I am its child. My thoughts are mine and it's ok if I think them."

Donna grew impatient with Jesse's poetic rambling.

"Fine, but now you're not living at home, and you can do and think what you want. Can't you figure out a safer time of the day to take a walk?"

Jesse looked exasperated as she listened. Donna had totally missed the point. "I can't get the calm and silence unless the city is asleep."

Donna responded, "Right, everyone is asleep, except for the murderers and rapists!"

If sex, drugs, and rock 'n' roll was the pulse of the times, Jesse had its philosophy running rampantly in her veins. Her attitude remained pristinely naive while she behaved like a bitch in heat. Sex was love, and love was one thing she had never been given. She hadn't been hugged, or rocked, or tickled, or had her eyes dried, or for that matter, been told "I love you. She moved like a vortex of emptiness driven by inexhaustible carelessness, and a furious need for sensual contact.

Donna listened, fascinated by Jesse's sexual encounters. Sometimes she listened as a friend but sometimes she felt more like a pervert voyeur who pays, then scoots down into the moist seat of a darkened theater, just to get a tasty glimpse of another reality.

Hollywood clubs were the stomping grounds for hippies and aspiring musicians. They provided Jesse with never-ending encounters. She would disappear whenever she found someone she liked. After being gone for a week, Donna finally caught her at home.

"Where have you been? I haven't seen you in days. You scared me; I was afraid something had happened to you, especially after that shit a month ago."

Jesse was her usual disheveled self except she was smiling all excited and talkative. "I met this guy at Pandora's Box. He was so cute; all I wanted to do was get to know him. We left and smoked some hash in the alley behind the club. Then we walked to his basement apartment about eight blocks away."

Donna wasn't sure she wanted to hear the gory details about this loser. "He didn't have a car?" she asked, rolling her eyes.

"No, that doesn't matter anyway. You know I don't care about material things. I care about what's inside a person."

"I'm sure he cared about your insides too. You didn't fuck him, did you?"

Indignantly, Jesse answered, "His name is Sean, and he turned me on to Thirteenth Floor Elevator!"

"What? You did it in an elevator?"

Jesse cracked up, "No, it's a group. I think he really likes me."

"So, you didn't fuck him?" Donna waited for an answer.

"Well, we rolled around on his bed for a while, then he took my hand and led me across the room to a mirror leaning against the wall and told me to get down on my hands and knees. I was so hot from everything else we had been doing, and I wanted to please him, so I did it, and he put his dick in me from behind. He started talking to me, saying, 'Look how good you look, I know you like it this way, just like a little animal. See how your tits swing. Umm... you're so good. See how I'm fucking you from behind, my big dick going in and out of your pussy. You need it this way.' I was watching closely because if I looked away, he would make me look back into the mirror. He came; then we got up off the floor. He is so cute; I can't wait to see him again."

Donna's anger flared. "You are so stupid. Do you spread your legs for every pretty boy who smiles at you? You must love being used."

Jesse did not comprehend. "He likes me!" She said defensively.

"How do you know? You didn't give yourself any time to find out. Don't you understand that getting fucked is not the same as getting love?"

They had been sitting on Jesse's bed, the pornographic image of her friend scorched onto her consciousness. Donna was suddenly disgusted as the smell of wanton sweating bodies seemed to drift up from Jesse's Indian print sheets choking her with its sour vapor.

"I have to go. I hope you're right about Sean. I'm tired of seeing you crying over some dude you slept with."

The two did not see each other for a while after that. Donna had a life. At the boarding house girls came and went, runaways, fading starlets and hopefuls whose ambitions had not yet been shredded in the machinery of the entertainment industry. Tinsel town swarms and abounds with every sort of hustler. All lies can be found somewhere on hungry lips. Everything is for sale; only a few make it, but not without scarring their souls.

Donna was headed for UCLA and her own share of pressures, so it was easy for her to stay clear of the quicksand where Jesse romped. Donna knew that this summer before school started would be the last of the unstructured free time until Christmas, so she looked forward to the times when Jesse would drop by to smoke a joint with her. That is, until the incident with the marijuana bugs.

Twigs were all Jesse had left at the bottom of the baggie of grass, so she pulled out a mesh strainer, poured the remains into it and started mashing. Sure enough, a few specks of leaf fell through. Jesse scrubbed; the seed hulls cracked and crumbled through, along with a colony of nearly microscopic bean colored scrambling bugs. So minuscule were these tiny bugs that the girls did not notice their existence until Donna tried to roll a joint. She sprinkled this pitiful grit on the paper when she noticed that it was moving. She yelled, threw the paper down, and without missing a beat Jesse rescued the half-rolled joint.

"Jesse, stop! There are bugs in it."

She looked at Donna earnestly, as if she knew what she was talking about and without missing a beat said, "It's ok, they'll get you high. We'll smoke them... they're marijuana bugs!"

Donna declined but watched in dismay as Jesse put a match to the end of the joint and drew in the smoke.

Jesse first smoked because of her curiosity, and afterwards laughed at the preposterous "Refer Madness," and its message of paranoia and hysteria. Even Donna, the straightest of straights could recognize pot's benign qualities, and the obvious hypocrisy of the laws, especially when Jesse showed her the amphetamines she got legally from a doctor for "weight control." Pot was where Donna stopped, but it was only the first substance in Jesse's life-long love affair with consciousness-altering drugs.

56

One afternoon she stopped by Donna's room just to tell her about the acid she had taken. LSD-25 was available on the streets in varying colors, shapes, and strengths. Jesse seemed determined to become "experienced," Jimi Hendrix's code for using acid. Until one trip catapulted her, like a stoned Alice, into a grotesque and threatening wonderland, after which, she never regained her full enthusiasm for hallucinogens.

"I did it! I tripped! This guy I met gave me acid," then she added demurely, "And I didn't fuck him, even though he wanted to, even though I wanted to." She acted like she needed a gold star, so of course Donna praised her for her restraint, welcomed her in, and handed her a Pepsi. Donna clearly had other motives... she wanted to hear about the "trip." She wanted to get 'experienced' second-hand, without the fear of possibly becoming permanently deranged.

"Well?" Donna prompted her impatiently.

Jesse began cryptically, "It was strange like there was a lot happening, and also nothing at all."

"Great! Am I supposed to know what that means?"

"Wait a minute, and I'll explain. This guy Sam came over with two hits of acid, and we both dropped it. It was such a tiny little tablet that I really didn't believe it would have an effect. Then I started getting nervous waiting for something to happen. Sam put his arms around me, but I told him I was tired of guys just fucking me. So instead of him trying to get to know me he sits down on the floor, wraps his arms around his bent knees, boxes his head and stays there motionless. I wasn't sure what the hell he was doing, but I didn't want to bother him in case he was getting into some heavy mental trip... meditating or something. I've heard some people like to go inside their heads when they trip. It looked like he just wanted to be left alone. About that time, I felt it coming on, like my head was filling up with helium, and I started getting restless like there was something I needed to do. It was about eleven-thirty at night by then, so I went out walking."

Donna rolled her eyes at her as she kept talking.

"The night air invaded my lungs. I walked, but I didn't have a destination, so I headed for the strip to see the sights. I know realistically that Sunset Boulevard is only two blocks from here, but there was so much to see along the way, it seemed like miles. Did you ever notice how the city noises will seem loud, but if you focus on the crickets behind the house in the ally, then they will drown out the traffic? Anyway, soon I could hear footsteps trailing off from somewhere behind me. It took me a few seconds to recognize that they were mine, because I didn't have a body. All I had was a big head, and it was swelling up as if it would absorb everything. I was floating up above the sidewalk. As my mind expanded, the stars and full moon up above were *inside* my head. I was absorbing galaxies and I wasn't afraid." Jesse had a peculiar look on her face, one of a childlike guru with a slight smile on her lips. "I just kept walking until I found myself a few blocks down the street at a fast-food joint. It was so bizarre. I felt like I was looking at an alien civilization on another planet, like I didn't even belong here. Someone was talking over a loudspeaker. At first, I figured out they must be calling names, you know, the food orders that were ready, except they were saying things that had nothing to do with burgers and fries. I was being surveilled; the voice was talking to me. It was making fun of me, for being stoned, watching me, and noticing that I was behaving weird. I couldn't focus, the words sounded like gibberish. I started to panic, like I was losing my mind. This reality was confusing, like a jigsaw puzzle that somebody had accidentally dropped. Well at that point it seemed like I had only two choices, brain hemorrhage or move on. As I turned my back, the loudspeaker was still blaring; I thought I heard my name, although I hadn't ordered anything. I hoped that if I ignored it all, the strangeness would disappear. I guess I was hallucinating like mad. I turned away from the assault on my senses, away from all the ant-like people swarming to Burger Delight. I had all this energy, but I didn't know what to do with it or where to go."

Jesse's monologue continued, mesmerized by her own voice, self-absorbed, and content to boast about her new drug awareness. Donna continued to listen.

"I ran across the street. I was aimless. I don't know why I walked into a coffee shop, I guess just to get off the street. There were so many cars that I felt like there was no oxygen, and I couldn't breathe. The last thing I wanted to do was stuff my mouth," Jesse said knowingly, "That's one thing, when you're high on acid, eating food is a very weird experience. It's like you can see yourself as a gigantic, evolved amoeba with these gross physical functions like chewing, and digesting, and shitting. Anyway, I must have been on automatic because, I sat down at the counter and ordered french-fries. And another thing; eyes... when you're stoned there are eyes out there, everywhere. Right across from me, staring out of a slit in the stainless steel, looking out from the kitchen were more eyes. Those eyes looked in my eyes and knew I was high. Those eyes were laughing when I stuck a grease-coated stick on my tongue. I swear I couldn't recognize what it was. The consistency was like oil dipped cotton balls. I felt awkward trying to casually swallow this clump in my mouth. Meanwhile, the world is looking on."

"Sounds like the usual paranoia that people sometimes fall into when they take acid," Donna reacted with a spark of hearsay expertise.

"Yeah, you're probably right. Then I decided to leave and almost forgot that it is customary behavior to leave money for the food purchased. I pulled what I knew was money out of my purse. I rubbed the dollar bill, feeling its texture on the tips of my fingers. It was unbelievable to me that every human on the earth was dictated by this stuff, this processed wood pulp, crumpled, faded picture of some dead politician. The dude next to me was staring at me. I guess I looked strange inspecting this five-dollar bill as if I'd never seen one in my life. I wanted to laugh out loud; decided it would be inappropriate behavior. Just the realization that every single person worshipped money, in large and small ways... and that no one could be who they wanted to be without its interference. You know, that is a lot of power for inanimate sheets of paper! Anyway, the rest of the trip wasn't all that radical. The guy that was staring at me... I told him I was stoned, and I didn't want to be alone, so he gave me a ride to his apartment, and we talked for an hour, until I got bored. He was a nerd, so I asked him for a ride home. On the way to his car, we walked by the swimming pool. I guess the acid was still affecting me, because the light coming from the pool was eerie; the ripples of color and intertwined thought were magical. I tried to look closer so I could see the little molecules drifting around and sometimes breaking away from the surface. I guess the guy was afraid I would jump in and drown, because he grabbed my hand and guided me to his car like he thought I wasn't able to do it myself. Imagine, him thinking that I would do anything so stupid?"

Imagine, Donna thought.

The Flesh Market

ed-up with always being broke, and tired of constantly dodging the landlady, Jesse began working a few blocks away in a nude modeling studio on Santa Monica Boulevard. The boulevard was scattered with heroin dealers, hookers, homeless panhandlers, gay hustlers, men with no legs, neglected runaways, alongside of desperate men hoping to feed on the likes.

This was a street littered with heartbroken, mind-shattered struggling souls. Every city has one, the maggot hill, a land of forlorn dreamers, survivors of the psychic wars. Jesse wondered how such a street materializes. It was as if there was a billboard over the area with a large invisible arrow, directing the lost and degenerate to come and hang out.

The John Carroll model studio wasn't the roughest or sleaziest one in the area. John was a good-natured father figure for most of his models, men and women alike. Of course, it did not stop him from being horny and exploitative. He was perfectly comfortable taking advantage of young girls, without families or jobs. He did not talk shit, no silly ideas about fame and fortune. He never promised more than the one hundred-fifty dollars for a six-hour modeling gig, big money for a girl with no experience or skills.

Jesse was fresh meat on the scene. Just eighteen with silky blond hair, vacuous blue eyes, and a chest that protruded like a shelf under her t-shirt. She instantly became John's favorite. For a month she was the studio's sweetheart, booked to capacity, going from photographer to photographer, until John Carroll's contacts were saturated with her image. Pictures of her Lolita face and every angle of her hard virgin-like breasts could be purchased and enjoyed in any number of magazines. The nearby adult bookstore carried them all. After the novelty and initial rush, every new girl was then encouraged to hang around the studio to be 'on call' and available to model for customers who walked in off the street. For a fee, a Polaroid camera and a private room were provided along with the girl of their choice. Full nude modeling was prohibited by law. The pornographic field had not yet been hit by the oncoming "sexual revolution." A typical cellophane enclosed girlie magazine was little more than a magazine version of the "cheesecake" shots on calendar pages that had so often decorated the walls of barber shops and garages after WWII. Maybe that is why Jesse didn't feel violated when she posed; no harm in showing some tit. Her hippie philosophy of freedom certainly included an aesthetic appreciation of the naked body. She had often said if people took their clothes off more often, they would be conscious of the shape they were in and would naturally take better care of themselves. This job gave her a chance to be true to her ideals, to live her philosophy rather than only paying lip service as she observed so many hypocrites doing, people who said they believed in freedom and then spent all their time faithfully adhering to someone else's standards.

Donna stopped by Jesse's place of employment one day, after driving past the building, and around the block three times while she bolstered her courage. Whatever Jesse's ideals of freedom were, the area looked dilapidated, maybe even dangerous. But it was the middle of the afternoon, and the only way to see Jesse was to go looking for her.

The waiting room was dingy. The walls needed paint; the carpet was streaked with layers of footprints. This was nothing like one would imagine a model studio to be, even a semi-nude one. The receptionist's desk stood empty, inelegantly positioned in the middle of the room. There were no pictures on the walls, no music in the air, which floated thick with cigarette smoke. Two girls sat on a colorless couch, one barely covered in a flimsy red kimono, the other with her feet propped up wearing dirty slippers and a ragged terrycloth robe. Neither girl gave Donna a second look as she walked in but returned to their magazines. She stood for a moment wanting to leave, when out of a doorway walked Jesse.

"Hey girl! It's good to see you. I've been meaning to stop by. But this place is keeping me busy. Everybody wants to see these tits." She pulled up her shirt and flashed her friend, making her blush. "Let's get out of here. I don't have a scheduled shoot today, and I'm tired of these perverts."

They walked out into the morning air that was quickly becoming hot, hazy, and toxic with the emissions of L.A. traffic. While her lungs grabbed at something resembling oxygen, Donna questioned her own sanity for remaining in such an unfriendly habitat.

"Where do you want to go for lunch? My treat!" beamed Jesse.

"How about the Nucleus Nuance? It's organic," replied Donna.

She drove them to a quaint health food cafe run by some rich Hollywood hippies. With a colorful mural of someone's psychedelic dimension covering the walls and the friendly utopian atmosphere, it was like a different planet compared to the studio they had just left. Jesse ordered a sunflower seed salad. Donna ordered her usual vegetables and brown rice medley and asked, "So, how are you doing? It's been ages!" Donna leaned a little closer and whispered, "I haven't been stoned... not since you and me. I don't miss it though... I've been getting a lot accomplished."

Jesse's eyes lit up. If there was one thing she liked to do, it was turn people on to grass. With her, it was a spiritual mission. "I have some. We can take a walk in the park later. I've been doing good... making some money. I meant to come see you."

"You don't have to sleep with him, do you?" Donna wondered out loud about the owner.

"Of course not." She paused reflectively, "I suppose he would like that. He is very friendly and gushes every time he sees me. I keep him at arm's length, although I think he knows that I don't go for old men."

"What's the job like? Do you really take off your clothes for men you don't even know?" Donna asked, trying to keep from sounding judgmental.

"Yeah, but that's not all. I go out on location with professional photographers. Like the other day, we went to this mansion in Malibu to do a shoot. It gets boring lying around and posing in negligees for six hours. They are giving me over a hundred dollars a day though. This one photographer, Nippy, really likes to work with me. I've been booked with him quite a few times since I started with the studio. Next week he wants to shoot a session in Laurel Canyon. I'm going to be the centerfold girl. Rock climbing with my tits hanging out, and I'll be wearing this silly little Swiss costume; sort of shorts with a bib and suspenders, with black stockings and a garter belt underneath. Strange, huh?"

The tone of her voice said she was looking for approval, but there was also excitement. She was making money for the first time since she had left her parent's house.

"I can't believe you're not embarrassed. Perverts are going to buy that magazine, and probably jack-off to it... looking at a picture of you!"

"I don't care about a bunch of perverts. First, my friends don't buy those kinds of magazines, and second, real friends don't judge me for taking my clothes off."

The waiter delivered their food.

"Wow, this stuff looks weird, like a scoop of glued together seeds, sitting on a leaf of lettuce. I thought it was going to be like a regular salad, you know, with tomatoes and cucumbers and stuff."

Between bites Jesse continued, "I hate to pose for those guys who come in off the street. The other day I got picked, so we went into the room and the guy shot half the role, then he asked me if he could see the bottom half. It's against the law; we can only let them see our tits. He begged me and offered me an extra twenty, so I let him snap a picture of my pubes too. Then I got paranoid, because I thought he might be a cop or a snitch for John, so I got dressed and went home. I didn't even tell anybody that I was leaving. I heard about that later. I guess I wasn't supposed to leave because there weren't enough girls available. I didn't get any bookings for a while after that... my punishment, I guess."

Donna was almost finished eating because Jesse had been doing all the talking when she looked up and saw the most beautiful man across the room. "Look at that gorgeous longhair over there. I would do him in a heartbeat."

"Don't lie" Jesse taunted, "I've never seen you meet someone and immediately go to bed with him!"

"Well, if I keep hanging around with you, it might happen. Your hedonist philosophy might rub off on me," Donna added lightly.

"I don't appreciate your value judgment, especially coming from a friend. I won't go to bed with just anyone. There has to be a connection!" Jesse had now switched to her defensive mode like all good Scorpios do.

Donna didn't feel like listening to her friend justify, once more, those surges of hormones that obliterated her next to nothing morals. Maybe she *was* being judgmental; Jesse needed the sex because it was a substitute for love. Once you got to know Jesse, you found out that she was one of those sad but existent humans who had never been loved. She had not been hugged, or rocked, or read to, or tickled, or had her tears dried, or for that matter, told 'I love you'. She was like a vortex of emptiness, driven by inexhaustible carelessness.

As they left the restaurant, Jesse locked eyes with the "long-hair." He was Mick Jagger.

Adventures in the Skin Trade

*T*he temporary employment agency had a job for Jesse helping the Blue-Cross Blue-Shield Medical Insurance Company with end-of-the-year inventory and organizing. Computers had not yet revolutionized record-keeping. She was still making fast money at the studio on weekends, but she decided to try the seven to five routine, which really amounted to five-thirty A.M. to six P.M. because of the bus ride into downtown Los Angeles.

There is no way to describe a daily trek on the bus except as drudgery. Jesse wondered how crowds of people could exist in the convoluted catacombs of these streets where the magic of morning light and the rays of dusk rarely reached the cement. Of course, the heat, like blasts from hell, reached the streets and remained fused in a toxic layer of bus fumes, human sweat, and rotting decay of garbage. Jesse imagined that the rotting decay of disillusionment and abandoned plans were partly responsible for the stench of the city. She made a mental note and stepped from reality into her ever-present companion, a book.

One evening on her trip home, a guy name Danny Swan, sitting adjacent from her, interrupted her reading. He was chubby, like a Charlie Brown cartoon character, not at all her type. She liked a boy to be thin hipped, with hair at least as long as hers. Usually, she would not give the time of day to a guy like this, but Jesse had begun to think about things like karma, and inequality, and choice versus chance. Danny was a thinker and a reader, and he offered Jesse his undivided attention. And as they talked, she thought he had a good rap. He spun pictures in her head, and he helped pass the time on an otherwise boring ride home.

He smiled sweetly to Jesse when he first sat down beside her. "Is that a good book you're reading?"

"Oh, I don't know. I love to read but when I go to the library, I can never figure out which book to try. It seems to me there are probably as many stupid, irrelevant books sitting on the shelves right next to the really important ones. It's kind of frustrating."

"I'm into reading too. I know a lot about literature. I'm a teacher... maybe you'd like me to recommend a book for you?"

"That would be great! You're a temp at the same place I'm working, right? I've seen you during break. If you're a teacher, why are you working at this place?" She asked with sincere interest.

"Believe me, I won't be here long. I'm having a hard time getting to job interviews without a car. Mine will be fixed soon, and then I'll have more mobility, and a choice about where I work."

The next time she saw Danny, he handed her *Adventures in the Skin Trade* by Dylan Thomas.

Their first dates included taking amphetamines, diet pills she got from her doctor, and discussing the fate of the world... taking amphetamines and discussing music and books. On a third date, they were also speeding when Danny suggested that they go out to a club, put on phony British accents and pose as music people from London.

Jesse used to say, "When I'm high I can do anything." It was fun pretending to be somebody she wasn't, until the night wore on and she felt bad about deceiving nice but naive people. Toward dawn after the come down was setting in, she woke up the couple who were letting them crash in their guest room to let them know that she and Danny were just a couple of hyped-up phonies who had fooled them. The catharsis of confession!

Danny was pissed that she had blown their game, especially after getting over on them for the entire night. The couple who had opened their home to them was terribly angry. But Jesse did not care; it just wasn't her scene... she didn't feel comfortable being a liar.

Jesse and Danny had become lovers shortly after they had met *even though* she was not physically attracted to him. He was the first in a long line of mercy fucks. After the British masquerade she decided he was too weird and intended to cut off the relationship, although she wasn't sure exactly how she would accomplish it.

The next Friday she and Danny went out for lunch and afterwards he wanted to show her where he lived. They drove out to the San Fernando Valley and climbed stairs to a second story apartment. As he gave her the tour, she thought she could see a woman's influence in the furnishings, although Danny asserted that he lived there alone. One room was obviously a nursery.

"I didn't realize you had a kid," Jesse said, her suspicion finding its words.

"Yeah, her mother and I are separated. I only have my daughter a few days of the month," he answered with reassurance.

"Why didn't you tell me before that you were married?"

Danny grabbed her hand and tried to pull Jesse close to his body, but she resisted, waiting for an explanation.

"I was afraid it would scare you away. You're the girl I've been waiting for all my life, someone I can really be in love with."

This little speech sickened her because she certainly did not feel the same way about him. He was nice enough and more interesting than many she had met. She loved the fact that he was turning her on to literature and art. Unfortunately, when he made love to her, she wanted to puke. As she stood in front of him wondering how she could let him know the truth, a knock on the door relieved her of the awkward moment.

Danny walked over and swung the front door wide open, and in walked the most beautiful male Jesse had ever set eyes on. He had a storm of wavy blond hair, intense brown eyes, thin hips and a black leather jacket. Danny introduced him as his best friend Carlos. It was all he got out of his mouth, when Carlos started telling Danny off.

"Look, Danny, Suzi has been calling me. She has suspected you were cheating on her." Then he turned to Jesse, "Danny has a wife and a baby. This is their home. She has been trying to make this marriage work and I suggest that you bow out."

This was Jesse's chance. Turning to face Danny, she spoke directly to him, "You lied to me; you have a wife and child. You involved me in parading for strangers as someone I wasn't. I don't want to see you again. I think you'd better get your head together!" Then she turned to Carlos. "Can you give me a ride home? I don't have a car."

"Sure!"

Without any more drama the two of them left. Next, Jesse found herself flying down the highway on the back of a bike, her arms wrapped tightly around Carlos' waist. She could smell the aroma of his leather jacket as she buried her nose in his back to keep sheltered from the wind. They rode, leaving the desert heat of the valley behind them as they snaked their way over the mountain, back to the coastal side.

Jesse had rented a small efficiency in Hollywood. She pressed her lips close to Carlos' ear so he could hear the directions. The two wheels finally rolled to a stop outside the apartment building. It was as if the bike had found its way home. Jesse hoped that he would come up and stay for a while; Carlos was hoping Jesse would want him to. They climbed the stairs. Jesse began her tour guide narration pointing out the highlights of the bizarre residents of this building, whispering and trying not to laugh but still ended up waking the landlord as Carlos and Jesse passed her door.

"People are so uptight. It's like no one has any fun, and because of it, they don't want anyone else enjoying life either. Fuck 'em. I am not living my life for them. I just can't be that boring," she whispered.

He nodded agreement but wanted to get behind a door away from staring eyes. It seemed to him that he could hear the clicks of doors opening and closing behind them as they walked up to the third floor where Jesse lived. Once inside he relaxed and the two of them began talking like they had always been friends. Such is the nature of mystical connections.

A Partner, A Lover

arlos stayed. They did not discuss it; she wanted him. Apparently, he was not bolted down anywhere permanent, so he spent the next few days bringing over his belongings which consisted of a few books, a few clothes and himself. Jesse felt delirious though she tried to be cooler than that. She could hardly believe that she had found someone with a brain, well-read, good-looking, and funny. In her mind, he was perfect.

"Jesse, do you want to trip together?" Carlos held out the tiny dot, and she stuck her tongue out.

The acid guidebooks with their guru authors suggested that a person should carefully choose the setting, and the people to be around during the sometimes eight-hour trek. The books never mentioned the euphoria that might be generated if two people were falling in love.

This is what Jesse told Donna... that she was in love. But Donna knew she did not know how to love. After all, she had never experienced it except in distorted forms. She thought that the shadowy residue of these abuses was hardly conducive to building a self that she could love. Donna wanted to tell her to slow down but restrained herself because, of course, Jesse would not listen anyway. After Carlos moved in, they lost track of each other for a while.

One day they ran into each other at a cafe on the strip. Jesse was very pregnant.

"My God, Jesse, I didn't realize it has been so long. Wow, you look like you're ready to pop." She had been sitting at a sidewalk table looking like the patron saint of Hippies in a flowing, dragging-on-the-floor length, empire waist dress of chocolate velveteen with a mauve lace shawl draped over her shoulders.

She stood and hugged Donna as she reached the table. "I am so happy to see you. You moved out of the Flores House?"

"Yeah, it was too monotonous after you left. They laughed.

"Are you still with Carlos?" Donna noticed a change in Jesse's expression when she spoke his name, kind of otherworldly.

"Oh yes. But you won't believe what we've been through. Do you want to hear about it? It's a long story." She looked at her only friend expectantly.

"Of course, but let's order first!" The waitress was friendly, and their food came quickly. Donna settled in and got comfortable.

"I got pregnant, and we got busted at the same time. It was so fucked up. Someone reported us... an anonymous phone call to the police said we had pot in our house. I answered a knock on the door at 7 in the morning. When I opened the door this man in a suit puts his foot in the door, forces me back, and says he has a warrant for our arrest. It was the worst nightmare, just like Nazi Germany. I couldn't believe they were going to take us to jail because we had a few stems and seeds."

"That's all, and they arrested you? That is so terrible. How long were you there?"

"Five days! It happened on a Thursday. They gave me one phone call and luckily, I got in touch with John Carroll, you know, the owner of the studio? He's the only person I thought might help us. He couldn't bail me out until Monday after the weekend."

"What was it like?" Donna asked.

"They treated me like I was a criminal. I don't see the harm in smoking a little pot, I'll bet they have a beer in their off hours... It's no different, except that alcohol is more harmful. After they took my fingerprints and a mugshot, they took me to a stall, and I had to strip. They sprayed me with something that smelled like DDT. I screamed at them... like, what do you think I have, bugs or something. I was so angry; I didn't want them soaking me down with their poison. But honestly, the worst part was when the guards were taking me to a cell. One electric gate after another opened and closed behind me... until I was so far in the bowels of that concrete and brick complex that it seemed like no one in the outside world would ever find me... like being in a medieval dungeon. Then, when I was going to the cafeteria, these chicks were saying stuff to me through the bars, and wiggling their tongues, you know, the same things men at the studio like to say... like, you sure look good, baby. They must have thought I was a lesbian since I cut all my hair off and I stopped bleaching it. Did you notice? So anyway, they were acting like I was dessert or something. In their dreams! It scared the shit out of me. I guess that's the idea... the pigs like to scare people. It probably makes them feel powerful, or in control. They fuckin' love to control other people, don't they?"

Jesse always got worked up when she talked about the cops, or pot being legalized. Passionate and naive, she believed in justice and freedom. They were not just words to her. She really thought that the world should function fairly and without undue restraints from governing agencies.

Donna managed to break in on her monologue. Pointing to her belly she said, "Yes, I know. So, when did this happen?"

"Well, I had just missed a period when we got busted, and I was planning to get some money together so I could get an abortion, but I wasn't really sure. Danielle, one of the girls back at the boarding house, got an abortion. Well, it really wasn't a complete abortion. You know it's illegal. So, she had her uterus scraped by this guy that she paid a hundred and fifty dollars to. He told her she would start to bleed and when she did, to get herself to a hospital right away. Well, she got an infection immediately and had a high temperature. Someone dropped her off at the County Hospital where she waited in the hallway while bloody bodies came and went, especially gunshot victims. She stayed there for three hours because they did not consider her an emergency; she almost died.

So, I think that in the back of my mind I had the image of Danielle going to that sleazy motel and being told to get some towels from the bathroom and spread them on the floor because the bed was too soft. He told her to lie down on them. She could feel the gritty, filthy floor against the bottom of her feet. Then because the lighting was so poor, he placed the bedside lamp between her legs with the shade removed. And all the while, she could see the shadows on the wall, as this stranger is digging inside of her." Jesse paused, whether to think about the seriousness of what she was saying, or only to catch her breath was unclear.

"One day I'd be talking about a baby, and the next day I'd be talking about finding a doctor. Carlos said that he had a hard time listening to me flip back and forth from one point of view to the other. I don't think I really wanted to get rid of it, because Carlos and I created it... and I am so in love with him! So, the minute I got out of jail, I knew I had to make a lot of money. The lawyer was going to cost eight hundred dollars, and he said he could get our offenses reduced so that we wouldn't have felonies on our records. I didn't care that much about myself, but I didn't want Carlos to have to carry that burden, since he's a man and being able to get a good job is more important for him."

Donna wasn't sure she agreed, but it was 1968, and the concept of feminism had just begun its emergence.

"I owed John our bail, and the lawyer wanted all of his money before he would do any work for us. I felt frantic, but I knew that there were clubs where girls danced with their tops off, and they made good money. John told me he had some connections. He knows the manager of the Pussycat Lounge on the strip. Well, I went over there with him, and the guy said that I looked too young. Talk about coincidences, around the same time I met this girl Pat McClarren who gave me her birth certificate because she got married and didn't care if I used it, so I went and got a driver's license. Groovy, huh? The fake ID didn't really work all that well, I guess because at nineteen I really don't look twenty-three like the ID says.

I couldn't get a job dancing in Hollywood for the big bucks, and by that time I was already three months along. I had to work at this place south of L.A. in Wilmington Beach where the vice squad weren't as watchful. It was a working-class bar, kind of grubby, lots of creepy guys, and long excruciating hours. We danced fifteen minutes on three stages, and then we'd get a fifteen-minute break each hour. I worked an eight-hour shift. By the time I got off work at 1:30 a.m. I thought my feet were going to fall off." I danced until I was five months, and then I really started showing, so I had to quit. All the dancers that worked there knew that I was pregnant and kept joking about it saying that the baby was going to come out doing the boogaloo."

Jesse gave Donna that self-satisfied look, the one that she had seen so many times, the look that typically accompanied some outlandish, disreputable adventure of hers. She talked with childlike enthusiasm, as if taking her clothes off, and dancing half-naked while many months pregnant were an accomplishment.

As they sat there, Donna trying not to judge her, she realized that it *was* an accomplishment. Jesse had come through regardless of the obstacles, or hardship. She had stepped beyond the boundary of her fear and had managed to keep both Carlos and her out of jail, had avoided felony convictions, without the help of a family. The only law she broke was falsifying her age.

"Jesse, I know dancing wasn't the first time you've taken your clothes off, but how did you make the transition from modeling to being in front of a live audience... in a public place?"

She moved closer, and her voice took on a more serious tone. "Well, it's no secret that I've always been a nudist at heart. So, I didn't go through any changes about showing my body, but the scary part about being up on a stage is that I'm the show, and all eyes are on me. One thing that helped was realizing that I am being paid to be on that stage and entertain, so I kept from feeling really frightened by concentrating on what I love... the dancing. I know you've never seen me dance but I'm good."

"I'm sure you're getting better with all that practice." Donna's interest pumped-up Jesse's emotional intensity.

"You know, sometimes I think that we can change the world with music, and dancing. Like when the Jessie Collin Young sings, "Com'on people smile on your brother, everybody get together and try to love one another right now," I mean, that's what Jesus was saying back in biblical times, wasn't he? I just imagine that when I dance to a song the words go straight into the people's minds, and they can't help but change."

"You think so?" Donna did not want to be cynical, but it seemed that it was going to take a lot more than some teeny-bopper dancing with her boobs knocking, to bring peace into the world.

"Obviously, you're not dancing now! How are you and Carlos making it?"

The food arrived; Jesse attacked it as only a pregnant woman can. Between mouthfuls she continued talking. "We're living in a little gardener's shack behind an elderly woman's house. I guess I shouldn't call it a shack. It doesn't leak or anything, but the roof is slanted so that at one side of it you can't stand up straight without bumping your head. It's a good thing neither of us is tall. It has three rooms, a bedroom at one end, the bathroom at the other, and a kitchen in between. I'm getting welfare help, and Carlos is driving a delivery truck for a stationery company. The money's tight, but I'm learning how to budget... like a dollar a day for food. I can do it too! I get a half pound of hamburger meat for a dollar a pound, a box of rice, and a frozen vegetable for a quarter a package, and we eat a good evening meal every day! I miss the money I made dancing, but it's ok. We've got my stereo set-up, and a few records. Listening to music is free, and the library is within walking distance, so I'm getting a lot of reading done. Also, there is this park where I go and swing just about every day. In fact, last Thursday I saw my old friend Jim Morrison there, walking with a chick, but he didn't recognize me. Remember how stoked I was on him, and how he was trying to get my virginity. Now he doesn't know my face."

The conversation shifted, "The only thing is... Carlos doesn't touch me much. I asked him about it, and he tried to explain that it felt strange for him to be with a pregnant chick."

Disappointment covered Jesse's face; she quickly changed the subject. "You know my friend Danielle? Well, we went down to Santa Monica last Tuesday, took some blankets, and slept on the beach. Here I am all fat and pregnant!"

"Why would you do that?" Donna asked with alarm, since it was the last thing on Earth she would do if she were getting ready to give birth.

"Well, to commune with the ocean and the sky... and besides, it's free. And I love the pounding of the waves, and the smell of the sea air, don't you?"

"Yeah, but in the middle of the night? You know what kinds of psychopaths, and perverts are walking around just waiting for a chance to jump on some pregnant girl who can't protect herself," Donna admonished.

"Don't you think you're being a little bit paranoid, and melodramatic? I mean it's the beach, not Hollywood," she said emphatically, as if it really made a difference.

After everything that had already happened to Jesse, Donna could not fathom why she would still take a chance like that, but she was nineteen not twelve, and Donna was a friend not her custodian. Looking at her watch and seeing that the day was getting away from her, Donna stood up.

"Jesse, I have to go. I still have a lot of errands to do." She scribbled her phone number on a piece of paper and left a twenty to cover lunch. "Call me. Let's not lose touch again, ok?" She bent down and hugged Jesse, big belly and all.

Donna cruised by in the car and Jesse waved from the cafe, radiating that smile of hers. She wondered out loud, as she pulled out of sight, 'would I be so enthusiastic and calm if I were accidentally pregnant, without family or support?' Well, at least Carlos seemed to be sticking around. She had not met him, but Jesse had shown her a picture. He was gorgeous, with his curly blond locks, sage eyes, and radiating smile! She hoped that his soul was as beautiful as his face.

Playing House

The L.A. summer was exhaling the last of its stinky, scorching breath, and in the second autumn week of October Jesse gave birth at UCLA hospital to a fine seven-pound boy. With no complications the birth took twenty-two hours, not unusual for a first baby. As Carlos and Jesse had previously agreed upon, the infant was not circumcised. Breast feeding came easy to Jesse; it just seemed like the natural thing to do, as if she had gotten instructions from a hippie handbook.

They were living in a small one-bedroom apartment, still close to the strip, and then moved in with Jamie, a friend Carlos knew from community college. All the while the couple was looking westward toward the ocean, only thirty thirsty minutes away. Jesse yearned for the beach and the sound of the surf.

Carlos continued to work second-rate jobs in delivery, and Jesse collected a welfare check with a hundred dollars in food stamps to help, but she soon grew frustrated living at poverty level, and began thinking about returning to the topless scene where she knew she could make enough money to move them out of the closet sized bedroom in which they were living.

There were high times at Jamie's place, good old fashioned pot parties. Jamie liked playing Master of Ceremony, so after using a cigarette roller (he did not have the patience to roll by hand), he would line up a few joints on the coffee table beside a bottle of wine and pass them around. After he deemed everyone properly altered, he would break out a new LP and collectively they would listen to the album. Often the group would sit and analyze, teasing out the 'true meanings' of the lyrics until the sparrows' twittering alerted them of dawn's imminence.

Jesse left the gathering early, softly padded downstairs, and crawled into the single bed which barely accommodated two adults. There she waited for Andre to wake-up, to relieve the pressure in her aching breasts. The infant's tongue was like sandpaper and feeding him every two or three hours had worn raw spots on both nipples. Inside of five weeks, Jesse had had her fill of breast-feeding regardless of how healthy it was for the baby. No one had told her how painful being an *earth mother* could be, and besides, she was desperate to make some money.

One night she told Carlos her intentions, as they were squeezing spoon position in the guest bed, trying to get comfortable. "I can't do this anymore. My nipples have sores on them from Andre's sucking. I'm going to switch him to a bottle, then I can go back to work and get us into our own place."

"Well, whatever you want to do..." He responded with hopeful resignation. Although he never talked about it, he too was tired of their living situation. But what could he do about anything, especially making minimum wage?

They had talked about getting out of Hollywood, out of the 'city' and away from the smog. The minute Jesse decided to take back her breasts she felt a sense of power returning to her. "We can look for a place down at the beach. Venice has a lot of cheap places for rent." The future looked brighter already. She pushed her butt up against him, and he tried to back up to get some room, only there wasn't any, just the cold wall.

The Grind

esse couldn't wait to get working. She found an agent who booked her into a club in Orange County. The place was a typical blue-collar beer bar with a clientele of rude, leering, loud mouths. Her first night back she was the only dancer to show up, so she danced fifty minutes on, ten minutes off, and then to top it off, the owner begged her to stay for the second eight-hour shift because another dancer had failed to show. Dead tired, her breasts still sore and seeping, but needing the money, she agreed.

"Damn, I wish I had more costumes," she uttered under her breath. She only had a few G-strings, garter-belts, stockings and a kimono she had bought in a Venice Beach hippie shop that barely covered her butt.

The manager of a topless establishment had to be in compliance with the vice squad's requirements of that county. The customer stayed 6 feet away from the performing dancers. Dancers could not leave the stage unless fully clothed, no pubic hair or nipples showing, no soliciting (from either side), and although sitting with the customers was encouraged because it increased drink sales, the bouncers watched for any infraction of the no-touching rule. Jesse put a smile on her face and limped through the grueling 16-hour shift.

With steady work for a week and money under the table Jesse and Carlos were able to move out of Hollywood.

They found a cute little two-bedroom house in Venice a block from the ocean for ninety-five dollars a month. They could not be happier, even if short-lived.

Jesse continued to work for the same agent who sent her miles out of town to obscure places she had never heard of, often outside of the city limits, where the vice was easily bribed, and the rules were conveniently lax. They had bought a '57 Chevy, for a couple hundred bucks, and Jesse would take off into the twilight never knowing exactly where she was going or what kind of club she would be dancing in. Carlos found himself a job at UCLA hospital pushing around a med-cart and following commands.

Tired of the commuting, Jesse decided to try her luck locally. She was still a little pudgy from the pregnancy, and her upstanding perky tits showed some wear from the breastfeeding, as well as a few stretch marks. Although she was young, there were girls who certainly had more "perfect" bodies than hers, and because of the competition Jesse did not get hired at the top-notch clubs. The honky-tonks she worked were not glamorous; in fact, her agent could not be relied upon to send her to any that *were not* dumps.

Carlos never knew what mood Jesse would bring home especially since her use of amphetamines continued to be a part of her work routine.

"God damn it!" She screamed as she stormed in the front door and threw her dance gear on the floor by the couch. "You would not believe the place Randy sent me to this time. First, it's in East LA; second, it's no more than a neighborhood slum bar, third, I get up on stage and the manager turns on a fucking porno flick *while I'm dancing.*

What could I do... I made a joke about not being able to compete with talent like that."

Carlos said and did nothing. He was not good dealing with the explosive emotions Jesse dished out. Not being experienced enough, he was unable to put reassuring arms around her letting her know that she was *not* alone in this unfair world teeming with exploitation and users. Although he was with her, she could not feel his presence. She could only sense an overwhelming fear, rage, and suffocation from a life without help, without connection or support, a perception so eclipsing that it tainted her whole being.

Reckless Behavior

t was before noon, and for a change, Jesse was up, her make-up perfect, her dance bag filled with clean fresh G-strings, cover-ups, and high-heeled pumps.

"Carlos, I'm taking the car up to Hollywood. I want to check out a bottomless club that I heard a dancer talking about. Supposedly they are paying twelve dollars an hour. It's on La Cienega in Hollywood."

Carlos looked at her, "When do you think you'll be back?" He had been up for hours taking care of little Andre, changing his diaper, feeding him breakfast, and now watching him hang out in the baby pool in the backyard. He was a dedicated father.

"A couple of hours," she replied. He knew that was a lie, Jesse notoriously could not be punctual or predictable. She had no sense of time.

The Runway was easy to find. Jesse walked in through the front door, as her eyes adjusted to the darkness, she could see that it was a big club, and catering to blue-collar workers. After ten minutes talking with Kenny, the manager, he handed her a work schedule for the week. It was as easy as that.

The club was nude, the first ever in Los Angeles; the first in Southern California. The owner and a posse of lawyers had decided to challenge the fact that there were no laws regulating nude dancing in public. As history would have it, it simply had not come up before this. Knowing they could operate until a test trial ensued and a verdict was reached, the doors opened. From the first night and each one thereafter, a line of men around the block waited to get into the club.

At the end of the week Jesse had made nearly a thousand dollars. She felt like she was finally getting somewhere, but the money came with a catch. She and the other dancers would be cited for indecent exposure. This seemed acceptable to her because she was using a fake ID. The owner had explained to all the girls that they would not be taken to jail, and that they would not have police records when the test trial was concluded regardless of the outcome. Being guileless, Jesse did not bother to ask how this feat would be accomplished, but rather took it to be the truth. She liked the idea that she was part of a movement for greater freedom, the freedom to dance naked, and the freedom to watch. This was in alignment with her ideals... besides, she already had a record.

Carlos was less than pleased.

"What do you mean you're going to be arrested for indecent exposure? Are you crazy?"

Jesse's anger started seething; she hated being criticized. She did not want Carlos or anyone else pointing out the gaps in her reasoning. Her rage made her unapproachable.

"Look! I pay all the bills. I'm making the money. It's more than what you're doing, sitting around depressed, and smoking pot every night. If I wait around for you to make something happen, I'll be an old woman. Anyway, it's none of your damn business, it's my life!" She screamed with all the rancor she could summon and walked out of the house slamming the door as she went.

The sun was setting; the beach was deserted. She walked a half-mile, her anger propelling each step in the sand. She felt deflated and ugly. She knew she was impulsive, and that Carlos was looking out for her, but she wanted to keep making the money. Her desire was like the core of a volcano; she could feel the power that the money gave her. She could do anything, go anywhere, build and create a life. And she was good at it! She did not give a damn if Pat McClarren got another misdemeanor; Pat had married and moved on. Anyway, she would never know. It was a tiny, insignificant incident in the greater picture of an entire lifespan.

As Jesse ruminated, she did not take notice of the six-foot-tall man with long blond stringy hair dressed in a dark colored raincoat who had slipped up beside her.

Startled, she began talking nervously, "Oh, hi! I didn't see you. It's dark out here tonight, no moon." Jesse began talking like they were neighbors.

"You live around here?" the man asked.

"Yeah, a few blocks that way," she said, pointing confidently.

"My 'ol man and I had a disagreement, so I came down here to the beach to cool off." She continued, not realizing that he was not responding.

Jesse continued talking and talking about her situation until she felt calmer and the emotional storm had subsided. At that point she stopped and turned around.

"Well, I have to get back home. My 'ol man will be wondering where I am."

The stranger stepped in front of Jesse and took a butcher knife out of his coat. Clearly, she could see the blade catching the light of distant streetlamps. Having been through this before she knew it was better not to fight.

"Hey, put the knife away. You don't need that. I'll cooperate with you. What is it that you want?" She quickly assured her assailant.

"I want you to do exactly what I tell you," he responded bluntly.

With the knife still in his hand he took off his overcoat and spread it on the ground.

"Now, lay down, and take your pants off."

She did as she was instructed. Only when his body was on top crushing hers did he reach over with his outstretched arm and forcefully insert the butcher knife into the sand up to the hilt. He inserted his hard dry penis. It felt like the end of a rough tree branch.

"Ok baby... that's good," he repeated until he had reached a climax. Then he zipped up his pants and said, "Get dressed. Let's get out of here!"

He offered his hand to help her up, and patronizingly brushed some of the sand from her sweater.

"Come on baby, I want to make sure you get home safely." The blond rapist cooed at her side. They trudged along silently, the semen and sand rubbing the skin of her newly violated vagina, until she was a block from her house. Then she spoke up.

"I just live a couple of houses down... I'd better go alone."

"Are you sure you'll be alright?" He asked as if he were her gallant protector.

"Yes, thank you." She turned abruptly and ran, cutting through yards to hide her retreat.

By the time she reached her front door she was hysterical. She burst in the front door crying. "A man with a butcher knife raped me."

Carlos put his arm around her, and led her around the corner, where he eased her down onto the bed. "I'll run bathwater for you," was all he said. It was all he dared say. He could hardly conceal his anger at her lack of common sense. He wanted to shout and scream, "you are so fucking stupid!" but instead closed the door after drawing a hot steamy bath and helping her into it.

He was in bed reading when the bathroom door finally opened. He looked up silently, studied Jesse for a moment, and returned his attention to the book. The gesture seemed cold. She sat down beside him on the bed. Her voice was soft like the breaking sea foam of the surf, her eyes watery as the seaside tide pools.

"I'm sorry I got so angry. I guess I let my temper get out of control... like my mother used to do." Her voice trailed off in tears, but then she noticed that Carlos was not paying attention. This caused her more anguish.

"Don't you care?" she cried.

He turned red and responded, "What do you mean, *don't I care?* I have told you that it is not safe to walk the beach at night and you did it anyway... and you know what is the worst part? I'm going to have to continue to hear about this. You're never going to let me forget what you went through."

Now Jesse was wounded twice, once when she was violated and now when she was being told that it was her fault. Her feelings of guilt overwhelmed any fight left. She was afraid.

"No, I can let it go. You won't hear about it again, really! I know I should have listened to you."

Jesse paused as a memory caught her consciousness, "Did I ever tell you about the time when I was ten? My mother flew into a rage; she picked up a metal trashcan in my bedroom and hit me over the head with it. She caught me off-guard. I fell and hit the bone above my eye on the foot of the wooden bed frame. Blood started dripping down my face from the gash. I didn't know where my mother had disappeared to. My stepdad put a wet rag over my eye. All I kept saying over and over is, "Does my mother love me? Does my mother love me? I promise I'll be better. I'll mind her, I wonder if she will forgive me and still love me? I guess she was sitting outside on the stoop of the backdoor.

Clayton took me to the doctor, and I got a few stitches along my eyebrow. I lied; I told the doctor that I was running and had tripped and fell. I said, I'm lucky I didn't hit my eyeball or break my occipital lobe. I wonder why I lied for her."

Carlos listened as he had been doing for the last two years, then he turned away with his back facing her, and drew the blankets up over his shoulder. He had tried to be content with Jesse, after-all she was the mother of his son, but her roller-coaster moods, and the dictatorship of her overbearing personality were slowly smothering the good feelings he had for her. It bothered him that his opinion did not matter; Jesse would do whatever she wanted.

The Jail

wo weeks later, Kenny approached Jesse. "Do you want to make twenty dollars an hour, guaranteed 10 hours, and you only have to dance fifteen minutes?"

Jesse was curious, "Oh really, how?"

"My brother has a club in San Diego, and we're doing the same thing there as here, testing the legal system. This time you will go out on stage, dance the first record clothed, then take your top off on the second record, and on the third one you lose the G-string. At that point, a member of the vise squad will come on stage to escort you off. When we have done this with fifteen girls, you will all be loaded into a van, and taken to a holding tank at the Sheriff's station. You'll be released after a few hours and we'll drive you home."

"And I'll be paid $200?"

"In cash before you arrive home!"

"My old man doesn't believe that I won't have a record. I tried to explain it to him, about getting it expunged."

"Tell him that we have seen this strategy work up in San Francisco, so we know beforehand what the outcome will be. It is a process for getting the ruling on the books. It is unconstitutional for the cops to bust us because we are set up like a private club with a membership fee. Believe me, if it were going to hurt the girls, we wouldn't do this." Kenny's concern was genuine. He had no desire to mislead

Jesse, in fact, he would be a terrible businessman if the girls he depended upon were hurt permanently by this experience.

The day finally came for the "gig." Jesse and the other dancers were picked-up in a long stretch limo for the drive to the club, appropriately named "The Jail." The mood of the group of women was optimistic since all of them had positive business relations with the club owner and the manager who had planned and choreographed the entire event, this opportunity for a 'test case'. True to his word, Jesse made her $200, and she never saw the inside of a courtroom.

The Golden Spur

er first private airplane ride came when Ray Deckster, a club owner from Modesto, flew down to the El Monte airport to pick up dancers for a three-week engagement at his rural bar. Recommended by her present employers, fearlessly Jesse stepped up into the Cessna and strapped in as directed by the pilot.

Flying above the patchwork landscape of the central California agricultural belt, it seemed to Jesse that she could reach out with her hand and smooth it over like a quilt on a bed. A wave of optimism and empowerment flooded her mind as she looked down, high above the Earth's surface.

The Golden Spur Club catered to farmers, migrant pickers and blue-collar workers of all odors, which unfortunately offended Jesse's sensibilities, which in turn caused her attitude to be quite arrogant. At this point Jesse was still only twenty years old and had not developed grace or an acceptance of those who appeared less "hip" than she.

Monday, the first night of her new gig she was nervous and animated as only she could get, but by Friday she was extremely euphoric, probably in a manic state induced by a two-day run with diet pills she had gotten from a pharmacist Carlos had met while working at the UCLA hospital. Methamphetamine Sulfate, what a great diet aid!

As she applied her make-up in the fluorescent glare of the motel bathroom her thoughts were on her ol' man. Carlos was driving up with Andre from Venice to Modesto in the pick-up truck and camper they had recently purchased. It was a test run, and the first step to actualizing their plans to visit central Mexico where Carlos' dad and his three young sons (Carlos' stepbrothers) were hiding out from his crazy wife.

The camper was a homemade shell they had snagged for 300 dollars from a man in the neighborhood. Jesse had made curtains out of prints from India and covered the ceiling as well. She had transformed it into a gypsy wagon. It was complete with a two-burner propane stove, and a camper size ice box (a block lasted about a week). There were tiny compact bookshelves for essentials like the I Ching, The Tibetan Book of the Dead, and Be Here Now, even a custom vase holder so she could always have a fresh cut rose as they rolled down the highway.

Jesse loved Carlos, his contemplative nature, his vocabulary, his depth of understanding, and his artistic literary eye. He was a philosopher, teacher, friend, buddy, and therapist. He was everything she wasn't. She loved to look at the contour of his cheekbones, his thick brown eyelashes, the dark luminescent chestnut eyes, and his lean swimmer's torso so like Michelangelo's David.

He also had characteristics that she could do without, his tendency toward melancholy, his seeming lack of ambition, not that she minded his nose buried in books, but his lack of enthusiasm, and he didn't initiate sex often enough. That probably bothered her more than anything else. She was a sex goddess in the eyes of the customers she danced for, but at home she rarely stirred Carlos' interest.

She tired of his constant nagging to get Andre' on a schedule, and not to let him sleep all afternoon, and not to spend money.

Just like her mother, Jesse wanted her way and total acceptance if she happened to change her mind unexpectedly. Exotic dancing fit her well. Deciding when she would and would not work gave her the freedom of self-determination, something she had never experienced in her life.

As Jesse placed the finishing touches on her face, and zip-closed her dance bag (her costumes were already hanging in the club's dressing room), she felt happy knowing that Carlos and Andre' would be here by the end of her shift. Carlos was such a good father, really a better caretaker than she was.

The club was spacious, with high vaulted ceilings. It was a converted barn, huge indoor space with room for pool tables, pinball machines, and basketball games, carnival style. The menu offered quick grilled items like burgers and fries, all freshly cooked, and kids were allowed on one side as long as their parents supervised. The room that showcased the dancers had an elevated stage, a long runway with customer seating all the way around it, and stairs at one end that led off into a dressing area behind the bar. Tables and chairs skirted the outer edges of the room against the walls for those wanting to watch from a distance. In one corner a fireplace with a half-finished checkers game in front of it, all-in-all a lively place at all hours. The majority of the Golden Spur's customers were in some way involved in the massive agricultural economy of the area. This was the hub for feeding the hordes in California, the metropolises of San Francisco, and Los Angeles'. Some customers were migrant workers much like the ones John Steinbeck brought to life in *The Grapes of Wrath.* Other customers were big shot warehouse owners, and farm owners, and heavy equipment salesmen and operators, and an occasional tourist or car salesman.

Whenever she crossed the threshold of a saloon, the stench of cigarettes assaulted her nose; she hated cigarettes. Her mother had smoked, and she had hated her mother. Yes, there were compromises dancing, but in exchange, Jesse was able to earn more money than most high school graduates. Plus, she loved the Burlesque atmosphere, the costumes, the rock 'n' roll music, the stage lights, the attention, the dance, the performance.

It gave her pleasure to muse, *Imagine, I earn money dancing; I'm required to perform, and entertain; my job gives me complete permission to do just that.* She was paid an hourly wage and received tips for dancing, for giving expression to the one passion she had discovered at age 4 in her babysitter's care.

"Hi Pat, go ahead and collect some quarters, you go on first." Jesse smiled; she was used to her fake name having used it since she began topless dancing. The bartender handed her a cup.

Quarters, she thought to herself, *who in the hell thought up that one? They want to run a classy joint but then ask the dancers to collect for the jukebox.*

The daylight outside faded as the beat resounded, the grilled beef aroma faded after the kitchen closed, the drinkers got louder, and it was more difficult for Jesse to find someone she could genuinely relate to. She had not yet learned how to play the "I'm-interested-in-you" game for tips and gifts, so she searched the crowd between sets almost frantically looking for a long-hair, or a 'head' to sit with. Instead, what she saw were cowboys; it was doubtful they read books or knew what protesting was. Then her wish was granted; Jesse spotted two longhaired guys by the pool table. What a relief... she was sure she heard the conspiratorial laughter of one of her own kind.

Rick and Andy lived in a communal house a couple of miles away. They lived with their band, and routinely traveled to San Francisco and L.A. to play the clubs. Both guys understood the limitations of the locals.

"I totally understand how you feel, Jesse; there aren't any hip people around these parts. Why do you think we chose this area to rent in? We knew we'd be able to focus on our music." Rick was dark haired with big lips, and fast-talking. Jesse felt so grateful that she could communicate with some one of her own culture.

"Yeah, no night life over in the town where we live; We're hard pressed to find a diner open after 9, but like Rick said, this place is exactly what we needed as a song writing team, no diversions, just eat, sleep, dream, and work music. No females, no hard drugs."

Jesse looked puzzled, "What about this place? It's rowdy."

"Yeah, true, we visit this place about once every three weeks just to see the new talent Ray brings in. But neither of us spends a lot of time and money in this place, plus neither of us really likes to drink, we're heads. He winked at Jesse.

She responded, "I know, alcohol makes people so sloppy and unaware. By the end of the evening, the men are so repulsive. I hide in the dressing room between sets." She wrinkled her nose and made a face. About that time, Carlos walked through the door.

"I gotta go," Jesse smiled at the long hairs. "I'll talk to you later. Will you be here when I get back?

"Sure," the cute one answered.

She walked away from them and over to the counter where Carlos had found a spot. He was not comfortable in bars; he thought the people attending were crass and unimaginative. Unfortunately, this attitude spilled over into his personality. Jesse loved him but got tired of his pessimism. It seemed like he was always down. Nothing and no one was good enough. However, his analytical mind was always busy, and it is what kept her fascinated with Carlos.

"How was the drive up? You didn't have any trouble finding the place, did you? It's so cool that the owner provides the motel room."

"It was ok; I just came in to let you know we were here. Andre' is asleep in the camper; I'd better go before he wakes up. Did you take some speed; you seem wired?" Carlos asked with irritation.

"Yeah, I didn't sleep very well last night. I guess I was too excited about the airplane ride."

"Ok, I have to go. I'll see you when you get off." He turned abruptly and headed out the door.

He was no sooner out of sight than she started thinking that he sure didn't act like he loved her. At least, these two long-hairs are friendly.

Before she knew it, the night was finished, and the diet pill hadn't worn off. The guys had stayed the entire shift. As she was heading to the dressing room to get changed and leave, Rick stopped her. "Jesse, do you want to come over to our place for a while; you'd really like it; it's beautiful." She had heard about it earlier, a house out in the middle of 50 acres of farmland. The owners were just holding on to it until the right buyer came along.

"You said it was close, right?"

"Yeah, about a fifteen-minute drive"

"Ok, but I can't stay very long; my ol' man will be wondering where I am."

"We'll be in the van out front."

As they were bumping along over a seriously rutted clay road, the guys were rapping about Led Zeppelin as they passed a joint. They passed it, but Jesse declined; a lot of times it made her paranoid. The drive was a little farther than fifteen minutes. The house was a gem, with a wrap-around screened-in porch, heavy hardwood floors, thick exposed beams, and a massive rock fireplace. Even in the starlight she could see the remains of an herb garden, grown over with voracious ivy, and a dry birdbath in the center.

"See those, we planted them." Andy pointed to rows of giant sunflowers leaning against the fence surrounding the yard and peeking into the windows on three sides of the house itself. Jesse had never seen such an enchanted place. Truly a find any hippie could be proud of. The

104

remainder of the wee morning hours passed quickly. They exchanged hitch-hiking stories, and Jesse answered their questions about how she got started dancing, and what it was like to dance around topless.

It wasn't until the sun's shaft pierced through the curtainless window that Jesse realized she had fucked-up. She had not intended to stay out all night. Luckily, Rick was alert enough that he did not mind giving her a ride back into town.

If Jesse had not been so freaked out, she might have enjoyed the rose mist drifting up from the fields in the dawn. Rick pointed out a local bird that, like an escort, was flying alongside the van as it barreled over the potholes leaving a trail of dust behind them.

Jesse hoped that she could slip in the door without waking either the baby or Carlos. No chance: Carlos was awake with the camper packed. When Jesse walked in, he gathered Andre up in his pajamas and blanket, and walked out of the motel door.

Before he left, he said, "I was worried, so I decided to wait until you got here. I was up all night wondering why I had driven 5 hours, 320 miles. I hope you enjoyed yourself." She watched as he drove away.

The rest of her two-week stint was unremarkable; Andy and Rick never came back, probably because they did not get laid. Jesse felt a terrible shame. She had let Carlos down, and he undoubtedly thought that she had had sex when she came in at sunrise. Regardless, Jesse believed herself to be a liberated, free, woman, direct, without games, and loyal to her ol' man. So, what was the big deal? She was only socializing. He was sleeping, and she was speeding. It made her angry that he did not trust her. Nevertheless, she felt guilty because she had unintentionally caused so much discord. Her pride stopped her from picking up the telephone. Now, it was her turn to worry.

At the end of their contract, Ray flew the girls back down to the Los Angeles basin. Carlos was there at the airport with Andre in tow, although his greeting was a bit frosty. With an hour commute home, it gave the couple time to discuss what happened, and plan for a more predictable future. Jesse begged forgiveness for her insensitivity to Carlos' feelings, and convinced him that she had not had sex with anyone else, which was indeed the truth. With the relationship back on even keel they returned to their favorite topic of conversation, the proposed trip to Mexico. It seemed that if Jesse kept dancing, they would be able to leave by the beginning of next summer.

Driving from El Monte airport to Venice sometimes looked post-apocalyptic, seedy intercity smog-stained buildings, the concrete metropolis of corporate wealth, alley after alley of rat-mazes, survival of the fittest, poverty-level disintegrating society, interspersed between miles of upwardly mobile housing developments of the middle and affluent classes. California's arid topography grudgingly gave way to the miracle called the Pacific Ocean.

Jesse always felt a great longing fulfilled when her eyes met the sea, the ultimate meditation, the unique, bio-rhythm attunement. Yes, the fertile farmlands of Modesto had charm, but nothing fed Jesse like the sound of the surf in Ocean Park. From her first memories of jumping the moody tide with her grandmother at sunset, she had connected with the ocean. She feared it but was comforted by its consistent nature. Standing on the seashore always renewed her. The sun was drowning and throwing its last waves of mad color on the horizon as they pulled to the curb beside their Venice cottage.

Mexico

The next few weeks Jesse outdid herself working many nights in a row, accepting dancing gigs anywhere, traveling out to the edge of the desert in Bakersfield, or deep in downtown L.A. She, Carlos, and the baby traveled together on some of the gigs. Both thought it was a good idea to take the camper for a few runs before they left for Mexico. It would have to be in cherry condition for them to feel safe once they got on the country roads of old Mexico. There were places where warring land barons and drug lords made the roads dangerous. Newspaper articles told of tourists being abducted with their vehicles and possessions confiscated.

Their projected departure date was quickly approaching when Jesse began doubting the sanity of driving through Mexico. And Carlos shared her belief.

"We did all this planning, and now we're going to take a train?" He complained. Secretly, Carlos was relieved because he knew his skills as a mechanic were limited, and a trip to Mexico in an old vehicle could be treacherous.

"Well, I feel relieved!" countered Jesse, "we'll be traveling in luxury with a sleeping berth, and it'll be easier with Andre too. Did you talk to your Dad? Is he going to pick us up in Mexico City, or do we have to take a bus to Cuernavaca?"

"I think he'll meet us in Cuernavaca."

"I don't remember him very well. I only met him the one time when we helped him kidnap his kids away from their eccentric mother."

"I'm hoping that his tropical fish business is thriving so that he can put me to work. Dad always said if he could have just 1% of the U.S. tropical fish sales, he would be rich. Two years he has been down there. In one of his letters, he was telling me about his setup. He says he's got over 100 tanks and I don't know how many species by now."

Jesse had not seen Carlos so excited in quite a while. Her hopes and expectations were high. She imagined a life of leisure living in the tropics of Mexico, a place where they had enough money that she would not have to sweat for a living. As the date grew near, and the suitcases were packed, her exuberance had no bounds.

Carlos's mom drove them through downtown Los Angeles to the train station where they said their good-byes. After months of planning, they were finally boarding a train for Mexico.

The first leg of the trip was uneventful, although wearisome for a two-year old. Carlos spent his time walking the cars and entertaining little Andre, while Jesse took in what scenery there was. Except in the ghettos of Los Angeles, she had never seen true squalor and dismal poverty. As the train reached the outskirts of the towns along the way, Jesse was shocked by the multitudes of families living in abandoned railcars, and lean-tos constructed from scrap lumber. Faces stared out of glassless windows, children and babies played in the mud and debris only yards from the rails. This was not exactly the picturesque Mexico she had imagined, with its mile upon mile of parched desert, and abandoned citizens. The train was slowing down as Carlos returned with Andre in his arms.

"This next stop will be a bit longer than the rest so we can get off the train and look around. Don't drink the fountain water in the station though, it can carry dysentery."

As they were stepping down from the train Jesse moved closer to him and spoke. "Carlos, it's hard to believe that people are living like this, I mean, we've only been gone a day, and it seems like we've traveled back in time to some primitive culture. How is it that these people don't have decent places to live, or clean water to drink?" she asked.

"The politics of power... a governor of a province can live in splendor, while the peasants in the same area have little. A man can pick the governor's food, but then not have enough on the kitchen table to feed his own family," Carlos explained patiently.

"It's so wrong," Jesse replied.

"Well, that's why when the social conditions get really terrible people aren't afraid to revolt. To those that don't have food, revolt is an acceptable alternative, and they're willing to fight and die in armed insurrection against the power structure in place."

Jesse agreed and added, "It's like what's happening in the states; the people who are protesting against the Vietnam War are activists because they know they will be the ones who are forced to risk their lives when they lose their college deferments."

"Exactly! Unfortunately, most Mexican peasants do not have the faintest idea about how to create awareness and change, and a revolutionary like Che Guevara has been dead for years. For some, the best solution is to somehow get across the border to the U.S."

"I don't blame them; I wouldn't want to live with no hope of bettering my situation," Jesse responded compassionately.

Just then a little boy rushed up to them, "Chick-le, Chick-le," he said while pushing a box of gum in front of them.

"No, gracias," Jesse responded, feeling awkward.

Before long, the conductor was calling for passengers to board. The venders with their ice cream, tamales, and fruits backed away from the open coach windows. The wheels grabbed steel, and the dust blew in thick swirls as the train started rolling again.

Their train ride ended in Mexico City, and from there they took a bus south to Cuernavaca, a popular tourist town for vacationing Americans. Jesse could see why. It was a tropical paradise; giant ferns and rhododendrons lined the walkways and spaces between the houses; fuchsia Bougainvillea covered the roofs; the humid atmosphere exploded with their sweet perfumes.

This was a busy little town, not the ugly overpopulated metropolis of the nine million plus Mexico City, but a bourgeoning center of commerce and culture none-the-less. Jesse and her family boarded a cross-town bus. At the next stop a fellow with a guitar hopped on, uncased his instrument, and began playing and singing. He rode for a few more stops probably hoping for some donations, and then disembarked as quickly as he had appeared.

"Wow, now that's something you don't see in L.A.," Jesse remarked.

"Yeah, I like the fact that the bus driver was willing to let him ride for the price of a song or two. Did you notice, even Andre was paying attention?"

After stopping for lunch, they were back on a bus again heading south. This was the short leg of the journey. The small village of Puente de Ixtla was only an hour and a half drive although it seemed longer because the bus was overcrowded. It seemed to Jesse that no one in these public places wore deodorant; the stink of body odor permeated the hot afternoon air.

It was dusk when the rusty, antiquated bus made its bumpy way on the rural cobble-stoned streets and parked in front of the post office with its conspicuous telephone line running to it. Geraldo was there with his three other sons, all considerably younger than Carlos because of the gap between the marriages. Jesse was surprised when they started walking, carrying the two suitcases and Andre across the town's main plaza. However, three blocks away they arrived at Geraldo's home. It looked like a mansion compared to the surrounding houses. Mediterranean white with blocks of Lloyd Wright glass in the walls

Jesse and Carlos steeped themselves in the unfamiliar setting, the tropical weather, the calm and simplicity of small-town living. Andre's three uncles looked after him and provided unlimited attention. This was a welcome relief for both parents, but especially for Jesse who was often irritated by the never-ending demands of motherhood.

The young couple was able to take a trip even further south to the coastal city of Acapulco, although, upon seeing its McDonalds' and Travel Lodges', Jesse felt as if she had been cheated and transported back to Los Angeles.

She was not impressed until they motored just ten miles outside of the metropolis. There they came upon a seaside vendor who provided freshly caught and roasted fish for dinner, and hammocks where they could sleep within yards of the rolling surf. The next day Jesse walked the pristine white beach. It was like a fantasy made more surreal by the pot she had smoked with some American backpackers they had met that morning.

The blazing sun and radiating heat made her question what she saw. From a distance she watched a rider galloping full stride toward her on a shiny black stallion. As he got closer, she could see he was clothed in shades of beige and white with a straw hat. The horse towered over her head, and she was quick to step away from its shiny haunches. After a few flourishes, the apparition disappeared back toward the direction it had come, and Jesse resumed her meanderings.

Stoned as she was, she half believed that the shells she was collecting had been hand-painted and placed in the sand by some set designer. Although she had spent years combing the California seashore, she had never seen shells this vivid before, pinks, lavenders, blues and mauves.

Those first few weeks in Mexico were filled with adventures. They met strangers on a bus, college students out for summer vacation, and tagged along with them for a weekend outing. Spirits were high, and the synchronicity brought the couple in contact with other hippies of like mind. Then the little bit of money that they had brought ran out, and they found themselves dependent on Carlos's father for their very subsistence, a role that opened a whole new side to his personality. Suddenly he got more demanding, belligerent, and dissatisfied with them, particularly, Jesse's behavior was often coming under his scrutiny.

One evening Jesse heard rock and roll music coming from the hotel down the street that housed soldiers stationed there for part of the year. She followed the sounds and made her way around back of the hotel where the pool was located. Sure enough, there was a semi-hip young Mexican band faithfully reproducing Creedence Clearwater's Proud Mary. Jesse had not heard American music for at least three months, and jumped at the chance to dance around, partner-less.

Back in the states a single female dancing alone became acceptable after Hippies staged Be-Ins, and hundreds of hippies and residual beatniks danced freeform and without partnering in the traditional mock-mating ritual. But here, deep in Mexico a woman alone without an escort only meant trouble. Jesse was, of course, oblivious to the town's cultural norms, and danced with abandonment even when the band played mostly local folk music.

After the band's last set at five (the streets were rolled up early, even on a Friday night), Jesse committed the next unspeakable sin. She invited two of the musicians to follow her across the street and visit with her and Carlos, her ol' man, or *"mi esposo."*

Carlos was surprised when Jesse appeared with two strange young men. After introductions he sat down with them like a gracious host and proceeded to speak with the two men, pulling from his college Spanish. Jesse bored quickly as the conversation between the guys developed beyond her scanty comprehension. She rose and quietly left the room to go find a book she was reading for a third time. Carlos joined her in the bedroom later after showing the guys to the door. They exchanged small talk and turned out the lights.

Two days later, Carlos approached Jesse in front of Geraldo chastising her for bringing two complete strangers to 'our house'. Jesse's sense of injustice immediately kicked in especially since Carlos had obviously enjoyed the company, a pleasant diversion from the doldrums they had sunken into.

"You are such a hypocrite, Carlos. If I was such a horrible person, why didn't you say something then, and ask them to leave. Instead, you sat and rapped with both for two and half hours; and I'm the villain here?"

Jesse's tone of voice had reached a shriek as she screamed defiant challenges, cursed him for his insensitivity, and for siding against her with his father.

Geraldo boldly intervened and announced to Jesse that she "Shut up, and show some respect toward me and toward Carlos, or go to your room."

Indignant, Jesse responded, "This is none of your fucking business, so why don't you just stay out of it. We'll work this out without you."

Geraldo stepped toward Jesse, and open-handedly slapped her face. The wicked crack of two surfaces well met. Jesse felt the sting. It was late afternoon. She ran from the veranda crying, dismayed and abhorred that this man had laid a hand on her. *The violent asshole! She would not stay under the same roof with someone so barbaric.* Jesse ruminated as she walked down the hallway to Andre's room.

Jesse did not hesitate; she woke her two-year old son from his nap, grabbed a bag of essentials, hoisted the sleepy toddler on her hip and headed for the front door. Carlos reached the door before she did. He did not prevent her from going out.

"Jesse, what are you doing?"

She screamed overdramatically, "You don't think I would stay in a house with a madman like your father?"

Carlos replied in a soft reassuring tone, "Jesse, you don't know where you're going to be tomorrow. Would you put our son through that?"

And with that, Jesse handed the boy to his dad, turned and walked away from the house. She made her way down the cobblestone street. She couldn't and wouldn't stay in a house with physical violence directed against her. But now, what could she do? She had no money and needed to get out of town. The middle of town was only a quarter of a mile away, and she remembered where the town doctor and his wife lived, close to the bus stop. Maybe they would help her.

The doctor's wife opened the door, surprised, but invited the disheveled girl inside. Jesse explained the situation in her inadequate Spanish and asked for enough money for a bus ticket to Mexico City. They were sorry to hear about her domestic conflict, and they were happy to help her.

Within 40 minutes Jesse was on a bus headed north to Mexico City. At least she was pointed in the right direction toward the United States and California, back home where she had more control over her life. She would worry later about what to do when she arrived in Mexico City, population, nine million. With the bus stopping in every small Mexican village between Puente de Ixtla and Mexico City, the relatively short distance had taken three hours.

Jesse looked out the dirty bus window in bewilderment at the sprawling city. With her minimal Spanish she was able to elicit help. The driver looked out for Jesse and made sure she got off at the central station so she could connect with another bus going all the way to the border.

"Gracias," she said with sincerity as she stepped off the bus. She grabbed her overstuffed suitcase and went looking for a schedule of buses. Once she located the window where she could buy her ticket to the states Jesse parked it under a bench and went scouting for an American who might assist in her exodus out of this country.

She scanned the waiting area filled with benches. To the right were two young men. She knew it was a numbers game, enough tries and she was sure to run into someone helpful. She took a deep breath and rolled the dice as she walked toward them.

She apologized for herself in simple sentences, and as articulate as her high school Spanish would allow quickly summarized her *problema* as an angry father-in-law who hit her, and she wanted to get back to California as soon as possible. The men, in their twenties, spoke between themselves, and one stepped away to make a telephone call to his father. Within 30 minutes the man's father appeared at the bus station, opened his wallet, and with his blessings had given Jesse enough money to buy a ticket all the way to

Tijuana. Then all she would have to do was walk across the border. No one could have orchestrated a more perfect getaway. In a few days, she would be back in Hollywood, able to work and generate money. Then she could save up and send Carlos enough for both him and her son to take the train back home to the states. She was irritated that Carlos had not stuck up for her, but not so irritated that she would abandon him and her son.

The Letter

ithin a week of being back in the states, she had saved enough money from dancing that she was able to send Carlos $250, enough to buy train tickets for Andre and him. She sent him a money order and a letter saying how much she missed them and could not wait for them to return. Perhaps it was a testament to her naiveté, but she did not imagine that Carlos would want anything else except to come back to the states. After all, they had expressed to each other their frustration at being stuck in Mexico with no money and no way to return to the states.

Since Jesse got back, she had picked up the camper and truck, and was now living in it, jumping from house to house when she needed to shower so as to not wear out her welcome. Jamie and Babs were renting a house in West Hollywood and welcomed her, giving her a key to the house so that she could use the bathroom shower without ringing the doorbell.

Jesse was feeling motivated, happy, in control, and anticipating the return of her family when Jamie handed her a letter postmarked from Mexico. She excitedly tore the envelope open expecting to get an arrival date; instead, the words she read ripped open her heart. She stared with disbelief, *"Anything you believe we had, is an illusion. Go on with your life."* Nausea overwhelmed her; her heart was racing; she felt like she had stepped inside of a living nightmare and could not wake up. She went to find Jamie who had disappeared to some part of the house. When she found him, she started talking frantically, uncontrollably.

"What does he mean, 'an illusion'? He has my son; that's no illusion. He thinks he can just say a word and I will go away. I'm not going to let go of my child. I would have taken Andre with me, but I didn't want to put him in an uncertain situation. Carlos is so damn arrogant! How can he just dismiss me as if I were nothing? I was good enough when I was supporting us, wasn't I? I can't believe he would do this to me." Jesse sobbed hysterically.

Jamie didn't know what to say. He had been friends with Carlos since junior college and knew that he could be hard and stubborn once he had made-up his mind. He had seen him simply make a decision and walk away, never looking back.

"Jamie, I'm going down there. I've waited long enough. I made money and sent it to him, and now he wants to play games? This is so unfair."

"Jesse, you know how much I like both of you, and I would love to see you two back together. I have been planning to take my vacation soon. I want to visit Carlos, so why don't you relax for a couple of weeks, and when I get back, I'll be able to give you a good idea about what's going on, ok?"

Among Carlos' circle of friends, Jesse had always liked Jamie the most.

Jesse thought about what he just said, "Yeah, well I guess sending out an emissary before the meeting is a good idea."

120

She stepped closer to Jamie and with lowered voice said, "Please put in a good word for me; tell him I'm working and putting the money away for us. I'm waiting to start my life over with them." Jamie gave her a brief hug to assure her.

That was the longest two-week wait in her life. Since Jesse had become a dancer instant gratification was the norm, so sitting back and having absolutely no influence on an outcome grated on her nerves.

In the meantime, she stayed busy working as many shifts as she could book. Finally, it was the day before Jamie was supposed to return. Jesse was calm and excited because she had already made up her mind that Carlos could not have fallen out of love with her that quickly, and that most likely he would welcome her back, give her a second chance, and they would be a family like they were before.

When Jamie told her that Carlos would not change his mind about their relationship, Jesse's stomach lurched as the reality hit her. She was alone on this earth, Carlos and little Andre were hundreds of miles away. There would be no reunion, no second chance, no wholeness, only Jesse's pathetic despondency. She walked away from Jamie doubtful that she could sustain her own life, full of sadness and self-loathing as she was.

That evening she tried to make herself comfortable in the camper bed where she and Carlos had slept, what seemed like many lifetimes ago. She cried and cried as if some compassionate god could or would make everything alright again. Pillow wet, eyes swollen, Jesse wished she would die in her sleep. Surely this was the hell she had read about, desolation and isolation, the place where no god would reside.

By noon the next day, she made her way to the modeling studio to see if she could pick up a gig so that she could eat and rent a place to live. Her thoughts flew wildly, and her emotions ran the gamut from anger and revenge, to transcendent optimism, and determination to become reunited with her baby boy. She knew she had not been a very good mother, but no one would convince her that he was better off without her.

She did not enjoy being employed in the flesh market but what choice did she have. She hated the shape of her body since giving birth. She thought it looked deformed, but as long as men were willing to look, Jesse would continue to take her clothes off for money.

In the past, the owner, John Carroll had been almost fatherly toward her, directing her and in some instances, protecting her. He had recognized a naive teenager when he saw one; enough of them had passed through the door of his studio. Jesse wasn't sure what kind of welcome she would receive now.

On her first day back from Mexico she walked through the once familiar doorway into the still decrepit waiting room, sensing that things were different. Three years had passed since her first illicit Polaroid and the innocent topless cheesecake. The industry had changed. Now in place of the classic semi-nude glamour shot was brazen raw sexual exploitation. As the erotic taste of customers grew, demanding more exotic faire, the sexual revolution blazed on. The industry rapidly changed to accommodate its voracious fans and loyal consumers.

When Jesse had first begun modeling, 'split beaver' shots had been illegal and prohibited. Now, no sexual display was too provocative. The world of vaginas was being invaded by the camera; the industry was wide open, so to speak. Jesse quickly made peace with her distaste, and scheduled a shooting for the coming week, eye candy for one of the dozens of pornographic publications who used John's girls in their layouts; it paid $150 cash for the day. All the models involved were required to sign releases. She signed, knowing that the image of her naked body was, again, no longer her property.

Initially, the sessions were tolerable, soft-core simulated sex with lots of 'pink', but no actual penetration. But before long John let her know that she would have to do hard-core stills and perhaps some movies if she wanted to have steady work. Jesse left the studio depressed knowing that he was right.

After a few weeks, Jesse felt like shit all the time. Even though it was still photography, she hated simulating sex, and spreading her legs for those eyes behind the camera. Her sense of self was disappearing in a haze of sweat. She liked sex, but she liked to have sex with partners of her own choosing, and she did not want to 'graduate' to movies. That idea disgusted and repulsed her; being rubbed on, slobbered on, probed, pounded, and climaxed on. No. However, the income and illusory sense of control it might bring, gave her pause for thought.

Jesse had a day off and her plan was to pick up a bag of weed, and head to the ocean. Hollywood always yielded a quick dollar; however, the beach was the place where Jesse could fill her emptiness with the sound of tons of water crashing and pounding the sodden shoreline. It seemed like the only spot on earth where she could throw off the heaviness in her chest, fill her lungs with its briny wind, and return inland rejuvenated.

My, My, My, Said the Spider to the Fly

ack in Hollywood Jesse bounced along Santa Monica Boulevard filled with a renewed sense of optimism about her future, meanwhile the tides of time and fate were converging on her. From the north across the street toward Jesse walked a young man with long blond hair, smoking a cigarette, and from the west at the exact same time walked another young man with dark long hair, tawny brown skin, both with their eyes on her. Jesse was inside her head otherwise she might have seen the hustle coming.

"Hey, hey, where are you going to in such a big hurry?" Jack spoke quickly and surrounded Jesse with his magnetism.

"Hi, pretty lady, don't talk to him, you want to talk to me." Marty, the dark-haired guy, came up on the other side. They were both vying for her attention and putting the other down in a friendly way that led Jesse to believe that they were friends. More than friends, they had pimped the same girls, hustled the same marks, and slept under the same bridge when they ran out of good ideas and places to crash.

Jesse smiled at both. It had been ages since she had been hit on by someone who looked good to her, and even longer since she'd had consensual, affectionate sex. While she lived with Carlos, he had had a low sex drive, but then she didn't have any other experience of living with someone to compare him to. All she knew was that he always seemed distant, and she always seemed to need more attention and cuddling than he could muster. And here were two dudes who were interested in this stray cat.

"Do you know where I can get a bag of weed?" Jesse asked with a smile.

Jack scored! Jesse, immature, unloved, and alone, was easy pickings for any half-assed player.

"Sure, follow me. I can get the best bag for the best price. See you later Marty, I'll catch up with you this evening." Reluctantly, Marty stepped aside as Jesse walked off with Jack's arm over her shoulder.

They arrived at Jesse's camper. Jack assessed the gypsy wagon that she lived in, stove, icebox, and pullout bed; everything but a bathroom. On the walk over Jesse was spilling over about her ol' man and her baby, *and how he thinks he's going to keep him, and how heartbroken she is, and tired of the flesh market,* and before long Jack was comforting her and telling her, "I'm with you now, baby. You don't have to worry about anything. I'm going to take care of you and help get your son back."

He said exactly what she wanted to hear. The comforting strokes on her back morphed into erotic caresses. Jack easily coaxed Jesse into the bed, and there he began to weave his magic. He required full passivity during love-making, firmly whispering into her ear, "Don't move. You're too aggressive. Let me give to you. Just concentrate and feel what I'm doing to you."

For the first time in her life, she was being pleasured. The romantic attachment was being woven. After sucking and tonguing her vaginal lips, Jack mounted her and rocked her to yet another climax, while he ejaculated wildly. Then he quickly got dressed. "Jesse, sweety, if you want that weed, I have to go now, or I'll miss my connection. Gimme that $50."

"$50 seems like a very high price," Jesse remarked, handing some bills to him.

"Not for this stuff, it's potent red-hair sinsemilla. Believe me you'll be happy when you smoke it." With that dismissive remark he stepped out of the camper door and was gone into the dusk, and darkening streets of the city.

Jesse lay amid the cluttered sheets and bathed in the energy of their lusty encounter. Soon she turned over, touched the light switch, and opened Lord of the Rings; and for the first time since she received Carlos' letter telling her to fuck off, she felt calm, and somewhat more optimistic. *Here is a man who is fascinated with me; someone to love and build a life with. He wants to be father to my child and said he would help me retrieve him.* In her reverie the hands of the clock spun. Suddenly, she bolted up worried and wondering where her prince could be. It was past well past 2 A.M.

He did finally roll in about 4 o'clock; Jesse was still wide awake.

"Hi baby, did you miss me? I'm sorry I got hung up, and then I got ripped off." Jesse had been anticipating a 'high' evening with her and Jack floating away in smoke rings, but at this moment she was so happy to have him back in bed by her side that she quickly forgot about the weed and the fifty dollars. Anyway, she still had some mescaline pills, she had stashed away (for a special occasion). They wound themselves in each other's body parts and fell asleep.

The next day they drove from Hollywood to a strip of beach in Malibu. During the drive, Jesse felt melancholy as her attention drifted to memories of her and Carlos excitedly making plans for the excursions in the camper that, at that moment, she was driving with another man. And there was Jack crashed out in back, wearing clothes Carlos had left behind. The sun-drenched sand, and familiar beach sounds soon brought Jesse out of her funk. She had stopped at a burger stand so she could wake Jack with a hot lunch; he seemed skinny.

Jack was theatrical, sometimes witty, and did his best to beguile Jesse. She slipped easily into believing his cleverly crafted disguise was real. He was entertaining, though more than once she thought his silliness was juvenile. Jack always finished off the evening by making love to Jesse, and with each orgasm her attachment grew. There seemed to be no limits to his erotic play, and since her unfounded trust had kept her blind to any warning intuitions that might have crashed into her consciousness, she continued to meet his sexual demands, even those with a slightly deviant taint.

Shortly, the mescaline was gone, and by noon the next day, the Jack with whom Jesse had been building a relationship with, disappeared. First his attitude changed, then his personality. He proceeded to pick a fight, screamed at Jesse for no apparent reason, and left the camper. Slamming the door, and running toward the highway, where he quickly picked up a ride with his thumb.

There was nothing left of him but a cloud of dust the car had kicked up as it drove away. Jesse sat in the doorway, crying, trying to figure out what had just happened. He simply began putting her down and listing all the ways she was deficient and saying some things she did not understand like Jesse couldn't keep a man like him.

She stayed one more night at the seaside campground and headed back to Hollywood the next day. She needed to generate some cash and had also resolved to find out where Jack might be staying; she knew girls at the studio bought pot from him.

It was a slow Wednesday; Melissa and Satin were sitting around doing their nails and watching the soaps. They both looked up when Jesse opened the door; the bell tinkled expectantly.

"Hi, which one of you has some spare time?"

"For you Jesse, deal of the day, two for the price of one."

"Bitchin', too bad I don't have any cash." All three laughed. Why not? The boss was gone, and there weren't any customers around.

"Do either of you know Jack, I think he sometimes models here?" Both women knew exactly who Jesse was referring to.

Melissa was the first to speak, "Yeah, we all know Jack. What did he tell you? You know, he's a chronic liar."

Jesse answered, "Well nothing really, except that I really like him, and I want to find out where he lives so I can visit him. We spent almost a week together, and got along so well, until..."

"Wait let me guess, he picked a fight, and disappeared, but not until all the money and dope were gone. Sound familiar?

Jesse looked dismayed.

"Oh please, are you simple? Jack is a small-time hustler with many bad habits. All of us have learned our lessons; we stay clear of him," Satin said backing up Melissa.

The romantic interlude with Jack was still fresh in her memory, in fact his smell was still on her. This attack on her newfound lover forced her to quickly tuck away her tender feelings for him. She said little while the two girls ranted on about someone Jesse was sure could not possibly be the Jack she knew.

Jesse stepped outside the studio doors headed for the truck with an address Satin had scribbled on a scrap of paper. The apartment was almost within walking distance of the studio. She parked in the same block, found the numbered door and knocked.

A lovely girl with pasty white skin and stringy black locks opened the door, and without waiting for Jesse to say anything, opened the door farther, and yelled at Jack. "It's for you!"

Looking past the girl, Jesse could see Jack holding a baby. "Hey Jesse, how're you doing, this is my wife, Gloria, and my son, Eli; he's, like, nine weeks old. This is the dancer I told you about, Gloria. Making a point to look at Jesse, he said, "We have an open marriage, that's the only way I can stay with one woman. She has her boyfriends who give her money and take care of us. It works out good!"

If Jesse had been able to express what she was feeling, L.A. would surely have registered another quake. Upon listening to Jack's simple explanation, like a trigger her anger and confusion welled up in nausea. Although on unfamiliar ground, she managed to keep her mouth shut while watching as the strange situation unfolded in front of her eyes.

It wasn't long before Jack came close to her neck whispering, "I missed you so much, Gloria and I are finished. That is why I left you in such a hurry. I knew I couldn't live in this lie any longer, not since I met you."

With these lies, all the uncertainty and hurt evaporated away. She lifted her lips to his demanding tongue. She was instantly wet. Jack stopped abruptly, turned his back to Jesse and walked away disappearing into what looked like the door to a bedroom. Jesse felt awkward. While Jack was gone, the baby Eli started fussing. Jesse looked over where he was lying in his bassinet. He had dark hair like Gloria, none of Jack's blue-eyed blond genes apparent. Jesse picked up the crying infant and drew him close. The remembrance of her own child was suddenly overwhelming, and she was glad there were tissues within arm's reach.

Jack and Gloria suddenly appeared. She reached for Eli saying, "Thank you for watching Eli, and please, make yourself at home." With that she retired to a back bedroom leaving Jack and Jesse alone.

"Honey, remember I told you about 'blues', well, I got some and I want all three of us to do some, and really get into the realm of love, together, ok?"

Jesse was game, she was with her man, and he loved her; what could be wrong with anything? Before she realized, Jack was using a belt to strap his arm off right in front of her. She watched, both repulsed and fascinated. Then it was her turn. She asked a half-dozen questions and when she was satisfied that it was a safe procedure, she let Jack inject her with 1/4 of the little blue pill dissolved in water.

The warm orgasmic-like rush hit her groin area and worked its way up her spine like a burst of fireworks into her brain. "Wow" was all she could say, and then Jack was removing her clothes, sucking her nipples, tonguing her navel, and finally doing both to her clitoris, and vaginal lips, but before she could climax, he stopped, and inched up to her ear telling her what he wanted.

"Gloria is in the bedroom waiting for you, and I want to watch and join in some of the time. This really means a lot to me, and it's our way of telling her that even though you and I are in love, we love her too."

Put like that, and horny as she was, it sounded reasonable. She took Jack's hand and followed him into the bedroom where Gloria was waiting within the mounds of soft comforters that clothed the king-size bed.

To begin with Jack lay down with both girls shifting his attention first to one, and then the other, but finally leaving them with each other to take a voyeur's view from an overstuffed easy chair only a few feet from the girl's playground. He talked to them, directed them to fulfill the needs of his lusty eyes.

Afterwards, they all slept, except for Gloria's trips to care for the baby. The following day, Jesse left with Jack.

He wanted a ride to a friend's house, and she needed to find a quick paying dance gig. Her camper would be needing gas, and food was low too. They agreed to meet back at the apartment when she got off work at 1:30 a.m.

She managed to land a dancing job off the strip. It was nude, but laying down on the stage was not required, so she took it. The manager gave her work; he liked to rotate the girls, keep the entertainment fresh. Only three shifts. It was the best he could do, take it or leave it. She started two hours later and walked away with $85 in tips, as well as another $12 an hour salary. She started early, the shift was done by eight, so she packed up her costumes and boots and headed to Jack's apartment happily musing about what a good time they would have tonight, maybe get some more 'blues', or catch a flick.

It sure was good to have cash in her pocket. After parking the camper, she climbed the stairs to number 8 and knocked. There was no one home. It did not surprise her; it was so much earlier than they had agreed to meet. No problem, she would relax in the camper and read a book until he got home. She fell asleep and when she awoke, she pulled the covers over her sheltering herself against the rising sun.

She slept as long as the noisy city traffic would allow and tried the apartment again. No answer. She felt the wave of disappointment, and queasiness hit her as she left a written note and headed for her truck. She did not have time to think about Jack. Right now, she needed to find a friend who would allow the use of their shower. Today she worked the 3-11 shift. As she left the name of the club on a note, she hoped he would stop in. This time her intuition had been right. He walked in toward the end of her shift, sat down front and tipped her. Her face lit up, and she rolled her hips provocatively to the beat of the jukebox.

Back in the truck with Jack and a pocket full of money, Jesse turned and asked, "Where to?"

Jack gave directions as they drove downtown into the streets of Watts. They had trouble finding a spot to park, and then had to walk a couple of blocks; it was well past midnight.

A black man clothed in boxers, white t-shirt, and socks answered the door, and left it open. As he faded back into the dark house the two of them walked in. Jack whispered into Jesse's ear to give him her money. This came as a surprise since Jack had not mentioned or asked her for money prior to this moment. She felt like she had no choice, but to dig in her bag for the wad of cash she had collected that evening. She handed it to him.

"Wait here; this won't take long."

Forty minutes later Jack reappeared. He seemed relaxed, probably high. She had steadily been getting more anxious as she waited. Jack introduced the black guy as Ty. Jesse was polite though not talkative. He invited them back into another part of the apartment. Jesse could see a low table set up with a spoon, and other items used to cook dope.

Ty offered to fix Jesse a hit, but Jack stepped in and told him that they couldn't stay. He put a protective arm around her, and they made their way out of the front door, saying their good-byes. Back behind the wheel, Jack told Jesse that Ty wanted to buy sex from her, and that is why they had left so abruptly. She responded irritably.

"And by-the-way, why didn't you ask me for money before we got there? I didn't have a choice."

"I was trying to please you. I thought you wanted to get high again, and this was the only place I knew I could get something. I'm sorry honey. I did this for you and me."

His tone of voice reached Jesse; she found herself softening as the anger left her.

"Alright, can we please get out of here? Did you get the blues?"

Jack did not answer right away, but instead began directing her out of the neighborhood and back on to the highway. Only after they were well on their way did he begin to explain, "I couldn't get blues, but I got us some Dilaudids. They're even better!"

He convinced her to stop in a grocery store parking lot. Once in the camper, Jack cooked her up a pill and injected her like he had done before, only this time, it was ten times stronger.

Dizziness enveloped Jesse: suddenly she could not talk, walk, or drive. This infuriated Jack who didn't know how to drive a stick shift and couldn't drive legally because of a suspended license. As she drifted in and out of consciousness, he badgered her until she got behind the wheel against her better judgment. Impaired as she was, Jack directed her through back roads until they were once again in familiar territory. If this drug was meant to be fun, Jesse was certain that driving a camper cross-town was not the way to do it. She kept nodding out and on occasion was bouncing off the guard rails.

Back at his place Jack became sullen and would not make love to Jesse but left her in the empty bed while he slept on the couch. She noticed that both Gloria and the baby were gone.

Next day, Jack made a big show of explaining how he cheated stupid people out of money, selling them catnip and charging the price of pot. Jesse was quiet; she had begun to tire of Jack. It was hard to remember the Jack she had fallen for. Since that first week they met, he had stood her up, lied to her, taken her money, almost gotten her raped, and been moody and non-responsive to the point of killing the tender feelings he had first evoked.

By evening Jack had again changed his attitude and had fucked her so good that she cried. As soon as they finished, Jack started talking about a rich guy he wanted Jesse to meet. "He will give you $250 for a blow-job, and I'll get some money too. I have known him for years. He's the grandson of a studio mogul. Ladies say he is good-looking and you would think that he can have any female he wants but he likes to pay for sex. He will be here in an hour. Why don't you clean up to meet him? If you don't want to do anything with him after you meet him, that's ok too. I don't want you to feel uncomfortable, I love you, and I love how much you show me you love me. I want to do everything for you. I just need to get on my feet."

Jesse felt sick, deceived, and just ten minutes ago she was moaning under him, "I can't believe you would ask me to do such a thing."

"Why? All I'm asking is that you meet him. You do not have to do anything with him if you don't want to. It's strictly up to you."

He moved closer and put his arm around her shoulder, "I'm sorry; I don't want to disappoint you, baby. I would never do anything to hurt you."

"I guess I could meet him; there's no harm in that," Jesse replied, still not entirely sure what she was getting herself into.

"My wife used to date Ronnie, and he treated her fine. But now she has another sugar daddy, and Ronnie's looking for a girl to display on his arm. He is very generous. His grandfather was Cecil B. De Mille.

Jesse felt motivated to meet this guy especially if he was young and rich. After all she was a reasonable, open-minded person, so she agreed to see him the next day.

The meeting was awkward, from the first hello, to Jesse's attempt at giving a 'professional blow-job'. The guy could not get off; maybe Jesse could not hide her revulsion. Prostitution was like acting, and Jesse had difficulty being a phony, pretending to be what she was not, or feel something that wasn't there. Ronnie felt sorry for Jesse and gave her $50 for her effort.

The ordeal of her 'first trick' made Jesse begin to think that Jack was more trouble than he was worth. She began to long for a stable home-base, a little shack somewhere near the beach, one where she could hang up some pictures, and carve out a meditation room, listen to some LPs, and sew a few hippie clothes on her sewing machine. Sure, this junkie gigolo satisfied her sexually, but it was all they had in common. She was already weary of the 'chase the dope' game. Carlos had exposed her to philosophy, sociology, and books that expanded consciousness. The life of a drug addict seemed so shallow, spinning wheels going nowhere. She had heard a lot of Jack's talk and had seen little action. But even as she thought about leaving, the tendrils of the poppy juices encircled her, and the next voice she heard was Jack's.

"Come on, Baby, I just heard about a new shipment just outside of Hollywood, my friend Charlie is saving me a taste.!" Unfortunately, it was a long trip, and his 'friend' did not open the door. It was late afternoon, with dusk approaching Jack's ugly side would appear as the effects of withdrawal changed his personality yet again.

Jesse's truck needed repairs, so she let Jack talk her into hitch-hiking with him. They stood on the access ramp to the freeway when a big black limo pulled to the side and the door opened. From the interior stared three olive skinned men dressed in suits. Ordinarily, Jesse would not take this ride, but she followed Jack's lead into the backseat, and slid across the smooth gray leather where she found herself sandwiched between Jack and one of the men. They all seemed friendly, but only spoke Spanish with an occasional English phrase on the side. Jesse understood enough to know that they were powerful and potentially treacherous. Jack and the most talkative of the three men were becoming fast friends. Jesse and Jack were being invited to the men's apartment not far away. Upon learning that Jack was looking for a bag of heroin, all three got excited and animated. Next stop, their apartment.

Jesse was hyper-vigilant taking notice that they were parking in a security garage. Jack grabbed Jesse's hand as they exited the car and followed the men through their private garden to an up-scale suite with more security. Jesse felt like they were in a risky situation. She knew they could be overcome or abducted, and no one would ever know.

The obvious head man of the group unlocked the front door, and immediately motioned to Jesse and Jack to follow him in and make themselves comfortable. Jesse wasn't thrilled, but she knew Jack would be able to get a fix if they were dealers. It was his one talent, talking people out of dope or money. She watched Jack turn on the charm. He could hustle anyone, even these Mexican drug dealers.

While Jack was talking, Jesse asked where the bathroom was. One man pointed. Thanking him, she turned the corner into the master bedroom. There on the gold satin bedspread were a couple of handguns along with a duffel bag and briefcase. Suddenly she felt afraid. Each escapade with Jack seemed to be taking her farther away from where she wanted to be, but her sad desperation leached life from her until she hardly cared what happened.

God sometimes she hated being right! Mexican mafiosos with big bags of heroin. From the bedroom door she could see the kitchen and the 'cooking' going on. When she stepped out the younger man asked, "Do you want a hit?"

"Sure," Jesse answered a little too quickly. She watched as he prepared her a spoon, the needle touching the bit of cotton, the tan liquid pulled up into the plastic syringe past the bars and painted numbers. He strapped her arm off and easily found her taut young vein. When he released the tie from the top of her arm, the warm wave of pleasure washed through her body. She felt herself slipping down a huge slide but remaining conscious. Vertigo engulfed her, and she wondered if it was heroin or something else he had injected into her arm. It was heroin, extremely pure with very little cut.

Jesse excused herself from the men's presence and headed for the big, overstuffed sofa in the living room. She soon became restless. About that time, Jack came in.

"We gotta get out of here right now!" he demanded. Jesse had never seen him frightened. She jumped up and nearly fell over from the dope. With Jack supporting her arm, they made for the front door. Retracing their steps they managed to find the way out onto the street. Not a word passed between them until they were a few blocks away, thumbing a ride out of east L.A.

"What was that back there?" Jesse asked.

"They wanted you to work in one of their whorehouses near Mexico City."

"What?"

"I wasn't sure they were going to let me take you. I told them you wouldn't be any good, but I knew three girls that would want to go, professionals, and besides, you were my girlfriend, and pregnant."

Jesse listened to the lies, relieved to be out of there, and just beginning to fully appreciate the close call. "You told them you would get them girls?"

"Yeah, I got their number; I'm supposed to call with the information. Fuck them, at least we got high for free, right? They even gave us a taste for the road." He was jubilant.

Jesse felt sick. Smack was the *last* thing on her mind, and it was all Jack thought about. Both exhausted, they made it back to her camper where she had parked it since the engine was smoking so badly. Jack insisted that they do some of the stash the men had given to them. Jesse wanted to save it for tomorrow, after all it was late, the dope would be wasted on sleeping.

"I don't care what you want. I deserve some since I put up with those assholes back there" Then he softened his voice, "You don't have to do any more if you don't want to. Just get in bed, and I'll make love to you in just a minute."

This was the other talent Jack had. She watched his transparent ploy to get a bigger portion of the powder. *Did he really think he had fooled her?*

He turned back toward her saying, "I'll leave you a nice wake up shot, honey."

Morning came. Jack started an argument so that he could walk out, taking the wake-up taste with him. Jesse was upset but decided that she had been wasting enough time with him. She resolved to get back to dancing, make some money, and return to Puente de Ixtla in Mexico to retrieve her son. Each day away from Andre was another day too many.

Jesse called a dancer she had recently met who let her use her shower and park in front of her house for a few days. It was close to the city and the clubs. Jesse managed to hold herself together during daylight hours when dancing and making money kept her distracted. But it was after-hours within the hollow walls of the camper that she cried until her pillow was soaked, her eye sockets scratchy and dry. After a few sleepless nights, an out-of-town gig sounded like a cure. She called an agent whose phone number she had stuck in her wallet. Her timing was impeccable.

Flower Seeds and Bombers

ext day she was on a bus headed north to the town of Lompoc for a dance gig at the Mirage.

Lompoc's two main industries were flower seeds, and bombers. It was the site of Vandenberg Air Force Base, and the base was the reason the topless club thrived in this small coastal enclave. The owner of the club provided a room for the dancer while she worked. He booked her for two weeks with an option of a second two weeks if the customers liked her. Jesse hoped that would be the case, but many managers did not like her because although she was young and pretty, she did not like to play the 'game' as she called it. She would not shave her armpits or legs because her hippie philosophy told her that society's standards of beauty were phony, along with most everything else that it held dear. She did not style her hair with the usual teasing and hair spray of traditional strippers but chose to leave her hair natural. Her stage presence exuded earthiness and an animal charisma that contradicted the image men were conditioned to expect. Nevertheless, Jesse had a following, and her fans were captivated by her intense creative energy, and her eyes. She had learned that if she made eye contact, it personalized the show. It invited the customer into her world and gave him hope.

As was her routine, she always managed to find a long-haired hippie to sit with between sets, and this gig was no different. Troy wasn't someone Jesse wanted to ball but at least he was somewhat hip.

"Do you know this area... I mean, are there any magical nature places around here?" she asked hopefully.

"Oh yeah, there's this big hot spring pool just outside of town. It's easy to get to, and not a lot of people know about it." Troy was enthusiastic. "When do you get a day off?"

"Sunday."

"Do you want to go there?"

"Sure."

"I've got some good acid; we could trip."

"I haven't tripped very many times. I'm afraid I might fall into some psychic adventure that I can't get out of," she replied with apprehension.

"I've been a guide on more than one trip. I wouldn't let anything happen to you, believe me, I'm one of the good guys."

The look on his face was sincere, and Jesse felt like she needed and deserved a diversion and relief from the obsessive dialogues inside her head, the incessant replay of memories, the hopeless, insistent, desolate mother, forever crying out for her lost child.

She had closed out the club at 2:00. The day was nearly gone by the time Jesse caught up on her sleep. Jesse and Troy dropped the acid anyway and took off for the hot springs at dusk. It was not pretty, the two of them stumbling along the poorly marked trail. When they finally reached the spring, they discovered the temperature was far from hot. Instead, it was tepid, and filled with mosquitoes. They turned around and headed back to the car, feet muddy and cold. Troy did not want to drive, and had turned into a sniveling, complainer. Jesse's perception was altered. She managed to pump Troy up enough that he was able to get behind the wheel and drive them back toward town. He couldn't resist one more stop; the local high school football game was at the stadium, and it was right along the way.

They parked and before she realized what was going on, she saw herself being pulled along by her clasped hand on a gravel road encircling an immensely huge coliseum. From within she could hear what seemed like thousands of voices rising and falling in deafening waves. Addled from the acid, Jesse suddenly thought that she had become an unwilling part of some ghastly Romans versus Christians blood sport, and she was being led to her inevitable death.

She stopped abruptly, "Troy, I can't go any farther. I'm sorry, but you'll have to drive me home. I'm way too fucked-up; I'm hallucinating like crazy!"

His face glowered with unhappiness. This date was not what he expected. He complied with her wish, dropping her off at the motel room. She never saw him again.

Jesse felt relieved to be back in her own space. She was still high. Sadness and regret of being far away from Andre seeped into her during these sunless hours. Although her body was weary from the week's dancing, sleeplessness kept her from the deep rest that she really needed. She pulled out her journal writing down her impressions of the town, the people, and the night's excursion. Relentless, compulsive poetry about her lost

144

child and loneliness, bleeding out onto the paper from the pen's tip and spotted by tears.

Shortly before dawn, Jesse left the motel room and walked a couple of blocks away to an all-night diner. It had been twelve hours since she had ingested the LSD. The hallucinations were subsiding, and her stomach grumbled with hunger. She ate a sandwich and stared at the gray outside the window. The longer she sat and stared, the stronger the feeling in her that the sun would never rise again. Her heart pounded; she looked at the clock. Shouldn't the sun be up by now? It was 7 a.m. Was this the existential hell she had read about? She looked around at the people coming and going, fast time lapse photography. An inner scream rose but was silent. Her eyes wandered the café searching for someone safe, someone to which she could pose such a stupid question, yet she was afraid, deathly afraid that the sum of her sins of her wretched life had caused the sun to stay in its place this morning.

Never asking anyone, she simply sat there in dread, in a drugged induced psychosis until she could sit no longer; out of the diner and onto the midmorning streets she wandered. Walking a few blocks, she came upon a bookstore that seemed to be peddling 'consciousness'. She pushed open the door.

Once inside, the peace was palpable, tangible, like perfumed oxygen coming through the pores of the walls. Jesse browsed the books and felt resonance with many of the New Age titles. One in particular caught her interest, so she dug for some money in the bottom of her purse and paid for <u>The Science of Becoming Oneself</u> by an East Indian author H. Saraydarian.

Jesse's suffering drove her to seek guidance, to mend her fragmented and emotionally tortured self. This spiritual textbook, a mental-health primer, an oracle, had found its way into her hands. She flipped through the first pages; her eyes slid down the Table of Contents: Toward Freedom; Harmlessness and Detachment; The Sea of Emotions; The Principle of Conflict; The Meaning of Silence; The Self; Joy; The Truth.

More than anything else she wanted freedom from the daily constant emotional pain. She had had a short reprieve when she believed that Jack was the real thing and that he would help her get Andre back. It was now, while she walked the mostly deserted streets in an unfamiliar town on a gray day, that the full weight of her loss all but squeezed the life from her. She sobbed aloud. Each moment she was missing her child's journey, his steps, his giggles, his words. He was somewhere she was not welcome; and the door to her little boy's life had been slammed in her face. Carlos's judgment of her was final, like a guillotine blade. He had murdered her, but only she knew. Try as she might, she could not throw off death's breath that surrounded, permeated, and seeped into her lungs.

She took the little orange book back to her motel room, and exhausted as she was, began to read. The words flew into her mind like welcome pieces to a puzzle she had been trying to assemble, chapters with messages of empowerment, creativity, and self-actualization. The concepts calmed her and brought enough peace that she was able to fall asleep.

Jesse finished the Lompoc gig and headed back to L.A. on a bus, with a pocket full of tips, and a good size paycheck as well. The last person she wanted to see was Jack, yet she knew he would probably come looking for her, dependent as he was on women. She realized that he had hustled her in the same manner as she had watched him do to others. These weeks away from his influence had freed her enough to focus upon what she really wanted. Jack was a junkie and a loser. Jesse was not in the habit of judging others, but this was a confirmation, a judgment that she needed to make for herself. She would not let herself be used again.

Nowhere to Go

esse stopped at Jamie and Bab's to pick up her camper and catch a shower, as she had done times before but instead of the usual friendly welcome the front door opened slowly.

"I'm sorry to have to tell you this but you're going to have to find another place to shower. We changed the locks. We don't feel comfortable with you having a key anymore." Jaime said stiffly.

Bab was silent until Jesse was heading toward her truck, "We heard through the grapevine that you're hanging-out with a junkie, and that's not the kind of influence we want around here."

With nowhere to go, Jesse headed to a park she and Carlos had once frequented. Just as she was turning the corner, red and blue lights flashed in her mirrors. "Fuck! What now?" She screamed out loud!

"Please step out of the truck," the cop said with memorized dialogue.

"Why are you stopping me?" Jesse couldn't believe her bad luck.

"Ma'am, it is illegal to display an American flag as a curtain, like you have it on the back of your camper door." He answered with his stiff professional voice.

"No, the man who sold it to me at the Army-Navy Surplus said it was called a Union-Jack," she offered contritely. "Really officer, if I had known it was against the law, I would not have hung it."

"I'm taking you in," the man in blue insisted.

Jesse began to cry but didn't resist as the cop handcuffed and guided her into the back of the cruiser. Once at the West Hollywood police station, they ran her name and license through the system. While she was waiting, a cop came by to announce what he had found in her tote bag.

"We found the tools of your trade in your purse. What, are you working the streets?" his voice stern and judgmental referring to a portable douche-bag she carried with her since the camper had no bathroom.

"I'm not a hooker; I'm a dancer," she replied indignantly.

"Well, we checked you out, and you're clear to go. The department is not pressing charges for the flag's display. But keep it folded unless you are going to run it up a flagpole.

"Yes sir," she replied, took possession of her confiscated tote-bag, and walked out of the station's glass doors.

Jesse drove to the studio hoping to catch a shower at one of the girl's houses. She walked into the lobby and there was Jack.

"Baby, I have been looking all over for you. I was just asking if anyone had seen you. I really have to talk to you." He put his arm around her waist as they walked outside. "I quit the smack. Gloria and the baby moved in with her sugar daddy. They left the apartment for me; it's paid up for a couple of months..." he rambled on. "You want to come over for a while?"

Still needing that shower, Jesse figured there was no harm in a visit. On the way, Jack tried to convince her that everything was different now, especially when he said, "As long as I have you, I don't need dope!"

Her heart jumped; her pupils dilated. Jesse enjoyed hearing it, but she was not so easily fooled this time. She readjusted her perception. His insincerity was blatant, the way he used words and lies with anyone who might provide him with resources and money.

Early the next day, Jack talking about 'easy money' drew her in.

"Jesse, there's a call for couples to do X-rated movies. They're not full-length features with dialogue and acting, just quick sessions of 20 minutes of sucking and fucking. It would just be you and me, and of course the camera and lighting crew. We'd each make a quick $250. The reels are used for the peep shows around town. You know what I'm talking about?"

She knew. Not crazy about the idea, still she followed Jack to the make-shift studio in a motel on the outskirts of the Sunset Strip in West Hollywood. There they signed standard waivers, consents to use their images once photographed, and sat on benches with other couples waiting for their names to be called.

"I'm nervous, Jack." Jesse sought his eyes.

He squeezed her hand, smiled, and kissed her lips tenderly. "Don't be. You don't have anything to worry about. You are beautiful and the camera is going to love you. Remember, it's just you and me."

Their names were called. A greasy looking overweight man directed them into a partitioned off room with bright lights and a red-satin bedspread.

"Go ahead and take off all your clothes. You can leave them on the chairs behind the cameras." This man was obviously the director, and Jesse did what she was told wanting to get through this ordeal as quickly as possible. She wondered how she had gotten so desperate.

The loud man began issuing orders to both, and the action began. Jack kissed Jesse in such a way that she almost forgot that cameras were set upon them. After caressing, pulling and sucking on her nipples, she heard the man say, "Ok, now move on down to that pussy." And Jack adroitly obeyed. After being commanded for over an hour about how to fuck for the audience, to lift a leg, or move her ass so that the floodlights could reach her pink wet vagina and clitoris, Jack ejaculated.

It was a wrap. Jesse was given permission to get up off the rumpled bed and leave the room. A bathroom was available, and she made use of it. Relieved to be finished, she felt a small bit of satisfaction when the secretary placed the money in her palm. Jack stuffed his money into his front jean pocket and immediately started talking about scoring.

Stepping outside, Jack made eye contact with a dope-dealer who was stalking the exit for newly paid junkies. Many of the porn couples were also regular heroin users. He discreetly made his purchase and grabbed Jesse's hand. They started walking back to the apartment. Jack had his dope and Jesse had the beginning of her nest-egg, so she could rescue Andre.

Jack disappeared early next day. She had an uneasy feeling that he would not be back to the apartment any time soon, so Jesse called her agent to set up some paying gigs for the week knowing that she needed to generate money with or without Jack.

As she had guessed, Jack did not return that day or night. Jesse felt relieved to be booked all week long at a club close-by, in Santa Monica. She made a promise to herself to maintain distance from him.

During her first shift at the Diamond Lounge, she noticed a man who looked familiar. As was her custom, she sat between sets with whomever she pleased, and this man, Joe Bukowski was intent upon getting and keeping her attention. By the end of her shift, he had tipped her a couple of hundred dollars.

He asked her to dinner, and soon they were chatting like old friends. Joe had seen her at another club a month before and had searched for her hoping to see her again.

"So, what kind of work do you do, Joe?" Jesse asked.

"I'm a pharmacist."

"Really? Could you get me any pills that would help me with my energy? Dancing every night is very tiring."

"Sure, the drug companies give me samples; I'll see what freebies I can find for you."

After dinner Jesse gave him a chaste kiss on the cheek. Joe told her he would see her at work the next day.

On the drive home to Jack's apartment, Jesse wondered what or who she would find when she arrived. Although it was early evening the apartment appeared deserted when she unlocked the door and stepped inside.

It was eerily quiet, and Jesse's conflicted feelings disturbed her calm. Her hurt and anger surfaced. *Obviously, Jack was not overly concerned about her, although he had given her the apartment key, but where in the hell was he? Didn't she deserve an explanation? Was she his dog?* It seemed that Jesse had lots of resolve when she was away from Jack but every time she came within his sphere of influence, she lost her own volition. She felt so alone with no one caring whether she lived or died.

After a hot bath, Jesse pulled out the spiritual book she had bought in Lompoc and tried to believe that her life would get better. The words between the pages told her it would.

The a.m. sun was harsh; Jesse's eyes were swollen from crying. She was scheduled to work the lunch shift, and it was already 10:30. She would have to apply her eye make-up in the taxi. This owner fired you for walking in late. It was only a two-week contract, so Jesse wouldn't have to put up with him for long.

The dressing room was like a closet; many topless clubs had not originally been designed to accommodate entertainers, so this was not unusual. She liked the stage at this club, uncarpeted wood with the requisite smoky mirror on the back wall. The place attracted *suits*, legitimate businessmen, as well as hustlers. Sometimes Jesse could not tell the difference; both types were blinded and consumed by material gain. Each had his own way of getting it, but both placed materialistic goals in an exalted place, and devoted precious time exclusively to those goals. Jesse thought that these men were parasitic, and pathetic.

Didn't they get it? Fancy cars and jewelry cannot feed the spirit.

Candy Man

The lunch crowd was less than inspiring, and not a generous tipper in the bunch. The afternoon dragged on. Finally, a familiar face, Joe the pharmacist; he was like a forlorn puppy dog, very lonely and homely. Jesse had no interest in him except as a diversion from the tedium of this gig. At least he was intelligent, and well-read. But she could tell that he wanted to possess her, to eat her up, both figuratively and literally.

She greeted him with professional enthusiasm, "I'm so glad you came in today."

Joe responded warmly, "I took off early so I wouldn't miss your show."

"I have been so exhausted!"

He fumbled with his jacket pocket and pulled out a packet, "Oh, look what I brought for you. It's a sample of something called Desoxin, an excellent diet pill, and it doesn't give you the jitters."

Jesse squealed like a fan and gave Joe a big hug. Seeing his chance, he grabbed the back of her head with outstretched fingers he brought her face close to his and spread her lips with his thick tongue. Jesse was startled and pushed herself away from him.

"I'm sorry; it's just that you are so beautiful, I couldn't help myself." Joe stammered.

"Ok, but you have to make it up to me, you know, for your bad manners." She chastised him lightly.

The club had ousted customers for less. She could have had him escorted out, but it was awfully hard to bite the hand that was reaching so routinely for his wallet. And besides, she sensed that he was a genuinely nice person.

"Alright, here's $20 to begin with; will that buy me any forgiveness?"

Jesse smiled at Joe, then looked around, and seeing that most of the men had left, probably home to their wives, decided that this guy deserved her undivided attention.

Right before the shift ended, Jesse saw Jack walk in the door. He looked too good; all of her 'realizations', and 'good intentions' disappeared like vapor. She thought she was immune to his words of poison. Still his smooth descriptions of 'the way life could be', found their way like seeds into her fertile and hopeful imagination. He was a well-practiced actor and knew exactly what to say for her to invest in him again.

Walking up to Jack, Jesse spoke without thinking, "You're not going to believe this guy I'm sitting with; he's loaded, and I think he really likes me. He's a pharmacist." Silently, Jack shifted gears and quickly brought his focus to what she had revealed.

"Honey, I've been clean for at least a week now, and I've been attending NA meetings, in fact, there's one starting around the corner from here in just a few minutes. Why don't you and your new friend, go back to his place; it's a chance for you to make some more money. When he saw Jesse's saddened expression, he added, "We're going to need extra money to get your son back, right?"

"Yes!" she said excitedly, "Thank you, for helping me stay on track. I feel like you really know me and know what

I need. I will see you in a couple of hours. Will you be at your apartment?"

"Sure will, doll." They kissed lightly before she turned deliberately and walked back to Joe sitting patiently in a booth.

Joe unlocked his apartment door and held it while she moved past him. His place looked like an attempt by a well-to-do bachelor to appear hip. He failed grandly. From the gold satin bedding, to the bar at the far end of the living room, everything shouted *lonely dork lives here.* Brass lamps with their pseudo gold shine added the last touch of tasteless gaudiness to the decor. He was so anxious that his mannerisms were comedic, apologizing for everything and nothing, while scurrying to the kitchen and back with a cocktail.

With the noise and bustle of the club stripped away, Joe's uneasiness was painfully apparent. She picked-up on his neediness like a neon sign strapped to his chest. Not being a veteran of the "streets," and not being in the habit of deliberately using people, Jesse did not immediately see the gain in hanging out with this homely man with his large nose, prematurely balding scalp, and pleading eyes. His desire to please and to be accepted exuded from his every gesture. Quickly Jesse fell into a pattern of saying yes to his numerous and insistent offers.

"Would you like me to fix you something to eat, or more to drink?"

In all her life, Jesse had never been treated with such attentiveness. He even gave her a foot massage. She found herself thinking that Joe really is a sweet guy and it is too bad he's so ugly. Sitting on the couch, eating a bowl of ice-cream and watching a Marx Brother's movie, (Joe owned a machine that played video tapes of movies; cutting-edge technology), Jesse thought she must be feeling like Marion Davies, when the wealthy stately twice-her-age Mr. Hearst took an interest in her.

Jesse set her empty bowl on the glass surface of the coffee table and stood up.

"Well, I've had a really good time. You're such a gentleman. Dancers don't get to meet many, especially of your caliber." She uttered patronizingly.

Joe jumped up, disconcerted, "Oh, I didn't know you were going to leave. I was hoping you would stay the night. I can help you with your bills; I have lots of money." His litany continued.

"Joe, I like you; please let's not move so fast." It was the only thing she could think of to say even though she knew the implications were not true. Eager to go, Jesse picked up her wine glass set it on the counter and headed for the door.

"Jesse, here's some money. I know you're not a hooker, and I really appreciate the time you spent with me." With that he stuffed a couple of hundreds in her hand, and she yielded to his insistent kiss allowing him to press his rotund belly up against her body.

His trembling betrayed his excitement as he hurriedly found her buttocks and rubbed them with his pudgy hands. She pulled away and said goodbye. As she was leaving, he called after her.

"Jesse, I'll see you tomorrow."

Without turning she raised a hand and waved. As soon as she was out of his sight she spit as if to rid herself of the memory of his amphibian tongue. Then she set out for Jack's.

The sex with Jack was outstanding; the orgasms came and came some more. By the time they hit the shower it was evening. With a pocket full of money, Jesse treated him to a fine dinner and a bottle of wine.

"Jesse, this guy you met is a pharmacist. We could get him to fill a prescription for Numorphan, you know, the 'blues' that we like, and I could sell them for $20 a pill. That would get us started saving for our trip to Mexico to get Andre."

Jesse was skeptical. "I don't know. Couldn't he get into trouble if he got caught?"

"Yeah, but you don't think he's going to take a chance if he can't pull it off, do you? You just let him be a man and make his own decisions. If he doesn't want to, that's ok too." Jack replied.

The next time she saw Joe, he hung around until she finished her shift at 6:30, and then took her to dinner at a fancy local restaurant presenting her with a big bouquet of roses. The waiters hovered around thinking that it was her birthday, or some other special occasion. Being treated like a princess was quite seductive, except that Jesse was repulsed by Joe's physical appearance, and she was painfully aware that he was lusting after her.

Like a newly acquired assumption, Joe automatically drove them to his apartment when they left the restaurant. She could feel the ropes of obligation tightening about her. While they were watching videos, and she was tolerating his occasional familiarity with her leg or back, she broached the subject that was the real reason she was spending time with this man.

She snuggled up to his rotund chest and stomach. "Joe, could you fill a prescription for me?"

Joe answered without hesitation. "Sure, just bring it by the pharmacy any day." The conversation ended there.

After a couple of hours, Jesse managed to get Joe to drive her back to the club so she could get her own vehicle. As she was saying good-night, she made a mental note to always drive herself rather than getting stuck in Joe's timetable. If he had his way, she would be staying the night in his bed, every night.

For a change, Jack was at his apartment watching some TV when Jesse walked in the door. He did not bother to look at her when she came in, and on closer inspection she could see that Jack was high. She plopped down on the couch beside him, and playfully ran her fingers through his blond locks.

He grabbed her hand. "Stop, I don't like that."

"What's your problem? You're usually in a good mood when you've got dope in your veins." She responded sarcastically.

Ignoring her comment Jack asked, "What did Joe say about the 'script'; will he cash it?"

"Yes, of course he will; he'll do anything for me." She answered.

Jack's attitude changed immediately; he rolled toward Jesse and covered her with his body, kissing her gently on her mouth, face and neck.

"You are the most amazing female I've met!" He jumped to his feet.

160

"I've got to connect with Marty. Common let's go for a ride."

"Jack, not now. I'm exhausted from dancing all day and dealing with Joe. All I want to do is take a long, hot bath, and rest. I'm not on the schedule tomorrow; we can run around town then."

Jack was impatient and not pleased with having to wait, but on this occasion, he gave in, and tried to put on a happy face.

Jesse soaked in the bathtub, already beginning to miss it, as she looked toward a future when she would not have a tub, unless they paid the rent that was due soon. Jack had not mentioned it; he seemed not the least concerned. He took for granted that her camper could house them during any emergency. That was only partially true because she had not spent a rainy winter in it, and considering it had no furnace only a couple of gas burners, Jesse doubted the camper would be comfortable when colder weather hit. The bathwater was quickly becoming cool, she ran some more, and watched the scalding liquid turn to steam. She hoped that he would not badger her about going out tonight.

"Honey, I'm going out for cigarettes; I'll be right back." She heard him yell from the living room.

Before she had a chance to respond, she heard the front door close. Wish granted. The tension began to leave her body. It was then that she noticed just how tense Jack made her feel. They were incompatible in so many ways. She could barely tolerate his smoking, and the drug hustle left little time to have a relationship. She was addicted to the sex, raw, experimental, submissive intercourse. Unlike other sexual encounters including Carlos, with Jack she felt total freedom and abandonment to her sensual proclivities. He knew this, yet she had no idea that this was a strategy he deliberately used to keep her coming back.

Jesse dozed off. When she awoke, she noticed all the tea lights had burned out; the apartment felt empty. She got out of the tub, groped for a towel in the dark, and found the light switch. Jack was still not there, and the living room clock glared 2:30 a.m. There on the couch was her dancing bag with her costumes scattered. The bottom of the tote usually lined with crumpled bills had been emptied of the day's tips.

She wanted to be angry, but she was so tired that she decided to sleep while she still had a bed. She would deal with him tomorrow, or whenever he dragged his raggedy ass home. As expected, he was nowhere to be found when she woke late the next day.

She was getting tired of these damn hide-and-seek games. Stranded with no money (he had left only the change), Jesse felt like she had no choice but to call Joe. She did not feel like putting up with his simpering, love-struck gestures but at least she wouldn't be stuck inland on her day-off. She popped a couple of Desoxyn samples; the speed would help with her attitude, and dialed Joe's number. Before leaving for the day, she quickly scribbled a note to Jack with the number and address.

The sun was sinking when she arrived at Joe's apartment. A stranger answered the door, and Jesse discovered a party in full swing. Joe appeared by her side, slid a drink in her hand and introduced her around. As she looked over the crowd it reminded her of a scene from one of Fellini's films; everyone was lying around in layers. There were women with few clothes on, and men lying naked on the furniture with huge hard-ons stroking themselves at leisure, and occasionally one would get lucky as some euphorically charged female would pass by and decide to straddle the opportunity. She even recognized a couple of workers from the "porn industry" which would explain the exhibition.

She let Joe take her hand. "Where did all of these people come from?"

He answered, "Mostly people I've met in bars, like I met you. These people are so nice; they would do anything for me. When I was sick with the flu, Nancy, the girl over there in the corner, came every day to make sure I had something to eat, and basically checked in on me."

The pills Jesse had taken were kicking in. She felt a sense of well-being; it seemed everything was as it should be. Her customary shyness around strangers melted. She found herself wanting to talk to people and wanting to hear what they had to say as if they could impart to her some long-awaited knowledge. An aura of profoundness permeated everything.

After an hour or so, Jesse passively followed Joe into his bedroom, into a hedonistic orgy. Without knowing why, Jesse allowed Joe to undress her. She found herself amid the down comforters, and satin sheets with other couples. Joe had eased his head between her legs and was hungrily lapping. Her thoughts were like flies buzzing in her head; first one, then another, images without order, without connection caught for a moment in her consciousness. Her bodily sensations shrouded in despair swelled and fell like the Venice surf, and there was no relief from the self-hatred and pain. In a bed with sweating bodies, and a strange man trying desperately to capture some illusive part of her, Jesse was alone in a space without meaning, without hope, a rag doll to be used and disposed of. She saw herself, an actor dragging feet in the parade of life, a lifeless shell of a person moving from set to set, vaguely searching for comfort and finding none.

As the effects of the drug began to wear off so did Jesse's tolerance. Weary of being poked and prodded with Joe's thick fingers and beginning to feel like the sensitive skin of her genitals was chaffed and worn, she pried loose and slipped out of the bed amidst Joe's objections.

"Jesse, please don't go." He pleaded.

"I'm sorry; I'm starting to feel sick," she lied. "I promise I'll see you another time."

Joe quickly put himself in order, "Well, at least wait long enough for me to get you something that you said you wanted."

By now, she had found her clothes, was dressed, and full of nervous energy. She wanted to be away from this place, with its smells, and its pleasure-less pornography. The shame was beginning to waft around her like invisible smoke. Jesse watched as Joe hurriedly rifled through the top drawer of his desk.

"Here's the blank prescription that you asked for. Bring it in to the pharmacy Monday afternoon. I'm the only doctor there."

Jesse held out her hand, only to have Joe grab it and pull her to him. She allowed him to nuzzle her neck, and clumsily knead her breast as he rubbed his crotch against her one more time in what seemed to be an attempt to keep her there.

"Joe, I need some money too."

"Sure, is a hundred enough?" He said while handing her a bill.

"Well, I need to do some grocery shopping too."

Without hesitation, Joe dug another hundred from his wallet. "I really enjoyed this afternoon. Maybe next time it can be just you and me without all the others around."

"I gotta go." She took the money, the 'script', and headed for the door.

Once outside, she inhaled deeply. Now, she and Jack would be able to cash the prescription and have 60 'blues' to sell. People paid $20 a pill, and it seemed like everyone Jack knew wanted to try them. Then they came back for more. Personally, Jesse liked a speedier high. She could not believe people paid money to nod off into a dream. She didn't need drugs to sleep... but to each his own. If Jack could make some quick money, they could travel down to Mexico to retrieve Andre a lot sooner. She had been away from her little boy long enough!

She stood out on the sidewalk watching cars come and go in the dusk of evening wondering what to do now. She felt dirty and wanted to go back to the apartment to take a shower. Not wanting to break a hundred to pay for a taxi, Jesse instead stuck out her thumb while walking toward what looked like a promising corner. It was a straight shot from the beach back inland to Hollywood. Just then a dark green van pulled to the curb. There was Jack hanging out of the window smiling.

"Hey gorgeous, you want a ride?"

165

He opened the door; she climbed up into the van and slid between the driver and Jack.

"So where were you all night; I thought you said you'd be right back." Jesse asked without masking her anger as she had done in the past.

"Marty needed some help moving. We got done really late. I knew you were exhausted, so I decided I'd let you have some time to yourself."

He put his head on her chest looking up at her face like a little boy. "You're not really mad at me, are you?"

Jesse could not stay angry for long when Jack sweet-talked her. She always gave him the benefit of the doubt. After all he had made a point to find her. She planted a kiss on him and turned to Marty.

"How are you? You two are going to be glad you picked me up." She said tauntingly and held the script between her fingers for them to see.

"Holy shit, you got it!" Jack exclaimed, unable to hide his enthusiasm.

"Joe told me to come in on Monday when he's the only one there."

As Marty hammered the accelerator, on the radio came Free singing 'All right now, baby it's all right now', and Jesse felt like, indeed, everything was all right.

Breaking the Law

Monday came. Jesse dressed in the most conservative clothes that she owned. She was nervous and had not really considered until now that she was about to break a federal law. Her only thoughts had been about the money they would make, and the upcoming trip to claim back her son! Jack was pleased. Soon he would be getting high, for free, on the best pharmaceutical morphine available.

As she pushed through the pharmacy door there weren't any customers but her. She approached the counter and was waited on almost immediately. As Jesse stood there, she could see Joe's face behind the glass. He glanced at her without recognition and moved quickly to fill the order. The clerk took notice of the prescription and asked, "Is this for you?"

Jesse responded coolly, "No, it's for my mother; last stage of cancer." The woman looked away embarrassed. Jesse's performance was convincing.

Outside the glass doors, slowly she walked down the street and around the corner to the waiting van wondering just how much money she was holding in this little white bag with its treasure bottle of turquoise blue pills.

Jack jumped out and helped Jesse climb in. He looked impatiently at Jesse. "Well did you get them?"

Jesse squealed, "Yes," and rattled the bag.

Jack grabbed it, pulled out the bottle, and started reading the label. "Numorphane, amount 60, take by mouth every 8 hours for pain. Yeah, baby, we are going to feel no pain. Marty, can we stop at your house; it's closer than the apartment. I'll give you a free pill... you got any new spikes?"

Marty, who had been quiet, finally spoke. "Sure, we can go to my house, but my mom comes home from work early today, and you have to be gone by then. You know she'll freak out if she sees you."

Jesse knew what Marty meant, and didn't want to impose on someone who would be hostile towards them. That wasn't her idea of fun. Jack was compelled to get high. He did not care about surroundings, or comfort, or who he made uncomfortable. His habit came first.

"Stop at the drive-through; I'll pick-up works." Jack directed Marty.

"Let me have the blues," he barked at Jesse.

"You said we would sell these and get some money to go to Mexico. Now it looks like all you're planning to do is get high" Jesse's voice was shrill with accusation and resentment.

Jack's voice implored, "Not now Jesse; everything is going exactly the way we planned. Just have a little faith in me. Believe me, we're going to get Andre back." Jack tousled Jesse's hair, trying to lighten things up. But Jesse still insisted upon holding the stash until they got to Marty's house.

The house was a remodeled, updated multi-leveled cabin nestled in the woods with a deck overlooking a wooded gully. It was a gem, so close to Hollywood and

Beverley Hills, yet hidden away in the canyons of Hollywood Hills. It seemed to Jesse that it was furnished with a flair for the dramatic like walking onto an Arabian Nights set, with hanging tapestries and stained-glass lamps, it was homey and inviting.

Jack got busy and cooked up a 'blue' pill. Feeling greedy, he fixed an entire pill for himself and hit it. After that he was good for nothing. Marty knew how to fix dope too, but he decided that a half would be plenty for him as he was clean; he hadn't been doing anything for a few days.

"Do you want me to hit you, Jesse? It looks like Jack's out of it." They both looked at Jack who was trying without success to light a cigarette.

"Sure, I appreciate it, but I only want a 1/4; I'm a lightweight." Jesse answered.

Marty hit himself, waited a minute and then fixed a quarter of a pill for Jesse. The two of them lay back in the sumptuous pillows of the love seat at the far end of the living room.

"You know, Jesse, you don't look nearly as happy as the first day Jack and I saw you bopping down the street," Marty said suddenly.

Jesse was surprised that he noticed.

"I try not to gossip too much but I just want to let you know that Jack is a junky, and a hustler. He has the gift of persuasion until you've heard him talk too long. He doesn't care about anybody but himself. That's why Gloria left him. He wouldn't help with the baby and stole money that was for diapers and formula. Don't believe what he tells you and look out for yourself; you can't depend on him."

"Thanks for your concern, Marty. I guess I have been fooling myself, but I thought these feelings I have for him were real. He is the best lover I've ever had in my life.

"You haven't had me, little girl." Marty teased.

"Can you give us a ride to the apartment pretty soon? Don't want your mom to catch us here, right?"

"Right."

Marty and Jesse managed to guide the very stoned Jack toward the van, wrestled him like an oversized rug into the back of the van and slid the door closed. Before dropping them off Marty said, "Can I get a few of those pills to sell? I'll make sure you get your money."

"No problem." Jesse counted out 6 and returned them to her pocket.

Jack had recovered enough to get himself to the apartment door. Jesse was silently thankful. Her thoughts were on her escape plan. She hadn't driven the camper in a while and wondered whether it would start.

Once inside, Jesse watched some TV while Jack stumbled around from room to room, and finally passed-out on the couch which meant the bed was free. As Jesse pulled the covers over her a deep weariness settled in. She knew this would be the last venture with Jack. Sure, she had indulged in the heroin, Diladids, and Numorphane, but she just was not a proper junky. She had aspirations; she liked to read and sew and raise houseplants. She longed to dress up and go to a movie or check out one of the clubs on the strip. Her life with Jack had been a sprint on a hamster wheel, hustle, run, score, sit around, nod off. What a bore it had become, empty sex and abundant lies. She felt cheated, betrayed, and embarrassed as she realized how incredibly

170

stupid she had been to think this man could be a father to her son or could build a life with her!

Jesse's plan was suddenly clear. With Jack's help and contacts, they would sell the pills, she would give him half the money, and then buy a ticket for Mexico. Until Jesse got her son back, nothing else would be right in her life. Marty's warning had given her cause to believe that she truly was alone. Jack's words were hollow, without truth, and devoid of intention. Whatever direction she wanted her life to go, she would have to get there by herself. Bitterness filled her. *You are alone; get used to it. You were not loved as a child, and you are not loved now.* The litany of her life droned on like an automatic soundtrack.

Next day, as might be expected, Jack's mood was expansive; Jesse listened distrustfully. Having heard it all before, what she wanted was action.

"Honey, I'm quite sure I can dump most of those blues within the week. I know a house where a bunch of out-of-work actors live. Sometimes a few of them like to get down between jobs." Jack looked to Jesse for validation.

"You do that, and I'll get in touch with my agent. I'll let him know I want to be booked full time. Both of us have to be making money for us to move ahead, otherwise we just spin our wheels."

Jack smiled. "Hey how much do you want me to fix for your morning shot?"

Jesse responded, "A quarter is fine."

After he got Jesse and himself off, he disappeared out the front door taking his share of the pills. Jesse noticed something flapping on the door as he left, an eviction notice. Jesse called her agent and booked herself solid for the next few days. Luckily, the truck started right up; everyone needs a vehicle in Los Angeles. Looking ahead, she thought they could use gas station bathrooms, but she didn't know where they would be showering.

Jack's specialty was his charm, and if you had something he wanted, he was your best friend. He managed to get in tight with a big household full of people in West Hollywood, and had Jesse running back and forth with the drugs. She was happy to do this knowing that with every pill sold she was that much closer to getting back to her son. In the week or so that Jesse had been their courier, a couple of guys at the house had nick-named her Jesse Blue. Getting more and more disillusioned with Jack, she found a sympathetic ear in Monty and Rene, the couple living there. They were primarily focused on their singing careers although they liked to chip occasionally, a term meaning to use hard drugs occasionally.

"Jesse, I don't know you very well, but it seems like Jack has no intention of helping you with your goals. It looks like he's stringing you along, telling you what he knows you want to hear." Rene offered in a concerned, sisterly manner.

"Rene, I have to figure out how to get away from him. My brain says he is no good for me, but my body wants him. I have never had anyone make love to me the way he does. I feel totally open, totally receptive to whatever sexual experimenting he initiates. It's like he has a psychic hold on me."

Jesse realized that she would have to break it off permanently with Jack if she were to make any progress on her own goals.

Rene offered her a hug. "Well, I trust you'll make the right decision for yourself. If there is any way we can help, you let us know."

It was not easy for Jesse to disentangle herself from Jack's web. For another two weeks she wavered. Her desire to be loved and her confusion between love and sex kept her going back to his arms, and the needle and spoon. She had never in her short sexual history experienced the heights of orgasm she had reached with Jack. It was his forte, skills that gigolos perfected, and women paid for. But more disturbing was Jesse's use of the synthetic morphine. Because it was drugstore dope it was easier for Jesse to feel secure about its purity and strength. Every time she was with Jack she got sucked into the vortex, the rush of drugs and sex. Before long Jesse was up to a whole pill, and more than once Jack had fixed a concentration so strong that she had nearly passed out.

Treachery

unday afternoon, Jesse was alone in her friend's house. Rene had given her an extra key so that she could use the bathroom at her convenience. Jack had been missing for over a week. The doorbell rang, followed by an impatient rapping on the door. Jesse answered believing it was one of the house mates wanting in. To her complete surprise, there was Jack and a stranger.

"Hi, Sweetheart, did you miss me?" This is Pete, he's been giving me a ride, and helping me get rid of the 'blues'. Wow, this place sure has a lot of stuff."

Shocked, Jesse watched Jack walk in past her as if it were his house.

"Yeah, a lot of musicians live here; Jack, I don't think it's a good idea for you to be here."

"And why not?" He snarled sarcastically.

"Rene told me I could stay here, and use the shower, but I'm not supposed to allow anyone else in the house."

"OK, we'll use the john, and then go."

Jesse could see Jack's hungry eyes looking around at all the equipment. His friend, Pete, followed Jack into the bathroom. Jesse felt her gut tightening with apprehension.

The toilet flushed, and the two men walked out of the bathroom, visibly high. Jack made his way to Jesse putting his arm around her shoulder.

"Jesse we're going to take a couple of these instruments and pawn them. You can tell your friends that the house got broken into. They trust you; they'll never know any different."

Jesse snapped. "You can't do that! These people have treated me good. I'm not going to let you steal from them."

She stepped forward to stop them from touching anything, but Jack shoved her out of the way and Pete ignored her. Both picked up the closest instruments in cases and walked out of the front door.

"Call me at Marty's. I've got another 'script' for you to cash." Jack said as he pushed past her.

Jesse was imploding. Up until now, she had felt like the consequences of her actions weren't hurting anyone else, but that was no longer true. How was she going to explain to her friends that her ex-boyfriend had ripped them off? She had never been in such a predicament. Jack and Pete drove off while Jesse sat and cried. She was so depressed that she went back to sleep. It was evening when Rene, Monty, and Sam returned. Embarrassed and humiliated, Jesse continued to cry while she explained what had happened. Monty was upset because the stolen tenor sax was a collectable. The other instruments that were taken were guitars belonging to Wayne and Felix, two studio musicians who also stayed at the house and needed their instruments to make a living.

Jesse was afraid they would tell her to get out, but instead they rewarded her honesty. Rene advocated for allowing her to stay. She had run into Jack's type before and knew that Jesse had been manipulated and lied to. Monty and Sam were ready to go find him and kick-ass.

175

"Jesse, do you know what Jack and his accomplice were planning to do with the instruments?" Monty asked, seriously.

"I'm fairly sure they were going to pawn them. Neither of them is a musician, and they don't know anyone who would buy them, right off." Jesse answered helpfully. "I think I might be able to get the pawn tickets from Jack. He said he had another 'script' he wants me to get filled. I'm supposed to hook up with him today."

She tried to look as reassuring as she could. She felt so awful; all of this was her fault. She could hardly believe that Rene and Monty were still being nice to her.

Jesse left the house that evening resolving not to return until she had gotten back the pawn tickets. It was not difficult to find Jack. He and Marty were camped out in the backyard of Marty's mom's house in his van. By the looks of the mess, they had been hanging out, getting high, and not much of anything else. As she approached, Jack watched silently until he could see it was her.

"Hi baby, I was hoping I'd see you this evening." He said to Jesse while casually draping his arm over her shoulder. "You want me to get you off?" Jack mumbled into her ear incoherently.

Not being able to hide her disgust, she answered, "No, I came to get the pawn tickets for the instruments you stole."

"Oh, those... Let me see... I think they're in my shirt pocket."

Jack stumbled to the van and climbed in. After a few minutes of shuffling-around, he found the crumpled tickets and handed them to Jesse, who was standing near the van.

"Here you go, no harm done," he whimpered contritely.

"How can you say no harm done? Rene and Monty gave me a place to shower, a comfortable bed to sleep in, and you brought your evil karma into their house. You have no consideration for anyone. I never want to see you again!"

Perhaps Jesse thought Jack was so stoned he would not react, but she was wrong. He jumped up and slammed her against the side of the van. Not being satisfied, he pushed her down with such force that she slid in the grass and gravel.

"Now get the fuck out of here you skanky bitch. I don't owe you or your new friends anything!"

Jesse gathered herself up, crying, and made her way out of the yard toward the camper. She suffered a few scratches but was happy to have accomplished her mission. She had the pawn tickets in her possession. Within a few blocks of her friends' house, the truck stopped running. Just as she was pulling away from a stop sign, she stepped on the clutch and boom, it gave way. She parked the truck the best she could and walked the rest of the way. Rene was already home and in the kitchen cooking.

Jesse quickly blurted out that she had tracked Jack down and had managed to get the pawn tickets from him. Rene noticed the dry blood on her elbow that wasn't there yesterday. Jesse gave a run-down of the events ending with her triumphant retrieval of the valuable receipts. Rene hugged Jesse and thanked her.

"Monty is going to be so happy to get his sax back!"

Jesse handed her the tickets. "I got the tickets for the other three instruments he took too! I hope you believe me when I say that I never wanted anything like this to happen; I told Jack I never wanted to see him again. I decided that I am going back to Mexico. I cannot give up my son. Maybe his father and I can talk and work things out."

"That sounds like a plan. When will you leave?" Rene asked.

"Probably, a couple of days" she replied with uncertainty.

"I think you're going to be fine. Monty can drive you to the bus station when you're ready to split."

Mescaline Meltdown

fter getting a new clutch for the truck, Jesse wasted no time securing a gig, though not the most convenient, an hour drive into the San Fernando Valley. The club was stuffed with a mixture of blue-collar workers and young rowdy college men. Jesse drank most of the afternoon with three long-haired hippies and agreed to follow them to their apartment after her shift so they could take some mescaline together. Reeling from the emotional entanglement with Jack and his deviant sexual hold upon her, Jesse decided to divest from his clutches by partying with these three young strangers. Following closely in her truck so as not to lose them, she did not question her behavior. They seemed nice. Once inside of their apartment she swallowed the mescaline and settled down on the couch to watch some TV, although it was the worst activity she could imagine while stoned on a psychedelic, too much going on to focus. The four of them discussed the state of the world, how wrong the draft was and the Viet-Nam war. Before long one of the men sat next to her and kissed her. High as she was, she could not come up with a reason not to succumb to her desire to be loved by this guy. She did not think about the other two but rather offered to him her hand and followed him into the bedroom where a mattress lay in the middle of the floor.

After dancing for hours, the mattress against her back felt good. The man in her arms was giving her, what she perceived as, much needed attention. The combination of the alcohol, drugs, and long hours on her feet knocked her out, not unconscious, but thoroughly relaxed her making her pliable for all three men who had their sights on her.

The first spoke to Jesse as if he were a hypnotist, cooing into her ear. "You are so beautiful. You are like the cosmic Earth mother who has come to alleviate our pain and loneliness. You are filled with love and compassion, and you are shining for all of us." When he was finished coming, he got up and left the room unceremoniously.

Another of the men came in and proceeded to ease himself into her, pumping as he exclaimed and praised her talents and bounteous love. Jesse hallucinated. She became the definitive Gaia mother, existing to nurture and bring life to the bone-dry horizon.

The third made his way into the dim room and took a sloppy turn. After a couple of hours, Jesse regained her composure, snuck out of the apartment downstairs to her camper, and drove away. A wave of self-hatred washed over her as she pieced together the previous hours. All she had wanted was comfort and a bit of socializing. She had inadvertently set herself up to be gang raped. In an emotional fog of anguish, she watched the lines on the highway hoping she would not have to seek treatment for an STD. Grateful to be back over the hills in Hollywood at her friend's house after her mistaken folly, Jesse took a shower and slept until late the next day.

After unloading most of the prescription drugs, Jesse had managed to keep some cash in her pocket and was ready to buy a bus ticket for Mexico, inexpensive, though certainly not the most comfortable way to travel.

Jack had not come back around since he pushed her down, and Jesse didn't care whether he was saving or spending his part of the drug money. She could make her own money. She felt like the game with Jack had run its course.

The Trip South

The next day Jesse boarded a bus from the Greyhound station in West L.A. headed for Tijuana. It smelled brand-new; the seats were fully adjustable and felt more comfortable than most people's couches. She grabbed an overhead pillow and scooted down for a snooze. It would be a seventy-two-hour trip once she reached the border. She was scheduled to arrive in Puente de Ixtla the day of Andre's 3rd birthday, October 12th. Traveling light with just one battered suitcase, Jesse felt contentment wash over her as she drifted into a fitful sleep.

The three-hour trip dumped Jessie at the border. All she had to do was walk over the bridge. She could see the bus station on the other side as she crossed the halfway point. At the border office the Mexican officials checked her I.D. scribbled out a temporary visa, stamped it, and pointed her toward the cashier across the tiny room who would exchange her U.S. dollars for pesos. Her wallet was bulging, she felt rich. At the time, the exchange was 20 to 1.

She had left Los Angeles at 10:00, and now she was getting ready to board another bus. The autumn sun had already topped its peak and was rushing headlong into afternoon. Jesse wasn't hungry although she hadn't eaten yet. She felt flushed, and her sinuses had begun to drip. She still had a three-day trip ahead of her; this was no time for her to come down with a cold.

She crossed the dusty streets and entered the double doors of a wooden building from a century past. This station had been built when the first bus route was established, and except for a change of the president's photo on the wall behind the clerk, Jesse figured that it probably looked the same, the scene frozen in time.

By the time she had bought her ticket and gotten help lifting her suitcase into the side storage unit of the bus, she was experiencing uncontrollable chills, shaking, and sweating. When a wave of nausea caught her by surprise, she excused herself, and ran for the public restroom. What she saw in the damaged mirror of the restroom sent her back to the toilet. How had she missed it, the gradual way her luster had faded? In its place a sallow, stressed, sad woman with dark circles under her eyes like the opium addicts in the black and white movies, her mouth a downward grimace. She had known that Jack always took the greater part of the drugs they used and had never even considered the notion that she might have an opioid habit. But here it was, and with the realization, another wave of nausea overtook her. With her stomach sufficiently empty, Jesse figured it was safe to board the bus that was waiting.

"Vamanos, young lady!" The smiling man called from the driver's seat.

She made her way up the steps of this old school bus requisitioned and repainted for commercial service. It was no luxury Greyhound with tilt seats, and padded arms. She looked around. It was a scene from a foreign movie, chickens in cages, mestizo women draped in hand-woven blankets, with their hordes of children, complements of the Catholic Church.

Jesse wished she had grabbed a sweater from her suitcase; suddenly, she was shivering. Feeling sick, she began to wonder how she would make it to Puente de Ixtla, seventy-two hours in the future. Unrelenting pain shot through Jesse's muscles and joints disrupted any possibility of sleep.

Yet the seventy-two hours did pass, and she arrived at her destination. The only food she had been able to eat along the way was a Popsicle. Grimy, because without air conditioning the windows of the bus had stayed open the entire trip, she was coated with three days dirt.

Though exhausted, her heart quickened with the anticipation of seeing her boy. She had been away from him for 6 months, and she had timed it so that she arrived precisely on his birthday. It seemed like a century since she and Carlos had first come to visit his father. Now she understood that she had had unrealistic expectations about the living situation. Geraldo had decided long before they arrived that he did not like his son's choice in women. He judged her to be no better than a common whore because she took off her clothes for a living.

She walked past the doctor's office and remembered fondly the benevolent couple who had loaned her the money to get to Mexico City. Turning up the street where Geraldo's house stood Jesse stumbled over the cobblestones, carrying the tattered suitcase. There, a half block away, she spotted Andre's blond curls, and started running toward him, calling his name.

"Andre, Andre, it's mama!"

The boy looked up at hearing his name called. His smile widened when he saw his mommy. He ran toward her, his chubby legs navigating the cobblestones of the street like a pro. Jesse swooped him into her arms once again. Little Andre hanging on to his returned Momma, asked her in Spanish, "no va, no va??" She certainly had no intentions of going. It felt so right to have her toddler in her arms once again.

When Carlos opened the door, his face was grim. It worried Jesse. She had honestly believed that he would welcome her back. After all she was the mother of his son. All she heard as she walked by him with Andre in her arms was, "What are you doing here? Why did you come back?"

"I just came back for my son's birthday," she managed to say through tears unnoticed by Carlos. With as much dignity as she could manage, she carried her son inside, and sat down on the couch. Carlos followed with her beat up suitcase.

He sat down in front of her and his voice softened, "I was just about to put Andre down for a nap. I guess you're tired and grungy from the bus ride? Do you want to take a shower?" Relieved at his changed tone of voice, Jesse relaxed.

"Come on Andre, you can talk to Mama after you wake up from your nap. Tell Mama night-night." With a hug, and quick kiss, Carlos and Andre walked off into the hallway.

Jesse toted her bags into the bedroom, and gladly pulled out her shampoo, clean underwear, and clothes for the much anticipated the shower. Once in the stall, it felt like all her worries were washing down the drain. As she lathered up and scrubbed her scalp, she began to feel human once again, even a bit optimistic. She had made it here. She had kicked the morphine, although she would not recommend a bus ride to inner Mexico as the ideal detox experience. She figured after a good night's sleep, she and Carlos could sit down and talk about their situation and come up with a good compromise. The steam, and the hot water smelled so earthy, no fluorine or chlorine, simply good clear well water hitting her skin.

After drying herself and dressing, she wrapped a towel around her head and quietly turned the handle on the door. The hallway was silent; she could not hear any voices, so she looked around peeking into the bedroom that she and Carlos had shared six months ago. It was empty. On impulse Jesse turned the knob on Andre's bedroom. It was empty too; he was not taking a nap. Jesse stood in confusion as Geraldo rounded the corner, his face stern.

"You have to leave!" He blurted out.

Jesse could not believe her ears. Her heart rate quickened. Startled, fear fired-up her nervous system. She wanted to scream at him and tell him what an asshole he was, but instead kept her voice level.

"What do you mean, I have to leave? I just got here."

"Carlos told me if you ever came back, he would go to Mexico City and disappear with Andre, and you would never see them again."

The terror rose unbidden. Jesse felt her throat constrict. She glanced around unseeing, her heart beat loudly in her ears. She was finding it difficult to breathe.

"I came back to be with Andre," her voice a mixture of dread and pleading.

"Well, he's not here now, and you can't stay."

He might as well have cut out her heart, and decapitated her, for she had no voice, and no arguments.

His words were poison, and she fed on them as a starving child might feed on dirt. She tried to comprehend, and came up with zero, a death sentence.

Jesse gathered the few items from the shower that she had unpacked. Sobbing aloud, she stuffed them in her tote bag, grabbed the suitcase, and left through the front door. Stumbling back down the cobblestone road that she had so joyfully walked two hours ago, Jesse made her way to the bus stop, her hair still wet from the shower. As fate would have it, a bus with a marquee labeled Mexico City pulled up and without further thought she boarded it.

The trip to Mexico City was a blur, but when she arrived at the same depot where she had been six months earlier, she made a different choice. Intuitively, she knew that if she returned to Hollywood she would not survive, so instead of purchasing a ticket to Tijuana, as she had previously done, her ticket destination read Juarez. Although she was not familiar with that town, she knew she could get a job dancing in New Mexico, and it was directly north from Juarez. Once back in the states, she would hitch-hike to Albuquerque.

The bus ride was without incident, same arid landscape, same hollow-eyed children vending gum, same dust, and poverty. There was a difference in Jesse. Carlos had stolen her life. Enthusiasm, lightness, sense of purpose, even the sense of a future, these were gone since her son had been ripped from her.

Back in the USA

esse stepped off the bus, bought a soda, and walked across the bridge into the United States.

Numb, emotions spent, a shell where there had been energy and plans. Jesse still had to function because she was standing on an unfamiliar road, with the sun going down. Instinctively, she stuck out her thumb.

As she looked around trying to get a sense of direction a police car approached and parked a few yards from where she was standing with her tattered suitcase. The officer got out and walked toward her. Fear was her first reaction, the sun suddenly pulled sweat from every pore.

"Excuse me; do you know it's illegal to hitch-hike from where you're standing?"

All Jesse could think was, *shit, I'm going to jail.*

Then as if she had read his mind he said, "You know, I could run you in for vagrancy? What are you doing here?"

Her nervousness took over and she began explaining her situation, talking fast.

"Do you mind if I search your purse? He asked directly.

Jesse felt suddenly lifted; her spirit and confidence arose. She was finally finished with drugs. She did not have any on her; her arms showed no signs of her escapades in L.A. Her former fear and self-loathing subsided as she relaxed and explained to the cop her situation, even offering to him the letter that she had penned while she was on the bus. It was addressed to her Mom and Dad in Los Angeles.

Remorseful for her wrongdoings, it outlined her plan of action to get her life back together.

The cop read the letter, gave back the tote bag, and offered to give her a ride up the road where it was legal to hitch-hike. The spot where she was standing now would only get her a ride to jail. Thankful for the intervention, Jesse gladly accepted, watching as he put her suitcase in the truck of his patrol car, and opened the passenger's side of the front seat. Her previous rides in cop cars were not in the front seat nor as lighthearted as this one. Still, Jesse was relieved when the policeman dropped her off and his patrol car was driving away in a cloud of dust. *Wow, dodged that bullet*, she thought as she looked down the long wide, empty road.

She was headed for Albuquerque, New Mexico. It was one of the cities she had visited back when she had an agent booking her shows. Not that she wanted to jump back up on stage naked, or breathe the nasty stink of yet another bar, but she knew some money was better than no money, and she would rather be riding the customer's cock in his fantasy than riding a trick's cock, for real.

A trucker heading to north Denver via Albuquerque stopped for Jesse. Enjoying his company, the easy-talking driver told Jesse stories of being on the road and the golden years when the best brothels were thriving all along the truckers' routes. She had always believed that if adults wanted to trade sex for money, it was their business. The miles rolled on; Jesse nodded peacefully dreaming of some past lifetime as a prostitute in a small Western town.

Before she knew it, the driver was turning into a truck stop in Albuquerque. Jesse said goodbye, with gratitude at being safely transported this far. Her next move was to telephone a hippie she had met one time when her agent booked her in this city. She hoped that his offer to put her up had been sincere. Within the hour Jon pulled up and loaded her suitcase in his V.W. He was an independent film maker who specialized in political campaign ads, and pornography.

"Jesse, I'm going to set you up in the loft of the studio. We're not scheduled to shoot anything for a few days, so no one will bother you. There is a club within walking distance. I can talk to the owner; we're on good terms. I'm sure he can fit you in to his schedule so that you can start making some money. It's not the swankiest, and the clientele are mostly Mexican but they're honest and they protect the girls. The manager doesn't allow any rough stuff."

They climbed the metal stairs, and Jon led her to a blowup mattress and sleeping bag. "Sometimes I sleep here if we're shooting for a long block of time." Jesse could see cameras and lighting equipment as well as various other items scattered about the warehouse floor below.

He helped her get situated and handed her some clean towels. Then he laid her back onto the makeshift bed where he gently and assertively fondled her breasts and buttocks, sucking sweetly and finally entering her. Then with her sounds of satisfaction still fresh in his ear he left a key and went home to his ex-wife who still lived in the same house. He would see Jesse tomorrow.

It was good to have a safe place to crash, and a nice man to help her a little. Jon was at least 25 years older than her with a graying beard and long hair he tied back in a ponytail. He had a wealth of information about New Mexico, and of course Corrales, the town where his hand-built adobe home was nestled.

The next day she put on make-up and heels, and followed him to the Wagon Wheel where, true to his word, he introduced her to the owner and manager. Both men asked Jesse to strip down to her panties. They wanted to see what her breasts looked like. Afterwards the bartender wrote her name on the schedule for the following day. Jesse knew that day shifts were usually slow, and the tips bad, but she had to start somewhere. Now with a job, she would be able to take care of herself.

Jon grabbed her hand as they walked out of the club into the bright midday sun. "Jesse, I really want to take you up on the Crest. You're not going to believe the view!"

The Sandia Mountains flanked the Eastern perimeter of Albuquerque and were over 10,000 feet high. It took forty-five minutes to travel around the back side of the mountain where it wound around up to the top. They parked. Jon knew of a huge flat rock that sat on the side of the mountain. It was there that he led Jesse and fucked her from the back as she bent over the ledge overlooking the city. Although, she felt like he was too old for her, she still enjoyed being treated like an ice cream sundae. His penis was small, but his tongue was persistent.

Jesse worked at the Wagon Wheel just long enough to find out where the better clubs were. She quickly learned that they were located on the East side of Central rather than down on the West end. Jon was busy trying to be a film director with little time for her. This suited her since she had no enduring interest in him.

Jesse planned to hitch back to Los Angeles because she did not want to lose the Smoky Topaz ring Carlos' mom had given her for her birthday. She knew when she hocked it, that the twelve-karat gold ring was worth more than the five dollars typed on the pawn ticket. It wasn't her idea, but being broke at the time, Jack had insisted. Now she had the additional hassle of returning fifteen hundred miles back west to retrieve it. The ring had sentimental value, as well as real value. She could not see letting go a five-hundred-dollar ring for five dollars. She was determined to buy it back.

The hitch to California was relatively smooth going. The route was well traveled, and Jesse was able to jump from rig to rig assisted by the driver who radioed another going in her direction. Despite the risks, Jesse never considered buying a bus ticket. She arrived in L.A. exhausted at the door of her musician friends. Rene welcomed her in and gave her the extra bedroom which Jesse gladly accepted. Without hesitation she was asleep before 9 p.m.

Lights in the Mirror

esse had decided to give the truck and camper to Rene and Monty when she got ready to leave the state for good. They had the resources to fix it up, and keep it running. It seemed like a good trade considering all the drama she had caused them.

She made a call to her last agent who remembered her and was happy to book her the following evening into a club in Van Nuys. Jesse was clean since she had detoxified on the bus to Mexico City. She still enjoyed smoking grass and loved the heightened sensitivity to music that it caused. As a dancer, her body became a living representation of the music, a fusion of sound, body, and consciousness. For Jesse pot facilitated this peak experience. She rolled a joint and slipped it into her right shirt pocket, intending to smoke it later.

Her shift ended at 7 and it was 7:30 when she saw the flashing lights in her rear-view mirror.

"Why did you stop me officer?"

"You've got a burned-out tail-light," he responded without emotion.

As the cop walked back to his car to run her license, Jesse wondered what he would find.

"Ma'am please step out of the vehicle." He had found a warrant issued for multiple parking violations that she had not paid, but no moving violations.

"I apologize, but I have to follow the rules and take you in."

He cuffed her wrists and called for a tow truck. Jesse's heart was in her throat, her breath constricted, skin burning hot. Her plan was to leave for New Mexico tomorrow. It was like California had an evil magnetic force field that would not let her go.

Jesse was sitting in the patrol car when she realized the joint she had rolled earlier was still in her pocket. Suddenly her misdemeanor parking-tickets warrant had morphed into a felony possession charge for a dangerous substance. Fear gripped her like a cold hand wrapped around her spine. She knew she would be searched when they booked her. Having been through this before she decided to throw herself on the mercy of the cop, after all it was 1969 and there had never been a death due to smoking marijuana. The times were a changin'; maybe he would be cool.

As the officer slipped into the driver's seat and locked his seatbelt for the ride to the station, Jesse stuttered a second before taking the leap.

"Look, I don't know how else to handle this. I have a joint in my pocket, and I know I'm going to be searched at the station, so you can take it and throw it away, or smoke it, but I know it's going to be found so I thought I'd let you know beforehand."

The young rookie was quiet, and Jesse did not open her mouth again.

After parking the cruiser, the cop lead Jesse by her cuffed arms into the valley station announcing as they walked through the door, "Look what we've got here, a controlled substance," and with that he brandished the joint like a prize for his captain to see.

Her breath escaped her; her nerves wound her up tight. Like a caged animal, Jesse's mounting instinct was to run. Instead, she was read her rights, fingerprinted and photographed. As luck would have it, she was released on her own reconnaissance. She cried from relief on the drive back to the house. Exhausted from eight hours of dancing and then hours in the jail with no chance of sleep, Jesse dropped off as soon as her head hit the pillow.

Close Call

The next morning at 10:30 a.m. Jack knocked on the front door, agitated. Rene opened it with caution, especially when she saw who it was.

"Have you seen Jesse? I've got some important papers of hers; I want to make sure she gets them," he managed to get out of his mouth self-consciously.

Rene knew he was lying. "No, I haven't seen her in quite a while. You can leave her stuff with me; It'll be safe here," she offered, carefully calling his bluff.

"That's ok, I'd rather put them in her hand," Jack continued deceitfully.

"Do you have a number; in case I see her?" Rene kept the chain lock on the door.

"No, I'm moving to a new place and I haven't put in the phone yet." He turned quickly to leave.

Well out of punching range, Rene called out, "Jack, don't come around here anymore. I'm taking out a restraining order so you can't come near my house!"

He threw her the finger as he got into the passenger's side of the car waiting with its motor running and sped away. Jesse had slept through the entire encounter.

She woke refreshed, but with a new dilemma, last night's arrest. Oddly enough, Jesse felt focused and motivated. She was ready to collect her hocked possessions and get the hell out of California. Knowing that if she ran, she would not be able to return to her home state, did not shake her resolve to flee. After all, there was nothing left to keep her here.

Rene offered Jesse a cup of coffee as she told her who had come looking for her early this morning.

"Oh my God," was all Jesse could say. If ever she had encountered an angel on earth, surely Rene was one.

Rene had seen Jesse crying daily since she had left Mexico. The rejection by Carlos and his disappearance with her son had kept her in a state of depression, and in this vulnerable state. Both Rene and Jesse knew that had she seen Jack; she very well might have thrown herself back into the maelstrom of that caustic situation.

Just a few feet from her head the serpent had approached, but Jesse had remained invisible and protected. She thanked Rene profusely and hugged her for this.

"I'm hitching out of here tomorrow. I'll be a fugitive from the law, but I don't care. I am not a marionette for them to manipulate. Just because I smoke pot, I am not a criminal and I refuse to play by their rules." Jesse was restless and anxious to get out of the Los Angeles snake pit.

Return to the Land of Enchantment

esse was ready for the trek. She had some money in her pocket. She had found her ID and birth certificate in one of the boxes in Rene's garage and she had bought back her smoky topaz from the pawn shop. Rene offered to drive Jesse to the interstate. She lifted Jesse's suitcase into the truck.

"This thing is heavy. What in the world do you have in it?"

"Just a few items I ran across while I was looking for my ID."

The truth was that she had found a trove of her favorite clothes, the black-velvet floor length hooded cloak, the fringed suede vest, the cranberry panne-velvet drawstring pants with the matching tunic, the see-through lace blouse, and a couple of dance costumes she had forgotten about. She packed every garment.

Rene took Jesse right to the best hitching spot. They waved to each other as she drove off to her job. Hitching with a suitcase wasn't a problem but getting out of L.A. could be. There were some dangerous inner-city off-ramps that dumped the hitchhiker right in the middle of the industrial parks wastelands, or worse.

This is exactly where her first ride took her. She looked around at the dismal underbelly of the freeway. Knowing it was illegal, she walked up on the freeway anyway, rather than staying on a deserted on-ramp. The next ride got her out past L.A., into the desert, but then the driver turned north, and Jesse found herself at a truck stop on I-40. Without having any kind of plan, or strategy as to how to find a ride Jesse walked straight into the roadside café, planted her suitcase, and announced that she was trying to get to Albuquerque, New Mexico and she would appreciate a ride from anyone who was going that way. A couple of drivers glanced at her from the booth, but no one spoke up.

The diner's many aromas drifted in from the kitchen. She was hungry. She had heard that if the truck stop was busy, that meant the food was good. After taking a stool at the counter, she ordered the breakfast slammer, served anytime. Before she had finished, the waitress mentioned to Jesse that the two men in the booth behind her would take care of her bill. Jesse turned around and smiled. One of them motioned for her to come over and sit with them. She obliged the two middle-aged truckers.

"Hey, Hon, I heard you say you needed a ride to Albuquerque. Me and my partner are going right by there. We'd be willing to give you a lift. There's plenty of room, right Max?"

The other guy nodded wordlessly. She had her ride. The first red flag hit Jesse as she stepped up into the cab. There spread across the floor of the passenger's side was a pile of pornographic magazines. Jesse took notice, but her need to get across the desert before night-time descended was paramount so she ignored the signs.

They were on the highway just a few miles out when one of the men said to Jesse, "Get in the back, in the sleeper. We're coming up on a weigh station."

Jesse could read the road signs as well as anyone, so she spoke up. "There's no weigh station."

The man raised his voice and yelled, "Don't argue with me and get in the back."

Not knowing what else to do, she obeyed. Before she could even get settled, in came the man who had ordered her. Suddenly his hands were all over her and he was kissing her neck. She fought, she kicked, as she lashed out she rolled in a summersault through the opening between the driver's cab and the sleeping box, nearly landing in the driver's lap, pleading with the driver who was sucking on an unlit cigar, and wearing a straw hat.

"Please don't do this, please let me go. I just want to get to Albuquerque."

She was frantic, and it seemed like no sound was coming from anywhere but the roar of the rig's engine. In that moment Jesse seized upon a thought. If these men did not let her go, if this driver did not pull over, she would kill them all. She would grab the steering wheel, use her dancer's legs and kick the snot out of the driver. They would damn well let her go, or they were all going to die. She had been raped twice and it was not going to happen again.

At that moment when she had those thoughts firmly in her head, miraculously, the driver turned to his buddy, and said, "Open the door Frank, and let this bitch out."

The truck slowed down, and Frank threw out her suitcase, then she stumbled down from the open door. The truck accelerated away. There on the side of the road in the middle of the desert, she wondered whether those two men thought that she would die, or maybe they did not give her a second thought. But here she was on a deserted road with little traffic. Undaunted, Jesse felt a sense of relief and replenished motivation, probably the residual adrenalin still pumping in her bloodstream. Standing all alone, not a soul knew where she was, but she was not sad. She had survived on her terms; she was uplifted and hopeful. The horizon was awash with colors of the setting sun.

Rather than walk she opted to sit for a while and wait for a car. Before long, an elderly man in a late model 'woody' station wagon badly in need of a paint job slowed down and stopped for her. Jesse ran over to the window to scrutinize her next ride; he looked safe.

"Here, you can put your suitcase in the back seat, kid." His kind demeanor was a welcome change.

As they started down the highway, Jesse told him about her close call. He listened compassionately and after an hour on the road they stopped at an Army surplus store, where he purchased for her a nice car-coat of faux fur. He also made sure that they stopped to eat, and that Jesse was full and satisfied. The miles zipped by and then he dropped her off right at her destination. She kissed him on the cheek in a daughterly fashion and dragged her tattered suitcase up to her friend's front door.

Murphy's Law

smiling face welcomed her as the door opened. During an earlier visit she had met Charlie at a bar where she was dancing. He was happy to see her and introduced her around to his house mates.

"You can put your suitcase in my room. We're all trustworthy around the house. We were going to play some cards, smoke a little grass, drink a bit of wine, and listen to some tunes; are you in?"

Jesse was looking forward to relaxing after the many miles she had been on the road. "Yes, absolutely! Can I use your shower to wash the road grime off me?"

"First door to the right." He pointed.

"Thanks." Jesse was glad to be back in the slow-paced south-west town of Albuquerque. Her other visits had been no longer than a week or two, but this time her plan was to stay. She knew she could find work dancing in this town since her agent back in Hollywood had sent her out this way more than once.

Refreshed and dressed after her shower, Jesse looked around. It seemed like everyone was altered in one way or another. The tunes were mellow, and the card game kept the laughter going. Not being a card player, Jesse was content to sit by and watch.

About two a.m. there was a knock on the door, and when one of the guys opened it, in streamed the police.

They had warrants for two of the guys who lived at this address. Because Jesse happened to be there, the police were taking her in for questioning too. Up until that knock on the door Jesse had not been drinking any alcohol. She felt her anxiety escalating, so rather than face it 'straight' she went into the kitchen, opened the refrigerator, poured herself a huge tumbler of wine, and guzzled it on the spot. By the time the cops were ready to transport Jesse, she had a serious wine buzz going on. She explained to the cops that she had just hitch-hiked in to town that evening. They searched her suitcase, and found no contra-band, however it did not stop them from taking her to the station. After passing out in the detainer cell she was released in the morning *pending further investigation.*

She showed up at Charlie's house to learn that the search of the garage had uncovered stashes of LSD, and marijuana. Nervous about hanging around the crime scene she picked up her suitcase, quickly said her good-byes, and headed toward the center of town where she knew she could find work. Before the day was over, Jesse had a dancing job at a combination restaurant/bar called The Fireside Inn, specializing in authentic Italian cuisine. The owner gave her afternoon shifts. Not crazy about it, but at least she was working. Afternoons were usually slow and too laid back for Jesse. *It is hard to make a tip if there aren't any customers.* One such slow shift, Jesse met Karen, who was a veteran stripper and topless dancer. They became friends fast and after a couple of weeks Karen insisted that Jesse share her large adobe house.

Encouraged by the steady work, Jesse purchased a used Volkswagen bug. Soon they were making plans to drive to New York City because Karen had an agent there who could keep them working at top wages, or so she said. Jesse had visions of coming back to Albuquerque with a suitcase full of money so she could set up house, and then she imagined that she would buy Carlos and Andre plane tickets. They would visit her in New Mexico and be a family again! She would get her second chance because she believed that God was merciful, and besides, she had learned her lesson about how not to behave in a relationship. She was eager to try out her new knowledge. Armed with irrational optimism, Jesse was often able to function without an emotional breakdown for long periods of time.

Before leaving for the east coast, Karen wanted to show Jesse the earthy culture of Albuquerque, so early Saturday morning she dragged her off to the flea market. It was located on the state fairgrounds in the middle of town, and accommodated hundreds of vendors. Jesse looked across a sea of international products, and diverse faces, Mexicans, Indians, mostly Pueblo or Navaho, hippies, gypsies, rednecks, and trailer trash, some vendors relaxing on their lounge chairs in the beds of their trucks, coolers respectfully hidden, waiting with their folding card tables full of junk from abandoned barns. Farmers stacked colorful produce, and local Chicanos unloaded bushels of red and green chilies. Indigenous artists sat with their portable glass topped display boxes of silver and turquoise Native jewelry.

Jesse had money in her pocket from a week of tips. They walked the rows slowly. She had never seen such an array of products at an open market.

"Wow, Karen, look at the antiques!"

"Yeah, the locals sell for pennies to buyers from L.A. and New York who inflate the prices and sell to city folks who will pay whatever's on the price tag," Karen remarked with distain.

Seeing a headboard with delicate carving and inlaid veneers of Birds Eye Maple, Jesse remarked, "It must cost a fortune?"

Karen asked the brown skinned man, "how much for the bed?"

"Twenty dollars, it's for a full-size mattress," he answered smiling.

Jesse just about fell over not believing her good fortune; she dug in her wallet for the cash. "How are we going to get it to your house?"

"Don't worry, I'll take care of it." Karen took the money and negotiated a delivery for later that evening. He knew exactly where the address was.

As they walked away, Jesse bombarded Karen with questions. Are you sure you can trust him? Why was it so cheap? Are there always great buys, or was she just lucky? It seemed to Jesse that this town where she had landed was exactly the place she wanted to be. The people were friendly, she could make some money dancing at the local clubs, the pace was slow compared with Hollywood and L.A., and she had found a friend and mentor in Karen.

Karen gave Jesse the living room of the house. She moved her newly purchased antique bed in a corner, laid down a huge round braided rug she had also found at the flea market, and set the beautiful maple rocking chair with the spindled armrests. All she needed was a bookcase, and some posters on the bare walls and the room would be complete. It was earthy, warm, cozy, South Western, and Jesse felt like after all her wanderings, and close calls on the highway she had come home.

Karen had a platoon of boyfriends who stopped by to provide her with all kinds of services, from minor plumbing tasks, to sexual gratification. She carried a noticeable disdain for men that went unnoticed by her suitors. Some of her mannerisms got on Jesse's nerves like when she dragged out the pictures of her surgery, snapshots of the tumor lying on a surgical tray after the extraction, passing them around like family photos, or her habit of blurting out that they were topless dancers, regardless of the place or setting. Karen prided herself on her honesty, and she abused it by being consistently inappropriate, and self-indulgent. She had been in the topless business ten years longer than Jesse. Being around Karen's know-it-all attitude reminded her of how she *did not* want to be. All in all, their relationship was symbiotic. Jesse needed a guide, and Karen needed to feel important; most of the time they got along fine.

The date for them to leave for New York was upon them. Jesse provided the ride, although the VW had not been road-tested, Karen provided expertise and guidance, since she had been there many times before.

They were both ill prepared. Jesse was no mechanic, and the VW was not under warranty, but she hoped the car was trustworthy. With the green bug stuffed with suitcases of street clothes and costumes, they wiled-away the day looking at a road atlas, passing a doobie, and wandering from room to room searching for overlooked necessities.

Nighttime fell and the other two housemates were sitting around the TV watching 'The Land of Point', a full-length animated movie with the main character wanting to find his identity because he was born without a point. This movie had become a hippie favorite, because of the underlying theme of 'the search for purpose'. Jesse wanted to leave early, and now if they watched the whole movie with the commercials, it would be 8 o'clock before they got on the road. With the car running, Karen and Jesse stood around the living room taking in the first few minutes of the movie, until Jesse pulled herself away.

"Karen let's get out of here. If we leave much later, we'll be too tired to drive." Jesse reasoned.

"I've been waiting for you." Karen answered defensively.

After quick hugs, the two of them climbed into the VW, and headed out to find the interstate. It was February, and neither of them had checked the weather forecast. It had not entered Jesse's California mind. She had studied the map and traced the route they had chosen. It looked like a straight shot, mostly interstate all the way.

Icy Roads

The first sign of trouble came when they hit snow and ice somewhere north on the Pennsylvania turnpike. The storm was long-gone; in its place was a bright crayon blue sky, with yellow blazing cold sunlight, and blacktop covered with an icy shell, rutted and shiny for long stretches. Jesse felt a false sense of bravado as she reached the speed limit. Then the tires slipped as she tried in vain to remember what she had been taught in driver's Ed. *Turn toward the skid.* But all she wanted to do was stop and so she stomped on the brake pedal, and the VW spun in a circle, out of control. The car directly behind Jesse's hypnotically followed, slamming into her right taillight. No one was hurt, and since Jesse carried no car insurance, information was not exchanged.

Jesse surveyed the damage; the back end and a taillight were crunched. If Jesse could get the car unstuck from the snow drift she had just slammed into, she was sure it would drive. With Karen directing, Jesse got the VW back on the shoulder of the highway facing east. They had both escaped injuries, but they weren't out of the woods. New York was still miles ahead.

"I guess I underestimated how difficult the drive would be," Jesse confessed to Karen after they were on the road for a while.

"Yeah, well I feel really bad because I couldn't give you better advice. I've never driven; I always flew." With that, each forgave the other.

Now, it was Karen's task to pull out the map and figure out a way for them to turn south away from the snow. Although they were both exhausted, they did not dare spend the little bit of money they had brought along on a motel room. Instead, they pulled into a rest stop to sleep. The minute Jesse turned off the VW engine the car went cold like the temperature outside. So, they rested their eyes for twenty minutes and then got back on the road so they wouldn't freeze. When Jesse thought she couldn't keep her eyes open any longer, she pulled into a parking lot behind a church, and both of them emptied the contents of their suitcases, costumes, under ware, socks, t-shirts over them, and tried to generate body-heat long enough to catch a nap. After a couple of hours Jesse got behind the wheel, and set out for Washington, D.C. New York was their destination, but Jesse wanted to see the Capital first. It was where her one and only uncle lived. The one she had not seen since she was 13. She thought she might like to drop in on him.

Just as they entered Washington, D.C. dawn broke over the city. Still too early for the church goers, the city was deserted. Jesse wove through the hubbed streets and found herself driving by the Jefferson monument as the sun's rays hit the sky tinting the clouds a frosty pink. She was feeling high from sleep deprivation, and the nation's capital looked to her like a reincarnation of the Roman Empire, floating arrogantly above all without answering to any.

She decided she would have to come back to visit her Uncle another time, and as she ended her thought, a sign drew her attention: TO NEW YORK. Six short hours and they would be in the Big Apple. Jesse did not know what she would find there. She needed to feel real, she needed purpose, like the kind she felt when she had a family. Now, she felt dead inside, sometimes replaced by dread.

Once they got near New York, Karen came alive; she knew her way around.

"OK, follow that car, and take the next exit. Let's go see my friend Maria. I called her before we left, so she's expecting us."

They were soon on Maria's steps; the kind of stoop that typified New York Brownstones. Jesse climbed the ugly, timeworn, stained steps following Karen after Maria buzzed them in. Walking down the dim hallway, Jesse could see why it was a locked building. The elevator that would take them to the seventh floor was a beautiful time-traveler's delight. Crafted around the turn of the early 20th century, it was ornate and ostentatious, like Cinderella's bejeweled carriage. The door of the cage opened onto a carpeted hallway; it was thick, plush, and the repeating design was like giving your feet an invitation to travel a magical walkway.

Jesse enthusiasm bubbled, "My God, Karen, this place is luscious, like an oasis appeared out of the ugliness outside."

Karen was stoked, "Oh, you're not going to believe what you can get in New York. All the stuff you see in Home & Gardens, or Vogue, that stuff you can find on any block near here. Sometimes you can find irregulars that you swear are perfect from vendors on the street. I will introduce you to Jerry, my agent. I think you will like him, and he'll keep us working. You might have to prove yourself."

"What do you mean prove myself?" Jesse asked suspiciously.

"Well, you probably won't get booked into the best clubs right away, because he wants to make sure that you are dependable, that you're not going to hang him up. He tells lots of horror stories about booking dancers and then they didn't show up. So now he makes the dancer prove herself. It's not such a bad system, and you work up the ladder very quickly."

Jesse did not like the idea of having to prove herself but what choice did she have. She entrusted herself to Karen to show her the ropes. After sleep, the world would look better.

By the end of the first week Jesse had oriented herself well enough that she could get anywhere on the subway by consulting the street map that she had bought in a neighborhood bookstore. And by the second week she felt confident that she could ride uptown or down and manage to make it back to their room at the Hotel Albert. Unfortunately, after the long ordeal on the highway, and the miles of being thrown together in less-than-ideal circumstances, Jesse and Karen were not getting along. Jesse's resentment increased the tension between them. She thought that Karen had painted an ideal picture of how they would be rolling in money. Karen, on the other hand, wished that Jesse were less hysterical. She always seemed to expect the worst, and wanted what Karen could not give her, a guarantee that they would not run into any glitches.

One evening Karen and Jesse got into a screaming match, over who contributed more, and who was getting used. Karen heard enough, packed her things, exited, slamming the door.

Jesse was dismayed. After the initial relief of seeing Karen walk out, and the rush of feeling like she had won the argument, she dropped across the bed and began crying. She had been on the road and had overcome one obstacle after another. The drama kept Jesse from thinking about Andre, how she was missing his first words, his big brown eyes, his curly blond ringlets. She wept over the prospect that she might not ever see him again, and that he would forget her. As she lay on the bed in the skid row hotel room with no connection to anyone, she let lose a flood of tears. She could die right there, and no one would claim her body because no one knew where she was. And now her only friend had walked out. As she lay there soaking the indifferent pillow, she wondered if there were a way, she could get something to ease the unendurable emotional pain, some drug that would give her peace. She put her coat on, and stepped out into the drab hallway, her destination the local diner. If she could not procure drugs, she would lose herself in the diner's daily special. She knew it was late, but in New York eateries were open all night on so many corners.

While she was munching her Rubin sandwich, slurping homemade tomato soup, and contemplating the dessert menu, a colorful man looking like Jimi Hendrix, slid into the booth seat opposite her, and introduced himself as

Buddy. Jesse listened to him talk about his band and surmised that he was a fast-talking hustler who thought he might convince her that he had something she wanted. Unimpressed, she finished eating and pulled out a book. Buddy got bored and left. With her sadness held at bay by a stomach full of food, Jesse walked back to the hotel planning to call Jerry in the morning so she could get a booking.

No Place for a Car

*M*eanwhile, having a car had become a huge problem because unlike other places Jesse had lived, there were no parking spaces. She met a very respectful and sweet man in the laundry room of the hotel; his name was Ernesto. After talking with him for a while, he asked if he could borrow her car; he had a family emergency. She gave him the keys; he promised to return them within two hours.

Good to his word, she heard the knock almost two hours later, to the minute. He was so grateful and insisted that Jesse accept a small laminated felt picture of the Virgin Mary. He told Jesse that it would protect her. She graciously accepted it, tucking it away in a satin bag along with other valuables.

"Where did you park my car?" She asked knowing what the parking situation was.

"In front of the catholic church just two blocks away." He answered with confidence.

"Are you sure there's a parking zone in front of the church?" Jesse asked with skepticism.

"Yeah, I'm fairly sure. I just figured that it's God's house and they wouldn't mess with your car there." Jesse was not so sure, and she had a bad feeling about Ernesto's story.

"Common Ernesto, let's go make sure the car is ok."

When they arrived at the place Ernesto had parked the car, it was empty. The sign clearly said no parking, tow away zone.

"Oh fuck, what am I going to do now?" Jesse broke down.

Ernesto stood looking at the curb space where he had left the VW parked.

"Jesse, I am sorry; I didn't see the tow-away sign. What can I do to help?"

"I don't suppose you've got money so we can go bail the car out, do you?" Jesse tried to make light of the situation through her tears.

"No, I've been trying to find work." Ernesto's anguished expression convinced Jesse that this was truly an accident. She found it difficult to blame him since she was the one who had made the decision to loan him the car. They walked back to the hotel. Ernesto said he would contact her when he had some money to help her get the car out of hock. With that said he disappeared, and Jesse made her way up the rickety elevator, and waited for the sliding door to open on the 4th floor. Utterly defeated, Jesse wanted to die. She was tired of trying, tired of being alone, tired of missing her little boy, tired of living a disappointing life, tired of encountering one more obstacle, tired of losing. The pressure behind her eyes hurt. As she stepped out of the elevator and took about five steps down the ugly, dirty hallway past the door to the janitor's broom closet, two fat rats ran across her foot, first one and then a second. She suppressed a scream since she didn't want to alarm the other tenants. She kept walking for a few paces and turned around to look again at the hallway. She knew the closet had a large trash barrel the janitor used to collect from all the rooms, so it made sense that the rats had figured out where the community dump was. They were traveling from the barrel to the hole in the floor under the radiator opposite the supply closet. From that evening forth Jesse always stomped the floor with her foot after she stepped off the elevator, and sure enough, the rats would go scurrying back to their home in the wall.

Jesse's room was down a hall and around the corner, last room on the right. Now, along with her depression, despondency and loneliness, she could add the pressure of having her car impounded. Well, either she could figure out a way to kill herself, or she would have to work extra hard to get the money that was steadily accruing daily on her VW. At least she did not have to worry about a parking space anymore.

Jesse loved working for good agents, They would scout out the best clubs and set everything up ahead of time. All a dancer had to do was show up. The agent paid the plane fees, the motel/hotel fees, and took his ten percent. In Jesse's mind it was a small amount to pay to keep working steadily. The agents in the big cities were more demanding, and competitive. Generally, Jesse did not command top dollar, because although she was relatively young during her one pregnancy her body had changed dramatically from the virginal to the frumpy. Pert firm round breasts morphed into sacks with huge brown nipples, and her tight stomach morphed into a doughy tribute to Rubens who immortalized the voluptuous overfed female of the 19th century. She had to be satisfied with what Jerry offered her, at least until she accumulated more elaborate costumes, and found a DJ to mix some sets of her favorite music.

Rural New York

erry booked Jesse for a two-week gig in Elmira, a small town in New York. She boarded the Greyhound bus full of excitement and anxiety. The first booking into an unfamiliar club, she never knew what to expect.

The agent told her to check in at the boarding house adjacent to the bus station. Most of the bus drivers stayed there between routes. The old turn-of-the-century relic stood on main-street next to the river; at this time of year, one could see huge frozen chunks of ice floating down the churning waters of the Chemung River.

After Jesse checked in, she noticed she could see the river clearly from the window of the communal bathroom at the far end of the hallway. Jesse's only silent complaint was that the building had an old smell. It was dark, and the wallpaper looked like it had been here since the Great Depression. But the sheets were clean, the room was close to the gig, and the married couple who ran the place was straight out of Norman Rockwell's world.

From their first meeting Jessie and Mrs. Wolf became friends. The old lady took to Jessie as if she were the daughter she had never had. Two weeks of winter in New York, and Jesse knew she needed a fur coat; it certainly seemed like an East coast necessity. Hearing that, Mrs. Wolf went to her closet and pulled out a beautiful fur coat; she said it was beaver. Jesse didn't care what kind of animal it was. She had to have this coat! Like a celebrity, she slipped her arms into the satin lined sleeves. It fit perfectly. With wide cuffs and a shawl collar she could turn up to keep her neck and ears warm, it was like a coat Julie Christie wore in Doctor Zhivago. In better condition than most she had run across while wandering the thrift stores in the city, and Mrs. Wolf only wanted one hundred dollars for it. After promising to pay at the end of the week, she lovingly cradled the fur coat like a new puppy and headed for her room in the boarding house.

Back in her room she admired the fur and found fleeting happiness in acquiring it. *Now she wouldn't freeze; it was a good addition to her flimsy and sparse wardrobe.* As evening fell Jesse began to feel the familiar sinking uncontrollable despair wash over her like ink, the aloneness with the unwanted tears rushed down her face. Her misery came; it stalked her and kept her shrouded. She knew it had become a pattern. In the daylight she was cheery and full of anticipation but as soon as she had a place to lay her head, a sense of destitution overcame her. If she were dancing, drinking, entertaining, and traveling, she was in the moment, and sadness didn't pervade her mind, but the minute she stopped, she was back in the hole. Glad to be working, she slept without the anxiety of the unemployed.

The club sent a car for Jesse. It stopped in front of a club with chasing lights that spelled out The Hub. The bouncer was expecting her and opened the door of the car.

"Hi, my name is Farmer. Can I help you with your suitcase?"

"Yes, it's in the trunk. I'm Jesse from the Galaxy agency."

He showed her through the heavy glass doors, and directed her toward Sandy, the manager behind the bar. The club had been an old wild-west saloon complete with dark leather booths, and an original refurbished proscenium with velvet curtains. Over the bar hung an oil painting of a saloon dancer leaning on the piano man singing and playing a tune.

After introducing themselves, Sandy pointed to the dressing room at the top of the stairs on the right side of the stage.

"Go on up and pick out a locker. I'll give you a key to it so no one can take your belongings."

Jesse said thanks and headed for the stairway. With each step up she felt like she was traveling back in time. She stopped at the top of the staircase; there were many doors along the hallway. Jesse thought she could hear the stories brushing her consciousness, voices, as she passed by the aged wood doors. This was where gunslingers, gamblers, prostitutes, politicians and landowners had played and laid their bodies down for one reason or another. She opened the dressing room door with the fading yellow star painted on it.

The Hub had once been a logger's oasis, and then a vaudeville house alive with entertainment. By the fifties, The Hub was headlining Gypsy Rose Lee and other strippers of celestial fame. Then in the 60's it transitioned without a glitch into a topless bar that was known for bringing big city acts out here to the sticks. The firefighters often frequented the club, kept it afloat during slow times, and raised hell all year. If there was a birthday, anniversary, award, or fire well fought, the local 84 would be there to celebrate.

Jesse worked the first week, took the allotted day off and started her second week on Monday with a matinee. Most days Jesse slept until noon, depending on how hung over she was, and then she would hit the pavement looking for the best local hamburger.

As was often her pattern, she would begin a gig with high energy, and intentions of keeping her consumption of alcohol low. Often as she neared the end of her contract, she became too comfortable, and drank excessively. Lately she had been engrossed in a book and had not been tempted to drag a strange guy to her bed while she was still in the middle of it. But the depression that haunted her when she was not indulging in her many diversions, weighed on her like a metal blanket, and the psychic pain felt like searing lava through her veins. She cried and often went to work with puffy, distended bags under her eyes. She hated it, so she trained herself not to cry, but sadness made her want to alter her consciousness even more.

Jesse had kept it together for almost two weeks. She knew it was the only way she could build a strong reputation and start commanding the big bucks. Upstate New York had tamed and soothed her. The close presence of so many trees, acres of wilderness, and the pounding tons of melting water thundering by on one side of the boarding house gave her a sense of peace, but on the last night of her gig she and Southern Comfort made a spectacle of themselves.

Eddie had been flirting with Jesse all week. He was an attractive paid firefighter with a killer body and was aware of the effect he had on women.

Jesse had begun drinking as soon as the crew arrived. Eddie created a permanent seat beside him and kept whispering into her ear.

"Jesse, I really want to be with you outside of this place. Why don't you come with me and some of the guys over to the firehouse? You can see the truck up close." Eddie teased.

"I don't think so. I'm usually exhausted by the end of the night." Jesse replied, not really believing her own words, and feeling in need of someone to hold.

"I promise I'll get you back to your room at a decent hour," Eddie pleaded seductively.

"How gentlemanly," Jesse countered.

"I try. Don't you want to see the firehouse, little girl? I'll give you the tour and send you home." It was his final pitch.

"OK, but only for a little while." Jesse did not want Eddie to think that she didn't trust him. She knew she was drunk, but she felt wide awake. Before she knew it, the night was at an end, and Eddie swept Jessie up along with her gear and helped her into the passenger seat of a big luxury car. As soon as Jessie hit the cold leather seat, she realized she was wasted, and probably shouldn't be going anywhere except back to the boarding house.

Eddie scooted in next to Jessie and began kissing her and fondling her chilly breasts. She tried to say no, but her need to be wanted, a quick substitute for love, seemed to be winning out. She opened her mouth wider to take in his exploring tongue.

Jesse had sex with Eddie in the firehouse bathroom arms stretched out, hands against the peeling paint of the bricks; and then he took her home.

She climbed the mahogany stairs to her room, thankful that the sun was still down. The boarding house was still. Jesse slid the key in the lock and breathed a sigh of relief to be back in her room. Her buzz was subsiding. She set the alarm for 9 A.M., since the Greyhound connection would arrive at 10 A.M. It didn't give her much time to get ready but, after all, it wouldn't take her long to throw her stuff in a suitcase and squeeze it shut.

Jesse lay down on the bedspread without bothering to pull back the covers thinking about the sex, and milking the last drops of its lusty nectar, before running the bath water. She did not feel used; she knew a guy like Eddie could not take her home to meet the family. Immersed in the still silent bathwater, she washed between her legs, as the certainty of her aloneness swept over her. She imagined how nice breakfast with a lover might be.

The morning came uninvited. Jesse smelled the fumes of the Greyhound as she boarded the bus that would take her into New York City, and back to her rat-infested room at the Hotel Albert, 22 E. 10th St. The news of Jesse's antics reached her agent long before she reached her destination.

The Apple's Wormy Interior

erry was livid. "I told you that you were on probation. Why would you fuck a high-profile guy like the fire chief and do it in the fire station where everyone could see and hear you? I don't run a whorehouse, or an escort service, and I require that my girls behave in ways that don't reflect negatively back on me and the agency."

Jesse felt his spittle spraying her as he lectured. She knew he was right. A deep shame crept up from her stomach like the impulse to vomit. Her face burned crimson, humiliation and anger kept her from saying a word.

Jerry continued, "It's really too bad, because up until your last night the manager had nothing but good things to say about you; now, I don't think I can use you."

Jesse lost it. "What do you mean; you don't think you can use me? I came 1800 miles, I don't have a cent to my name, my car is impounded, the woman who brought me here abandoned me, and now you tell me I don't have a job?"

She was hysterical. "I might as well kill myself, what hope is there?" She slipped into a nearby chair sobbing.

"Alright, alright, I've got some clubs in New Jersey that you can probably work at. Calm down. Don't freak out."

Jerry was rarely conciliatory, and probably could feel his angel wings sprouting.

Jesse straightened up and blew her nose, genuinely relieved. Jerry reached over to her and held out an envelope. She took it and tore it open; it was her paycheck.

"If you want, you can endorse it now and I'll cash it for you," Jerry said sincerely.

"Yes, that would really be helpful." Jesse sighed with more relief, "Thank you... and thanks for giving me another chance."

With a pocket full of hundreds, Jesse's attitude improved slightly. So, after paying her rent, she entertained herself by wandering around town feasting her eyes on the fashions, store windows filled with clothes she had seen in Vogue magazine. The more she explored Manhattan's streets, the more she could see the bustling historical seaport market, only bigger.

Jesse had read about the danger of over-population. It had been a concept on a sociology test somewhere in her past, but she had never experienced it until she found herself being poured out of the theater following the movie credits into a wall of people. Sidewalks swelled with bodies, involuntarily squeezed together, shoulder to shoulder, in an ever-moving sea of people.

Jesse, not wanting to go straight home just yet, headed to the diner close to the hotel. Sitting in the booth before she ordered, relief flooded her senses and for the moment she became more understanding about the value of a job. She had been in tight spots before, but her prior life in California was a vacation compared to being unemployed in

New York City. She wondered what kinds of gigs Jerry would give her now that she had botched it with him.

After fielding some unwanted looks, Jesse walked home. The lobby was crowded with tenants, and friends of tenants watching a Sunday night game. Jesse passed invisibly across to the elevator. Upstairs, she found herself again facing the hallway of rats, rat metropolis, the rat subway station, or just rat heaven, for short.

Reaching her room without a vermin encounter, she finally collapsed on the big, dilapidated bed with no thought for the rats that slithered up through the flooring, rustling and gnawing on a loaf of bread she left on the table. It was a broken sleep full of warnings and persecutions.

Motivated by her anxiety, Jesse arose early and gave Jerry a call. His answering service picked up.

"Will you let Jerry know that Jesse called and I'm ready to work."

"Sure, I will. Thank you for calling," said the pleasant though impersonal voice.

Jesse felt panic; what would she do if Jerry would not book her? *Fuckin' Karen; she brings me to this place and abandons me, I wonder how she'd feel if I turned up dead, I can't believe she treated me this way, I wouldn't do this to a dog.* Her thoughts fed her desperation, and her desperation fed her feelings of fear and hopelessness. It was a murderous downward spiral, killing confidence in its path. Her anxiety prompted her to call again, with better results this time. Jerry picked up.

With a sense of lightness, she heard herself say, "This is Jesse, I'd like to have my schedule for the week."

Jerry acquiesced and gave her three gigs. None of them were topless, they were all clubs in New Jersey where the laws prohibited uncovered nipples. The tips would be less; the commute would be longer. Take the subway train under the channel after three in the morning, because it's what time the bars close.

The first night Jesse worked, she was persuaded to take off her top after-hours when the manager locked the doors. She made a few dollars, and then was dropped off at the subway station. On the wall, the hands of the round school-clock clicked to 4:30 as Jesse stood alone in the empty concrete cavern waiting for the train that would take her back to mainland Manhattan. She was acutely aware of the potential jeopardy of her situation, vigilant and heedful of every movement within her sight. This was an easy task as the only human she encountered was sleeping against a wall. She was relieved when the train finally appeared, although she did not like that it traveled in a tube under water. It was just another reason why this gig sucked.

Once she was back in her own neighborhood, she realized how lucky she was to have made it back unhurt. She made a note to herself to let Jerry know that she would not work there again.

Another gig was in the Bronx; the club was Latino owned by Mr. Mendez. The only music on the jukebox was salsa, and traditional ballads with sugary lyrics, all in Spanish. Jesse loved the place, although the cab ride from the station was pricey. Since she was able dance to any kind of music, by the end of the night the owner asked if she wanted to work exclusively for him. Jesse liked the place, but a diet of strictly Latin music, not likely. Since

Jesse was full breasted, and a bit over-weight, Mr. Mendez's customers loved her and tipped her generously. Jesse felt satisfied. She seriously considered his offer, sure that her Spanish would finally improve.

The third gig was in Jersey City, and like the last two jobs, Jesse had not been told the details. The Diamond Club was all black. Jesse had no qualms but hoped the customers would be hospitable, not like a club in L.A. where she had not made one dollar while the black dancer had been showered with money. Edwin, the buff bouncer directed Jesse to the dressing room and then up to a stage about four feet in diameter covered with shiny linoleum, raised four feet in the air behind the opulent wrap around bar.

"You have got to be kidding me; I'm a dancer," Jesse remarked with irritation.

"Well, Miss Jesse, we have some of the finest entertainment and none of our other dancers have complained," Edwin retorted insolently.

She checked her sarcasm. Was everything, she said and did, being reported back to Jerry? She could not afford to alienate him again. By the end of the first set Jesse had adapted to the stage and was even reasonably successful collecting tips as she made her way around the booths in the lounge. Jesse's main complaint was the music. She really was a hippie at heart, so she wanted to hear music that rocked, music that had a political message, not the sexy lull of Issac Hayes. But she managed to tolerate it, and the rest of the evening passed without incident. She collected her wages, hoping she would not be booked here again.

She called Jerry for her next week's schedule and was told that he didn't have anything for her.

"Jesse, right now I'm hurting for clubs," he explained without emotion, "and I have to give priority to my dancers with the most seniority. You are a new dancer, so I can't use you this week. I am sorry it worked out this way. Call me tomorrow; I might have something." And with that he hung up the phone.

Jesse did not utter a word and sat with the receiver in her hand. Her rent was paid, and she knew she would not starve, but how could she get her car out of hoc if she could not work steadily. She spent most of the night trying to lose consciousness, and then awoke before the sun. The anxiety flowed in her brain; her thoughts jammed up, and it felt like her heart was going to crack her rib cage. *I'm pretty sure it's way too early to call Jerry*, she thought, before falling back into sporadic sleep while waiting for a decent hour to call him.

The morning sun was relentless. Jesse's eyes were puffy and burning from the previous night's crying; she listened intently for her agent's voice.

"Galaxy, Jerry speaking."

"Please don't hang up. Jerry, I really need to work. You know I'm a stranger here, I don't know anyone," her voice sounding little and weak.

"Who's this? Jesse? Look Jesse I have some work for you. I have a couple of friends who make adult movies, and one of their models didn't show up. Do you want the gig?" Like a good salesman, Jerry did not say a word until Jesse responded.

She had done pornography and hated it. She had hoped to leave it in her past, but here it was being presented as an option again. Stagnate or make money, stand still or progress toward her goals, starve, get thrown out of the hotel, or generate money?

"Sure," Jesse heard herself answer flatly.

"Good! Can you stop by the office and I'll give you the information?" He said abruptly.

"Jerry, I'm not sure I can do...."

"Jesse, honey, don't worry about anything, just come on over and I'll give you the details. This is no big thing, and the pay is great. Ok, I'll see you in a little while, right?"

Turning down work and not generating money, was not an option. He held the power. She felt sick, nervous, all the feelings that arise when you have to do something despicable, something you really don't want to do, and yet there is no other way.

Jesse rode the subway to the agency, dreading what was in front of her. The trip across town seemed shorter than usual, and the glass on the front door seemed greasier than usual. Galaxy Entertainment needed her services.

Both Jerry and his business partner Al greeted her as she walked in. "Hey baby, come over here and make yourself comfortable," Al patted the chair beside him.

Jesse complied.

"Listen, I'm going to give you a ride over to my friend's apartment. Randy and Mitch are going to give you $400.00 cash to have sex with Rachelle while they film you. She is a classy lady, and she will tell you, most of the time she is a clothes model. However, Rachelle agreed just this once to act for us, and then the other girl didn't show." Al rambled on. "Have you acted in adult movies before?" he asked.

"Not really," she lied. "But I've had a lot of sex."

Jerry snickered, and Al lost it.

"You're going to do fine," Jerry reacted patronizingly.

Jesse was tired of them talking down to her, and she was getting restless to get the damn job done. "Al, do you mind if we leave? The sooner I get started, the sooner I'll be finished."

Al had volunteered to transport Jesse to the shooting location since her VW was still impounded. Every point in New York City is accessible to every other point, and if the men had really wanted to be mean they could have insisted that she take the subway.

Al would not stop jabbering, and Jesse was forced to submit to his constant assault of banal verbiage.

"Jesse don't be surprised if they ask you to show them that you can take a dildo up the ass. They had problems with girls getting cold feet when they hauled out the double headed vibrator." Al laughed as if he thought he was a comedian.

Jesse wanted to say fuck you, and your sleezy friends, but instead she said nothing. If she protested, she would lose the gig, and possibly the agency's support; she wouldn't chance it.

When they finally arrived, they climbed the brownstone and were greeted at the door. After introductions, the cameraman led Jesse into the bedroom. It was setup with lights, a movie camera, and the obligatory red velvet bedspread.

The producer who doubled as the director told his brother, the cameraman, to go ahead and introduce the two actresses.

Jesse liked Rachelle immediately; and there was no doubt that she was indeed a model from her full Nubian lips, to her long brown legs that carried her to 6 feet tall. Her soft black hair was styled to wrap around her face to perfectly frame a radiant smile. She smelled good like silken baby powder. She was a few years older than Jesse, and a native New Yorker.

"You know pornography is not my usual gig. But I haven't landed any modeling jobs recently, and I really needed this to cover my living expenses. Her attitude was nonchalant, and pragmatic. Jesse was reassured by her cool confidence, and Rachelle was generous in guiding the young neophyte.

"Alright you two, come sit on the bed, and let's get rolling!" The director had a name that Jesse promptly forgot. She silently uttered a prayer of gratitude that she would be filmed having sex with Rachelle instead of some skank.

Al decided to stay and watch the show after all, this was one of the perks of the business.

For Jesse, pornography was a bizarre world, a dissociative experience where strangers mimic passion, and the most sacred acts of intimacy are showcased like pathetic human anomalies, freaks in a carnival side-show. She was mildly repulsed by the sex, a fact that she knew would surprise the men who were watching, and she performed it all without a drink or drug in her system.

The time dragged, but 2 hours later she and Rachelle were both 400 hundred dollars richer. By the time they walked out of the shoot, they were talking and laughing like long-time friends, a phenomenon that occurred frequently in the pornography industry.

They agreed to share the cab fare to Rachelle's apartment in Manhattan. It was still mid-afternoon, and they wanted to continue their conversation. Jesse could not believe how beautiful her place was. It oozed comfort and sensuality, rich hand-woven tapestries from exotic and hard-to-reach enclaves around the planet. Rachelle was a woman of many talents. She pulled out her portfolio, or rather her stack of portfolios. The woman was a clothes designer, a model, a dancer, and an artist. Jesse was fascinated by her assemblages; encased in glassed wooden boxes was a mix of paint and real items like ticket stubs, eggs, bottle caps, pressed and dried flowers, pinned butterflies, and sepia photographs pilfered from the many antique shops that littered Manhattan. Rachelle sold her boxes to high-end retailers like Macy's. Jesse was surprised at the prices these one-of-a-kind three-dimensional collages commanded. Rachelle pulled out her modeling portfolio; it was filled with her promotional images. She also had some stills of the different commercials she had done.

Here was this hugely talented artist who had to resort to lesbian skin flicks in order to support her lifestyle until the serious gigs came along. One more reason to be depressed. Jesse hid it around strangers that she felt dead inside, empty and devoid of energy. It was some relief to spend a few hours with this sweet person who listened intently to Jesse's story of bitter love, and the kidnapping of her little boy. Jesse always cried when she told anyone about Andre.

This evening was no different. Rachelle hated to see her new friend suffering so much torment. "Hey, Jesse," she said gently slipping her arm over her shoulder in a big sister way, "I know something good will work out for you; just don't give up hope." And then pausing, she said, "You know what? I have some valium. It will make you feel better and let you sleep."

Jesse was no stranger to drugs. She knew exactly what Rachelle was offering her but thought it best not to say anything. "I would be so grateful," she said.

Rachelle brought her a whole prescription bottle full of valiums. "Take as many as you like. I have an open prescription with my doctor, so I can get a refill whenever I need to," she said as she tossed the prescription bottle to Jesse.

As she fiddled with the cap, she wondered how many she could take, and still be considered appropriate. Knowing the wonderful feeling of relief that just one little tablet could offer, she poured ten into her hand, and quickly went back to the conversation with Rachelle.

After they had thoroughly processed the day's "work," both came to the same conclusion. They were not thrilled about making skin flicks, but both were happy that the other one was a quality lady. Jesse did not want to overstay her welcome, so she got directions to the nearest subway entrance, and headed back to the hotel.

Jesse's sense of aloneness began to seep into her senses the minute she stepped out of Rachelle's apartment, her feelings sinking like ice cubes to the bottom of her feet as she made her way down the stairs, and out of the locked lobby.

"Bye," she said as she walked past the doorman. By the time she arrived home the Valium were calling. She could hardly wait for that rush of relaxation and forgetfulness to wash over her.

She reached her door, and dropped the keys trying to unlock it. Tonight, the awful faded wallpapered walls whispered stories, making it hard for Jesse to settle down. Her tears were relentless, as they were most nights, but tonight was different. Jesse had a hand full of yellow tablets. She knew where her relief lay. She started with one, and after a while she took one more. At some point she could not remember how many she had taken, and yet she noticed, the pain remained, so she took another one.

Jesse raised her head from her wet pillow; she had no idea what time it was. She had to pee, and of course the bathroom was outside her room down the hallway. Standing with difficulty, she decided to brave the trek. Dizzy and drugged addled, outside the door she walked the wrong way and turned the unlocked doorknob of her neighbor's apartment, to his surprise. Blurry from Valium, Jesse excused herself, but then fell slightly against him; he caught her as she snuggled against his chest for a few seconds.

"Where's the bathroom. I can't find the bathroom," she whimpered pathetically.

Being a junkie himself, the neighbor pointed her in the right direction. Semi-conscious Jesse precariously made her way down the hallway, and managed to find the commode, but she was again turned around when she exited. Her other neighbor woke up hearing Jesse scratch around at his keyhole, and unlike the previous encounter this man saw an opportunity. The Valium had made Jesse so submissive and accommodating that it did not take long for him to get Jesse out of her clothes and on the bed where he proceeded to exploit her. She was passed out for the greater part of the show. When she came to, the digital clock glared green 5:00 a.m. The dark bearded man next to her was snoring, his dick hanging placidly on his hipbone. Jesse tried to piece together last night's scenario. She remembered bits and pieces of what looked like slides for a book of Kama Sutra. She felt sore, everywhere. Her clothes were scattered around the bed. She moved quickly gathering and dressing not wanting to wake the bear. She found the door and was out in the hallway once again.

Her head somewhat cleared, Jesse was able to negotiate the corridor back to her own apartment, and easily open the correct door with her key. She felt like an asshole. She had been used like a receptacle for her next-door neighbor's semen and couldn't even remember most of it. These musings did not lift Jesse's spirit instead she felt the pull of the vial of pills at the bottom of her bag. She found it, and without caring about losses, schedules, or obligations she popped two more, and waited for the relief. She lay down on her bed. The last sound she heard was the crunching of plastic wrap, *damn rats!*

Jesse lay deathlike for 24 hours. By the time she was fully awake, another day had come and gone. Her eyes were still blurry, and she wondered just how long she had been passed out. She also wondered whether she would be able to avoid the two neighbors she had inadvertently visited during her Valium binge. One thing she did know was that her time for self-pity was quickly running out. If she ever expected to return to New Mexico, she would have to pull herself out of this suicidal dive, get her car out of hock, and drive away from this God-forsaken city.

It seemed that Jesse's video performance had placed her back within the good graces of her agent, because he gave her a full schedule to work when she reached him on the phone. Only one catch, most of the clubs were a long way out, lots of traveling time.

Weeks later, Jesse bumped into Karen at the Red Barn, a Jersey club on the circuit. Karen had been through a few adventures of her own and admitted that making money in New York was no longer as easy as it once had been. She also was ready to head back to her Albuquerque homestead, and had long since forgiven Jesse for her temper tantrum. Jesse told her friend that she would have enough money saved after this week to get her VW out of hock, and Karen agreed that they would leave the city the Sunday after that.

Jesse's reunion with her car was emotional; she could not believe how trashed the beetle was. It had been impounded for ten weeks. The left front end was still mashed-in from the accident traveling here, and the inside looked like it had been ransacked more than once. Jesse did not care; it was her ride out of this place. She paid the impound fee and secured the keys. Even Karen was excited and ready to go. Jesse figured that she had been working her regular gigs the entire time that Jesse was off and on, plus Karen stayed with a girlfriend for free, and Jesse had been paying weekly at the Prince Charles since they had arrived almost 2 ½ months ago. Jesse felt a little bit jealous, but quickly shifted her attitude, glad to have someone to share the ride home.

On the Road Again

Threading her way out of the city was easy. It was as if a giant crow had been living inside Jesse's chest, and as the wrecked VW made its way west, the giant black bird took flight out of her being, and headed southwest ahead of them. With the window rolled down she filled her lungs with the wind from the sweet horizon.

Karen's voice interrupted her daydreaming behind the wheel. "Jesse, how long will it take us to get back to Albuquerque?"

"Maybe 5 days… this bug slows down over mountains and we must drive through the Smoky Mountains, and the Blue Ridge Mountains. That's a lot of climbing."

Karen seemed satisfied, and let Jesse go back to her daydreams. The trip back promised to be a lot smoother than the trip to New York City. They had arrived in March at the tail end of winter, and here they were traveling South West almost 3 months later; the temperature was mild, no need for a heater. The I Ching would say something like *'fortuitous.*

Somewhere in Kentucky the right front tire blew. Jesse screamed and mistakenly jerked the steering wheel left. Across the median in midday, the car careened. The momentum bounced it off and, on the highway, more than once, into oncoming traffic, until it landed in a ditch facing on-coming cars, trucks, and tractor-trailers.

The car had stopped moving but Jesse and Karen remained locked in each other's arms. Neither was hurt only shaken.

Quickly, a state trooper appeared. He called for a tow-truck, and the two of them were rescued. Jesse worried over the cost of the tow and the tire. She had a small amount of cash left from the impound transaction and wondered if it would cover everything. Fortunately, where the women had landed in rural America, the labor and tire were cheap. Karen contributed.

Soon they were on their way with blessings from the Sheriff, and lots of lewd looks from the mechanics in the garage. Karen had to prolong the departure by flirting copiously, exchanging numbers and addresses that she would never look at a second time. Jesse was fatigued but wanted to push on. Karen was hungry so they stopped at a truck stop diner on the outskirts of town.

The rest of the trip back to New Mexico was notably without incident. The miles unrolled, the desert panorama engulfed the two relieved females, and the sunset danced enticingly in front of their sleepy eyes. Home to Albuquerque, and it could not go by quickly enough.

"How well do you know Leann and her friend Mal? Jesse wondered out loud. "I mean have you talked to them since we left almost three months ago?"

"Well, to tell you the truth I haven't known them all that long, and no, I didn't talk to them, but I left a couple of solid numbers and they didn't use them so I'm assuming everything is alright," Karen replied optimistically.

Jesse had to be happy with that answer even though it made her uneasy. She didn't have much for anyone to steal,

240

but she would hate to lose the great flea market loot she found. She decided that she was not going to worry about any of that stuff; it was not worth it.

Welcome Home

The reception was cordial. Karen and her friends went off toward the house gabbing, and Jesse unloaded the VW. Standing in the archway of her room she lovingly looked at her few belongings. It felt like home, but the peace did not last long. Karen was a drama magnet, and her new friends cared only about getting what they wanted. Although Jesse tried to be friendly, Mal and her sidekick Leann aggressively teased and mocked her until she felt compelled to move out.

The euphoria she had felt when she thought she had an ally, left her. Jesse was again cast off and looking for a place to live. She remembered saying, I would rather be on the streets and homeless in Albuquerque, than be working in New York City. And so, she searched and found a small duplex that she could afford not far from the university. Danny, the manager of the Fireside Inn continued to put her on the schedule, and after all the problems in New York, she felt relieved that she had a regular dancing job.

One slow afternoon a blond bearded man with long hair sat at the front of the stage. He looked like a hippie, or a hillbilly. Between songs Jesse leaned over to start a conversation. "Hey, hippie, how 'bout buying me a beer?

He blushed. "Sure. Can you sit down, or is that against the rules?"

"No, it's ok. I have another ten minutes before I'm done with my set."

Jesse returned to him when her music ended.

"I'm John. You dance really well." Jesse appreciated the compliment and before long they were chatting like old friends.

"I live in this adobe hacienda out in Corrales."

"Where's that?"

"It's on the outskirts of Albuquerque in a rural community of horse lovers, professionals and recently, hippies."

Jesse welcomed the affinity of spirit she felt as the two talked.

"It's so cool that you dance and sew. You're an artist! You have to come out to the Welcome Home and check it out."

"What is the Welcome Home?" Jesse asked.

It is a 200-year-old hacienda. The legend says that Pancho Villa lived here with his gang. My brother and I created a commune and tea house. My brother David is an artist, and Jeff is our resident cook who wants to open a vegetarian restaurant. I think you would fit right in.

"You said it's a commune; what if the other people don't like me?" Jesse asked.

"Oh, don't worry, everyone will like you. When my brother and I first thought about starting a commune, there were about 9 or 10 friends who wanted to go along with us. Now, a lot of the original members have left to do their own things. The people who live at Welcome Home come and go; they don't quite have the same vision as the original group, but it's still a communal effort," he explained.

Jesse liked John but wasn't sexually attracted to him; she hoped that the help he was offering was without obligations.

Early evening when Jesse was finished with her shift, John came back and gave her a ride to the Welcome Home in Corrales. Within the week she had moved her flea market bed, vanity, sewing machine, box of books, and clothes into a rustic, unfinished cubicle with a high ceiling.

Jesse gave him what she would call a charity fuck, and two weeks later he moved a girlfriend into his bedroom. Jesse was hurt, but realized it was for the best since he wasn't her type.

Jesse's room was tiny with unfinished walls. She draped panels of lace, and immediately hung a photograph of happier days, a summer day on the rocks at the beach with Andre, Carlos, and herself. It was positioned right above her bed. She could see her child, and her ol' man, before Mexico, before the slap that had driven her into the world, and away from her little boy. She felt like the photograph gave her direction, away from the grave, but it also fueled her daily crying spells.

It seemed that no matter where she was sleeping, or whose party she was in the middle of, she felt disconnected and empty, incapable of feeling anything but pain, not able to truly engage or care.

Cinco de Mayo was soon approaching, and a few people from Welcome Home were driving north to Santa Fe to join in the festivities. Jesse hitched a ride with them. Once the car arrived everyone scattered, and Jesse immediately became separated from the others. She drank a few cervezas and attracted a sinewy thick lashed Mexican with a beautiful fro and an intoxicating bright smile.

"Say, Chiquita, you look lost. Can I be of help?" He glided up on her, and she took the bait.

"Yes, my friends are here somewhere." Manuel grabbed her hand like a boyfriend, and she followed, loving the feel of his hand in hers. They walked around most of the night and got squeezed in the rush to watch the straw man burn. There it was in the center of the adoring crowd, two stories high, Zozobra blazing; the community's hopes and fears, ignited, transmuted, and offered in pagan fire to the hungry souls surrounding it.

Jesse had never seen such a spectacle, the atmosphere was exhilarating, and her new friend was romancing her, buying her corn on a stick, and green chile burritos. She talked non-stop about her life, her journey, her losses, and her past heroin chipping. They finally ran into her friends and without much talk, Manuel followed along to the car and crunched into the back seat with Jesse on one side and a hippie on the other.

It was an hour between Santa Fe and Corrales, but the ride seemed short with this dark, brown-eyed man beside her. Jesse was anticipating, and Manuel did not let her down. They were compatible in bed. And afterwards he pulled out a piece of leather, unrolled it, and meticulously laid his works on the nightstand. Jesse knew exactly what all the paraphernalia was for. There was the bent spoon; the strap used to tie off; the syringe; needle and a balloon-end knotted, all sitting neatly like props on the set of an off-off Broadway play. Jesse thought about protesting, hearing in her mind words like, *"No thanks, I'm clean."* Instead, she snuggled up to his naked back with her bare breasts and looked on with eagerness. He fixed her and then fixed himself. They both fell back into the pillows for more games and bed talk.

By next morning Manuel called a friend who lived in close-by Albuquerque to come and give him a ride back home to Santa Fe. Jesse had no phone number to give him. She had no interest in seeing him again either. They kissed lightly as his ride pulled up to the front door. The sex was a quick diversion from her loneliness, but she knew better than to get hooked up with another junkie. Jesse wondered why of all the people on Earth she attracted another heroin addict. Within a few days Jesse's lower abdomen was aching so that she could not stand up straight. She made an appointment at a community clinic in town. While the doctor was taking a sample from her uterus, he spoke to his nurse, "Looks like he left her a few other visitors," talking as if Jesse were not in the room. It took ten minutes for the lab results. The nurse came back with a syringe full of penicillin for her hip, and a prescription for pubic lice.

Although the weather was beautiful, Jesse felt tainted, rotted inside. She quickly found a drugstore to buy the needed poison and hitch-hiked back home to exterminate the crabs trying to live on her.

Welcome Home was unusually quiet and deserted when she arrived. David the un-appointed leader often invited people to do many kinds of workshops, massage, meditation, acoustic guitar, Tai Chi, and more. With eleven renters, and the weekend scheduled activities and performances, there was always something going on.

Since she had moved out of the city, Jesse's motivation to drive back and forth had dwindled. She began wondering if she could make money without depending entirely on dancing. Comparing Albuquerque with New York Jesse could see that this was not a big money town. There were a handful of topless and strip clubs, and the economy was nowhere booming. Perhaps she could put her sewing skills to use.

She found a consignment shop called The General Store, right on the plaza in downtown Albuquerque. Her first garments were country print aprons and jumpsuits for toddlers, appliquéd, and embroidered. It took her many hours to design and execute her projects, and they were always unique and well made, but she figured she was earning about fifty cents an hour because she did not want to ask an exorbitant amount, especially since the policy of the shop hiked the price one hundred percent. She soon grew tired of that hamster wheel. She continued to search around town for places to dance other than The Fireside Inn. There was an all-nude club on the southwest outskirts of the city, but Jesse was hoping to find something classier. She would go bottomless, but her experience in Los Angeles told her that she would again be pressured to dance on her back rather than on the platform heels that she loved so much. So, she stayed where she was for a couple more months until a fellow dancer told Jesse about The Body Shop.

As soon as Jesse entered the lobby, she knew that this place was classier. She could see the elevated stage, and red spotlights. The owner asked her to audition and gave her a three-day schedule for the following week. Before leaving she looked over the jukebox to see what kind of music selection she would have. Jesse harbored one complaint about dancing, she was not able to play her own preferred music. Most clubs had jukeboxes that reflected the tastes of the owner or manager, who in most cases was certainly not a dancer. Jesse prided herself on being able to dance to anything, even country music, but that didn't mean that she liked it.

When Jesse had to work at a club with a bum jukebox, she felt trapped in an existential hell. One time she took a two-week gig at a cowboy bar with the worst country trio she had ever heard and found herself required to dance topless while the singer crooned such favorites as Your Cheatin' Heart complete with steel guitar and yodeling. On occasion Jesse had tried to get some of her 45's put on the club's jukebox, but to no avail. Her music was not welcomed, too radical, too political, or too raw. She quit trying and nestled into her new job anticipating the needed stability.

Artistic Expression

One smoky Friday night Jesse had just finished dancing her set, one of the songs being Proud Mary. Every hippie knew that Mary referred to marijuana and of course Jesse, the ever-flamboyant activist, liked to mime the act of rolling, lighting, toking, and passing a joint while she was dancing to this overplayed 45. While making the customary rounds to say hello, and collect tips, one handsome hippie man pulled her hand and whispered, "Your dancing was great, and I loved your choice of songs." He slipped a thin joint into her hand which she quickly transferred to the front of her G-string. Jesse thanked him and moved along since it had been the final set of the night, and the bright go-home lights would soon be turned on.

She made her way to the dressing room with the two other dancers in front of her pulling on their jeans and talking about money and guys. Jesse changed clothes and slipped out of the club as was her routine. At home when she dumped out her dance bag to count her tips, she remembered the joint. It was gone.

Jesse was scheduled to work the afternoon shift on Saturday; afternoons could be slow, it depended on the planets. The place had a good number of customers by the time Jesse's turn to dance came around. She climbed the steps and proceeded to do what she loved, entertaining. Sometimes she danced, sometimes she clowned, and sometimes she tried to be a parody of sexual desire, because she believed it was ludicrous for anyone to spend their leisurely sunny Saturday inside a smoky bar watching naked women who will likely never be anything more than allure. She finished her set and was confronted by the owner and a stranger dressed in a suit who accompanied Jesse to the office.

The man introduced himself as Officer Reicher from the vice squad. "You are being arrested for lewd and indecent conduct."

Jesse recovered from her initial shock and instantly became inflamed. "What are you talking about? I didn't do anything different from any other dancer," she pleaded.

"Follow me," he said as he directed her to the owner's office. There he instructed her to empty her dance bag. She did this, hoping it would be over quickly. Not finding anything but G-strings, make-up, perfume and tampons. The detective again instructed her to pick up her belongings and get dressed. "We're going downtown to the police station to process you and then you will be released on your own recognizance. You'll be charged with lewd and indecent conduct."

She was enraged, frightened, panic-stricken and lost, all at once. Being arrested and held for a bogus charge seemed like the height of absurdity. She practically spit with resentment as she retaliated with words. She knew that she still had freedom of speech to tell them what she thought of their repressive, archaic laws and the Puritans who authored them.

"I know why I'm being hassled, you thought I was a drug dealer, and this ridiculous charge would give your boys a chance to rummage through my smelly G-strings thinking you would find serious drugs."

She paused long enough, to assemble another tirade. "You're really just perverts with a good cover, hassling an innocent person when there are plenty of real criminals out there; I'm easy pickings for you, and your so-called vice squad. What a bullshit charge! You know I wasn't being obscene."

"Well, the law says that you were," Detective Reicher retorted.

"Believe me, if I were being obscene you would have known it," she said as she dropped her eyes to the detective's crotch.

The cop just stepped up his pace and stopped talking to her.

Jesse figured that if she couldn't stop them from following through with this ridiculous charge, at lease she would speak her mind. Their forensic expertise and fervor could be better utilized than in terrorizing a young girl alone in a strange state, trying to support herself with no help and no marketable skills.

An officer booked Jesse and gave her official papers explaining what she was charged with and when to show up for the trial. Jesse was so incensed that she had again been harassed for no significant reason, that she decided she did not need a lawyer, and would represent herself.

The day of the trial came. Jesse got up on the stand and explained to the court that she had not actually been grinding on the stage support pole but rather suggestively to those watching as a *parody* of sexual coyness, insinuating that the pole was better than anything a customer might show her.

Judge Robbins paraphrased Jesse's words, "So, you're saying that you feel it's a matter of artist interpretation."

"Yes sir, I do!"

"Thank you, you may step down."

Jesse stopped breathing to pay closer attention to Judge Robbins verdict.

"Dismissed, by reason of first amendment right to expression."

Jesse stepped out of the courthouse relieved and vindicated. She reminded herself that she was ahead of the times. Her philosophy of freedom, especially sexual, and freedom for her own bodily expression whether nude or otherwise, was not mainstream in the sleepy town of Albuquerque. This was not West Hollywood, with its tolerance for eccentric artistic types. This place was one step above a wild-west stagecoach stop. Jesse saw authentic cowboys and ranchers in the audience all the time. She sometimes fantasized that a rich one would fall in love with her and take her away from dancing.

Now it was back to the pavement. She felt disappointed that she could not continue working at the Body Shop; it was better than most of the dives in town. She especially did not want to work in the video houses, smelly, sleezy, disgusting places where the dancer didn't dance but rather tried to persuade the customer to give all of his money by assuming various positions while masturbating. A one-way mirror allowed the customer privacy. Jesse supposed the custodian earned his paycheck. Scrubbing booths had to be the worst.

She had heard from other dancers that the money was abundant, but she just could not force herself to demean herself like that in public. True, she had done pornography, but she had either been "in love" and had followed Jack's lead, or had been desperate, besides, making love on camera was radically different from masturbating.

Jobless and penniless did not set well with Jesse; she liked to stay working. Ever since Jesse had discovered dancing for money, she thought little about her future, only happy to be paid for something she loved to do. Jesse knew that having a baby at 19 had not been kind to her body. Breastfeeding had stretched her breasts; they would never again be the pert pair she had sprouted at fourteen. Jesse had never been petite. She had a Marilyn Monroe body, big rib cage, and hour-glass figure. Many club owners wanted females that looked like virgins, or tomboys, pencil-thin and waif-like, trends fueled by Vogue magazine, and models like Twiggy and Penelope Tree. Jesse often felt dejected because she did not fit the mold; she felt obese. Dancing was all she knew... and sewing.

Miles of Stitching

This was the summer when the streets of Albuquerque surrounding the university erupted. Students joined in a nationwide effort to stop the Vietnam War and overturning a police car gave the government justification for calling in the National Guard. Although she sympathized with the anti-war movement, she did not see how violence would help.

Instead, Jesse attended a massage workshop given by some vagabond guru. She remembered what Timothy Leery had taught, "Turn on, tune in, drop out." She felt like her time was better spent blowing on her recorder or designing a dance costume. Her specialty was embellishing her pieces with hand-strung glass beads. They were unique wearable art and gave the dancer an air of class. In a spotlight, they reflected like diamonds.

Ever since her very first dancing gig in California, Jesse had sewn her own costumes, shiny brocade bras, tiny bottoms, cover-ups, robes, jackets, and capes. In 1966 there were few specialty shops for strippers. Occasionally Frederick's of Hollywood sold clothes that a dancer might be able to get out of gracefully, but rarely. Sewing was one activity that her mother had encouraged; in response Jesse had continued to sew and had become quite proficient since her junior high sewing class. Now she thought she might be able to use the skill to her advantage. She could design and sew some costumes and see if she could sell them in town.

Limited in funds, she hit the thrift stores and found a couple of prom dresses for a quarter each with enough material for an entire outfit. She had perfected sleeves that stayed on with elastic even after the bodice was removed; the puffy full skirts made angel sleeves easy. With a few glass beads, and ribbons Jesse knew she could get top dollar for her creations.

Her co-workers admired her costumes. Sometimes she designed a costume around a prop that she had found. It might be a snake arm bracelet, or a rhinestone broach she picked up at the Good Will. She enjoyed assembling the parts and pieces, watching the outfit take shape, and then seeing her costumes on the dancer, her own creations and handiwork. Her costumes sold quickly, and she took orders for more. If Jesse could have cloned herself, she might have made a living, but she worked slowly and soon realized that spending all her waking minutes sitting at the sewing machine did not suit her. Before long Jesse was looking for another place to dance.

Jesse thought about the first club where her agent had booked her in Albuquerque, and wondered whether he was still flying in women from out of state, or would he hire her off the street? Would he even remember her? She could not remember his name, she thought it was Rusty. The club was about a mile from the college on the main strip through town. As she walked in she was disappointed to hear the same tired records that were already ancient when she had worked there before. At this point if somehow, she could stay on her feet, keep her bottoms on, and make some cash, she was not going to be particular. Maybe she could sweet talk the owner into putting some of her favorite records on the jukebox. Rusty did not seem to mind that Jesse had relocated and wasn't being represented by an agent. It gave him an opportunity to pay less money without the middleman agent. Rusty asked Jesse to jump up on the stage and dance a couple of numbers. She obliged, and happily left the bar with a few tips, next week's schedule in hand.

Relieved at having work, Jesse wondered if her VW would hold together to make the trip back and forth to the city about 12 miles from rural Corrales. The gig she found fit her temperament, a couple of day shifts and a Friday. Perfect, giving her enough time to join in some of the activities at Welcome home.

Each weekend Welcome Home showcased live acoustical music in the massive living room which doubled for audience seating and performance area. The place was always packed. Jesse's bedroom was right off the front room. She loved being around the performers and traveling hippies. Welcome Home became an underground hotspot for students and curious tourists.

Lure of a Cult

O ne day Jesse hopped a ride into town to see Charlie, the guy whose apartment had been raided on her first night in town. They had just happened to see each other while sitting in the audience at the Welcome Home; she barely recognized him because he had grown a beard. After hearing that he had become a Jesus freak; she wanted to hear more.

He told her the bizarre story of being robbed by gunpoint one night as he was walking to his house.

"The man said he was going to waste me, so I said out loud, *Jesus, if you're real, then get me out of this.* At that very moment the dude lowered his piece, and ran away.

A few days later, I met my spiritual family. We call ourselves *The Children of God.*"

Jesse and Charlie had been walking when he said quite impetuously, "Jesse, I want to introduce you to my people. I'm sure there is a meeting today over by the university."

"Sure, I guess so but you know I'm not sure about the whole savior thing," Jesse stammered.

She did not want to seem close-minded, but since leaving home Jesse was so done with Jesus. She was more interested in Eastern religions. After all, Jesus had not helped her. He had not protected her from heroin. He hadn't protected her from being raped, nor protected her from her stepfather's predatorial lewdness, nor from her mother's emotional and physical cruelty, and certainly he had not reclaimed her kidnapped son for her.

Charlie and Jesse arrived at a house in a neat middle-class neighborhood. The moment Jesse stepped inside she was besieged with ten or more people, males and females putting their arms around her, each whispering loving statements to her. Then she was ushered over to a dusty sofa and offered food and juice to drink which she declined.

The obvious leader, a strikingly handsome young man with long dark hair began speaking about the all-powerful love from Christ that is available to every single suffering person. He asked all of us to feel the love we had for each other and to imagine this feeling millions of times over: This was what Jesus had to offer each of us. We need never feel lonely, hungry, sad, desperate, or hopeless. Jesse felt the words seep into her ears, and into her consciousness, and the tears welled up as the strangers around her groped and hugged her, making her feel even weirder. She learned from the Children of God, that Christ would always take care of every single detail, and that Jesse like the others in the room was welcome to stay and partake of their collective efforts. Within minutes Jesse felt like she was being suffocated, and excused herself from the group, found her coat, and hastily exited the front door.

Her bearded friend came running after her, concerned that she would freeze. "Are you going to be alright?"

"Yes, I'm going over here a couple of blocks away to visit another friend. Thanks for the introduction to your spiritual family. They seem very loving."

Jesse turned, eager to get away from him and the vortex of religious fanaticism. She had no desire or need to be enveloped in their world or be told how to live. Her reaction was so strong it had propelled her outside into the dropping temperature of the late afternoon.

Forrest wasn't really a friend yet. She had met him earlier in the month at a party. He seemed genuine, smart and as far as she could judge, he was the best-looking and most accomplished of the group. But he wasn't home, so she planted herself on his steps and waited. She was nearly frozen by the time he pulled up.

She jumped up as he approached. "Hi, I hope you don't mind that I stopped by. I was two streets over listening to these kids. They call themselves The Children of God. They say that they are being directed by Jesus. They do not work they just wait for the Holy Spirit to provide. It was creepy. They all wanted to hug me and tell me how much I was loved; it felt like a cult."

"I'm glad you remembered where I live," Forrest responded warmly as they walked into the house.

"I was going to hitch to Corrales, but I didn't realize how quickly the temperature drops around here."

"You can stay here for the night if you want, or I can give you a ride home."

"I don't have anywhere to be; it would be great if you could drive me home tomorrow."

"Can I draw you a bath? You look cold."

"I'd love that!"

Forrest lit some incense and drew a tub of steaming bathwater for Jesse. She loved the pampering and laid back to let the music surround her like the warm water. Later amid bed trays, blankets, and tears she told him about her journey and her utter aloneness, and anguish that enveloped her regularly. It seemed that he felt her pain, so he made love to her to the meditative sounds of Asian flutes, and she allowed him to lift her legs high over her head, pressed back, her athletic body, flexible and uninhibited.

Jesse slipped into sleep fully satisfied and awakened to breakfast in bed. Forrest was thoughtful, educated, and musical. He came from a well-respected family of four children, all of them educated, and professionals or married. He was probably the most adventuresome of all of them being the youngest. Jesse was just exotic enough from the pagan land of California to interest Forrest. He had no idea that their casual coupling would result in a child.

True to his gentlemanly demeanor, Forrest gave her a ride home. He called to Jesse as she slammed the car door, "Jess, I'll call you, let's go out. Think about where you want to go."

Jesse smiled, and mouthed ok as she kept on walking toward the front door. Back on her own turf she felt a wave of relief as her room welcomed her like an old friend. Jesse avoided a phone call from Forrest. Something about his hands had turned her off; they were clammy, dripping sweat. Valentine's Day came and went, and Jesse had no idea that Forrest might want to visit.

Heavenly Blues

esse wanted to test what she thought might be a hippie myth about the psychedelic properties of morning glory seeds, specifically Heavenly Blues. She had heard that if you crushed and then ingested them, they would get you high. She and one of the other residents at Welcome Home, a college student, ground seeds, and putting the dust into capsules, discussed how many they thought would be sufficient.

Every time Jesse took a hallucinogen, she was afraid, afraid she would get stuck in some recess of her mind from which she could not escape. It was worrisome because she knew Schizophrenia ran in her family's genes. She had tripped previously, and it wasn't always fun.

Motivated by her libido, this time Jesse's objective was Cassidy, the fine, bearded, long-haired man directing the experiment. Swallowing twenty monster capsules she had stuffed full and washing them down with orange juice Jesse looked forward to hanging out with Cassidy. Unfortunately, he said goodbye and disappeared before Jesse realized he was leaving. Left alone, she wandered into the living room with its tall ceilings, and fireplace still sizzling from earlier. She lay down on the woven rug in front of it. Before long she was floating, until her stomach lurched and she ran to the toilet just barely making it. She wretched until her stomach was truly empty.

The nausea was the beginning of the Morning Glory high. Jesse returned to her reverie watching the cinders and flames, like looking deep into her own private volcano, becoming distracted only when Cassidy returned with John.

"We're going up to the Jemez Mountains to pick up some wood, and then we decided that since the San Isidro springs were nearby, we'd go there afterwards. You want to come along?" Jesse had visited the springs one other time, but not at night.

"I'm kind of fucked-up."

John offered a hand up. "Don't worry. I won't let anything bad happen to you. The springs are a sacred place to the natives. They leased it to some hippies, and they've got a cool commune going. Their common goal is to keep the springs open and create a self-sufficient independent cooperative."

Jesse remembered the first time she had visited the springs when she first arrived in New Mexico. "I had just smoked some pot and my attention was captured by an unfamiliar sound, a buzzing scream that almost deafened me. It reminded me of a science fiction movie I had seen when I was 7; it scared me to death. I admit I am a light weight when it comes to grass. It really affects me. Sometimes it makes me feel afraid... I guess paranoid. So, my reasoning self was telling me 'nothing has changed', you have a drug in your system. But I still felt afraid because I could not identify that incessant sound like a beam of energy piercing my brain. I went exploring away from the buildings and found a couple of huge bugs facing each other engaged in what seemed like an intense electronic audio-exchange."

"Oh yeah, they're called cicadas, definitely weird insects," John replied.

"I was convinced that I had found aliens communicating out there on the mesa. I can see how people go crazy and end up in institutions. I watched those two and realized that they were in the middle of a mating ritual.

"So how fucked-up are you?" John interrupted Jesse's musings.

"I wouldn't want to drive."

John chuckled saying, "Okay, just follow me, and relax. You won't be required to get behind a wheel."

The drive was fun. Jesse had not been brought up with older brothers or a family where team spirit was cultivated. This was like nectar to her soul riding in the back of a pick-up with friends to scour the forest of dead wood so they could heat the house. The wind was nippy, but the layers of clothes under her navy-blue pea coat kept her warm enough and John kept his arm around her.

Passing the San Isidro Springs on the right the truck continued north to a spot where the wood was accessible. Jesse traipsed around and did her share of bending, carrying and pitching logs into the bed of the Chevy. When the men were satisfied that all available spaces had been stuffed with wood, they piled inside, and everyone got cozy for the short ride down to the springs.

They arrived, paid their fees, headed for the dressing rooms, and out into the pool area. Jesse opted for a bathing suit bottom without the top, wrapped a towel around her and stepped out on the cement.

As her eyes adjusted, she could see that most of the bodies were her friends from Welcome Home and a few others she didn't recognize, hippies with their long hair, except over to one side a Native family was bathing. Jesse found a spot in the shadow near the edge, spread her towel and sat on the edge for a minute before slipping over into the dark warm liquid.

The effect of the seeds gave her enhanced sight. She noticed the concentric circles around the knots in the wood pillar supports. Their aliveness struck her consciousness as the colored grains in the wood undulated and wove patterns under her watchful gaze. The hallucinogenic effect of the seeds had leveled off and it seemed to her that she could drift into an alternate consciousness or dimension, and then snap to her present-body reality as needed. Floating on her back in the deep steaming hot pool of spring fed water the star-crowded sky was the only reality. She was Kubrick's embryo suspended in the amniotic sac of the starry universe, she the primal female fetus of the cosmos. Jesse felt incredibly supported by Mother Earth, so calm, protected, and comfortable, without thought, without desire, without pain, forever traveling on this spaceship, into and through the galaxy. Her lungs absorbed the sweet oxygen; she experienced her body accelerating, silent forces propelling Jesse, a small speck, spiraling amidst the heavens. Cassidy walked to the end of the pool to check on her.

"Are you alright?"

Jesse could not decipher his language, nor attach meaning to his sounds and syllables. Her intuition told her that he was concerned about her well-being. She smiled, figuring it would suffice for communication. As if on cue, he smiled back and faded back into the shadow.

When it was time to go, wrinkled and waterlogged Jesse struggled to get her damp and sticky skin inside her jeans. Her sense of being was clear and she felt like her insides shimmered with energy. Strangely, she found her way back to the truck with perfect timing. The others loaded up and they all headed back to Welcome Home.

Another Chance

esse missed her period; she hadn't been with anyone since Forrest. Thinking back to the night when she had taken the Morning Glory seeds, *No wonder I threw-up, thinking it was the seeds; instead it was from being pregnant! She wondered why is it that a woman's first reaction to pregnancy is to vomit?* The irony was not lost to Jesse.

At first, she was disbelieving and then shocked. Days passed, her breasts began to swell, her nipples got sensitive and she knew without a test that she was indeed with child. This time there was no uncertainty. Jesse wanted this baby. There were no thoughts of abortion. She knew the father well enough to recognize good intelligent DNA, and she had grown so tired of the daily crying, of being miserable and feeling guilty about losing Andre. Now she would have a child in the here and now to think about. No longer caught in the nightmare of her past mistakes, Jesse could have a second chance to nurture a child, and to be a successful mother.

It was the middle of the week when she decided to tell Forrest. She telephoned and without much of a warning said, "I'm pregnant."

Forrest was calm and without hesitation replied, "I can give you the money for an abortion."

"No, I'm going to keep it. Don't worry, though, I'm not expecting anything from you." Jesse thought that she heard an audible sigh of relief but maybe she imagined it.

Jesse hitch-hiked to her first prenatal appointment, a few miles away, at the Bernalillo County Clinic. She had not given up the habit of sticking out her thumb, mostly because she didn't own a car anymore, and couldn't depend on any of her housemates or acquaintances. Hitching often put Jesse in the "zone," a vibe that she stepped into when she gave up control. It was a kind of spiritual pocket where she felt buoyant, elated and caught in the stream of love consciousness that transported her from here to there. After all, it was an act of kindness that compelled a driver to slow down and give her a lift. To those who had never experienced this sublime art of travel it seemed like a dangerous activity, for Jesse it was natural.

The nurse practitioner confirmed what she already knew, gave her some sample vitamins and iron pills, and scheduled her next appointment. Stepping outside the door she felt her heart quicken as she imagined the few cells dividing furiously inside her, soon to be her baby. It was late morning; the sun was reaching its peak. Jesse thought that she had better get some help from the state. The clinic she visited was free for poor people like herself, but she was going to need some financial help. Soon she would not be able to dance on a stage, although she had danced into her 5th month with Andre.

The department of social services was packed. It took her three hours to fill out paperwork and wait for an interview. Subjected to the judgmental snooping of a stranger so that she could receive a monthly check of one hundred and sixty-nine dollars, and another hundred and thirty dollars in food stamps left Jesse feeling dissected and demeaned. Still Jesse was grateful for the little bit of supplemental security.

This pregnancy was different from the first one. Jesse did not want to dance; her body immediately felt heavy. Her intolerance of smells increased, and it became impossible for her to spend even a small amount of time in a smoky bar or club. She knew that the small pittance issued by the state would not be enough to get by. Although she had never had to depend entirely on selling her costumes, she decided that it was worth a try. At least she could stay home and make her own schedule.

One thing was becoming apparent. She needed to move away from Welcome Home and back to civilization, at least somewhere with a thermostat, and quick heat so necessary for an infant's stable environment.

Chanting: Connection with a Community

ext day Jesse headed for town; she was on a mission to find some inexpensive material so that she could get started sewing some G-strings and tops. While she was browsing at the thrift store, Jesse fell into a conversation with a young woman named Margie. Margie had a wide blue-eyed stare that made you feel like you had been listened to for the first time. With reddish-brown hair, freckles and a fresh open smile, hers was the type of face that Norman Rockwell loved to paint. If she had been a boy, her friends would have called her Tom Sawyer. Jesse and Margie were instant best friends.

Walking down the street Margie kept encouraging Jesse to talk about her adventures. Then there in front of them stood a tall dark-haired man with deep intense eyes, and a resonating voice.

"Ladies, did you know that you can have anything you want just by chanting Nam Myo Ho Renge Kyo"? Walter spoke with a gentle authority.

Both Jesse and Margie were instantly interested and followed him to a house a block away. They were directed to remove their shoes, and the three of them knelt in rows in front of what looked to be an altar. In front of the altar were assembled the artifacts of the ritual, incense, a vase with a rose, and a bowl that rang like a bell with a small wooden mallet.

269

A middle-aged Asian man entered the room and requested that the group follow the words from the tiny paper-back books that had been distributed to everyone. He hit the side of the bowl, and so began the flurry of words, the liturgy of the service. Jesse listened to the symphony of voices all around her chanting the phrases in what sounded like ancient Japanese. It seemed to her that she was in the center of a powerful galloping voice machine with each wave of words rising and falling in unison.

Within the hour both became converts to Nichirin Shoshu Buddhism, the same religion that had fascinated Tina Turner. Walter seemed to think it was a powerful way to become Self-Realized. Margie and Jesse thought it was worth a try. After the ceremony they walked to the Morning Glory Café to drink coffee and talk about what they had just discovered.

"What just happened?" Margie said turning towards Jesse.

"I know; I really felt some kind of power come into me while we were chanting," Jesse answered.

"And can you believe how beautiful Walter is? Margie remarked.

"Yeah, and smart. I loved the way he explained how chanting works," Jesse answered contemplatively.

"Do you want to go to the next meeting together? Margie suggested in her take charge way.

"Absolutely," Jesse responded. "This religion says if you put in the devotional time chanting you will get what you want in life, and they dare you to try it out."

"What about the people who got up to tell their stories? They were amazing!" Margie continued.

"That's what makes a person want to try it, hearing those stories of how they asked for something and their lives were changed, and God knows I need some magic or power in my life." Jesse looked helpless as she uttered the words.

"You seem down. Are you okay?"

"I'm pregnant, and I've got to find a good place to rent, and I have very little money. I'm a topless dancer, and I don't think anyone is going to hire me in this condition," Jesse disclosed anxiously.

"You know, my parents just got divorced, and my Dad says he'll rent their house to me if I want to find some roommates to help share the expenses." Margie offered sincerely.

"You're kidding me; what's it like?" Jesse asked

"It has 5 bedrooms, 3 bathrooms and a swimming pool. I think he wants eight hundred."

"That would be doable if we can find 2 more people; then we would pay only $200 each. Jesse said excitedly.

"You're not going to believe this, but I was already talking to Walter and his friend, Tom. They are looking for a place to rent and they are willing to pay a little more because they want the garage as a shop to build furniture in," Margie replied.

"And this, with only one hour of chanting!" Jesse quipped. "Imagine the potential!"

The house was a rancher shaped like a horseshoe with 3 bedrooms on one side, a huge living room/den and dining room at the bottom end, and the kitchen, another small room and the master bedroom on the other side. In the center of the house was an in-ground pool with a diving board, and surrounded by grass. Jesse was charmed by the beautiful wood molding, and the rich tile floors that embellished the Southwestern theme of the architecture. She and Margie agreed that they could manage this big place. Margie collected the money, and they were given a key. Jesse was elated to have her own retreat, a place to go when she felt invisible. She liked her room; it was away from the others with a big window for plants. The space was large enough so that she could spread her sewing projects around.

Jesse and Margie were both attracted to Walter. He was an enthusiastic teacher and guru. The first few weeks were luscious for Jesse. Her enjoyment of life increased when she was around Walter. She felt hope and thought that the Spirit had brought her to this place. It was easy to slip into reverie while envisioning the blooming relationship between them. Psychologically, she had severed the tenuous ties with Forrest, the baby's biological father, because she wasn't attracted to him. Jesse's belly was swelling. She wondered whether Walter thought she was pretty, or sexy. His voice resonated in her ear, and reached her body chemistry, its sound stirring her desires.

Despite their mutual attraction for Walter, friendship grew between Margie and Jesse. Sisterly love had been another missed experience in Jesse's upbringing. The two had long conversations fueled by espresso, about the spirit world, consciousness, and how strange humans are. They gave each other the audience that the other had been missing.

Once all four converts moved into the same house, their involvement in the Nichiren Shoshu movement intensified. Going to meetings and chanting filled the days of their lives. Walter was promoted to a leader and was committed to bringing in more members because he believed this form of Buddhism to be the next evolutionary vehicle for mankind.

Walter introduced Jesse and Margie to the couple who had recruited him. Jesse described them as two of the happiest people she had ever met. Richard was black, Rosalee was Pueblo Indian. They had 3 children, all talkative, smart, and high achievers. Jesse loved hanging around their house before and after meetings. Richard's van was the unofficial shuttle. He was always doing God's work, helping people, shuttling members to services, and meetings. Ready to discuss spirituality anytime, Richard had studied Zen Buddhism in the Army, as well as other Eastern religions. He felt gratified by what chanting had added to his life. His wife had a welcoming way about her with a generous smile and receptive ear. Most of the time she let her husband do the talking, except when encouraged to tell her stories about how the Butsudan could intervene in a person's life. This practice did not promise everlasting life like the Christians, but apparently it did deliver gifts to the daily chanter. Eighty million worldwide chanted Nam Myo Ho Renge Kyo and had become disciples of Nichiren Shoshu Buddhism.

Jesse was surrounded by more loving people than ever before in her life. She continued to chant regularly, alone and at meetings that she attended with the rest of the crew. She was taught that the more hours she invested in chanting, the more she would see the results. She imagined leaving her poverty behind, and as a bonus she would have enlightenment. Jesse's misery had once again brought her to the wishing well. She wanted to believe that if she chanted enough, her prayers would be answered. She wanted Walter. He had become for her the gold standard in men, spiritual, intellectual, funny, handsome, and gentle. He reminded her of Carlos. She had begun building an immense castle of dreams all based on a perception that love was growing between her and Walter.

They lived in the same house, yet he had never visited her room. She often closed herself in her room, and wrote tortured bad poetry intuiting his utter lack of romantic interest in her. Her stomach showed its six months grandly. She had no idea that her pregnant condition might not be a turn on. Her dejection knew no limits; she was caught in a hell of her own making.

Although Jesse's mood often shifted without warning, still the luxury of her surroundings did not escape her. Jesse's own middle-class upbringing had not included a backyard in-ground pool, so it was with appreciation she swam every warm clear day during the summer, and most evenings she sat by the pool blowing melodies into the wind with her recorder, the southwest colors awash in the sky. She cried less often since getting pregnant but the sadness, and disappointment that had pervaded her life since childhood still had its influence on her. She often wondered what kind of person she might have been if she had been cherished and nurtured, rather than resented and abused by a jealous mother.

A memory surfaced. She was standing in front of a full-length mirror in the hallway looking at herself and perhaps admiring herself a bit. Louise, her mother, who had been standing by silently staring at her daughter, startled her.

"Think you look pretty good, huh?" she uttered sarcastically. Jesse's fifteen-year-old frail ego was throttled for the sin of appreciating her own image. Blushing and properly humiliated, she recoiled from the mirror, retreating to her bedroom.

A kick brought her back to the present moment, to the growing wonder inside of her. She knew without a doubt that she would be a better mother. She was due to deliver in the first part of October, and now in July, Tom and Walter were going separate ways. Margie and Jesse were not having luck finding new trustworthy roommates for her father's property. Then like synchronicity, Richard told Walter about a little adobe house available in Corrales. The owners would rent it to Jesse for $100 a month. It had two bedrooms and was surrounded with mammoth sunflowers. Sitting twenty feet from the road, it was perfect for someone without a car. The path out from the back screen door led to a dirt road along the ditch. Jesse saw it and thought that it was charming,

She continued to chant, attributing her good luck to Buddhism rather than to the kindness bestowed by Richard and Rosalee, and their insightful timing. She moved to the new house with the help of her Buddhist friends. When the last box and hanger were off the truck, Jesse thanked them, said goodbye, and then was alone.

Jesse's idea was to have the baby at home. She talked to a midwife who lived down the road who agreed to help her deliver when the time came. But as the due date approached, she had not met with the woman even once.

Thinking about all the problems that might arise, she changed her mind. Her decision came one evening a week prior to the due date. Jesse stood naked in front of her dresser mirror, turned sideways to see the huge mountain of belly-baby, and said out loud to herself, somewhat facetiously, "What have I done? How am I ever going to get this baby out of me?"

It was October 6th; she hitched to her prenatal appointment. The doctor reached inside to loosen the mucus plug at the neck of the uterus.

"Now, I've just loosened the plug so you will go into labor within twelve hours. Then get yourself to the hospital and have that baby! Everything looks fine, the baby is turned around and ready to deliver."

Painless Childbirth

The wait was almost over! The last month the baby had grown substantially, and Jesse was more than ready to give birth. She called Margie, and Margie called everyone else. They were going to have a 'labor party'.

That evening about ten people in Jesse's chanting community showed up with food and sodas. Jesse was the center of attention talking about her labor pains and what the doctor had said. By eleven most had left except for a handful who stayed long enough to chant midnight gongyo, a ritual Jesse had grown so accustomed to that she had memorized the entire liturgy.

She had been having contractions since late afternoon. By 1 a.m. she had borrowed a watch from Julie who owned the house. Stretching out on the living room floor with the wristwatch to concentrate on her breathing, Jesse watched the illuminated second hand. Her contractions were regular though not close together. She found herself "in the zone."

Each time a contraction started; Jesse would begin panting just like she had read in the Lamaze book. She had tried this breathing technique a few times during her pregnancy, but it had seemed so simple that she had not actually practiced for more than a few minutes. Now the time for practice was past, and Jesse did what she always managed when she was faced with having to endure an unfamiliar situation. She found her determination, and doggedly rose to the challenge. She lay on the floor with a couch pillow beside her, and proceeded to pant, the in and out puffs of oxygen moving her lungs and stomach and slipping her into a zone of mindless reverie.

She had been lying there for a few hours when she suddenly became aware that her contractions were coming much more quickly. She stood up and went to the guest room where Margie was sleeping and woke her up.

"I think we'd better drive to the hospital... my contractions are three minutes apart." Just as she got the words out of her mouth another contraction started, and now the labor pains were a minute and a half apart.

Walter, Tom, Margie, and Jesse threw on jackets, bundled up and piled into Walter's VW bug, Jesse panting in the backseat with Margie. He drove through 5 red traffic lights, the time was 4:45 a.m. and the streets were empty. They arrived at the entrance to the emergency room of the Bernalillo County Hospital. Jesse looked at the clock over the nurse's station as she was being helped into the waiting room; it read 5:00 a.m.

A man in a white coat asked Jesse if she felt like pushing, and she said "sure." He said quickly, "Well, don't push yet; let's take a look and see if you are dilated." A quick probe revealed to the intern that Jesse was fully dilated and ready to deliver. With no time to prep her, two orderlies helped Jesse onto the rolling bed. They reached the elevator; one punched the button to the delivery floor.

In the delivery room, Jesse did what the doctor told her and pushed with all her might. The doctor stopped her to perform an episiotomy, and then she pushed three more times, and her new baby boy was born at 5:20 a.m. Jesse looked over to the infant that the nurse was handling, putting drops in his eyes, and checking his vital signs. Jesse noticed that whites of her baby's eyes were blood red. She asked the nurse why? "Oh, that's just from the pressure of being born; sometimes the eyes will get small, ruptured blood vessels. His eyes will clear up in a few days, nothing to worry about."

Jesse's tears welled up as she felt the relief from months of preparation and anxiety. She had done it! She would name him Jules, eternally youthful, and she would give him a second name of Shonin, which meant Buddha, after the great spiritual leader and prophet Nichirin Dai Shonin.

Jesse stayed overnight and was released with her newborn son midmorning. Richard came alone to pick her up, as most of her fellow Buddhists were working. It was a perfect October day, bright slanting sunlight warmed, and a tiny breeze stirred the autumn leaves as Jesse carried Jules toward the front door of the small adobe house. She stepped inside the dark cubicle, but before Richard left, she grabbed her camera and asked him if he would snap a picture or two. Her life with Jules had begun.

The rigors of tending a newborn kept Jesse busy, but between breast feedings every two to three hours she was able to focus on her own goals. Jesse knew that she would have to sew and sell more costumes in order to get by. She still had her machine. The money and food stamps she received from the state welfare system was so minimal as to be ludicrous. Never-the-less Jesse was content; Jules was a perfect fit for her. His fussiness was minimal, and he laughed easily. She found herself looking into his eyes, and appraising every pore, and subtle curve of his face as he lay back on her bent legs. For the first time in nearly five years Jesse did not think about Andre. She was able to stay in the here and now.

Her little adobe house was next door to a farm, and every day she would walk over and pick vegetables out of the wooden bins and leave her money. The roadside stand worked on the honor system; the customer was trusted to leave the correct amount in the box. Jesse was enchanted. It seemed like she had landed in a corner of Eden, fresh vegetables daily, and if she wanted to see some innovative architecture, all she had to do was walk out of her back door, toward the clear ditch (the same clear ditch by which she had planned to shoot herself, before her pregnancy), across a few dusty driveways, and through fields by any one of her neighbors houses, Southwestern designed estates, and mansions, with red tile roofs, foot thick adobe walls, cathedral ceilings, and shiny 18 foot windows bordered with the local artist's stained glass imaginings.

One day while walking up an unexplored lane Jesse came upon an empty adobe house. The doors were unlocked so she wandered through from room to room. In the last bedroom she found hanging on the wall a Japanese print. Sure that no one would miss it from the abandoned digs she carefully pried it loose from the flaking wall and carried it home. It looked like a watercolor painting of a man fishing from a small wooden boat moored among grasses. Nearby on land are large rocks and outcropping from the side of them is a tattered yet still thriving tree. It shelters the man in contemplation over his pot of tea. The backdrop mountain's base is shrouded in mist. The orb floating center in the sky leaves an unanswered question; is it noon or midnight's full moon? The print had a bit of water damage; maybe that is why it had been left behind. It looked to Jesse as if it were a print of the illuminated Nichirin Daishonin immersed in the Spirit, communicating from another realm, and that the universe had left it specifically for her to find because she could appreciate its message and ambiguities.

Web of Self-Delusion

ight weeks passed; the OB/GYN told Jesse it was safe for her to resume sex. Jules was healthy and thriving, and Jesse had continued investing in a fantasy involving Walter. During a past trip with the group of Buddhists to a regional state gathering they had sat next to each other on the bus Jesse had experienced, for the first time, a remote orgasm. Tonight she wanted to feel his touch, and open up to him sexually. She telephoned Walter to ask him if she could visit him after Jules was fed and sleeping for the night.

He was hesitant, but still said yes. She arrived at his front door around six-thirty, the sun had already set. He was welcoming, always the consummate host, so compassionate, attentive, and striving to please. They talked about the Buddhism they were involved in, and Walter disclosed how he had first become aware of chanting, and how significantly it had altered his life. In the presence of her champion, Jesse felt like he had opened the door to his personal world, and requested that she step in. Walter's intended austerity showed in the style of his bed; it was a pad on a platform. Walter and Jesse disrobed, and she slid onto the smooth fresh smelling sheets. He pressed himself up against her hotness, and began to slowly play with her nipples, gently following his finger-tips around and about the curves of her body. Right before he entered her, he looked into her eyes and said, "No illusions here, right?"

Jesse knew what he was saying but refused to believe it. In her mind, this coupling was the culmination of months of anticipation, chanting, and hope, and it had the effect of validating Jesse's fantasy. Walter would see how beautiful, sexy and intelligent she was, and fall in-love with her. They would be together and live happily ever after. Truth, they never had sex again.

For a while, Jesse was ecstatic experiencing a wave of energy and optimism. She was attending the Buddhist meetings and group chants. Margie and Jesse had memorized the Japanese liturgy and were leaders in their group of inductees. The two women collaborated on artistic projects and fed each other's esteem, which they both needed. Margie did not know that Jesse and Walter had sex. Walter continued to tutor and guide every female novice who crossed his path, his brown eyes, and seemingly genuine personable smile, a ready light in their spiritual darkness.

Jesse of course believed that their relationship would grow; her slide into depression began when he did not call or spend any additional time with her. After a month of minimal contact from Walter, and with his standard answer being, I have an event I must attend, Jesse felt abandoned, heartbroken, and hopeless. She decided that if Buddhism really worked then she would chant until she had the definitive answer. She had all the time in the world, so she sat one afternoon after she had put Jules down for a nap, and began to chant, Nam Myho Renge Kyo, Nam Myho Renge Kyo, Nam Myho Renge Kyo.

Hour after hour she chanted, droning, vibrating, focusing, concentrating, invocating, willing; four and a half hours later Jesse decided to go see Walter. After all, he still was her spiritual counselor, and she was a disciple seeking help. Jesse wore her chanting beads around her neck, a common practice. She calmed her heart, walked up to the door and knocked. Walter called out for her to come in.

Stepping through the front door Jesse saw Walter sitting on his couch holding hands with Claudia, a woman newly converted to chanting. Walter did not try to hide their obvious affection for each other. Jesse stayed only a few minutes, escaping from the intense shock of seeing them together. She stopped on the porch outside of his front door, stood resolutely, took her beads from around her neck and threw them as far into the trees, bushes and darkness as she could. Struggling under the weight of her shattering illusions, she felt it was the only way she could regain her independence, and composure. In that moment she threw away eighteen months of living in a world dominated by her desire for Walter.

When she arrived home, she opened the altar that he had built for her. It was a rugged log that had been hollowed out, the doors cut from its bark and hinged back on. Taking the sacred scroll from its tack, she rolled it up and stored it away in a velvet pouch she had sewn for it. Tearing the Butsudan off the wall where it had been secured, and opening her front door, Jesse flung it out into the snow drift that had accumulated by the walkway. There the altar sat waiting for the fireplace.

Jesse had gotten her answer. She knew that she could not detach from Walter and all the related memories if she kept all of the trappings of Nichirin Shoshu Buddhism. She was done. Another dream up in smoke, and Jesse's delicate emotional stability was challenged again.

Back to the City

On Thursday evening came a telephone call from Forrest. He had pulled ligaments in his spine, and asked Jesse if she could come into town to help him. The doctor told him to stay still on his back for at least a month.

"You don't have to stay here all the time, just be around enough to fix me a meal once a day, and maybe do a load of laundry. I would really appreciate it. Most of my friends work every day at jobs."

"Sure, I can do that. Is it ok if I use your car while I'm in town helping?"

"Yeah, I don't mind. I won't be driving it."

"Do you know anyone who can help move the crib from my house to yours?"

"I'm pretty sure I can find some help."

"OK, as soon as you can make that happen, I can be there."

She and Jules, who was not yet three months old, moved into the Crest house, so named because of the street it was on. It was an upper middleclass home with five bedrooms, a den downstairs, fireplace on the main floor, huge kitchen, and immense cedar fenced back yard with a mature apple bearing tree in the corner. In back was a double-car garage; separate but attached was a workshop, with its own heating unit, and by the door, a huge picture window allowing sunlight back into the deep box of a building.

Initially infant Jules and Jesse slept in the same bedroom as Forrest. This was the first time he had seen his son. Since Forest was hard to read, it kept Jesse guessing about his state of mind and his feelings about Jules until she asked him one evening. His answer was straightforward.

"Jesse, when I offered you money to get an abortion, you told me that the child was yours, and you wanted it. I accepted that. I've never allowed myself to get attached because I knew you could leave at any time, and that Jules would go with you."

Forrest and Jesse slept side by side on two floor mattresses with Jules a couple of feet away. He never made a move on Jesse, and Jesse never approached him. When the six weeks had passed and Forrest could get around again, Jesse asked if she and Jules could move into the workshop. The other members of the house agreed.

It was empty and its concrete floor clean. Jesse found some outlet carpet pieces to cover the cold floor, sewed curtains, hung plants in the window, and turned the furnace on to a toasty 78 degrees. She moved in and began designing costumes to sell to the topless dancers in town. She played classical music for baby Jules and sewed whenever sleep eluded her. It was the perfect match, sewing and listening to music. One did not interfere with the other and she could bounce her attention back and forth.

One day Forrest asked Jesse if she wanted to help his mother sew for The Shire, a leather shop that he owned in town. Since she was always looking for opportunities to expand her skills and generate money, she answered, "Yes!"

In the days ahead, Jesse dressed her infant warmly for the drive to the shop. She derived pleasure from the mixed aromas of leather, oil, and dyes hitting her nose as she stepped across the threshold each day.

Elinor, Forrest's mother, was a woman whose love of life and family emanated strongly. She and Jesse became fast friends as Elinor showed her tailoring tricks and taught her how to sew leather. From their creative partnership came capes, ponchos, backpacks, belts and purses, all handmade with quality designs and craftsmanship.

Jesse thrived in this atmosphere of acceptance and productivity. Elinor was supportive and nurturing in a way she had not experienced before from a mother-figure. Before long Jesse wanted to share the secret that Forrest had asked her not to divulge. It was impossible for her to work with Elinor every day, and their friendship growing, without letting her know that Jules, this little angel, was her first grandchild!

Not intending to cause discord, Jesse blurted out, "Elinor, your son and I were involved for a while, and he did not want me to say anything to you, but Jules is your grandson. I just couldn't keep it from you. I thought it wasn't fair to you."

Elinor looked surprised, but realizing what she had heard, quickly focused on Jules admiringly. "Oh! It had crossed my mind. Well dear, I'm so happy you told me." From that day the two remained friends and Jules was welcomed as a member of the family, although Forrest never quite forgave Jesse. She had ruined his "perfect son status."

The brutal winter was almost past. Jules transitioned easily from breast to bottle so Jesse could again focus on dancing. While making the rounds in town, a fellow dancer told her about a gig in Santa Fe. All she needed was a car, and she had recently been given a decrepit VW bus, but it ran. Her schedule would be Monday through Thursday with an afternoon matinee on Friday, and then she was off Saturday and Sunday. It paid $250 clear a week and the owner provided an apartment at the back of the club. Jesse would be able to bring Jules with her, because her schedule allowed large blocks of time in between sets in which she could care for him. It would pay the bills for the summer until she could find a job closer to home. It gave her a new environment, and the men who frequented "The Round-up" were challenging, mostly middle-aged Mexicans with wives at home, or the occasional child-man, part hippie, part gypsy drug dealer.

She liked being able to do a shortened week and have her weekend for herself for once. Usually, she missed all the parties and fun because she worked nights. Now, she would be able to socialize with the other members of the household, seven in all, including Forrest with whom she remained on friendly terms.

Unintended Desert Pitstop

t was summer, 1973, Jesse was bicycling around the university neighborhoods in Albuquerque, when she spotted a guy sitting out on his front porch with what looked like a grocery bag full of books. He was shirtless with cut abs, dark skin and black curly hair. His face was etched with distinct cheekbones and a large Mediterranean nose perhaps broken once or twice. He was not classically handsome, yet he emitted charisma from his open smile to his athletic body. Coincidentally, Jesse had recently been browsing in a History of Art textbook, and there between the pages staring out from centuries ago was an ancient mosaic portrait of this same dark eyed man that she now saw before her.

She was wearing shorts, halter and a tan. She biked up the driveway and stopped abruptly, her sleek Motobecane 10-speed between her legs.

"Hey, what are you doing today?" Jesse forged forward impetuously.

"Oh, just watching some soccer and getting rid of some books."

"Really, can I take a look?"

"Sure; you can have the whole bag. I was just going to drop them off at the secondhand bookstore a couple of blocks away."

Vince had an easygoing way and the most intense deep-set brown eyes. Jesse was beguiled. She asked him all sorts of questions, and he was happy to talk about himself. Jules was with friends, so when Vince asked, Jesse said yes to staying the night. His waterbed was like an oasis, and his life was full of accomplishments. He had a Master's degree in Clinical Psychology, played on the community soccer team, climbed up the sides of mountains, read voraciously, spoke three languages, and skied. He had a position as a therapist at the local mental health clinic. He had created a program called, *Hoods In The Woods*, in which he took inmates into the wilderness. There they had to get real with themselves, there in the mountains where the games of the city streets could not save a person, only a clear present awareness, problem solving skills, organization, and cooperation might.

Jesse had not met such a complex, fascinating man since Carlos, deep and pensive. She listened with rapt attention, hardly aware that he did not ask about her. Smitten by her desire to be hooked-up with this motivated and accomplished man and believing that his interest in her was more than simply sex, expectations loomed. She believed that Vince might simply step into the role of 'daddy' for baby Jules. They would get to know each other, continue to have great sex, and then they would move in together, and live happily ever after. One catch, Vince clearly said that he wasn't interested in any long-term commitment. Jesse did not hear his words.

Vince introduced Jesse to running, rappelling, cross-country skiing, and camping. She bloomed with the attention. Under Vince's tutelage she had applied and been accepted for a federal program which paid for college tuition and books. Under President Johnson's 'War on Poverty', it was intended to help the disabled get training so they could have a chance in the work force, but since the program was new Jesse was accepted because of her welfare status. *Finally, I can get out of the flesh market,* she thought. *I'll have a way to make a living without taking my clothes off.*

Vince seemed pleased. "Congratulations Jesse, you'll do well in college, I'm sure. Meeting you confirms what I have always believed that a person doesn't necessarily need college to be aware. It sure helps in the job field," he added chuckling.

She was flattered. Since they had met, Vince had been a driving force. She thought about him daily, exclusively.

It was August, and as she had previously planned, Jesse packed Jules into the VW bus, set the compass for due west, destination Santa Monica, California and her parent's house. Jules was almost a year old and her parents had not seen him yet. The trip from Albuquerque to the coast was about eight hundred miles. She could make it in fifteen hours.

Outside of Albuquerque, she picked up Garrett, a hitchhiker. He was a 'Rainbow person', a member of the hippie-gypsy tribe that gathered around the country, their full name 'The Rainbow Family of Living Light'. He was headed for California for a gathering in the Redwoods, and Jesse was happy to have some company for the ride.

Half-way to their destination the old bus started having trouble. The engine light blinked as the engine lost power forcing Jesse to get off Route 66 at the nearest town. She pulled into a service station where the owner personally assessed the problem.

"It needs an alternator."

Jesse dropped her head so he would not see the tears welling in her eyes. "I don't have money for it."

"No credit card?"

She shook her head.

Seeing Garret by the bus who was holding baby Jules, the owner responded, "Well, you should be able to get to the next city on the charged battery."

Her mood brightened. "Then I'll be close enough to the coast to make it home."

Jesse fed Jules a bottle, laid him on a baby blanket behind the driver's seat between some pillows. Garrett grabbed a granola bar from his backpack. They pulled back onto the highway.

Forty-five minutes out, Jesse's anxiety began mounting. Restless, worried, and overwhelmingly sleepy, she glanced over to the dark curls and angelic face nodding in the passenger seat, and then turned around to check on her baby. It was at that moment, Jesse forgot she was driving. Unintentionally turning the wheel to the left, the bus rolled over the embankment tipping as it went. She held onto the steering wheel and seeing that they were going off the edge she closed her eyes. After the first revolution and a deafening crash she was catapulted out of the driver's seat, slicing open her right arm on the metal doorway as she exited, jettisoned through the air.

In her weightlessness she thought, *oh no, I've killed myself.*

During the vehicle's first roll, Garrett and Jules were thrown somewhere in the dirt and rocks along the ditch. From above Jesse hit ground. She opened her clenched eyes. She had not killed herself. Where was Jules? Her heart pounded; then she saw them. Garrett was sitting cross-legged holding Jules Garret was sitting cross-legged with Jules in his arms. Jumping up she ran over to them.

"Oh my God, I'm so sorry I almost killed us. Is he hurt?"

Undamaged, Garrett looked up at Jesse face. "No, not a scratch, just a couple of light bruises."

Jules was not crying. It looked like he might have slept through the whole thing. Suddenly, Jesse noticed her right arm was ripped, and from the gash a steady pulsing stream of blood was shooting from a severed vein. Backing away from Garrett and Jules, she tried to cover the gash with her left hand. Instead, her hand slipped inside the flesh of her arm. She could feel pebbles and twigs inside where they did not belong. In a manic state of shock Jesse's nimble fingers picked the rocks and sticks from inside the wound throwing them away from her body in revulsion.

"Shit, I'm going to bleed to death. We've got to stop the blood!"

They tried in vain to get a make-shift tourniquet on her upper arm; the blood continued its flow.

Then, unexpectedly, they heard the whine of an approaching siren and within minutes Jesse was being attended to by professional EMTs. Garrett and Jules got a ride to the hospital in another vehicle. He didn't leave the scene until Jesse's parents were called, and her stepfather arrived to take over little Jules's care. Then Garrett disappeared into the Indio desert. She never saw him again. She was eternally grateful that he had been there and had not been hurt.

On the other hand, Jesse had come a millimeter close to severing the radial motor nerve of her arm. With an unresponsive dead wrist and arm it -would have been the end of dancing, the end of her ability to give full expression, and end her ability to support herself. Coming from surgery, Jesse's dad was told that everything went perfectly; her recovery should be complete. Impressed that the hospital had been able to get in touch with her parents at all, she was relieved to be in the car safe with Jules and headed west.

It had been about five years since Jesse had last seen her mother. Time had not changed the woman's ever-present crankiness. The toxic mood and bitter attitude were still there, veiled in compassion and sympathy. Jesse's mom could shine in situations that required her to act decently for a limited amount of time. This accident allowed her to be the loving mother she had not managed to be in the past. Jesse certainly appreciated the warm hospitality, no matter how superficial. She remembered being thrown out and told not to return. This was by far the preferable treatment.

Jesse visited for a month, and then was back on a plane with Jules in tow. Before leaving Jesse and her dad made a trip back out to the desert to visit the crash site. She wanted to rescue a few possessions that might still be in the vehicle, especially her notebooks full of poetry. What she saw disturbed her. The inside of the bus was destroyed, the shattered crib, a pile of dangerous daggers, shards, and toothpicks. The bus had rolled at least two, maybe three, times down the hill before resting where it was now. Jesse thought, *it looks like no one survived this crash.* It was at that moment she realized what an anomaly their survival had been. Back under the medic's blanket she had vowed to be a service to humanity to pay back the excellent care she had been given during her ordeal.

Vince was surprised when he heard the details of her trip.

"Wow, I'm so glad that you are alright. I can't believe I could have lost you and not even have known about it."

Those words helped Jesse continue weaving the web of self-deception. Once a week Vince would call; they went out to eat, and see a movie on Friday. The two always ended the evening in bed, and always, to Jesse's dismay, Vince would be up and gone by 8 or 9 a.m. the next morning, not even waiting to eat breakfast. It was as if he avoided any possibilities for true intimacy. She told herself, *he is a busy person.* He always had soccer practice, or another rock to climb, or a seminar-retreat to attend. He never had time to spend an entire weekend with Jesse and her two-year old son. Still, she believed that love would find a way. Then she got pregnant.

Classes all week long to satisfy the double major of Dance and Theater Arts, then dancing at the bar every Friday and Saturday night, left Jesse little energy for anything else. Her roommate watched Jules some of the time to help her save money. Fortunately, the university had a daycare-cooperative on campus. Parents volunteered four hours a week, and in return were given quality daycare while they attended classes.

While taking the Theatrical Makeup class, Jesse's eccentric personality and artistic talent made her stick-out. She was selected to design the ghost makeup for Strindberg's classic play, *The Ghosts*, a significant honor in Jesse's mind, but a huge burden on someone who struggled daily with unending disorganization, low self-esteem, lack of consistent motivation and depression. Now she tried to focus on how she might design the schematics for the ghost characters in the play, coach the other students, and do it all fearlessly having never attempted anything like this in her life. Meanwhile she needed to be a mother to her toddler, maintain her grades in the academic courses, and, of course, drink and dance weekends so she could survive. Rent, food, electricity, none of it free.

She knew the first morning when she lunged for the toilet that she was pregnant. She loved Vince and wanted to have his child. He was her whole identity; present or not, his being sat on her shoulder day and night. He accompanied her during classes, while she studied, or buried herself in the library doing research. Jules gave Jesse the desire to create a more secure and legitimate way of generating money, but the real hidden energy behind her motivation was the love she felt for Vince. She wanted to be the most amazing female; accomplished and successful like him. It seemed like within two weeks her clothes were getting snug, and her breasts were swollen and tender. The professor was pressuring Jesse to submit drawings for the play and to attend meetings with the other production managers. Rehearsals would start in four weeks.

Jesse suffered debilitation. She missed classes and slept instead of studying. She feared her limitations, and it clutched at her solar plexus, making it difficult for her to breathe. The teacher saw potential, but Jesse had reached her coping capacity. She scheduled a meeting with her Professor.

"I'm sorry to disappoint you but I am overwhelmed! I am pregnant, and I need to get an abortion. I'm in no state-of-mind to be able to do a good job on the play. You'll have to choose someone else."

"I'm sorry to hear you're having personal problems. I can certainly find another student, and I do appreciate the notification. We still have plenty of time. Don't worry; just do the best you can. I'm sure everything will be fine."

Jesse left with the greatest sense of relief. However, her sub-conscious whispered that it was not the undecided abortion that overwhelmed her, it was her own terror at being given such a responsible position with such an extraordinary opportunity to fail. The assignment had been too much obligation. She knew she could not fake it, and she didn't want to be publicly humiliated for her ignorance. All her classmates would then know what a loser she was. That was a risk she was not going to take.

She picked up Jules and bicycled home; it continued to be her main mode of transportation. That evening after Jules had been fed, bathed and tucked into bed, Jesse told her roommate Lauren,

"I'm going to keep this baby."

"Who's the father?"

"Vince"

"And what did he say when you told him you were pregnant?"

"He told me that I would be on my own, that I couldn't depend on him to be around. He said it would be better if I got an abortion."

"So, why are you thinking about keeping it?"

"Seems just as easy to take care of two babies as one!"

"Are you crazy? You already have two children, and, what? You're just going to keep having them? You can't even take care of the ones you have?"

Lauren was right. But it was easy for her to be rational. Jesse wanted to have this 'love-child'. When she closed her eyes, she could see the child's dark curly hair and olive skin, nearly smelling its newness and innocence. But taking care of Jules without help was proving to be a challenge. Although she thoroughly enjoyed motherhood, she recognized rearing two children would be twice the work. If intention and the desire to love were all that is needed, Jesse would have gotten an A plus for parenting.

She made the call to the local Planned Parenthood Clinic, grateful that she did not have to resort to a back-street abortionist like her friend had done years earlier in Hollywood. The voice at the other end was professional and reassuring. Jesse was scheduled for Monday, the following week.

The complete procedure, from the signing of the paperwork to the recovery room took only three hours, and the cost was covered by her welfare status. This unique community clinic was an adapted residential home. Jesse was wheeled into what was once a personal bedroom with two twin beds. She had the room to herself. The blue skies through the window kept her attention as tears began to flow. The doctor walked in and sat down beside the bed with his clip board and release paper.

"You know, Jesse, usually at this stage of development, the fetus has a fine velvety coat of fibers, and this one didn't. The chances are that even if you had not had this abortion you would have miscarried anyway."

She was sure the doctor did not understand why she was crying. She wanted to tell him that she was crying because she knew what it was like to be forever waiting to get on with your life, and then to have to wait some more. She could feel the disappointment coming from the spirit of the child who now must delay and stay suspended in some etheric waiting room. Jesse felt that neither she nor any force could stop the evolution of a soul. If the soul needed to incarnate, it would await the next similar situation for the needed life-learning experience.

Vince had agreed to drive Jesse home. She was quiet. He was solicitous and affectionate, unlike his usual aloofness. Jesse felt dead, tempered by relief, her tolerance for Vince's disingenuous demeanor was low. She welcomed his goodbye when he finally shut the front door and left her tucked in the covers of her bed. Lauren, her roommate, had flown-off to Hawaii with the owner of a kite store, and Jules was staying with Lauren's mom.

While she lay there recuperating, she asked herself if she was finally ready to let go of this man who had so callously turned his back on her and his potential child? When she imagined the end of the relationship, she felt an immediate rush of nausea. She decided that she would not make any decisions while she was healing. Now was the time for repose and leisurely reading, a luxury she had sorely missed. She would jump back on the treadmill in a few days.

Jesse recovered, and Vince was eager to resume their sexual routine. While she was not entirely trusting of him, living without him was not yet a consideration. One afternoon with Vince's penis in her mouth, and sunlight streaming in through a gap in the drapes, Jesse saw a wee illuminated crab crawling on Vince's pubic hair. She pushed him away from her and sat up, "Oh, no, you have crabs! Who have you been fucking?"

"No one," he answered defensively heading for the bathroom. "I probably got 'em from the toilet at the clinic. I use the same bathroom as our clients. Some of them live on the streets."

Jesse wanted to believe him, but she knew that he had other admirers, and there were many nights when he was not sleeping with her.

That was the end of the sex for the day. Jesse left to buy Pyronex-2000, shocked to think that Vince had cheated on her, and had cheated with someone who had crabs. She felt disgusted, her illusion rug ripped out from under her. After three years chasing a fantasy, the stark reality was clear, she was merely a glorified fuck.

Bitter and reeling from Vince's infidelity, Jesse planned a trip with Lauren in an effort to stop focusing on him. The D.H. Laurence ranch was located north of Albuquerque in Taos. Having recently read The Man Who Died, Jesse felt Laurence's presence, restless and disincarnate, stirring in her mind.

Lauren's family owned a cabin in Taos. It was the perfect wilderness retreat. After a day of hiking the Laurence ranch and touring his immense log cabin estate including the studio where he had created huge canvasses with lots of paint and little talent, the surrounding area offered nothing for night-time entertainment.

"Shall we check out the local bars? If there are any..." Jesse asked her friend when they were back at the cabin.

"Sure, I'll see if I can use my mom's car. I don't think she will mind." Lauren assured her.

Soon they drove off into the New Mexico sunset. Within four miles they noticed a red neon sign flashing Cervezas-Comida-Musica. The parking lot was busy but not packed. As they approached, Spanish music blared from the cantina, as the door opened and closed.

The two found a booth in the dimly lit interior and scooted in, ordering shots of tequila from the waitress who arrived a minute later.

"Here's to adventure and love," Jesse toasted as they clinked glasses, licked salt, linked arms over the table, slammed the Cuervo, and grimaced at each other after the burst of limey sourness hit their taste buds. Before they could order another, two Chicano men asked if they could sit with them.

"Sure," they chimed in unison, happy to have some male attention.

Three rounds later, with everyone's judgments impaired, the men convinced Jesse and Lauren to take a ride with them.

"You come with me. I will show you a place where you can see the Milky Way from a cliff!" Roberto had introduced himself and seemed nice enough.

"Ok," a drunken Jesse replied.

He was insistent that she go along with him since Tito wanted to show-off his low-rider hydraulics to Lauren. Although Jesse was not entirely comfortable with riding separately, she agreed after consulting Lauren. Outside the building, the sky was clear, stars so dense within the complete blackness of their canvass that it seemed like the planet had no atmosphere. Loaded with their passengers, the cars drove off in opposite directions. Jesse tried to keep their discussion going to ease the tension that had suddenly crept into the silence, but Roberto was no conversationalist. He had stopped talking and continued driving into the dark hills across arroyos, beyond streetlights and warmly lit houses. The car's engine droned on down the road away from civilization.

Jesse panicked.

At that exact moment streaked a huge meteor out of the sky crashing into the earth off to the driver's side of the car. Reflected in the cornea of their widened eyes, the rock exploded on impact, pieces flying from behind the ridge of mountains. Neither one of them had ever witnessed such an event as this. Jesse's head pitched forward as Roberto hit his brakes. Without hesitation or words, he made a U-turn and headed back to the cantina. It seemed Jesse had been saved, this time, by a celestial intervention.

Like synchronicity in action, both cars reach the bar and the two girls hurriedly said their goodbyes, glad to be back in the safety of their own car.

Jesse continued to be sexually available to Vince until the day he said to her, "I'm going on vacation to Greece for a month. I'm leaving next week." After he left, Jesse's anger and resentment boiled. *Why didn't he ask me to go with him? Sure, he had strayed, but they were still officially together.*

The day before his flight he came over to see her one more time, to say that they were breaking up for good.

"I guess I always knew that I couldn't give you what you wanted," his insipid explanation dripped from his mouth.

Jesse interpreted. *He took me out, fed me and fucked me once a week for three years, never once intending to take it to a more serious level.* Pain like lava pulsed through her heart.

With the relationship officially ended, Jesse's academic performance plummeted. Her depression came back and would not leave. It was then that she ate an entire Pepperidge Farm cake, and slipped into a stupor of weeping, stopping only to care perfunctorily for little Jules.

A month had come and gone. Jesse knew that Vince was back from his vacation. She had lunch with one of his 'other' girlfriends, probably the one who gave him crabs, to learn that Vince had brought back a French woman whom he had met on a boat in Greece, and moved her in. Jesse could not believe what she was hearing, having convinced herself during their separation that Vince just needed time.

Now, her delusionary perception gave way to another bitter awakening.

A letter from Jesse's landlord informed her she would have to move out immediately. Another renter was waiting in the wings. Overwhelmed, with no one around who could help her move, her anxiety mounted. It was the middle of the semester with mid-terms coming. She had no extra money; *extra money, what an oxymoron.* Her fermenting cynicism poisoned the atmosphere where she lived and breathed. She was self-pity's poster child. Jesse had been living in her two-bedroom house in a stable middle-class neighborhood, and the only reason she had paid such a small pittance for rent was because the landlord was Vince's friend. Now that they had broken up, he wanted to charge more.

The Mouse House

n a rundown area of town, Jesse rented a tiny house she nick-named the 'mouse house'. It was under-insulated, but affordable. The electric floorboard-heat escaped through the gaps in the ancient wooden windows leaving little warmth, and a big electric bill. Jesse quickly learned to block off the coldest rooms and moved her bed into the box-sized living room where she could keep it toasty for Jules and her. During the summer months Jesse took Jules to a huge city park just a few blocks away. It was a bonus since the house had no yard. The lack of space inside the house frustrated Jesse.

One morning as she stepped out of bed running late for her first class, her heel caught the sharp edge of a wooden block Jules had left scattered. She twisted her ankle in an effort to keep her balance. Her mind raced, *hadn't she just talked to Jules yesterday about not leaving his blocks everywhere, but here they are again, and she couldn't go to school or dance on weekends if she broke her ankle.* Jesse's anger flared as her thoughts fed her powerlessness. She mistakenly believed that her bright little three-year-old could comply with her rules. and keep his blocks picked-up. She could not understand that at three years he was not mature enough to keep his toys off of the floor. Jesse, who had rarely hit Jules, picked up her leather belt and whipped his legs. He cried as she angrily jerked on his clothes.

She loaded him on the bicycle toddler-seat, strapped him in, and peddled off to yet another college class.

That afternoon Jenny, one of the daycare teachers, pulled Jesse aside when she was picking him up.

"Did something happen at home this morning?"

"Why do you ask?" Jesse responded.

"Jules wanted to be on my lap all day; he seemed to need comforting."

"I'm going crazy." She proceeded to explain how she had reacted that morning, how difficult her single life with a child had become since beginning college.

"I had no idea how much additional work I was in for when I started."

"Yes, that's why I don't have any children. Managing the daycare center reminds me every day."

Jenny listened; Jesse needed to talk to someone who cared. Without a support network, she kept all her anger inside, and today Jules got the brunt of it. She was not proud of herself, but after all, Jules had to learn to listen. It was the parenting she had learned from her mother.

That evening, with a new onion skin writing pad, Jesse penned a one-act play titled The Confession. She imagined a dark stage lit only by a single spotlight focused on a coffin (center-stage) awash in a warm glow. An elderly woman lies as in an open coffin viewing. A character walks on, the audience assuming the forthcoming sad soliloquy. The young woman seems to look around the room, perhaps checking to see if there are any listeners nearby, and then nears the coffin and places her hands on the edge to begin speaking to her dead mother.

"You fucked up Mom! You took a sensitive intelligent child and turned her into an inept non-functional being. Aren't you proud? You turned me into a replication of you. I might have been a maker of music. I could have floated through life if only you had helped me just a little. But you insisted on hating me. You didn't know that you were filled with poison, but still that's what you gave me to live on. I grew sure of my worthlessness. I was your little doll to dress and show to your friends. Too bad I was a real human being.

You never bothered with my brain, my thoughts, my identity, consequently I have found it difficult to have an identity. All the crucial points for development into a healthy person, you mistakenly ignored... and since I left your house, I have tried hard to build a foundation on which to establish this thing called self.

I never knew I was raised inside a bubble. I only knew I did not feel happy. The bubble was transparent, but I could not touch anybody or anything. And when I spoke, only my thoughts bounced off the interior and echoed back to me unchanged.

Why did you condemn me to a cell? Me, your baby girl that you say you loved. I didn't even know I lived alone, but I did know there was something missing. I must have died from suffocation, from lack of warmth and psychic nourishment. I wish you could hear me. Would you be surprised to find out that you had killed your first born or would you deny that you had done such a thing?

I was helpless at the receiving end of your vicious whims. After what you have done to me, it is a wonder I believe in the existence of a benevolent force because no great intervening hand came when you were beating me amid one of your holy rages... and it seems your rages were indeed sanctified. You were always so righteously committed to your maniacal temper! Truly a sight to behold, such grandiose hatred. Not a person could stand up to you, to stop your demonic force. So, I was crippled by repeated bombardment. What! You think because my smile is not crooked like your cleft palate made yours that I am free of deformity. You have twisted my spirit, and knotted this being until no brace, cast, nor remedy, can bring it from the state of disease and pain it is in. I do not like to hate, but what you have done to me disserves hatred. I have been walking for years in your shit all the way up to my forehead. Sometimes I think when it is only knee-deep that soon I may escape the mire that you pitched me into.

I still cry. That was your gift to me, tears, frustration, self-doubt and discontent. You were a tainted woman, ego-centric and selfish, especially selfish. You were so dreadfully alone because you had no interest outside of yourself. Yet, with all the mess you were, I tried to love you.

Such a pathology! I tried to gain your love, and always you rejected me. What a pattern to establish in one's life."

(She finishes her dialogue, and slowly wanders off stage as the lights dim.)

Two days later, Jules had again scattered blocks all over the floor, including right under the edge of the bed where Jesse would be stepping. She took note and seeing that the leather belt had not been effective, promptly decided that she would never use it again, ever!

A Return to the Past

The last time Jesse had visited her parents in Los Angeles, she made a point to look-up Jamie. She had not seen him since he had handed her Carlos's rejection letter when he returned from Mexico, what seemed a lifetime ago. He probably didn't even know she had fled California. Oddly enough, he was easy to find through the phone directory for the area.

She dialed the number.

"Oh my God, Jesse, it's been forever! Where have you been?" Jaime asked enthusiastically.

"It's a long story. I was wondering if you want to get together for a visit. I'd love to hear what you've been doing too." Jesse replied.

"Yes, of course! Let's meet at my house tomorrow evening. I will give you directions. Do you remember this area at all?"

Excited about the prospect of seeing an old friend, Jesse assured him that she could find her way to his house and said goodbye.

Jamie lived in the Hollywood Hills up above Sunset Strip on a steep road lined with old trees and thick woods, surrounded by the hidden yet crowded hillside community.

Her finger shook slightly as she rang the doorbell. Jamie opened the door with such an authentic and genuine smile, Jess was instantly glad that she had come.

"There you are! Come in, come in. Wow, it's so good to see you." They hugged as she crossed the threshold.

"This is a beautiful place you have, especially up above the city!" Jesse remarked.

"Yeah, I followed my brother's lead and stayed in the film industry," Jamie replied softly.

"Really, what do you do?" She wondered out loud.

"Oh, a little of everything, writing, editing, directing, whatever is needed, wherever I can use my talents. The people in this town thrive because of coalitions and networking. After so many years I've got a good reputation and resume so I'm able to stay working... one project at a time." Jamie paused.

"It sounds fascinating," Jesse said.

"Hmm, I guess... to someone outside the business. Believe me it can be maddening.
Everyone has to work, might as well do something interesting, right?"

She nodded in agreement. Meanwhile, the aroma from Jamie's cooking filled the air.

"I made us something simple, just rice and veggies. Are you ready to eat?" He motioned toward the dining room.

After dinner, the two sat in the plush living room, and as the evening progressed Jesse told Jamie about her extraordinary journey after she had left. He listened with quiet focus. Finally, she began wrapping up the story.

"So, I'm relatively happy these days, although I'm way too busy with full-time college, and being a mother. But you know, I am still sad because Carlos took my baby away from me. I know it has been years, but I can't let go of the thought that he never gave me a chance. Maybe I was hard to get along with. I was emotional and unpredictable at times, but I wasn't a horrible person and I didn't deserve to be treated like I was a piece of shit. People make mistakes. They learn; they grow. And I will never believe that Andre is better off without me." Jesse was weeping now; Jamie touched her shoulder.

"I know you've been through a nightmare; I'm sorry you've had to endure so much pain," Jamie responded as though he harbored his own silent loss.

The hours had passed quickly. Aware of the time, Jesse gathered up her jacket to leave.

"Thank you so much Jamie. I appreciate that you spent time with me. It means a lot that I could talk to you about my past. You're someone who knew us back then."

"You're welcome. I have your information. We'll keep in touch."

Jesse smiled, they said goodbye, and she made her way back down the mountain, back to her parent's house. The next day she flew out of LAX back to New Mexico.

Back home in Albuquerque, Jesse returned to her frantic schedule. Never did it cross her mind that Jamie was still in contact with Carlos. He had not mentioned it once during the hours of conversation and reminiscing. Checking the mailbox, Jessie found a letter from him saying he had talked to Carlos and told him that it was time for Andre to be reunited with his mother! She had gotten so used to being without her first child that it was hard for her to grasp that she would again be able to spend time with him, especially during the summers. She looked expectantly for the letter from Carlos to arrive.

However, when it arrived, Jesse's joy was dampened as she read the words. It explained that she could see Andre if she signed the legal adoption papers within. Kicked in the stomach! After enduring emotional torture at his hands for years since he had kidnapped and hid her child from her, now Carlos was causing her more pain. How could she sign these papers if Andre would at any point in his life think that his mother had not wanted him? She would only sign them if he knew that she had done so under duress. Attaching the stamps to the packet of adoption papers, Jesse felt a strange unfamiliar feeling of relief and closure. Jesse made plans to visit Santa Cruz, California where Andre lived. In an unaccustomed synchronicity, Jesse was able to get a ride with a friend right to their door.

The reunion with her son was sweet but made awkward by the attention Carlos was giving his present new girlfriend. However, Jesse had no desire to bring up the unfairness and resentments of the past. She was simply happy to at last be with her son Andre, who was still a kid. She would have years ahead with him.

Theater Arts and Dance

esse continued her harried routine attending academic classes, Physiology, Math, History, and French in addition to modern and ballet classes, and to satisfy requirements for a double major, additional theater classes. She danced topless on weekends, and drank enough beer to keep herself friendly, an essential personality trait if she wanted tips. Her car wasn't dependable, so she took the bus up the main drag to the club and bummed a ride home either from a customer or from the manager.

One evening she danced for a man named Ogle Golden; he must have been 70 and to hear him talk, he was a wealthy man. Jesse went out with him a few times for hot fudge Sundaes, and he listened to her talk about her dreams and her politics. She never knew whether he was trying to get her in bed, or just enjoying being with a pretty, young woman. Jesse was approaching thirty and looked eighteen. After they finished their sundaes Ogle would drive her home to the minuscule shack, and hand her a twenty-dollar bill. She would say thank you, and walk in the house thinking, *you talk like you are a philanthropist who is really interested in helping me, but then you hand me a $20.* If Jesse had tried, she probably could have gotten more of the man's money, but as it was, their exchange was chaste and wholesome. She liked the simplicity and being able to easily live with herself. As long as she had a dancing job, she didn't have to sell sex. Eventually she would graduate, and life would be different.

Getting a degree was a sound plan but Jesse struggled with an avalanche of responsibilities. Juggling motherhood, the slew of homework assignments, and the obligations of the theater arts component which included doing overtime on the plays either as a stagehand, lighting person, costume-assistant or usher, kept Jesse reeling. Her poor study-habits and procrastination did not help. Then at the end of every week came the drinking, dancing, and hustling. Though she tended to be an introvert, Jesse became adept at entertaining. No one would tip a dull dancer, so Jesse became known for having the most audacious mouth. She had a repertoire of topics that she added to and refined until she had created another persona, the loud-mouthed know-it-all sex kitten. Jesse could be bold and rough like a biker broad, or soft and gentle like an innocent child, and she loved to dance. Dancing fed her spirit. Re-inventing herself on the stage, she worked the space like someone possessed with the joy of rhythm, movement, and music.

Jesse did not delude herself. She knew that dancing on a raggedy linoleum stage in the two-horse southwestern town of Albuquerque would never make her a star, but she felt satisfied knowing that during daylight hours she attended college including many hours of studio dance classes. She hoped that her efforts would result in a career, but just what it might be, still eluded her. She could see herself owning a dance studio; still she had no clue how to make that happen.

Every semester the University of New Mexico dance department put-on a student recital. Students choreographed, auditioned their pieces, were judged and chosen. The dancers who made it into the Dance Department's Program had the opportunity to exhibit their creativity and add it to their resumes. For Jesse, the opportunity to choreograph beyond the confine of a topless bar, to be on a university stage dancing with her clothes on was irresistible. Jesse was thrilled when she was chosen but unaware of the additional work she had inadvertently taken on.

The house she moved to had a large hardwood floor. Jesse bought two huge pieces of quality glass and had them hung on the wall. This was her studio. This is where she chose the music Long Tall Glasses by singer Leo Sayer to use for her audition and choreographed the steps and dance phrases that she repeated over and over until she was confident it reflected her vision. After rehearsing the piece, she was ready for the audition.

Auditioning cannot be about competing unless you are competing with yourself. It is, instead, about losing the judges and audience from your awareness, to step inside of your effervescent transitory dancing body. In reaching this place of communication with oneself, one also universally touches everyone else.

Taking on this extracurricular project and stepping outside of her comfort zone was accompanied by Jesse's ever-present anxiety. It was severe but not easily recognizable to her. Many of her behaviors like procrastination that caused so much disorganization and internal conflict were related to her underlying fear.

316

Regardless of the forces working to impede her progress, Jesse remained steadfast.

Years later she wondered if taped recordings of her fleeting image were archived somewhere in the Theater Arts library at UNM?

When Vince exited Jesse's life, so did her ability to contain the inky depression that followed and kept her defeated, haunted, and miserable... except while she danced. Climbing the stairs to the stage, it was there that she transcended her despair and cynicism. Art transformed her. Her Muse, the Queen Dance freed her. She felt and enjoyed her stage presence grow powerful with each performance, with each dollar bill stuffed into her garter.

Between sets customers bought the drinks. Jesse drank hard liquor or beer depending on her mood. The liquor phases came and went like the moon's; one week her passion was shots of Cuervo Gold, and another Uzo, then on to Long Island Ice teas. The assault on her liver never assailed her consciousness.

The customers liked Jesse. She listened with genuine interest to every story, and never hustled to the point of greediness. If asked, Jesse would only tell you quietly, "I'm looking for a guy who will help me and my son and will also help me get where I want to go; in exchange I will help him in the same ways." Lots of men wanted to help Jesse, except, they wanted to possess her. But with her mother's haranguing voice so deeply buried in her psyche, Jesse fiercely guarded her freedom and autonomy.

Unfortunately, she was a slave to her sexual proclivities and had never understood the difference between love and sex. Just because a man wanted to touch and subsequently fuck, that it did not mean trust and long-term love. Because Jesse had a child, men were even more likely to fuck her once and never call back. She never understood how few men were willing to take on another man's child, yet there were an abundance of men willing to tell Jesse anything they thought she wanted to hear in order to get a piece of ass. She craved to be caressed and did not always catch on. Instead, she was repeatedly victimized, reinforcing her tattered self-image with its corresponding low self-esteem. After these sexual encounters Jesse would be left feeling unworthy of even the low-life man with whom she had shared one night.

While attending school, the hours that she could work were limited to weekends, and an occasional Saturday matinee. The money was better because she was dancing near the foothills, the up-scale part of town. Jesse had not run into any hard drugs for a few years. Feeling so happy with Jules, she had stayed clear of them. She was smart enough to know that no chemical would assist her with studying, memorizing, and writing papers. Luckily, she had no compulsion to drink alcohol outside of the club. She was the perfect weekend-warrior, student and mother during the week, wanton wench on weekends.

The Ring of Power

ithout help, Jesse wasn't able to keep the pace to fulfill the roles of student, provider, nurturer, parent, dancer, seamstress, and spiritual seeker. Help came in the form of crystal methedrine. Hope, a tall ebony-black man, the bouncer at the club, introduced Jesse to "doc."

Larry's customers called him "doc" because of his meticulous handling of everything related to the methedrine experience, from measuring, to preparing and using. He slipped on latex gloves when he was touching any of the surfaces or the powder. When Jesse walked into his house, she felt like she had walked on the set of a photo shoot. What a picture of organization! A place for everything and everything in its place! High quality furnishings and lighting had turned each room into a page from *Home & Gardens*. Dr. Larry invited Jesse and Hope to sit down at the dining room table while he left the room and quickly returned with his scale and a baggie full of white powder. Jesse was vaguely aware of her feeling of anticipation, fluttering stomach, not unlike the nervousness she used to feel when she was going with Jack to cop heroin. Jesse had always liked a speed high; she could get things done. At work, she could dance and entertain like a superstar. Back when she had lived with Carlos, a pharmacist he had met at the UCLA hospital, was very accommodating and supplied

Jesse with generic diet pills. She loved the endless energy, euphoria, the feeling that she could do anything.

"Jesse, have you ever injected methedrine before?"

"No." She left it at that, deciding not to talk about her heroin days in Los Angeles.

"You are going to love this," he nearly cooed over her with his bad breath.

"So, how do you know how much the right dose is?" She asked, suddenly feeling protective of her life.

"I use myself, so I can gage each batch I get by how it feels to me, and then I compare my weight with the other person. I've never had any complaints yet." He smiled closely. He was charming in a ferret, fawning, Wormtongue kind-of-way, but Jesse trusted him. She had to. She was going to let Dr. Larry inject methamphetamine sulfate into her vein.

She watched him mix about 10cc of distilled water in a spoon with what looked like a few grains of the white dust; it dissolved instantaneously. Dr. Larry rolled up a little piece of a cotton ball and dropped it into the liquid before sucking it up with the brand-new insulin syringe.

Jesse let him tie her arm off; the needle-prick was nothing with a new rig. When he pushed the plunger in, she felt a rush of pleasure, not unlike an orgasm running through her body until it reached the base of her spine, traveling upward and flooding her brain with endorphins and euphoria. Jesse felt like liquid love. She thanked Dr. Larry. He was close by to get a hug because he knew how first-time users tended to be pliable because of all the pleasure they are feeling.

Jesse felt expanded beyond her body, fusing with the power of Life, closer to the Source than she had ever been before. Then the thoughts and impressions started. Her brain bubbled with ideas, spontaneously inspiring and generating derivative ideas. She found herself wanting to scribble her thoughts on paper. It began with her announcing to whoever would listen that she was a spiritual empiricist meaning that she sought proof of the metaphysical realm through empirical evidence, not realizing the paradox, or how foolish she sounded.

Jesse, immersed in feelings of sustained euphoria, moved through the house entranced by all the beautiful artifacts. In her sensitized state she easily picked-up on the influence of a female. Larry explained that he was separated from his wife. Jesse smiled internally acknowledging that Dr. Larry's wife was likely responsible for the lovely décor. Larry followed her around giving her the narrated tour. She soon grew tired of his sniffing like a dog. He obviously thought she was in heat. Drugged as Jesse was, she was not attracted to Larry. He seemed arrogant with his too-close-together eyes, and pointy nose, and besides, she was certainly not in need of sex. She could always get someone hot to scratch that itch. Larry was not the first mediocre looking guy to drool over her. It would be easy for her to play him, only he really did not have anything she needed. He was a good connection in case she wanted to speed again. He was nice, so it was easy to be nice in return even if her friendliness transmitted a mixed message.

An hour had passed, and she could feel the high flattening out. Jesse felt restless.

"Do you think I could have a little more, unless you think it's not a good idea; I have money."

Larry didn't ponder for long, "Well, I could, but it won't give you the same effect because your system already has some in it. What you should do is, go ahead and buy a gram, that is 80 dollars, and wait until tomorrow when you've had some sleep, and you've eaten. Because you have to remember, when you do speed, you use up a lot of energy and if you don't sleep or eat, you don't get high."

Jesse took it all in, "I'm glad you let me know. Can you show me how to shoot up? I've snorted speed, and I hate the way it burns; the rush isn't as good either."

"Sure, I can do that." Larry was accommodating.

Larry gave Jesse a quick instructional lecture about how and where to buy Insulin syringes, how to estimate an amount and prepare the liquid meth, and then the technique for injection.

"First, just say to yourself, I'm buying these for my diabetic grandmother... that way, you're going to stay relaxed when you're talking to the clerk at the pharmacy."

Jesse understood.

"You ask for a 10-pack of 100cc insulin syringes... they're really inexpensive, and using a new, sharp needle every time will prevent bad tracks from forming on your arms, and of course, protect you from anyone else's bugs you might get if you were sharing. Did you see how much I put on the spoon... about a match-head amount? Draw up the filtered water from a glass, and that amount of water is how much you are going to squirt into the spoon with the crystal. You know you don't need to heat it, just swish the cotton ball around with the cap of the works until it's dissolved. Then touch the needle point to the cotton and carefully draw up the liquid." Jesse paid further attention.

"I've already showed you how to tie-off, right?" Larry asked. Jesse nodded. She remembered not to actually make a knot but to simply wrap the belt over itself, holding pressure with her arm and knee, then it would release automatically without having to be untied with one hand.

"Make sure that you hold your fingers under the works for leverage as you inject, and don't slam the whole vial if you're not sure of the strength... that's how you blow-out your heart." She gave him a peck on the cheek as a thank you and asked for a ride home.

Jesse unlocked the front door and stepped into the empty house. Her heels echoed as they clicked on the old maple floors, Jesse's make-shift dance studio had no furniture.

Jules was still next door at the babysitter's house. She walked in circles from room to room trying to select a hiding place for her *works*, her Ring of Power, the little baggie of meth. Jesse recalled from Tolkien's book that whoever held on to the *ring* became dependent upon it. The ring had absolute power over its keeper. Up until now, Jesse had always needed someone to inject a drug into her vein, but now she would have full control, and could be alone when she shot-up. Jesse had turned a corner in her drug use.

Speed brought out Jesse's boldness. Under its influence, she could summon her college Spanish and speak with ease to her Mexican neighbor who lived with her husband and two young children. The woman didn't know any English and was probably an un-papered immigrant.

Using speed, Jesse felt her ability to empathize was growing, merging with another person, her compassion increasing. She had always envisioned many wonderful futures for herself, and humanity, but the methedrine produced an exhilarated delirium. When the molecule hit Jesse's brain she was inundated with neurological magic, streams of ideas.

Her imagination stimulated, her mind's eye gaping, she envisioned solutions for humanities problems. Artists who wanted to live in the country, and still generate money by offering classes and services to people in the city would be shuttled by electric vehicles. A hundred-acre artistic community, complete with the artists' cabins within easy distance from the bungalows where the workshops are facilitated, and classes taught. The Esalen Institute in Big Sur, California was a forerunner in the Human Potential movement, and functioned in a similar manner since its conception in the 1960s. Jesse felt her psychic connections embracing and synthesizing the knowledge of her cultural teachers such as Baba Ram Das, Fritz Perls, C.G.Jung, and of course the charismatic Timothy Leary,

Around the corner from where Jesse lived was a huge brick church and school attached. She began to visualize an afterschool artistic recreational center housed in these buildings. In her mind she saw the dance classes, and yoga training, rooms filled with kids from the community. She envisioned arts for the community, photography, silkscreened T-shirts, pottery, music, clothes design and sewing, as well as classes in sustainable living that included gardening, and canning. She could see healthy families getting the support needed to create environments and opportunities for their empowerment. Jesse clearly saw the end product, the gestalt. She did not question how she would manifest these grand ideas. Because when she did, a great unhappiness would descend upon her, a sense of impotency, powerlessness, insecurity, anger, self-pity, self-denigration, blackening, self-defamation, belittlement, and disparagement, all of it would wash over her like a toxic river.

So instead of entertaining self-doubt, she did speed. The chemical steeped and baptized her in the awakening of gladness and pleasure, such unfamiliar feelings. With the miracle of amphetamines Jesse felt alive, unfettered, unchained, her strength of mind flown free from the cage of limited self, every minute a delight, a flurry of thoughts. Without direction, Jesse meandered in the crevices of her imagination. Energy fed into awakening circuits created a biochemical flow of endorphins. Elation, this is where she wanted to remain forever. She realized that heaven is a state of consciousness rather than a physical place, and that this level of consciousness was, at once easy to attain, though difficult to sustain, and nearly impossible to explain to another person who had not experienced it, like trying to describe the flavor of vanilla.

Jesse followed Larry's instructions and waited a day before doing more. She soon discovered that after the high had subsided, and often for hours later, she could not turn her brain off. After a night of dancing, bits of lyrics would repeat endlessly on the tattered circuits of Jesse's brain. Wide awake, though exhausted, unconsciousness would not come. So, she learned to use the time to meditate, to stop giving her thoughts audience. She had read this, s*ee the thoughts as clouds and simply let them float by.*

Another time, feeling frayed of body and mind, and again not being able to sleep, Jesse began to give thanks for everything, item by item, category by category, for five hours until the sun rose. She felt uncannily well-rested though she did not lose consciousness at all.

Saturday night at work, Jesse was speeding her ass off, and behaving more boisterous than usual. Jesse could drink large quantities of beer while under the influence of meth. After an intense dance set Jesse spotted a biker sitting down front. He wore a black leather jacket, shoulder-length black ponytail, and beard. She slipped into the seat next to him, grabbed the just-poured pilsner of beer and with five or six gulps imbibed the entire glass. Since it was her last set, she said thanks, kissed him on the cheek, and disappeared. Robbie was angered and intrigued. But that was last call; he and his buddy were directed out the front doors.

The tables were scrubbed, chairs up, and bright overhead lights were blaring. Jesse waited to get paid. Her boss Shirley, a good-looking woman who had once been a lawyer, asked her to stay for minute.

"Jesse, I know you used to dance nude, and I need a girl at my other club on the edge of town. It pays more than here." Then she didn't say another word, like a good saleswoman. It took only a moment for Jesse to respond to the sound of *more money*. "Sure, but I don't have a car."

"That's not a problem," she answered brightly, "we'll pick you up. I think you might have danced there when you first were hired out of the agency. That was when my ex-husband owned it. It's called the Raceway because the drag strip is nearby."

Jesse remembered the club; it was her first *bottomless gig.* The jukebox was horrible, stocked with the worst songs, the majority Country-Western, and a few worn-out top forty hits from decades ago. "Do you think if I bought some singles, you'd put them on the jukebox?" She questioned cautiously, not wanting to be told no.

"Well maybe; it's not that acid-rock stuff, is it?" Shirley wrinkled her face in loathing.

"No, just some music that's more up-to-date," Jesse answered hopefully.

Shirley did not want to make promises, but she also needed Jesse to stimulate business at her other club. It was always good to bring in new bodies. She had another reason for wanting to move her feisty dancer. Jesse tended to get mouthy from the stage, she cussed like a street person, and talked about contentious issues like civil rights, marijuana legalization, and withdrawal from Viet-Nam, in a town born and sustained by Kirtland Air Force Base. White Sands testing grounds was a day's ride away as was Los Alamos nuclear facility northwest of Albuquerque. Silently, Shirley felt that Jesse was too rough around the edges. She wanted girls who were two dimensional, not controversial, to dance at the Silver Slipper. She had her club's reputation to think about.

The move was both good and bad. The Raceway was closer to home and she would have an automatic ride with the manager. Totally nude dancing paid more. The downside was that since the club was on the outskirts of the city limits, the clientele was mostly blue-collar, and tended to get lewd and raucous, not exactly Jesse's turn-on, the smell of cheap cologne and diesel fuel. Still struggling with school and on the verge of dropping out, she turned to meth more often.

Jesse had a previous history with speed, from her first prescribed diet-pill at 18 to its latest incarnation. In the tiny zip-locked baggie, a little over an inch square in measurement, the sandy substance sparkled like the fine dust of Austrian crystals, hence the drug's street name, *crystal*. She knew its properties and had a healthy respect for its power. Making a promise that she would use it to get ahead for Jules and herself, she worked double shifts and doubled her earning power giving her a foot-up. She still needed a vehicle. Jules had become so heavy that her knees could not handle the additional pounds while biking to school or the grocery store. Determined and fortified with a gram of crystal, she set out to finally take control of her life. In the words of Tom Petty, she was tired of living like a refugee. To stay focused and drug-free during the school week, she kept her pouch tucked away on a hook in the closet. When Friday night arrived, Jesse packed a tote bag for Jules, walked him around to the back house where Mrs. Flores watched him while she danced. Then she hurried back home to perform the 'ritual' before work.

She dissolved the grains in the spoon watching them disappear into the clear water, then tied-off her arm allowing easy access to the puffed-up vein. Taking a deep breath anticipating the psychic acceleration, like a scientist she was attentive and exact, although her hand was not as still as she would have liked, a phlebotomist in training, she was still jittery. She always followed Dr. Larry's instructions so that delivery of the methamphetamine sulfate via intravenous injection was a success, no missed veins, no tracks, no infections. Jesse felt the rush, the orgasmic prelude to the "crystal-meth experience," and then the onslaught of optimism and resulting positive attitude along with a manic flow of ideas, plans, visions, and of course, motivation. With speed, everything was easy.

Jesse mentally catapulted herself, speed-of-light, into a beautiful future, one that was certainly possible. However, the gap, between where she lived and functioned, and where she envisioned herself to be, was a chasm. A therapist might have labeled Jesse's ranting as drug-induced delusions.

Filled with euphoria, Jesse got ready for work. She carried a notebook and pencil because she liked to scribble pieces of poetry, characters she wanted to develop, and ideas for classes and workshops. The evening went as planned and true to form, Jesse made almost two hundred dollars, twice as much as she usually pulled in. It might have been the speed, it might have been the crowd, and it might have been payday for the local workers. She repeated this formula for a month, always making sure she had eighty dollars, her meth money, before she added to her car-savings, and soon she had saved about eight hundred dollars. It was not an easy plan to stick to. Jesse was *boosting* crystal on a regular basis and was not accustomed to the extreme changes both physical and emotional that the drug was putting her through. She had lost at least fifteen pounds, at one twenty-six she was satisfied with her flat stomach. Sometimes her inability to sleep drove her crazy, and she broke out in boils on her thigh that she tried to hide with makeup as they turned to scabs.

Jesse's experiment was almost concluded. She had intentionally used the meth to work double-shifts so that she could finally buy a car. This weekend she would own the sunshine-yellow Vega that she had seen in a driveway two streets away.

She felt buoyant, walking up the gravel driveway to the owner's house. The man was bald, middle-aged, and overly friendly, with a belly like he was getting ready to give calf. Jesse had little experience in the art of purchasing an automobile, and as a friend later remarked, "What? Did you walk in backwards grabbing your ankles?"

Jesse was enamored with her snazzy new ride. It looked like a miniature station wagon, with twin portholes in the back. She thought it would be perfect for transporting her Amway products that she had recently begun selling. Ten days from the moment of acquisition, the car stopped running. Jesse marched back to the house and knocked.

"Hey, how are you doing?" the same man greeted Jesse contritely.

"Not too well. The car you sold me isn't running; it just stopped."

The man's faced turned red. He did not pause before responding. "Look, I told you when you bought it that it was a used car. It was running fine when you drove off in it."

"You lied to me; you told me it was a good car."

He got up close to Jesse's face, "You better not be calling me a liar. I will call the police. Now get off my property." He turned his back on Jesse, walked through his front door, and slammed it.

Victimized once more, she had trusted and been betrayed. She mused, *'So alone on this planet; I never have help like normal people, now all of this effort for nothing. The crook just sold me a bum car, took the $450, and slammed the door in my face when I protested.'* The anger generated tears pressed hard from her eyes. She went home and stared in the mirror. She had a big fever blister on her upper lip, a reaction from the speed she had been taking. She felt defeated, also a reaction from the withdrawal.

It took her another month to accumulate enough cash to buy another clunker; this time a Dodge Dart with a V-8 engine. The seller told her upfront that the block was cracked, and that it overheated. Jesse did not understand the seriousness and bought it anyway.

Phone Call from Santa Fe

bout this time Jesse met Dean. He had a pretty face and a gentle demeanor. With her usual abandonment she bedded him, and he was smitten. She also turned him on to the crystal she was doing. Jesse had a way of making it seem like it was ok; it was simply expanding one's consciousness.

Thursday came round and Jesse was scheduled to work, so she asked Dean if he would watch Jules. He had already met little Jules; he knew the three-year old would not cause any problems. It gave Dean more time to spend with Jesse, besides, he had always liked children. Jesse said goodnight to Jules, and kissed Dean, "I'll be back by two-thirty," she told him happily. Jesse always felt upbeat when she was involved with a man, surer of herself, and calmer.

At ten-thirty the manager had a dancer relieve Jesse from the stage.

"You've got a phone call from the Santa Fe Police Department." She said while handing the receiver to Jesse.

"Yes, this is Jesse Bell."

"We have your son in custody here at the Santa Fe Police Department," an authoritative voice said.

"No, that can't be, my son is at home with the babysitter," she responded, trying to keep the hysteria out of her voice.

332

"Well, apparently he was taken along for the ride when a Mr. Dean Brown was making a drug deal."

"Oh my God, is Jules alright?"

"Yes ma'am, the officers gave him something to eat, and made him comfortable. He is anxious to see you."

"Yes, I'm sure. It will take me about an hour to get there."

She got directions, hung-up the phone, and quickly explained the situation to the manager who told her not to worry. The other girls would cover.

Jesse's car could make the 10-mile trip from her house to work without trouble, but to take it on the highway for a 60-mile drive was risky. She searched the bar for Allen, a guy that she had been talking to earlier, and approached him. After explaining the situation, she asked, "Can you drive with me up to Santa Fe? My car has a cracked block, and I don't want to get on the highway alone; I don't trust it."

"Sure, I can help you out."

"Will you drive? I don't see that well at night."

"Yeah, I guess so. We should get a couple of gallons of water and carry them with us just in case it starts to overheat."

Jesse smiled with relief, "Thank you, I really appreciate this."

Within minutes they were on the road north to rescue Jules. Santa Fe was deserted at midnight; just a few cars, left-over tourists winding their way through town. Allen was familiar with Santa Fe and found the station easily. Jesse jumped out of the car while Allen found a parking place.

She approached a woman behind glass. "I'm looking for my son. The police called my work and told me he is here."

The dull-eyed woman pointed and buzzed her in. "Just follow that hallway all the way back."

Saying thank you Jesse hurried to find Jules. He was sitting on a wooden bench with a bag lunch next to a big desk with a large Mexican policeman shuffling papers. It took minutes for them to release Jules into her custody. The Santa Fe Police did not want the liability.

Jules looked exhausted, so Jesse told him lie down in the back seat so he could sleep. As they pulled out of the cop shop Allen said reassuringly, "I filled the radiator, so we shouldn't have any problem with the engine overheating."

Jesse looked over her shoulder at her little golden cherub. She felt so grateful that he was safe with her again. Once at home, Jesse put Jules to bed and thought about Dean. How could he have jeopardized the safety of her son? Too much of her life had been tied up with legal problems. She was wary, and wanted no part of it. Jesse never saw him again.

Two Marbles in a Shoebox

esse continued to do crystal, and she quit school. She was at the end of her seventh semester, and she knew she was failing at least two classes. It would bring her GPA below the accepted level for the state financial help that she was getting, and there was no way she could pull it up. She told herself that the dance class she was teaching at the YWCA was the beginning of something important, that she did not need school. What was a degree in Theater Arts worth? She did not want to waste anymore of her time in school. She never had time to read the books she wanted, or for that matter, to write. And sewing was nearly a forgotten skill.

With more than one psychology class under her belt, Jesse was still unable to see that she fit the description for clinical depression and was self-medicating. Part of her "depressive schema" went something like this, *I was never loved, I have never been given any help in my life. I am alone in the world. As a child, I was never allowed to be happy, nor encouraged to laugh.* These thoughts joined other beliefs that kept her victimized, sad, and depressed. Yet those beliefs had no power over her when she was high. Crystal made her normal. It made her act like the real Jesse, instead of this powerless, pitiful, abandoned, worthless person who paraded around in her body most of the time. Speed was the chemical that gave Jesse substance, a feeling of confidence. She could do anything, explain anything. She had a knowing about her worth. She was compelled to write, and dance... and dream.

Saturday night toward the end of Jesse's shift, Robbie walked in with his helmet in his hand. Jesse gravitated toward him and asked him if he would buy her a beer. "Yes, I'll buy you a beer so that you don't drink mine."

Jesse looked at him strangely.

"You don't remember me. I saw you a year ago uptown. You came over, sat down, and drank my beer in four gulps."

"Really, I might have; I really don't remember. Do you want me to buy you a beer?" She asked apologetically.

"No, but I couldn't believe you did that. It was my last two dollars, and I really wanted that beer." He had a smile on his face, and although he was big like a bear, Jesse did not feel threatened. In fact, she wanted to get to know him better. They talked long enough for Jesse to find out that he used coke.

"Robbie, I'm going to give you my address. You come over to my house when I get off work, ok?"

"Sure, I have to make a quick stop, and then I'll be over. Give me your phone number."

"No, just come over; I'll be up," she said handing him a coaster with her scribbling on it. Jesse hated getting 'excuse' phone calls.

After Robbie left, Jesse asked Starr, another dancer if she wanted to come over after work.

"This guy I know is coming over to my house after work. I thought you might want to come over too. He's bringing coke," she said excitedly.

Starr agreed, especially when cocaine was factored in. She brought her pearl handled revolver; she never traveled without it. Jesse and Starr waited at the house and talked until about 3:30, but Robbie didn't show.

The next evening Robbie again walked into the club.

"Hey lady, I ran out of gas just as I was coming over the railroad tracks, AND I didn't have your number so I couldn't call. I'm so sorry; I was really disappointed."

Jesse accepted both his excuse and his apology. He hung around for the rest of her shift, bought her beer and tipped her well. By the end of the evening, they had agreed to meet this weekend. He would stop by on the bike, and he could show her his house. They made a tentative date.

Since she had been speeding, Jesse noticed that her leaner body attracted younger, foxier men. Wednesday evening, one such man walked into the club just as her use of speed had become routine. Ryder was six feet tall, thin, a beautiful, chiseled face, long dark locks, and he rode a Harley.

"Do you want to ride with me out to Grants? I gotta visit a brother out there, and do some business?"

"Sure, when are you leaving?"

"Tomorrow early. Why don't I pick you up tonight after work? You can stay at my place, and we will leave in the morning... plus, you do crystal, right? I've got a little bit I'd like you to taste."

"Ok, I have to ask my babysitter if she can watch Jules; it'll cost me extra," she said, not expecting a response. To her surprise, Ryder volunteered, "Don't worry about the extra for the babysitter, I can pay for that."

Jesse called to arrange for her neighbor to keep Jules so that she was free to spend the night with Ryder. As the bar was shutting down, and the dancers were leaving he arrived promptly. Ryder was the perfect gentleman, grabbing her dancer's bag full of costumes, makeup and tips, simultaneously opening the door so that she could glide into the black leather seat of the money green Cadillac he was driving.

"Yeah, I'm not sure I'm going to buy this car. I like it though. I'm going to see how it feels on the highway."

Jesse liked the way his long dark brown hair framed his face, and his mustache hugged the side of his lips. He must have read her mind because as she was getting settled, he reached his arm around her, and pulled her close for a kiss.

"Come here."

The attraction between them warmed her insides; she felt the power of lust and yearning. After their energetic session, Jesse spent a sleepless, uncomfortable night. The trailer smelled of dogs, and her handsome escort had turned out to be a dud. He was nice enough but didn't take any time to satisfy her.

The next day time dragged for Jesse. The drive to Ryder's meth manufacturer was long, as were the silences between them. She listened to Ryder's story. He was 26, and his primary job was drug dealer. Mostly he wanted to talk about buying the car they were in. He did not seem to be interested in her, although he treated her with respect. Jesse wasn't exactly a fountain of conversation either; instead, she found herself censuring herself because she didn't want to bore him with her intellectual musings. At that time, she had been reading a lot of books on Existentialism, a philosophy that refuted the existence and need for a supreme being; instead it rested responsibility for an individual's life solely upon the individual. To the Existentialist, concern for one's immortal soul was considered a waste of time as there was no empirical evidence of an afterlife. Ryder seemed more like someone who would appreciate talk about sports, and Jesse could not deliver.

Shortly after they arrived, Ryder and a couple of other bikers walked out toward the back of the property to shoot a dog that was old. Jesse was horrified and elected to stay behind looking at tattoo and biker magazines, the only reading material available. Finally, they all returned, the drug transaction was completed, and Ryder and Jesse were able to get back on the road toward Albuquerque.

It was easy for Jesse to back away from Ryder, handsome rake that he was. She was aware that he could not provide any kind of predictable security for her son. When he asked if she wanted to spend another day with him, she declined and instead called Robbie for a ride.

Father Figure

They met-up a few blocks from Ryder's trailer park, and Jesse rode away on the back of Robbie's bike. With her arms firmly around Robbie's waist, he roared down the street heading for his home.

Robbie's house was located in the South Valley, a part of Albuquerque whose population was mostly Latino, Mexican American born and reared, with a sub-population of illegal immigrants, who managed usually through family or friends to establish residency and obtain work. The three-bedroom adobe was on five acres of farmland that he leased to a neighboring farmer; the revenue he collected paid the taxes. The most prominent feature of Robbie's living room was his hundred-gallon salt-water fish tank where he kept a lionfish, angel fish, a triggerfish, and a spotted grouper. All of them were aggressive and fed on live "feeder" goldfish.

Jesse felt right at home in Robbie's house. He welcomed her with friendly affection. Genuine affection had been absent from Jesse's life so much, that she hardly realized it was missing. Their first time alone as they sat on his couch close to each other, Jesse felt bathed in comfort and warmth emanating from Robbie. He seemed to agree with Jesse's point of view, he laughed at her cynicism, and was slow to approach her sexually. What more could she ask for? He was a gentleman and he worked. Her attraction grew, as did her sense of immediacy. She needed a surrogate father for Jules, and a man that she could love. She didn't want to wait any longer; at thirty, she thought she was old.

Besides the tank, the other impressive piece of furniture in Robbie's house was his brass bed. Everyone on the earth had heard Dylan sing "Lay lady lay, lay across my big brass bed." Robbie dropped back to the mattress demonstrating that his bed was solid. It did not squeak! Impatience overwhelmed Jesse. She practically jumped out of her clothes into his outstretched arms.

Robbie accepted her just the way she was. He did not judge her because she did speed occasionally, nor did he think she was a whore because she took off her clothes for a living. In fact, he lavished attention on her. Jesse had been working non-stop with the pressure and obligations of being a student and a single mother. Suddenly Robbie's arms felt like a safety net, and much needed support.

Jesse moved in. She stopped dancing for a while, and she stopped using meth. She cooked walnut vegetarian spaghetti, and baked cookies. Robbie was more than willing to playhouse with Jesse. She loved to fuck, and he didn't mind having her and her little son at the house. He didn't mind when Jules decided, out-of-the-blue, to call him daddy. When Jesse asked, "Do you care?" Robbie answered, "No, It's ok with me."

The first act of nesting that Jesse did was refinishing the hardwood floor in their bedroom. When she explained to Robbie what she was going to do, he lent his hand and expertise; the sanding, filling, and 3 coats of polyurethane were accomplished within a week's time.

One morning while Robbie was away at work, the telephone rang.

"Hello, this is Albuquerque National Bank. May I speak with Mr. Ramirez."

"I'm sorry he's not here right now; he's working. May I deliver a message?"

"Yes, please tell him that we will be auctioning off the house and property, and for him to make sure the house is empty and ready for possession."

Jesse stomach cramped as a sense of foreboding overtook and crashed her world. Her newly found home, and lover were not as certain as she had imagined. Mind racing, Jesse started thinking about all the work it was to move, and why didn't Robbie tell her that they would be moving soon. Why did he let her refinish the bedroom floor if he knew they could not stay there? Suspicion bled into her nerves; she worried and wondered all day until Robbie walked in the door from his job.

After telling him about the phone call and venting the huge reservoir of anxiety that had been collecting all day, Jesse waited for Robbie's response. He reached out with his arms open saying, "Now honestly, do these feel like the arms of security or what?"

Jesse buried her body in his, and he proceeded to explain away her fears, however, it was true that they would have to find another place to live.

Robbie had already found them a place in what was called the 'Northeast Heights', it was a modest 3 bedroom in a suburban neighborhood within walking distance from the elementary school Jules would attend. Living in a development never appealed to Jesse, but now that she was getting help with her life, she didn't want to complain.

She began waitressing without pay, at Chile World, the Mexican restaurant Robbie and his brother had recently opened. Both brothers could make authentic Mexican cuisine in their sleep, hands tied, having learned at the side of the 'master', their dad, who had owned a taco stand in the South Valley for decades. He and his wife had raised three sons and paid-off a nice two-story house with the earnings from the business.

Before long Jesse began gaining weight. She wasn't dancing, and every day was a culinary temptation, fried bread and honey, fresh green Chile, and cheese enchiladas. To bolster her willpower, she turned to legal diet aids, over-the-counter Epinephrine. Her skin erupted in allergic reactions, and she felt nervous rather than high. She could not tolerate being overweight. Even while she danced, she could never get below one hundred forty, and now that she was not sweating every night she began to bloat.

Chile World's business was increasing, so with Jesse's encouragement Robbie applied for a loan to buy property in the South Valley. They moved to the newly constructed adobe-style house on a half-acre of desert, with a mortgage of 500 dollars a month. She was thrilled. No bank would give an exotic dancer a loan, but she could enjoy this home as her own with Robbie's help. Nesting was one of Jesse's better skills. No matter where she lived, her house became her art gallery, her personal museum of unique 'finds'. Not having a stable income meant having to decorate with pennies. Even so, Jesse had an eye for the unusual, and could spot treasures under their layers of dust, hidden among the junk on the tables. She threw all her energy into the new house. Robbie came home one day from Chile World.

"Jesse, you know those red velvet drapes that were in the restaurant?"

"Yeah?"

"We're getting rid of them. They make the place look like a whore house."

"We need something for our bare living room windows. I can dye them!"

Jesse had yards of heavy gauge bright red washable velveteen. Robbie was right. With the red and silver flocked fleur-de-lys wallpaper (that had been quickly stripped when the brothers bought the place), and these candy-apple red drapes, the place had the air of a brothel, though it had previously been an Italian restaurant. The material was washable, so Jesse bought brown espresso dye, and threw the pounds of textile in the machine to await the results. The drapes came out a dark rich maroon and perfectly complimented the chocolate wall-to-wall carpet. The sunken living room now looked warm, homey and inviting. Jesse was pleased.

Bit by bit the house began to reflect Jesse's style. She discovered that by framing a poster she could get a more refined look instead of the usual student dorm, tape and thumbtack presentation. She hung her stained-glass trinkets in the bay window and punched holes in the new ceiling, to Robbie's protests, so she could hang her plants everywhere. The sterile house began to look like it had a personality. She renewed her fire tending skills, and kept a fire going in the fireplace. Turning this house into a home took most of Jesse's energy.

Every day for a month during the summer, Jesse could be seen out in the back digging in the sand. She had never had an opportunity to garden and had always wanted to grow her own food. She unearthed rocks and tumbleweeds and cut out a garden bed. While digging she thought that the sand didn't have many nutrients, so she called the local dairy located just two miles away and arranged to have a truck full of manure delivered. Then she spent a couple of days hand turning the sand and manure with a shovel. Optimistically, Jesse planted corn. Within the week small shoots had appeared in a neat row. Jesse's hippie heart soared! Then she woke up one morning to find all the inch-high plants laying on their sides, sawed off at dirt level. Confused and upset, she thought, *What the fuck?* After asking around she found out that fresh manure always has cutworms in it, and for it to be used in a garden, one must prepare it by mixing in Sevin dust or Malathion, insecticides that kill the cutworms before they have a chance to decimate your garden or crop. Jesse bought some of the poison, and her second crop of new corn shoots did not topple over immediately from the onslaught of cutworms. Instead, the brutal winds racing over the prairie battered the little saplings until they dried up from exposure. Jesse's experience with gardening gave her a fresh appreciation for the vegetables she bought at the grocery store; and renewed respect for the farmers who grew them and did constant battle with voracious insects.

Jesse liked staying at home. She had time to cook, sew, and write. Regrettably, she didn't have a dime in her pocket. Chile World was still struggling in a slow New Mexico economy, so she could not ask Robbie for additional money. They had agreed that he would pay the $469 a month mortgage, and Jesse would pay everything else. She returned to dancing.

For years, the Raceway was on the south side of the city, in fact it was one of the first clubs Jesse's manager had sent her to when she still lived in California. It was the same club where she had reconnected with Robbie, and it was only about a mile from their new home. Although Jesse was no longer 'prime flesh', she was still a good entertainer. She gave eye contact in a way that made a man feel like she was dancing for him alone. The owner hired her again, and Jesse resumed exotic dancing.

The restaurant never did take off. Robbie and his brother struggled to pay the bills, and on more than one occasion borrowed more money from their parents. One day Robbie brought home a business envelope with a brick of uncut cocaine in it. This was his effort to make some money on the side. Jesse did not realize that the mortgage was in arrears. She kept up her side of the deal by providing food, and utilities, and never imagined that Robbie had not paid the mortgage for a year. When Jesse asked Robbie for an update on their finances, he would always answer, "Don't worry about it; I'll take care of everything."

Three years had passed since they had first moved into the house. One morning as Jesse lay in bed Robbie quickly got up and was getting dressed.

"Well, I guess the bank will be auctioning off the house today," he said abruptly and without much emotion.

Jesse was still groggy from sleep. "What did you say? What are you talking about?"

He repeated what he said, and Jesse jumped out of bed, grabbed a robe to follow Robbie out of the bedroom.

"We're about a year behind on the mortgage. I've been trying to make a chunk of money so that I could get caught up, but I just haven't been able to do it."

Jesse's heart pounded; all the effort she had expended was for nothing. She had been sinking every penny she made into improvements for the house, railway ties to provide boundaries for some lawn in the front yard and back, and grass seed. The trees she had bought at a local nursery had cost more than $100 per tree. She was so upset. Her world was imploding, and she could do nothing about it.

"Why didn't you tell me? Why did you wait until we were so far behind? If I had known, we could have gotten a roommate; I could have done something."

By the end of the day, she called her Pappy, the man who was her biological father. At age 30, she had met and visited him for the first time. When she met him in California, he spoke as though he were very well-off. He told her had money stashed in CD's, but when Jesse asked him to loan her money to help them with their mortgage, his answer was, "Oh, I'm sorry sweetie, I just deposited the last of my money into a CD and I can't access it."

For the first time in a year, she remembered what she had said to herself when she noticed that Chile World was not generating enough capital, and they had to borrow from his parents. She had told herself then, *if we ever lose the house I will not stay in this land-locked state, I will leave,* and now it seemed that her intuition had been right.

Jesse was silent most of the time now. She was silent when Robbie showed her the house, he had found to rent in a run-down south valley ghetto. She was silent when he brought home an unwelcome Springer Spaniel puppy. She was silent as the saltwater fish went into shock and died. She was silent when the dog ran away and was not found. Chile World went bankrupt. Robbie's parents lost their house that they had put up for collateral for their sons' business loan. One day Robbie came home and announced that he was going on the road, that he and TB (short for Time Bomb, an old biker) would be remodeling Pizza Huts. He was leaving for Louisiana, and Georgia in a couple of days. Jesse's world was crashing, shattered. It was the middle of summer and Jules was not in school. This gave her some time to find another place to live, one that she could afford by herself. She and her son would now have to downgrade since she was not working, having been fired for exhibiting a temper tantrum in front of the manager, who was also the owner's daughter.

Jesse found a tiny adobe house in the barrio; one she could afford. The front wall was strafed with bullet holes. The street was not paved so when it rained it became one big mud puddle. She accepted her circumstances and figured that she could put up with just about anything for a short amount of time. This would do until she could get working full time. Borrowing a truck and two cousins from Robbie's family, Jesse managed to get the large pieces of furniture moved into the tiny adobe cube of a house. The rest of the boxes were still on the truck when some children from the neighborhood asked whether they could help.

"No, I've got most of the stuff moved into the garage, and it's going to take some time for me to figure out where to put the rest of the boxes. Thanks for offering."

The four kids moved aside as Jesse went inside to use the toilet and get a drink of water. When she came back out, she felt like something was amiss. Looking around she noticed things were not where she had left them. Her jewelry box and the 365-day clock were missing. It had taken only one minute for her to be fleeced by the scavenger children. Like professional thieves in a Dickens novel, they had taken the items that were most valuable and disappeared like smoke.

Jesse never generated enough money to have disposable income so buying expensive jewelry was not her habit, however she had been given two or three beautiful and unique pieces in her lifetime, and now they were gone.

This was not the first time she had been robbed. One time she recalled walking down the street a block away from her house. When she returned, her only transportation, a 10-speed bike had been stolen from her front porch. Again, her trusting naiveté had caused her to overlook vulnerabilities. When would she learn that there were nasty dishonest people who would take advantage of you if they had a chance?

Alone again, Jesse's despair returned. Frantic and without help, her surroundings compounded her feelings of hopelessness. With seemingly deliberate synchronicity, gray and black mold began creeping up the walls from the floors behind the sofa and beds, a phenomenon she had never encountered before because she had not lived in a house so poorly built and designed with no ventilation. The adobe was airtight like a mausoleum.

Her welfare check was stolen from the mailbox. She bought a mailbox with a lock, but the vandals quickly broke it and stole her check a second time. No money for food or gas, and she had not been able to find a job dancing since being fired from the Raceway. Thirty-five years old and competing with women in their twenties, in dire straits, abandoned, and without hope, this was Jesse's life. Robbie had been a disappointment. She never expected the house to be auctioned-off, for them to be kicked out of their home, all because he could not talk to her like an adult or communicate that they were in trouble. Still, she felt an obligation to support Robbie out on the road, and when the phone rang Jesse answered as pleasantly as she could, considering her situation.

"Hi, Jesse, how's it going?"

"I'm ok, you?"

"It's hell out here. The money's not what I thought it would be. The out-of-pocket expenses are way over what we estimated."

"Are you going to be able to send me any money? Jules and I are just getting by." "You promised me that you would help me, and I've been faithful to you." Jesse hated hearing herself beg.

"I know, but things aren't working out like I planned."

She heard herself say, *he can't be counted on, why did I invest so much time in him? More excuses, things never work out with him, he attracts bad luck.*

350

"Well, I think I got a job at the Chapter II. It's an up-scale gentlemen's club in the heights. They only scheduled me three shitty slots during the week, but at least I'm working. I can sell some Avon on the side too."

"I'm sorry baby, I promise it'll be better, just hold on."

Jesse thought, *'what options do I have?'*

They hung up and Jesse felt loathing and disgust for everything. She was sitting alone wanting to build a home and stable atmosphere for her son yet found herself unable to provide even the barest of essentials. She wept.

By the third month of battling the unsupervised juvenile thugs in the neighborhood, Jesse was primed to explode. The school Jules attended was sub-standard as one might expect because of the predominantly Mexican American population in the area. The economic class 'caste' system was so apparent to anyone who had eyes to see. The system for distributing the wealth was faulty or broken altogether. After reading The Communist Manifesto, and understanding its premise, she could never again experience life without seeing the class perspective. She had always wondered why a few short-sighted power-hungry industrialists had managed to hi-jack the entire economic system.

Robbie returned to New Mexico sheepishly humble with little cash expecting Jesse to reject him. Jesse's philosophy was 'don't kick someone when they're down', so she welcomed him, fed him, comforted him, made love, and enjoyed him, however she had decided long ago that as soon as he was on his feet she would leave. She wasn't sure how, or to where she would flee.

After he returned, Robbie landed a position working as a driver for Budweiser distributing. He found a fabulous three-bedroom home with a huge garage, and the sweetest floor plan she had ever lived in. A row of cabinets suspended from the ceiling between the kitchen and the dining room created a large serving area beneath, immense counters. She had never lived in a house with so much space. There was an extra room with white carpeting that Jesse claimed for her sewing. For once, she would be able to make a mess and close the door on it.

After tolerating those few months alone in the ghetto, by contrast her life felt secure and predictable when she was with Robbie. The neighborhood was middle class compared to the awful rental she had just left. Soon Jesse, Jules and Robbie settled into a routine.

One day close to Jesse's birthday, Robbie announced that he had saved a thousand dollars and wanted Jesse to buy a new car. While a new car was exactly what she needed, Jesse was nervous about the big car payment. Their relationship had cooled-off to the extent that Jesse wondered why he wanted to help her acquire the new Nissan sports car he insisted that she test drive.

Robbie rarely talked to her anymore. He worked all week-long delivering beer, and every evening, the moment he walked in the door he would switch on the TV, before anything else! 'Couch Time' was their 'special' time together. If she wanted to be with Robbie, she could sit next to him and watch TV, or she could sit with him during the endless football games. He worked and he watched TV.

Jesse managed to dance a few shifts. During the fifteen years she had lived in Albuquerque it seemed like she had worked every club, excluding the X-rated bookstores. She was running out of new places to try.

Again, Jesse turned to designing and sewing dancer's costumes in order to supplement her almost non-existent income. In hopes of making a sale or two she took her costumes to the Round-Up, a huge club on the North West edge of the city and left with a dance job.

Its interior was set up like a playboy club with three raised stages, the dancers' waitressing and moving between tables giving personalized attention in the form of clothed, touch-less table dances. Two feet from the customer was the rule. The Round-Up employed ten dancers a shift, two bouncers, and an M.C. named Rio. In fact, every dancer had a stage-name, a handle. There was Midnight, Killer Kathy, Cocoa, Star, Crystal, Satin, Stormy, and Pumpkin, but Jesse didn't have a stage-name. She felt left out, and immediately began contemplating a catchy name for herself. When she was younger, she had told David Crosby that her name was Celeste, but now she was thinking of EZ, or better yet Easy. By the next working shift, she let the announcer know what her new name was. When customers asked why she was called Easy, she responded, "Because I'm easy to get along with." Or another time, when asked, if she was easy, she answered, "My name is Easy, not easiest!" The list of retorts was endless, and she felt a degree of anonymity behind her silly name. While being a new face, she still did not make as much money as the women who were dancing and hooking on the side. They made the big money in the club, and Jesse felt dejected and unattractive. She did not realize what was going on behind the scenes. She watched other girls count twenties and fifties, while she counted ones and fives. It was difficult for Jesse to keep up with the car payment she had recently acquired.

One particularly slow evening she did accept an invitation by a truck driver to make some extra money. And when she got out of the truck right before the sun tipped the horizon with only fifty dollars, she hardly felt it was worth it. She would have rather slept, and then there was the nasty business of having to sneak into the house with the smell of another man on her. She headed straight for the bathroom for a soak in the tub and denied any wrong doings when Robbie looked in before going off to work. It seemed to Robbie that Jesse had stopped trying to get along with him; she rarely cooked dinner even on her nights off. And when Robbie rode to the Sturges Bike Rally she was not invited.

The East Coast Pull

One of many boring nights at the club Jesse was lined up with the other girls at the floor to ceiling mirror checking G-strings, makeup, and money. Her ears perked up when she heard one of the women say loudly, "I'm sick of this shit; I'm going where I can make some real money." Jesse moved nearer and although she was not well acquainted with Valerie, she struck up a conversation in order to learn more about this land of plenty the woman was talking about. They exchanged numbers when Jesse offered to drive the two of them to this place called Waldorf, Maryland on the East coast.

They had decided on driving when Valerie changed her mind at the last minute saying that it would be a much better idea to travel by plane and arrive rested so that she and Jesse could begin dancing and making money right away. Jesse pulled together the money feeling a surge of hope. She was willing to try yet another lead, especially since Valerie said she knew her way around the East Coast. Waldorf was close to Washington, D.C. where all the museums were. Jesse's wanderlust stirred.

Somehow, Jesse did not recall the catastrophe she had endured when she followed Karen to New York. Instead, she imagined the absolute best scenario and followed with anticipation. It was not until they landed that Jesse found out Valerie liked to shoot heroin, in fact, she was a stone-cold junkie, completely dependent. Heroin was not Jesse's drug of choice. She had experimented with it sufficiently in the past, and did not feel the least bit compelled to join in. However, she did try the smoking rage of the east coast ghetto scene, 'Green' or 'Angel Dust', formaldehyde-soaked parsley rolled like a joint and smoked. Sprinkled on pot, it altered consciousness often to the point of hallucinations and delusions. Sold as 'love-boat', Jesse was not impressed. It set her nerves twitching, like short-circuits along her spine and out through her limbs. Under its influence insomnia loomed and presented like a disorder.

The second evening on the east coast Valerie, Candy, and Jesse went to their friend's' house, and Jesse watched as someone's brother came in smoked the *green*, and fell asleep in a living room chair. Right before dawn, the older brother woke him from his drugged sleep to warn him that their parents were arriving home soon. He nearly got hurt as the younger brother "went off" like a bomb. The man destroyed everything, splintering bookshelves with their rows of fine glass collectibles and crystal, ripping pictures off the walls, and drapes from the bay window. His final gesture was to pick up the lazy boy in which he had been sleeping and throw it through his parent's front bay window.

Jesse watched from upstairs. "I feel like this trip has been a mistake."

Valerie tried to reassure her. "I'll call a taxi; we don't have to stay here. I've got another friend; we can stay there."

They fled before the police arrived.

Reb's Fireside Inn was another shock. The table dances were not the austere two feet away show. Instead, the club (and the vice) turned a blind eye to the rubbing and fondling that took place during the table dances. The club became renowned for them; even the vice squad visited regularly to receive the same non-judgmental treatment as a civilian. The alcohol and money flowed. The owner wanted to believe he ran an upstanding club, but everyone knew it was a dive, and for a few dollars you could suck on nipples and stick your finger up some strange crotch.

Generally, Jesse had deliberately stayed away from places where the management wanted soft pornography, lots of spread-eagle lying on ones back. In this joint it was not unusual for a dancer to get just drunk enough that her G-string would slide to the side to give spectators a better view. It wasn't Jesse's style, never-the-less, the customers were generous. The first week Jesse received a fifty-dollar tip, and the second week she received her very first one-hundred-dollar tip in her entire career. In the past Jesse had turned a desperate trick or two, but as long as she could generate money by dancing, she wasn't interested in the many opportunities for extracurricular money. Jesse felt like she could never be as desperate as when she was running with Jack the junkie. With steady tips and a tax-free salary, Jesse maintained a standard of behavior that was openly mocked by the other girls. They thought she was a prude. She believed that the money she made was sufficient without having to prostitute herself.

While watching the women who were engaging in, what looked like, public foreplay with their customers, Jesse decided that, as comfortable as she was with sex and her body, she did not enjoy the phony exploited way that she felt when she engaged in prostitution on any level. Having been around countless dancers who sold their bodies, still Jesse could never figure out how to not be repulsed. She had to be attracted for the act of sex to feel right. However, Jesse soon discovered that she would have to engage in the high-contact table dances she had seen if she wanted to make enough money to justify this trip. She watched and learned as one dancer eased-up between the legs of a sitting customer and leaned over so that her breasts were on either side of the man's face, on his cheeks, his nose was in the middle of her sweaty sternum. Then the dancer typically covered her nipples with her own hands, protectively, and brushed the man's cheeks, whiskered or shaven, with the mounds of her breasts. The quicker a woman could learn to do the perfunctory movements, the more dollars she could rake in.

Jesse was a quick learner and soon was heading to the dressing room on her breaks with her G-string stuffed full of bills. Jesse was exhilarated, she thought *for the first time in my life she I am finally making what I'm worth* as she slammed the metal door of her locker. She still didn't make the hundreds that some of the dancers pulled in, but she made two hundred a night consistently, and if she continued doing well, she would make her goals, and head back to Albuquerque. Being a homebody at core, she always looked forward to returning home after she had earned money to pay bills. Already she felt ready to fly back and she had only been gone a few weeks.

Valerie stayed behind in Maryland while Jesse flew back home to New Mexico. She did not plan to stay long in Albuquerque. While picking up a few shifts back at the Round-Up Jesse met another dancer who was hungry for a better paying gig. Still primed with the memory of the tips she had made, Jesse offered to drive Nova to Maryland and back. This time Jesse was the one who knew the ropes. She even managed to rent a whole basement apartment for them from a waitress she had met at Reb's on her first trip.

It was a busy Saturday night; Jesse was working the room when a couple of good-looking men caught her attention. The one chubby faced blue-eyed man called her over and whispered in her ear that she could have the dollar or what was under it. The dollar was folded lengthwise, and up on its ends. Jesse picked it up to see a rail of powder sitting there.

She leaned over and asked, "What is it?"

With glossy eyes, he smiled and answered, "Coke."

He quickly handed her a two-inch straw, she bent over from the waist, put it into her nostril and sniffed. Within a minute she felt a surge of energy.

"Can I have the dollar too?" she asked with newfound assertiveness.

"Sure, if you do me a favor and ask your girlfriend to come over and have a drink with us.

Jesse was happy to accommodate him not stopping to wonder how it was she always attracted drug dealers. Tracy was not your stereotypical dealer. He looked like a college student. He had three friends he had known since high school who liked to go in on an ounce of cocaine a few times a year. The price was $1600, a mere four hundred apiece. Tracy commented that he was coming back from a run to Florida where his contact lived when Smuggler's Blues came on the radio. Jesse wondered, art imitating life, or life imitating art?

Nova came over to the table; she was an immediate hit with the guys, Tracy and Mike. The coke was euphoric. Jesse was not so familiar with cocaine and had forgotten how good chemicals could be. Nova and Jesse agreed to go out and party with them after work.

Jesse was oblivious to the fact that Tracy was enamored with Nova. But when it became apparent that Nova did not want to have sex with him, Tracy turned to Jesse, and she jumped at the chance while Nova crashed on the couch.

Tracy invited Jesse to stay at his house. It didn't hurt Nova's feelings because she preferred having the rental to herself. For the next week, every chance they got, Tracy and Jesse hung out. Jesse liked to drink white Zinfandel wine to help her come down from the coke. A bottle wasn't enough, a box was too much.

Nova had made a pile of money and was in a hurry to depart back to the land of enchantment. Jesse had become enchanted with Tracy, so she told him that she would be back to stay as soon as she could. He didn't believe her.

The trip back to New Mexico was without incident, the Nissan SX200 performed; Jesse raced a Corvette in her four-cylinder car, and both of them flashed their tits at truckers as they flew down the highway back to New Mexico. Jesse was jubilant; she was in-love, she thought.

Nova had made her quota and had yearned for home almost from the first day they had arrived in Maryland. All Jesse wanted was to turn around and go back to Bowie, Maryland to be with Tracy. When she arrived home, she was cold toward Robbie, and kept telling him that she was going back unless she could make enough money to pay her car payment and credit card bills. But she already knew that the club scene was dried up and that her return to the east coast was inevitable. She did not tell him that she had found someone else. She emphasized her financial woes and was resolute in her decision to leave. This time she would take Jules with her. Within a couple of weeks, she had closed her accounts, and transferred responsibility for utilities and rent to Robbie. It was the first time in eight years that he had to be responsible for all the maintenance details of living. She had been the shopper, cook, accountant, domestic help and bed partner but did not feel loved, cherished, or protected enough to continue to stick with him. She was deliberate and clear with her intentions to depart; only Robbie could not see her clarity. On the day she was preparing to leave, Robbie cornered her and dropped to his knees.

"Jesse, please don't leave; we're good with each other." His eyes were red with tears.

"I can't Robbie, I have to go where the money is; you can't support me and Jules," her voice obstinate and bitter. She had supported him through the last eight years, and now she was tired of what he was, and tired of what he wasn't. She felt like she needed to go looking for an opportunity to progress more quickly instead of simply existing. Like times before, the road called.

361

Jules was not thrilled with the prospect. "I don't want to move to the east coast," he complained to Jesse. She could only offer him her logic, "I can't make enough money here in Albuquerque anymore. I found this club where I can make better money than I ever have before. We will be able to get ahead, besides there are good people everywhere. You'll have new friends... it's like an adventure."

She wished, like an insistent mantra, for power, a greater ability to control the events and progression of her life. She felt like she was forever at the mercy of outside forces. She was at the mercy of the club owners, and she was painfully aware of her deficits in such a competitive field as the flesh market. Her support network was tenuous at best, and not having time to cultivate friends who might have helped, she doggedly did what she knew had not failed in the past. She danced.

When first she started dancing with her clothes off, she explained to those who asked her why she did it, "If I could make a living dancing with my clothes on, that's what I would do, but it's not possible for me, so I do the next best thing."

Jules accepted his mother's non-conformist nature and spontaneous decision-making because he had to; he was twelve. He packed up his clothes, and favorite toys. Jesse stuffed the car with her uniforms of the 'business', the capes, costumes, beaded bras and G-strings, and they left New Mexico.

Jesse had bought a gram of methamphetamine for the road. She did not have back up money for motel rooms or any accidental contingencies, however she felt that having speed was essential for getting her through the next 1800 miles of driving. Jesse's propensity for making poor decisions escalated when she was under the influence of amphetamines. Somewhere on a long stretch of highway in Oklahoma Jesse started playing road tag with a truck-driver which resulted in both pulling over and chatting a bit.

"Hey, where are you headed?" He asked, obviously intrigued.

"I'm headed for Maryland; I found a gig in Waldorf where the tips are really excellent; I'm a dancer. This is my son Jules."

The trucker, whose name she didn't know, asked Jules if he had ever been inside a big rig tractor trailer.

"Nope," Jules answered directly.

"If it ok with your mom, you can ride with me for a few miles; would you like that?"

Jesse's intuitive scanner didn't pick-up on anything weird, so she left the decision to Jules.

"Do you want a ride in a big-rig?"

"Sure." And up into the cab of the truck Jules climbed. He looked so small. Jesse was thinking that here was an opportunity for him to have this unique experience that he probably would not otherwise have. The trucker and Jesse agreed to meet-up ahead five miles at the next exit.

The minute Jesse slid into her seat she felt apprehension; the speed had her second guessing and questioning herself. Then the reprimands began, *what a stupid, risky stunt to pull,* and as her warnings to herself got more persistent, and the huge inappropriateness of the situation became a worry, and then a fear, Jesse calmed herself and followed closely reassuring herself that she wouldn't lose her son; that man did not want a twelve year old to care take. The exit finally appeared. They pulled into the rest stop, where Jesse retrieved Jules. Jules said thanks and disappeared back to their car.

Jesse felt stupid and vulnerable as she talked with the trucker, "Well, thank you for giving my son a ride in a big rig; it's probably the only chance he'll get."

"Do you want to meet at the Cracker Barrel just a few miles ahead? I'll buy you and Jules lunch." He asked sincerely. Jesse felt dread, wanting to escape. "Sure, that sounds good," she lied.

When they got to the exit Jesse kept going straight. She explained to Jules, "I really don't want to waste the time stopping to eat right now. You don't mind, do you?"

"Nah, it doesn't matter to me. He seemed like a nice guy."

"Yeah, but I realized if I intend to get to Maryland and start working, I'd better keep going."

Jesse felt such a surge of relief to have Jules beside her, back inside the car. She did not say to him that she was afraid that he could have been hurt or kidnapped. Yet those were some of the worst thoughts pulsing through Jesse's brain as she had followed closely behind the rig.

They finally arrived in Bowie in the middle of the afternoon on a Sunday after being misdirected south when they should have continued north. Jesse's took a deep breath as she turned the car into the dirt and gravel driveway. Tracy greeted them; Jesse was exhausted but exhilarated at having ripped up her fifteen-year roots in New Mexico. She felt excited about life and energized by the prospect of making decent money for a change. And none too soon, she was about to have her thirty-eighth birthday.

Jesse was beaming, "See I told you I'd be back in a month; this is my son Jules."

Tracy a short, chubby man with thinning blond hair and bright blue eyes welcomed Jules, put his arm around Jesse and led them on a tour of the cabin. His screened in front porch was hung thick with drying animal pelts, mostly raccoon and fox. The kitchen was kept toasty in winter by a vintage potbelly stove fed with sticks. The rest of the house was equally rustic with a huge wood burning stove in the middle of the living room that required more tending and maintenance than the kitchen stove, so was not used unless temperatures dropped.

It was summer, so the first thing Jesse and Jules did was go for a hike behind the cabin where there was a four-acre pond and wild land surrounding it. Jules seemed to welcome the change, and as soon as he made some friends, he took every opportunity to hang-out with them. Jesse visited the house of Jules's newest friend, Eric, who was a couple of years older, and spoke with his mother who was divorced and worked as a nurse. Jesse felt relieved that Jules had met a friend; he would not be lonely and miserable.

Tracy had a good paying gig. A friend from high school who was now a major land developer, hired him for post-construction cleaning, making houses pretty for the realtor and prospective buyers. He pocketed seventy-five dollars a house and could stay busy, sometimes knocking out three or four houses in a day. Enough work to allow Tracy to buy an ounce of cocaine and split it. He had his quarter to divide into sellable packets so he could make back his investment and have enough to play with.

Jesse had tried coke before, but since it was not readily available in the southwest, she was unfamiliar with its addictive properties. She soon found herself looking for Tracy's stash when it seemed like he wasn't sharing.

One day while Jules and Jesse were sightseeing in Washington, D.C. Jules told his mom outright, "I don't want you doing that stuff!"

Jesse answered her son knowing that she did not have a limitless supply of money to feed a chronic coke habit, "Don't worry, it can't hurt me, and I'm just enjoying it while it's available."

Jules thought his mom might become a statistic. He did not know that sniffing coke was mild compared to the crystal ships she had been sailing in Albuquerque. He was becoming a teenager, and never having been sheltered, his mother's behavior was not unusual, only a cause for anxiety and concern. He was still getting used to being away from the home he had known, and the big man he called "dad." He missed feeling like they had 'back-up', but a new state and a new school kept Jules too busy for him to become melancholy.

Tracy taught Jules how to shoot a rifle and play skeet. Eric taught Jules how to smoke cigarettes. Being so enthralled with her new boyfriend, Jesse didn't notice anything different about Jules, only that he wanted to be with his friends most of the time, and why not, he was almost thirteen.

What had caused Jesse to migrate to the east coast? She said it was because she had never been there before and had an idea that the area would be vibrating with creativity. Perhaps a calendar picture of December with snow, and the warm glow from windows in distant houses had planted its image in her mind and had come to fruition at last. Jesse's need for money and her propensity to chase cock is what compelled her to a dot on the map in Southern Maryland.

For the first few months Tracy introduced her to the Chesapeake Bay culture. They went boating, water-skiing, snow-skiing, and to Baltimore's Inner Harbor where she ate fresh shucked oysters for the first time. He wined her, fed her, drugged her, and then began to neglect her. On her thirty-eighth birthday Jesse was alone. A customer had given her a rose the night before. She looked at it in the vase by the window, the rain accumulating and dripping down the pane of glass like tears she could not stop.

Chesapeake Beach

esse knew Tracy's infatuation with her was short-lived when she got a card with the word *ephemeral* written on it. Jesse countered by giving him a card that said *tenacious*. But separation was inevitable when Tracy announced that he would be moving to Washington State. Jesse and Jules would have to find another place to live. Jesse went into alarm mode for no good reason because immediately one of the dancers at work offered to split the rent with her on an apartment she was renting in Chesapeake Beach. She was not keen on apartments. She had always managed to find a cheap house, or split the rent on one, but Jesse was anxious to find a place so she figured she would keep her mouth shut and see what Blondie's place looked like.

Blondie lived in an apartment on top of a liquor store. It was designed to look like a light house, octagonal in shape with windows all around the outside where the bedrooms, closets, and kitchen were. The inner room was carpeted bright green and was divided to accommodate both a couch for the living area, and a table and chairs for the dining side. The center of the apartment had a glass attic-type room where the green working lighthouse lamp could be turned on. Jesse wondered if the neighbors liked the spinning flashing replica. This arrangement lasted three months before both Blondie and Jesse were sick of each other. Blondie's idea of funny was to fart and then walk away.

During her walks around town, Jesse had found a quaint fabric and quilting shop. She had fast become friends with Christine, the women who managed it. When Blondie flew into a rage, Christine came to the rescue by offering her front room until something permanent would present itself. Her husband had died a year earlier, so it seemed like she welcomed the company. Jesse offered to help her clean out his room that had not been touched since his passing.

She and Jules camped out in Christine's living room. From the open front door, they could hear the waves of the Chesapeake Bay slapping the dock that substituted for a front porch. After tucking Jules into bed, Jesse listened to the soothing murmurings of the wetlands, caught in a net of safety.

Then a small inexpensive efficiency apartment became available near the quilt shop. Jesse and Jules moved again. This little cardboard box was miserable, hot and humid. Since it had only one bedroom, the living room was officially Jules. Jesse got the room with the paper accordion slide door. At least she didn't have to put up with an inconsiderate roommate. The Chesapeake Bay was close by. It was like living in a resort area with a steady bustling crowd of speed boats, sailboats, skipjacks, and jet skis.

Jules was adaptable and resilient. He attended Junior high school, found a couple of friends, and took to exploring the beach with them. Jesse felt fortunate that Jules was not a juvenile delinquent. He wasn't a great academic achiever, but he got Cs and a few Bs in art, so she didn't worry about

369

him too much. He liked to do what he wanted to do, but he didn't demonstrate explosive anger, or exploitative anti-social traits like meanness and insensitivity. He would hang out with his friends, listen to music, or play video games.

He liked to ride his bike and watch a TV whenever one was around. Although Jesse felt like Jules could be performing better in school, having experienced the oppressive parenting style of her mother, she was inclined to leave Jules alone because it seemed like she was criticizing him whenever she tried to talk about his grades.

Her incessant yearning for a companion never left. It only receded at times when she had to deal with a crisis, and then returned unrelenting during quiet times. A Sunday afternoon with the community alive; families gathered around picnic tables, the sound of mowers, smell of grass, and stereo boom boxes thumping rolling down the road, Jesse had time to look around and notice how empty of romance her life was; except, of course, for her thirteen-year-old son, no one cared whether she lived, died, succeeded, or failed. It had always felt like this, scraping, scratching, and here she was at 39, with nothing and nobody.

She walked three blocks toward the Chesapeake Bay; she had her thirty-five-millimeter camera hanging from a strap around her neck. Her recent arrival to this picturesque water town motivated her like a tourist, and with an artist's eye, she was steadily capturing images of still life and becoming a proficient photographer. Today she felt sad and dejected from Tracy's boot. The day was gray; she saw what she feared was her destiny, a sign: Dead End Street.

Carol Lynn Jones, MSW

Don't Mess with the Missionary Man

*D*ancing at the Fireside Inn Jesse met Bradley, a blue-eyed pretty-boy with confidence and charm. He would never be the Air Force One pilot that his father had been, but he was a damn good computer salesman, and was making exorbitant money for a twenty-five-year-old college drop out. Riding the crest of the personal computer boom, everyone from student to professional had to have one. Bradley worked in a computer showroom and caught the money as the customers threw it at him. His sales bonus for one week in November was five thousand dollars.

He came on to Jesse like an infatuated high school student for his teacher, but he was tipping heavily so she returned to his table again and again. He bought her drinks and kept insisting that she give him table dances for which he paid generously. By the end of the night, she gave him her phone number.

When Jesse walked out of the club Brad was standing by his customized VW bug.

"Jesse, I wanted to tell you how much I enjoyed your dancing, and your company. You're really interesting to talk to."

"Well, I spend a lot of time reading books when I'm not dancing. I guess you could call me a philosopher," Jesse responded without much egotism.

Their faces close, they kissed. Turning to leave, without under ware she flipped her skirt over her head Can-Can style, mooned him, laughed and disappeared into her open car door. She smiled and waved, believing she would never see him again.

To her surprise, he called and invited her to dinner. She made reservations at her favorite bayside restaurant. He did not take his eyes off her. He ordered wine; they devoured lobster bisque, and crab cakes. The Chesapeake Bay rocked the boats sensually against the dock outside the restaurant. Toward the end of the meal, Brad excused himself, and went to the bathroom. Jesse thought it odd that he did not return for over twenty minutes. Meanwhile she drank wine thoroughly enjoying the ambiance. When he returned, he leaned over and kissed her on the neck. She took him home to her lonely bed, and they made lusty love. She had not been driven to such climactic heights since leaving Robbie in New Mexico.

Brad courted her and told her all the words a struggling single mother wants to hear, similarly, words a frightened aging topless dancer wants to hear. Brad was her knight in shining armor not considering what their fifteen years age difference might mean. They cruised to Ocean City and swam in the clear, turquoise opalescent surf. At the Baltimore Inner Harbor, in a five-star hotel they rode up to the third floor bar in the glass elevator kissing and caressing each other. She became intensely attached to his attention, his sexual inventiveness, and drive.

After two weeks of non-stop dating Jesse stopped by the quilt shop to share her happiness with a new girlfriend.

"Janie, he's too good to be true. He is sweet and caring and has a great paying job! He wants me to stop dancing so he can take care of me. I'm so happy."

In the spirit of a true friend, Janie responded, "Well Jesse the only thing I can say is that if someone seems too good to be true, maybe he is."

Jesse did not want to hear it. She was convinced that Bradley's intensity was proof that finally she had found real love. Brad came over on a Monday; he said he had taken the day off work because he had something important to tell Jesse.

"I fought with myself, but I love you too much to continue on this way. I'm married."

The rug flew out from underneath her feet.

"Ok, well, thank you for letting me know." She responded stoically, and turned away from him, but he stopped her. He reached and brought her into his arms. She could not hold back her emotions.

"I am so sorry; I didn't want to lie to you. You are quite different from what I imagined you'd be. I fell in love with you," he whispered.

Brad's words were hurting her even more, until he said, "I'm going to divorce my wife. We haven't been sleeping together for at least a year."

Then he said something that gripped Jesse heart. "I thought about this and realized that if I let you go, I might never find love again."

At that moment Jesse felt a wave of relief and contentment. They kissed long and deep. She was home.

Brad swept into Jesse's life and started making changes. He found her a two-bedroom house in North

Beach and gave her the deposit and first month's rent so that she and Jules wouldn't have to live in the tiny cracker box that was all she could afford. He moved in, bringing a computer and some clothes. Jesse continued to work while custom designing her schedule to suit Brad's wishes. Before Jesse left Robbie, her attitude had been imperious and unrelentingly selfish, now she was allowing this youngster to run things. She was beginning to learn how incompatible some of their values and beliefs were, but she remained vested in their mutual fantasy. They would get married, move to rural Pennsylvania, and live happily ever after.

Brad's divorce was granted. They waited in the courthouse to find out how much child support his ex would get for his two boys. Then they walked out, free to be with each other.

Having Brad around was wonderful and annoying. Since Jesse was used to having complete control over her life, especially over the money. She tended to be obsessive about paying the rent and bills punctually whereas he tended to spend money frivolously buying what he wanted and paying bills with whatever money was left over after his sprees. He liked to laugh about his addictions, all of them. He was addicted to food, cigarettes, alcohol, and sex, just to name a few. Jesse indulged in drinking when she was with him. They drank Tanqueray and tonic and seduced each other again and again.

Now that she had "her man" at home, she resented having to go to work at all. Brad was relaxed and talking about his day. She felt warm listening to him share his thoughts with her.

"I hope you don't mind but I masturbated on your bathrobe while you were gone. I couldn't help myself. I just love the way you smell, and your pink satin robe was hanging on the door of the closet."

It struck Jesse as being so creepy and obsessive. "What! Why? Why would you waste your time? After all I am right here. You knew I'd be home in a little while?"

Brad had a hurt look on his face. Later she supposed that he might think it was sexy or flattering to her that her clothes provoked the lust in him, but right at that moment she felt disgusted. Not one to hide her feelings, she honestly could not fathom his actions. Did he really think that story was a turn-on?

The next day Jules brought home a study sheet about dinosaurs and the different periods of time in which they existed.

"Brad, look what we're studying in school?" Jules said, trying to relate to him.

Brad took the sheet from Jules hand, looked it over and threw it on the floor saying, "This is all bull-shit! If you study the Bible, it tells us that the world is not as old as what that paper says."

Jesse responded, feeling protective toward Jules, "What about carbon dating, is that bull-shit too? You think all the scientists and researchers, they're all liars; none of them know what's going on, huh?"

Brad did not answer. This was the first time Jesse realized the extent of his ignorance. When they first met, he had told her he was a Christian, but she didn't know to what degree he had been indoctrinated. Jesse had read books that proposed alternative explanations to the ones postulated by the Bible thumpers. She had read The Passover Plot, a book that hypothesized Jesus's resurrection as a staged event, and Those Incredible Christians, another book that shed light on the inconsistencies throughout the Bible's pages.

Jesse had long ago given up the idea of a savior. It seemed likely that humans were required to save themselves through the process of incremental awakening of consciousness. That Christians could simply utter a few 'sincere' words about accepting Christ, and magically one's life would be "straightened out," their immortal souls saved from eternal damnation, seemed like a hustle, a lie to keep people strapped to the church. Jesse was interested in this present life, not some hypothetical one, after death. It seemed ludicrous that Christians would deny their present desires in order to offset the danger of some speculative hell fires.

Jules was almost fourteen. Jesse asked him what he thought of Brad, and he answered, a bit sarcastically, "It's cool. You brought home a playmate for me," alluding to the eleven years that separated them.

Though untraditional, Jules and Jesse's relationship was solid. Her parenting skills were few, she treated Jules more like her kid brother than like a mother, admonishing, and threatening corporeal punishment. Jesse maintained an interest in what Jules was doing in school, though she was vaguely aware that her lifestyle kept her from fully engaging in his education. She was always working evenings when PTA meetings were scheduled, and if asked she would admit that she expected Jules to do his best. Deep down, she trusted him, perhaps naively. He was smart and would be able to recognize trouble. Practical in her thinking, Jesse knew that she could not ride on her son's shoulder. He would have to walk his path, with or without her consent. It was his individual journey.

She was already practicing the Buddhist principle of 'detachment', that is, not being emotionally attached to a particular outcome. She realized that it is a set-up when we constantly want reality to comply with our expectations, and then allow ourselves to be unhappy when we "don't get what we want." No wonder half of the population is depressed.

Having a live-in boyfriend kept Jesse home nights, and much of the pressure of being the only income was alleviated. She breathed easier, and a renewed sense of loving life infused her being. After hearing reassurances from Brad that their age-difference was not significant, Jesse began to enter the ongoing 'forever-fantasy'. They planned to marry.

Brad's lust was a wonder to behold. He was romantic too, bringing her flowers, making reservations at the fanciest restaurants in the area, and initiating sex in the car on the way to the date-place. Many drinks later, they would find woods, or an alley to continue their antics. They got stopped by the D.C. police for circling the rotunda in front of the capitol building too many times while mutually pleasuring each other. Jesse enjoyed their sex games and went along with Brad's goal of beating their highest number of orgasms in a weekend. He took her to a comedy club on a Monday night near Georgetown. Afterwards, the two of them staggered back toward the car. As they passed along the edge of a park full of trees, bushes and walkways, Brad pulled Jesse's hand, guiding her back into the grassy, lush interior. There he fondled Jesse until she was wet. He spread his jacket on the grass, took off her panties and told her to sit on his erect cock. No one could see because Jesse wore a long skirt, and although it was apparent what they were doing, no flesh was showing. Jesse was Brad's sex slave. No place was too public. If he could devise a way, they would try it, including driving down the highway with her straddled across his lap. Mostly, she enjoyed these semi-public displays; though at times she felt humiliated, still she was willing to gratify his every sexual wish.

Brad wanted to set a date mostly because as a fundamentalist Christian, he was not comfortable living in sin. Hypocritical as it seemed, she agreed. Apparently, Brad had forgotten that he began the illicit relationship with her while he was married!

They had just finished making love and were lying entwined when Brad said, "You know Jesse, one thing that I have never experienced, and I have been wanting to try, is a ménage a tois."

"Really?" She knew exactly what he was asking.

He continued on, "I really would like to experience it once before we get married. I bet you could find one of your girlfriends who would do it with us. I could pay her. What do you think?"

Jesse was immediately conflicted; on one hand how could a man who was supposedly in love with her be thinking about having sex with another woman? Jesse could understand Brad's desire. She had no interest because she was satisfied being a couple. But love is compromising and even long-suffering, to quote a biblical term and far be-it for Jesse to deny Brad what she herself had already experienced.

"I guess I could try. I'm not into women; I would only be doing it for you," she answered rather sadly.

Brad pulled her close, and started massaging her breast, "It would mean so much to me; I would know that you really love me."

Every self-sacrificing woman has responded to similar words, and pleas. It is a woman's nature to accommodate her mate. Jesse's self-esteem was dependent on Brad's love and acceptance of her. She wasn't aware of it, but it motivated her behavior all the same.

I don't know, I'm not very close to any of the dancers. I doubt if I can get anyone to go with us."

"The girl with the long black hair, she seems to like you."

"Yeah, actually she might do it. I think she has turned tricks; she'd probably do it for a hundred."

That night when Jesse posed the question to Deena, she was surprised to hear her answer.

"Sure, I'd like to do that!"

"Well, we could give you some money for your time, or if you'd like maybe we could get some coke."

"No, I don't need all that. Why don't you introduce me to this fiancé of yours?"

Deena and Brad hit it off; Jesse had to manage her jealousy as she watched the two of them chatter. It was arranged for Saturday; no one had to be anywhere the next day and fourteen-year-old Jules would be staying at his friend's house who had an X-Box. It was the perfect opportunity for the planned event.

380

Jesse felt like heavily drinking Saturday afternoon. She was nervous. Deena laughed at her, "It'll be fun; I don't bite."

They had both arranged to work the early shift and were done by eight. Brad picked them up and they headed for the city. Washington, D.C. was filled with bars, pubs, and sidewalk cafés. Just about any musical genre was available, the blues, bluegrass, and rock. They dined and Jesse felt the sexual tension arising. This was not her idea of fun; she didn't want to share Bradley. So, she drank enough to put her critic asleep, and another persona took over who said life is an experiment. *It won't kill me.*

When they arrived home, everyone was ready for bed. Jesse just wanted to get it over with. She had decided she would enjoy it, but this was not something that she wanted to incorporate into her lifestyle. Brad had promised that it would only be the one time, so Jesse had made a concession knowing it was time limited.

All three players were invested in giving the others the best time. Truly, a circus could not have had any more suspense, acrobatics, climaxes, and death-defying leaps. At one point Jesse was underneath licking Deena's clitoris, while Brad was ass-fucking her. It was kinky. Jesse wondered how she endured the pounding and was glad it was Deena and not her. Finally, the ride slowed down and skidded to a squeaky stop. Everyone drank water and said good night. Jesse lay beside her husband-to-be in the dark, awake and bored, listening to them snore.

The next day Brad showered Jesse with admiration for giving of herself and being so loving with Deena. Jesse was relieved, and eager to get on with planning their wedding.

Deena was addicted to crack. The dancers called it rock because it looks like, a crystalline pebble. She spent a lot of her time hooking-up so she could buy, transport, or smoke 'rock'. She had often traded sex for the drug, and after a great big drag of the chemical smoke, she would brag about escapades with tricks, johns, and cops. She was the opposite of Jesse. Jesse liked to get high and visualize what a Utopian society would look like, and she could go all night if she had someone to talk to about the many kinds of significant societal changes that are possible. Only once did Jesse make the mistake of getting high with Deena. Suddenly she was Deena's captive audience bombarded with non-stop talk about her many scrapes with the law, and the last time she had assaulted a cop. Being self-centered she dominated the entire conversation, not allowing anyone else to take it in a different direction; it was Deena's show.

Jesse was reminded that it was not only the drug that made a person high, but it was also the company. Some people were not fun to be around; she called them kill-buzz people. Deena was like that, her beauty drew you in, and then her harshness and arrogant cynicism pushed you away, hopefully before you got burned.

It was in Jesse's nature to want to help and nurture people. Probably years of her own neglect had sensitized her to the universal need. It was in that mood that Jesse asked Deena if she wanted to stay with them for a while so that she could take a break from the crack. It wasn't as available in this bayside town as it was in the city. While she stayed here, her access to 'rock' would be limited.

"You told me you wanted to slow down, detox, right? Well, you can stay here, relax, take a break from the crack. We will feed you, and you can hang out and watch some TV, get your mind off your problems. If you can stay away from that shit for about a week, it'll give you a head start on your recovery."

"I suppose so, but I can't stay here long. Bills don't pay themselves. I've got to get back to work soon,"

Then the two of them figured out what the sleeping arrangements would be since last evening's romp was a one-time event. The living room couch folded out into an adequate bed. They decided Jules could sleep out there and that would give Deena the privacy of Jules's room for the short time she would be here in recovery and retreat.

That evening after dinner they all gathered around the TV and chattered like any family might, the one difference being that this was not just any family. Somewhere during the commercials light bantering started. Jesse goaded Deena into giving her teenage son, Jules, a piece-of-ass; innocent, though risqué, teasing.

The next morning Jesse unexpectedly walked in on the two of them engaged in sex. Turning away, she walked back into the bedroom and naively blurted out to Brad what she had witnessed. He was barely awake and began to rant about the immorality of it as he headed for the bathroom. Realizing her mistake, she charged into the living room and lied that Brad had seen them and wasn't very pleased. Then Jesse told Jules that it might be a good idea to get dressed and take a bike ride.

"I don't know why Brad is reacting like this; it's stupid! I'm sorry." Jesse felt awful.

"It's OK mom; I'll be over at Wayne's house." Jules quickly saw the sensible action to take and was out the door.

"Deena, I don't see anything horrible about what you guys did. I sure didn't expect Brad to lose his mind over this, especially after our threesome."

"What a hypocrite! After he indulged in his own a-moral sexual fantasy how could he judge either Jules or me?"

Agreeing, Jesse knew for a fact that Brad had lost his virginity at ten to a neighboring teenager, a few years his senior. She had not heard him complain about its ill-effects on his life.

Being insecure, and doubtful enough of her own behavior to feel guilty, Deena shifted into flight mode, a survival instinct Jesse was well acquainted with.

"I'm sorry Deena, I feel like this is my fault."

"Hey, don't worry. I'm going out for a little while; I need some fresh air." She gathered up her tote bag and left.

Police Brutality

*T*wo hours later, Jesse heard Deena knock on the door. Jesse opened it exclaiming, "You don't have to knock; this is your house! Besides, Brad's gone; he went to work to get some holiday-weekend, over-time pay."

Deena walked in, and started ranting, "Fucking pigs! That mother fuckin' cop Charlie Brown raped me."

"What... what are you talking about?" Jesse asked startled.

"When I left this morning, I decided I'd hitch back to D.C. to score, maybe pick-up a trick and get some rock. Instead, I got harassed by the local pigs."

Jesse could hardly believe what she was hearing. Chesapeake Beach seemed like such a sleepy little town to her.

"He forced me to have sex with him; or, he said he'd take me to the station for soliciting." So, I bent over in the back seat with the door open and that pig fucked me."

Deena did not appear to be traumatized, only angry.

"I hate mother-fucking cops." She glared at no one in particular.

Jesse recalled Deena's boasting about the time she had beat-up a policeman. She could not help but wonder about the karma she was carrying. It was odd that a woman with so much animosity attracted that which she hated most.

"This is terrible. I'm so sorry you encountered that asshole." Jesse offered weakly.

"Cops like that should be shot," Deena continued unabatedly.

"Is there anything you can do, like report his abuse?"

Deena threw Jesse a look that said don't be stupid.

"Do you want to go grocery shopping for some food since you're going to stay for a while?"

"No, I appreciate the offer, but I've got to get back to my life; I'll see you at work." Deena was animated, and Jesse could see she was ready to get back to her own stomping grounds.

"Alright, let me find my keys; I'll give you a ride to D.C. That's the least that I can do."

On the short ride to Oxen Hill, the outskirts of D.C., the two of them discussed Brad's strange reaction that morning.

"Was he jealous because he had just had sex with you, or was he thinking it was immoral? It happened on his watch as substitute dad, maybe he thought it wasn't good parenting?" They snickered.

"I think he was acting like a territorial male," Deena offered. "He probably reacted from a gut-level instinct. The little bull challenged the big bull!"

It seemed like Deena knew men, and why wouldn't she? She had danced for 12 years and had more often than not resorted to sex as a bartering tool for drugs, money and whatever else she needed. Where could a predator like Deena find a more fecund hunting ground than the clubs where she danced?

Jesse was not in the habit of deliberately using men. First, she did not consider herself all 'that', and second, she focused primarily on developing her potential, getting training, refining her skills, rather than focusing on what others could do for her. It separated her from most of the other dancers. She hated referring to the women she worked with as dancers, mostly because they were not. They sauntered around with their clothes off and tried to trick men into paying. Most discovered that it was easier to date a guy and lead him on to get her rent paid or a refrigerator full of food, than to beg dollar by dollar during a shift.

Jesse dropped Deena off. Suddenly relieved of her presence, she felt like a dark entity had stepped out of her car. On the drive home Jesse thought about the last few days. Over-all, she felt good. She believed that Brad deserved to have his fantasy satisfied and was happy that she was the one to do it. That said, she did not want to dwell upon it. Sharing her man was not agreeable to her.

The Move

rad and Jesse had talked about moving up to a small town in Pennsylvania, Fairfield, near Ski Liberty. In fact, Brad's dad had a home on the other side of the mountain's ski slope. A custom log cabin with a pentagon shaped living area, and a fireplace in the center.

Brad loved to ski and wanted to show Jesse the delights of the slopes. Dancing was her livelihood, and her interest in learning to ski was minimum. The prospect of breaking a leg was not attractive, but under Brad's spell, she was convinced that she could learn. He was so insistent that he made it impossible for her to say no. She quickly graduated from the 'bunny slope' to the intermediate where she could share the chair and mountain with Brad. He had been skiing since he could walk and had the opportunity to continue through high school. Poetry and balance on the slopes, he could snow dance, and enjoyed showing-off. Jesse watched him with fascination and admiration.

One evening Brad came home and announced that he had rented a house in Pennsylvania right near his dad's house. Jesse was not accustomed to being left out of the decision-making processes that impacted her life and Jules'. She tried to stay quiet, but then Brad was going on and on about this place and how close it was to the slopes, Jesse responded.

"When did all this happen; you just decided on the fly that we would move? How am I supposed to make money? Are there any clubs to dance in up there?"

As Jesse presented her case and accused him of being insensitive, she also was aware that she might be pushing him away with her whining. She had never depended solely upon a man. It was uncomfortable letting Brad make decisions. Noticing she had less time to pursue her own soul-sustaining activities, she dismissed the feeling telling herself that their lives would settle down once they were married. She did not yet recognize that their differences would increasingly be impossible to ignore.

Brad did not like what Jesse was saying and stormed out after telling her that he had to go and think about things. It felt like a slap. She wasn't scheduled to work, so this gave her time to think about whether she could trust Brad enough to throw her fate in with his and take the leap to another state. She was making enough money to get by, but not enough to get ahead. She wanted Brad to rescue her, to take her away from all of this. However, a cautionary voice told her not to burn her bridges, not to depend entirely upon him.

He did not call or come by for a couple of days. It was just enough silence for Jesse to become uncomfortable. When he finally did stop by (without calling first) she felt such a relief that she practically jumped into his arms. Their lovemaking was especially exuberant and passionate. Afterwards, they made plans to look at the house Brad rented. Jesse felt subdued, and passive. Not having heard from Brad, she was reminded about the bleakness of being alone again. Her quality of life was so much better when she had a partner. Alone, the struggle was enormous, and always clouded with depression. Those few days convinced her that whatever Brad's shortcomings, she would rather be with him than without him. Jesse was charmed with the house the minute she saw it nestled in its wooded, rural majesty, surrounded by idyllic rolling hills and apple orchards.

"It's like living in a postcard!" She exclaimed.

As suspected, there were no clubs or topless bars anywhere near Ski Liberty, so her dependence on Brad was secured. He told her smiling, that he wanted to take her away from her ability to dance in bars, and added that luckily for her, he was making enough money for all of them. She did not argue with him but wondered about his two- and half-hour drive to the computer showroom every day. She was going to marry this guy yet was having trouble trusting him.

They married at the courthouse and promised each other that they would have a regular wedding at a later date.

Jesse tried to recreate a stable life, like the one she had with Robbie; she cooked, and did laundry, and he brought home his paycheck. Married three weeks, one night Brad did not come home from work. Sick and worried that he was in an emergency room somewhere, Jesse could not sleep. When he finally did call, he told her he would be home shortly, and not to worry. The scene was a replication of an age-old drama. She is the adoring and dependent, betrayed wife. He is the self-serving, manipulative husband.

"I went by the Playhouse; Deena was working, and we had a few drinks. When she got off work early, she convinced me to buy some 'rock' and party with her," he narrated with a sincere look cloaking his face.

"You fucked Deena? I thought you said you were over all that?" Jesse was hurt and feeling vulnerable; not only did he deceive her, but she was in a position of not being able to leave easily.

"I am over it... I won't be stopping by there for a drink anymore; it was a mistake," his voice contrite.

"So, this won't happen again?" Her voice, laced with threat and anguish, caused Brad to put his arms around her, a technique every player masters.

Poor Jesse was exhausted from the all-night ordeal and needed sleep. It was Brad's intent to placate Jesse, and he knew all he needed was to get his lips on her genitals. Jesse allowed Brad to apologize in this manner and exploded, her climax a combination of anger, relief, and yearning fulfilled.

Soon, the ski slopes consumed Brad. Jesse did not mind; it gave her time to read and sew. For Christmas he surprised Jules with a complete setup of skis, boots, poles, snowsuit and gloves. Jesse's heart was warmed by the opportunity Brad was giving to Jules. Turns out, Jules strong legs from running cross-country in high school and a natural ability for skiing made the mountain a good place for him to channel his teenage hormones. Brad bought Jules a season ski lift pass. He covered their living expenses, however Jesse needed to continue paying for her car to the tune of $400 dollars a month, payment and insurance.

Even though Brad knew that Jesse had depended upon dancing for years, he had moved them out to rural Pennsylvania where she was out of her element. She felt uncertain and insecure about her abilities. Pressure increased, driving her to find a job, but deeper still, she felt compelled to become something more than what she had been in the past. She wanted meaningful work; work that paid her the amount of money that reflected a lifetime of effort. At age 40, she was weary of her own limitations, and the mundane routine of her life created by them. She was forever on the gerbil wheel never really getting ahead. Many times, she had asked the Great Spirit to help and guide her so that she could get away from exotic dancing. It was like quicksand, once you got used to the fast money and short hours it was difficult to justify working a regular job, gaining weight, and making less. Here was her chance to make the break.

The most obvious place to apply for work was the ski resort. It had the slopes, rentals, a snack area, restaurant, and a hotel. Jesse had hoped that Brad would be able to cover the cost of her car; after all he drove it daily. Brad wanted her to get a job at Ski Liberty because then the family would be eligible for free lift tickets. Truth be told, Jesse was afraid. She had worked a few straight jobs, and the outcome was always the same; minimum wage, boredom, disappointment, and depression. She did not fit in; she could not be punctual, and she certainly couldn't tolerate stupid people telling her what to do. Working retail, Jesse had walked off of the job screaming at her supervisor whom she had pegged as an ex-cheerleader seeking money and power and reeking of elitism and entitlement.

The lobby of the hotel was busy. Jesse took a deep breath, walked up to the front desk and asked a woman with strawberry-blond hair.

"I'm looking for work; do you have any positions open?"

The woman responded, "We have a part-time housecleaning position."

"Oh, I need full time, thanks," Jesse smiled and left. Mission accomplished. The woman had people waiting in line. Like most, Jesse hated searching for work. With dancing she had always been able find a job and didn't have to fill out a million papers; just jump up on stage, audition, and get her schedule for the week. Now she was in unfamiliar territory. She thought of herself as having no marketable skills, except for typing... slowly. Jesse felt as she did when she was a teenager, that society seemed closed and unwelcoming. She blamed her mother. She had gone over it a thousand times, if she had only been raised with love, affection, and support, her confidence and self-worth, hence, her life would have been so much better. It was a mantra that inevitably brought tears and kept Jesse in a haze of depression for years. At least she had some help now.

A week later, Brad started nagging Jesse about getting a job at Ski Liberty.

"What about the slopes? I know they need help."

"I just went over there last week, remember?" She answered defensively.

"Well, go over there again; you never know when things change."

"Oh, for crying out loud, I'll go! It's a waste of time; they told me they don't have any openings!"

She walked into a bustling lobby, not unlike the previous week. Jesse thought she saw a glimmer of recognition on the face of the woman behind the counter.

"Do you remember me from last week; I was looking for full-time employment."

"Yes, tell me, have you worked with money before?"

"Yes, I've worked retail."

"You have? Can you make change?"

"Sure," she answered, thinking, *couldn't everyone?*

The woman had a thick German accent, and a friendly smile.

"If you wait just a minute, I'll get you an application. Can you start right away?"

"Yes, I can start tomorrow!" Jesse was flabbergasted; she took the application and set a time to be interviewed the next day.

Suddenly, Jesse felt hopeful again. Her anxiety crippled her so. When it subsided, a surge of energy coursed through her. It was nice to have good news, and the belief that she could survive took front and center as fear receded.

Brad took the news without much celebration. Having come from an affluent family and background, he did not comprehend her drama.

The ski season was fast and furious. The hours of time Jesse spent at work flew by. The perks of the job were the free ski pass, and the employee Christmas party. Although Jesse rarely drank now that she was not working in bars, she still enjoyed getting hammered with Brad. It was then that their differences disappeared. They flirted, danced, and seduced each other, and then went home to fuck wildly.

Spring brought stillness to the ski resort, at least until summer when the rooms were filled with vacationers and golfers. Jesse stayed employed for a year, spending long hours of solitude watching the desk on the second shift with few customers. She vowed to finish a short story she had begun, and this was just the right situation conducive to that end.

In the meantime, Brad had gotten restless, and began talking about how he wanted them to move to Colorado. Jesse was opposed.

"Damn it, Brad, I just left that part of the country. I'm not finished with the east coast yet; besides I think it's really insensitive of you to even consider jerking Jules out of school in his senior year."

"Well, I'm going. If you don't want to go with me that's your choice."

She thought Brad was kidding; she was mistaken. By their next conversation, Brad was packing his WV bug, heading off to Denver.

Abandoned in a Pennsylvania Postcard

*T*he wreckage of her marriage overwhelmed Jesse; she looked at the wedding ring, realizing that it had been no guarantee. Brad left her with the nearly new Subaru Justy that he had recently purchased. It was a three-cylinder car with predictably excellent mileage. Brad might have realized that Jesse would need to drive to a city to work. She was relieved and in no small way grateful, even though it did not sooth her broken heart. The car never got washed for the entire time she owned it. Brad had been driving her beautiful Nissan sports car when it got reared-ended and totaled so she wound up with his little tin-can on wheels. She treated it like a trash-can; it could not compare with her lost Nissan SX.

Jesse and Brad had frequented a local bar, so after he left for Colorado, she found herself there on a barstool flirting with a man named Tom. They became lovers for a couple of months. The relationship wasn't sustainable; he had just turned twenty-one. It seemed funny to Jesse that when she and Brad had fought over his unfounded jealousy, he would throw it in her face that she was looking for a younger man, which of course she wasn't. But here she was having sex with a man four years younger, Brad's worst fear!

Jesse went back to the kind of work she knew. Her reputation as a dependable hard-working dancer got her rehired at the Playhouse, a club two hour's drive south from her Pennsylvania home. It wasn't long before Jesse found a waitress willing to rent her a room so that she didn't have to make the hundred-twenty-mile round-trip drive every workday. The manager scheduled her shifts consecutively so she could work in three- or four-day blocks, and then drive home to be with her teenage son for a few days. Jesse wanted to work the busiest shifts on the weekends which, regrettably, left Jules alone. Jesse named the house The Hotel California; it became the clubhouse with no adult supervision, the tales of the parties, legend.

Brad's leaving tripped Jesse's long cultivated panic button. Being thrown back into a position of financial responsibility escalated her anxieties. How would she manage to pay rent, utilities, gas, food, and provide her son with the extras that he needed?

Occasionally she went off with someone to snort cocaine after her shift. Jesse still suffered daily from Brad's departure. Sniffing coke and engaging in social discourse provided distraction from her misery. Men were curious about the dancer they called Easy. It wasn't unusual for her to be invited to do free cocaine. She quickly discovered that cocaine was everyone's drug of choice on the east coast. Twenty years after her first encounter with mood altering drugs, she found herself dropped into this cocaine culture. Jesse was not a cliché; she attended parties with the understanding that she would not provide sexual services; they wanted her company anyway. Jesse's insatiable hunger for books, and knowledge along with her uncanny ability to see the underlying connections made her a hit among these cocaine users. Few of them had much education whereas Jesse had been to college. Her impulse to teach and offer advice was easy to act upon during these chemically charged social situations. She became aware of her desire to bring people to the light, to facilitate the expansion of their awareness. She was intuitive in knowing what a person might need to hear.

Hours of coke and mind-melding conversations depleted Jesse's reserves. With everyone asleep and Jesse pacing at dawn, she called Jules and broke down asking for forgiveness.

"Mom stop crying. Are you alright?"

"Yes"

"Why are you crying?"

"Because I feel like I'm a horrible mother. I stayed out all night and I'm not there. Instead, I'm here with a bunch of passed out people who I don't give a shit about."

"Did you spend a lot of money on the coke?"

"No, none, my friend invited me."

"Then why are you crying? You work hard and you deserve to party once in a while."

Like a sacred absolution, her son's assurances gave Jesse the needed energy to pull herself out of the self-hatred and despondency.

"You are such a great son! Thank you for being so understanding. I am wired so I'm going to get out of here and drive home. I'll see you soon."

"You be careful on the road."

"Yeah, no problem, I'm definitely awake." They both laughed.

Invite the Trouble In

ules had begun running with an older crowd, and one of his new friends needed a place to live. The additional cash was attractive to the struggling Jesse, so he moved in for a month. She didn't realize that Toby was dealing pot out of her house. It was especially convenient for him with Jesse gone days at a time.

Sunday morning 7a.m. Jesse answered a knock at the door. Looking out she saw a young man with an earring and thought it was one of her son's friends. When she opened the door in came the Gestapo, his weapon drawn, gangster style.

"State police, anyone else in the house?" he bellowed.

Jesse was half asleep, and could not believe her ears, so she asked him, "What did you say?"

"I said, State police, anyone else in the house with you?"

She heard him that time, and responded, "No, there's no one else in the house. What do you want?"

Then he said what no citizen ever wants to hear, "Ma'am, I have a warrant to search the premises for illegal contraband."

Jesse made a spontaneous decision. "Sir, I have a tiny little bit of pot. Rather than having you and your men tear my house apart, how about I just go and get it for you."

"Alright, go ahead," he responded with a smirk.

Jesse looked where she thought it was and could not find it. The search was on; no corner left untouched. They tore apart her closet finding nude pictures, and her vibrator. She became enraged as the cops ripped off the head of an expensive porcelain doll, and trashed her house, looking for the pinch of weed that she had hid from herself, and did a fine job of it too!

Midway during their search, Jesse's teenage roommate Toby, the source of all this harassment, walked up the driveway not recognizing that the Z-Roc belonged to the local drug-enforcement officer, and got nailed, though he had nothing illegal on his person. His name was on the warrant.

The task squad's major contraband haul of the day paid for by hundreds of tax-payers' dollars, was a dirty bong that Woody the narco-dog was able to discover in plain sight beside the TV.

"That's not mine; it belonged to my husband who abandoned me last year." Jesse offered weakly, though it was true.

After a quick arraignment in front of the Magistrate, Toby and Jesse were released on a back road in rural Pennsylvania. Since neither of them had people they could call, they walked home extending their thumbs to the occasional passing car.

Jesse turned to Toby and said with a laugh, "You know, they never found that bud I've got hidden. I hope I can locate it. After the crap those cops put us through, we deserve to get high!"

Back home Jesse surveyed the mess the police wrecking crew had made of her home. Since getting high always motivated Jesse to organize, finding the evasive bud was first on her list. She looked underneath her roll-top desk in the shallow round woven basket that served to catch her desktop clutter. It was crammed with business cards, bookmarkers, bills, emery boards, bubble-gum wrappers, fortune cookie predictions, and scribbled notes. Rendered invisible deep in-between was a thin tin that one might use to carry breath mints, and inside it was a small compact resinous bud.

Toby and Jesse shared tokes as between comrades, laughed and marveled at the cop's inefficiency. The next day Jesse was abhorred to discover that the 'big bust' at her house was front page news of the small-town newspaper, complete with a photograph of Toby in handcuffs. The story alluded to a romantic relationship between the 18 years old and the 42-year-old woman. Jesse hated her life, and now she had even more reasons for her vitriol.

This was not the first time she had had a run-in with the police; she knew the drill. There would be endless court dates, demands and deadlines to be met, hours of community service, fines, fees, addiction counseling, and urine testing. But since this was Jesse's first offense (in this state) Jesse would have an opportunity to complete the first offender's program successfully, resulting in the offense being expunged from her record. The entire process would take at least eighteen months.

Before long Jesse became infatuated with another young man, and resolved to save him, to give him a place to live, because somehow, she knew that that is all he really needed was for someone to genuinely love and cherish him. He loved his alcohol; Jesse was blind to his addiction. His long black curly locks, his blue-eyes, and his voice conspired to weave a rock and roll spell. Jesse drove him to her home in rural Pennsylvania to recreate some earlier ideal, two hippies in-love working together to create a life. Mark was looking for a sugar-mama so he would not have to grow-up and become a man, a fantasy about how a woman would want to support and keep him. Their two fantasies were on a collision course.

Jesse's relationship with substances was unique. She abused alcohol but never developed a dependency upon it, yet the men she was attracted to were always steps up on the abuse and dependency ladder. Mark was a binge alcoholic; he would abstain for a week or two, and then plunge into a two-day debacle. Jesse was a sucker for a pretty face; he was exceptional and 15 years younger. She repeated her usual pattern and ignored the fact that she had little in common with him besides a love of rock music. To compensate for the deficit, they drank. Not liking bars, Jesse acquiesced, dipping to Mark's comfort level, accompanying him to the local hot spot in Emmitsburg, a town known for its firefighter's training academy where they could drink beers, shoot pool, and not be burdened by the necessity of conversation. They had made an agreement that Mark would not get plastered, but he easily forgot it and proceeded to mix beer with liquor, the results of that combination, predictable.

To control Mark's drinking, Jesse confiscated his last-call mixed drink from his hand and downed it, believing that she could handle it better than him. She was driving; within a block from the bar, the cops pulled them over. They knew Jesse's car.

The police stuck a breathalyzer in her face; just one drink over the legal limit. She was being arrested. Mark was also too drunk to drive so the car was impounded. It was like watching a bad re-run. She had certainly done this before, now here she was again facing the legal system, and all it entailed.

From the minute her rights were read, Jesse was an angry victim. She determined at that moment that since they felt the need to stalk her, and make her life miserable, she would say exactly what she thought about their fascist, cowardly strategies. She began the harangue in a low-key, sarcastic tone.

"So, I'm the best you could do?"

"Excuse me?"

"So, I'm the big criminal you guys are paid to apprehend?"

"Ma'am, I do my job, and you broke the law."

"You didn't answer my question; am I it? Taxpayers, including me, are paying you to find and capture criminals! I am a single parent trying to support a teenage son and myself, and you're about to disrupt my life! I hope you get paid a lot for this important work that you do. I think you go after people who cannot or won't fight back. There are big-time drug dealers, cutting up pounds of cocaine and distributing it right here in Carroll Valley. Why don't you go after someone who is worthy of your attention instead of a woman who is barely making it?"

"Can you shut her up?" the cop practically pleaded with Mark.

"No, Sir," he answered.

All the way to the station, through the fingerprinting, and until they were released, Jesse did not let up. She kept reminding him that he was a punk picking on the wrong people. The only comfort she felt was having Mark there, even though he was the reason they were out drinking that night.

Jesse had just spent six months going to drug counseling with Miss Irene, now with this second bust, it would invalidate the number one rule of the first offender's program, no arrests. Not only would they recharge her for the possession of paraphernalia, but they would also add the DUI. She would have to spend at least a weekend in jail. She decided, after that, she would leave this area. The cops had terrorized her with their witch hunt long enough. If they wanted her gone, she would oblige them. They had harassed her son numerous times to the point where Jules played with them. He knew all their hiding places and dirty entrapment tricks and outsmarted them with every encounter.

When Jesse told Jules what had happened, she ended the story by telling him that she needed to get out of Carroll Valley, and she was going to leave.

"Mom, it's my last semester! I don't want to change schools."

"Alright, it's up to you. I understand, but you have to understand too, that I can't stay here. I have to move closer to the city so I can make money."

"I think Robin's mom might let me stay at her house until the end of the semester."

"Is this the same Robin whose mom handcuffed her to the bed?"

"Yes, but that's all done with. They have an understanding now. If Robin wants to party, she can have friends over, and her mom agrees to stay in her bedroom. It's a good compromise."

"Are you sure you'll be able to handle it. You won't be able to smoke cigarettes or pot?"

"Yeah, I don't have any money for that stuff. Anyway, living there will introduce me to a different crowd. I have been hanging out with the pot-smokers, and a lot of Robin's friends are straight. That's ok with me; I need a change."

Jesse did not like leaving Jules but felt reassured that he would be in a safe household. Robin's mom was a retired schoolteacher fiercely dedicated to her three children, still adjusting to the sudden death of her husband five years prior. She lived in her bedroom surrounded by books.

With Jules settled, Jesse escaped the community that had captivated her with its postcard idyllic landscape of covered bridges, battlefields, and apple orchards, to head back to the outskirts of Washington, D.C. to an enclave called Brandywine. Initially unnerving to be again looking for a place to live, Jesse quickly found Tanya, a kind-hearted waitress at the Playhouse Lounge who offered her a room to rent. She and her husband were buying a house nearby and needed the money. In fact, with Jesse's encouragement, Tanya decided to try dancing. The Playhouse featured topless dancers; she jumped right in and took to it with much enthusiasm. Being a woman with a long horsey face and too many teeth, Jesse imagined that she quite enjoyed being flattered and fawned over. Tanya had silky long natural blond hair, a friendly demeanor, and a lean tall body. She was a hit and made lots of tips.

Jesse had brought her boy toy along but was finding out that he was not responding to her efforts to rehabilitate him. His binge drinking and weak sex drive frustrated her. Just looking at his pretty face and curls made Jesse want to love on him, but his interest was elusive. She was paying for both of them because he couldn't keep a job, even the one that Tanya's husband, Pete, had graciously provided.

Jesse felt strangely distant when she told Mark that she could not support him any longer. After all, he didn't even make the effort to fuck her. He was not much of a gigolo if that's what he was trying for. She never saw him again after the day he climbed into his brother's truck and drove off.

The 'flesh' business was going through its usual cycling, new women coming and old ones leaving. Jesse watched as a nineteen-year-old girl raked in hundreds of dollars each shift. She was allowed to dance but prohibited from drinking. There was no competing. It was time for Jesse to seriously take the needed steps to finish her degree so that she could finally move on. How many years had it been that she was sick-to-death of the hustle, sick of the drunks and the losers?

One of Jesse's favorite customers came in. Bob Silver was quality! She had met him when he was still an Air Force One pilot. Each time he was in town he would come into the club to see her. She was captivated by his stories of flying the first lady to Hawaii for a fund-raiser or hearing the inside information about the White House.

"You're so accomplished. What must you think about me taking off my clothes for a living? Not very impressive, huh?" she remarked in her self-demeaning way.

Bob quickly quelled her self-doubts. "You know, Jesse, when I was in Vietnam, I bombed the country for 8 hours a day. I killed innocent people, and then went to the hotel to take a shower and have dinner. I really don't have a right to criticize others."

Sometimes after she had spent an evening with him, she wished that she could love him. Military was not her style, but Bob treated her with such respect that she grew quite fond of him, though never enough to be sexually assertive toward him. His home was clean and organized like one would expect of a military lifer, and she imagined softening its atmosphere with her presence. But as much as she visualized, she could not bring herself to make a move on him. So, they spent time together, watching movies, enjoying restaurants. Bob was the first to support Jesse's effort to finish her degree. He loaned her half of the $400 dollars she needed for a night class at the University of Maryland in College Park, and when she tried to pay him, he told her to keep it.

The class was titled, *The Psychology of Intimate Relationships*. She aced it, not a difficult task with only a single class to focus on. She could vaguely recall the anxiety she had experienced while attending the University of New Mexico; but now she felt empowered. Completing one class was like eating a delicious piece of intellectual candy; she wanted more. The only way she could make it happen quickly was to secure a student loan, something she had not been able to accomplish despite the many times she had tried. Each time she filled out the application, it was turned down, usually because of some minor omission. Her latest effort was no exception. Jesse was extremely frustrated, and as was her pattern, she drank to oblivion on several occasions.

An inebriated Jesse pulled a wall of metal lockers over upon herself while trying to dislodge her wedged costume bag. She was so depressed that she just laid there crying silently, wishing she would die, until the owner and manager came in the dressing room to rescue her.

Another time, Jesse was scheduled to work with Deena, and drunkenly confronted her about fucking her husband, who was now gone and presumably living in Colorado. Jesse forgot for a minute that she was just a non-violent displaced hippie from the west coast. Without protecting her face, she screamed at the raven-haired bitch who had seduced Brad. Deena, having been previously arrested for assaulting a police officer, punched Jesse in her right eye without hesitation. She could not work for a week while the swelling and bruising healed.

The last event before Jesse was fired was mild in comparison, but unforgivable because she challenged and humiliated the owner's daughter, an intellectually vapid, spineless, spoiled rich girl with trailer-trash non-style, and an understandable inferiority complex.

Once again Jesse found herself without a job, a status that, because of her age, was becoming intolerably frightening. Her reputation as a quality entertainer and dancer had earned her goodwill. She recalled a conversation with a club manager near D.C. who had offered her a job. It was a 45-minute drive, but she figured it was worth a try.

Linda didn't require an audition. She remembered Jesse and welcomed her warmly.

The Captain's Lounge was a dive, a place that smelled of urine outside of the bathrooms, and was known for its homely, loose dancers that Linda hired out of pity. Jesse was like a movie-star among this line-up, and she drew customers because they had never seen the likes of her. Throughout the years, somehow, she hadn't lost her enthusiasm. She did not look like a burn-out; her eyes still reflected hope, and she loved to dance. At 140 pounds she was too heavy to work the pole, but she did kick up into a handstand, and throw herself into a backbend as her creativity demanded. She wasn't boring to watch. She still measured her choreography by the moves of the MTV dancers.

Jesse was taking only one class a semester. Progress felt excruciatingly slow however it allowed her to do her best without the stress that usually taints the education experience. Since she was pursuing a Psychology degree, she had her pick of any psychology classes offered. The class titled *The Psychology of Women* gave Jesse a reason to interview the bartender at the Captains Lounge for her term paper and presentation. Lucy was a cynical, middle-aged woman with the filthiest mouth of any she had worked with, and she suspected that her story was an interesting one. The paper earned her an A for the class.

An Unlearned Lesson

omeone had once remarked that if Jesse had not been drinking all those years dancing, she would not have stayed in it for so long. The alcohol made it tolerable. The downside was that she had to drive home, more times than not, drunk. Driving under the influence was illegal, a rule she broke without a thought, a lesson she was slow to learn.

Speeding home on a Friday night after drinking and dancing all afternoon, engrossed in the moment, Jesse was jockeying for position on a crowded beltway at 70 miles per hour when she caught the attention of a cop, who from her passenger window side waved her over.

No matter what chemicals, genetics, or simply a hard life predisposes a person to distraction, seeing that strip of lights in your rear-view mirror sudden puts everything else into perspective. Jesse's stress level was off the chart, primal fear flowing, Cortisol spewing. This time there was no witch-hunt; she knew there was no one to blame but herself. It would be her fourth DUI, a number worthy of mandatory incarceration, and an automatic year's suspension of her driver's license. The thoughts began their haunting. What would happen to her son, to her little pile of possessions? The bottom line was that in order not to simply go insane, she would have to pull some coping skills out of her ass. Her perception of herself as a rapidly aging woman with few options terrorized her. When she surveyed her life, she couldn't identify many successes, only a long string of vain efforts, disappointments like bloody clothing hanging, skins of former selves. One thing was certain, she knew how to complicate and sabotage her own life.

Since the next day was Saturday, Jesse had to wait until Monday to call the best criminal lawyer in Maryland. He had represented her when she got a second DUI. With the recently adopted reciprocity between Pennsylvania and Maryland Jesse was concerned that this would be counted as a fourth instead of third.

Sitting in his office the lawyer was reassuring but emphatic about his fee being paid before going to trial. Jesse figured that if she could make an additional hundred dollars a week beyond what she needed; she could pay off the twenty-five hundred within six months. Mr. Andrew Houlon agreed to those terms; she signed the papers and left the office.

On to the next step of the plan; so, some distant day in the future, Jesse's life would again be hers. She needed a second dancing gig. She could not make the additional money at the Captain's Lounge, and because of her age it would be difficult to land a steady dance job anywhere else. But she had to try.

Downtown Washington D.C. had its share of all-nude exotic dancing clubs; however, the competition for the upscale bars was fierce. They wanted women in their twenties, or women with major breast implants! For the latter, club managers had a wider acceptable age range; Jesse did not fall into either of these categories.

The first club where she auditioned was on an obscure side street close to a metro station entrance. It was all nude. The owner hired her for two weekday lunch shifts, certainly no quick money, but desperation has a way of shoring up one's courage. She knew the lawyer's fee would not get paid unless she generated another job in addition to the gig at The Captain's Lounge. Jesse felt sick as she got a good look at the "stage." It was no larger than a square yard, carpeted and elevated so that a customer could be eye level with the dancer's vagina as he slipped a tip into her garter. The clientele were black lower-income men whose tastes were far more pornographic than Jesse was willing to play-out. The other dancers watched with disdained amusement as Jesse danced so hard, she broke a sweat. Not one customer rose from his seat to tip her. She was aware that she was not giving this audience what it was accustomed to. Edgar, the owner noticed and tucked a ten-dollar bill in her garter as she stepped down from the stage on her way to the dressing room. It was discrimination; she was the only white woman in the bar. Not only were the tips non-existent, but she hated the music, a whole jukebox of ballads. The only reprieve she found was Pink Cadillac by Aretha Franklin. The rest of it sounded like background music for a pornographic movie, exactly the right music for the other dancers who didn't mind spending the fifteen-minute set, naked on their backs, legs spread wide, or on their knees, doggie position, pumping rhythmically, easily milking the men of their dollars. She worked the two days and quit.

The next place she tried was at the corner of 5th and K Street downtown. Washington, D.C. had a handful of gentlemen's clubs. They ranged from the most exclusive with a line-up of beautiful women, to the tarnished and decadent place where Jesse was offered a job. The stage was once the showcase of burlesque revues. It reeked 'antique'. Complete with now unused velvet stage curtains, a hidden door with a staircase to the wall-to-wall mirrored dressing room and lockers above the stage, this theater had once hosted the great vaudeville acts. Now, undisguised stripped bare pussy was the entertainment, labia major and minor. Vickie, a big white, blond woman who had once been in the army, contorted her body and flexed her muscles in such a way that the view was complete from her rectum to her clitoris. She made piles of money.

Again, Jesse stayed on her feet and did what she felt she did best, dance. Fortunately, she was able to work enough shifts to accumulate the additional $100 dollars a week her lawyer required. Like a good soldier Jesse showed up at Mr. Houlon's office every Monday. It was like a special ring of Dante's hell, having to wait with the future looming dangerously every day. If she allowed herself to think about the real possibility of incarceration for a year, her heart would pound, the acid in her stomach poured, and her nerves burned.

Drinking made Jesse sociable, and she was required to sell a quota of drinks every shift whether she drank them or not, so of course, Jesse drank. There always remained the risk of another DUI when she drove home after her shift.

It was a humid hot summer night 2 a.m., Jesse, drunk and too tired to change into street clothes had stumbled out of the club dressed in the white satin cami and bedroom shorts with sequins, beads, and lace she had worn for her last set. When she got into her car, she powered down the windows and immediately passed out. 3:30 a.m. she awoke startled, realizing with disbelief what she had done. Scrutinizing the empty sidewalk outside the club, the chain-link fenced parking lot across the street, she saw no people, no cops, and no moving cars. Her heart raced; she wondered if she had lost her costume bag with the tips she made last night. But no, it was there behind the seat with the pile of dollars stuffed inside, untouched.

All the way home she wondered about the stories she had heard of guardian angels protecting people; maybe she had attracted one in its off hours, keeping her safe, cloaking her in invisibility. She felt stupid and reckless to have taken such a chance. She thanked the forces of luck and promised herself that it wouldn't happen again.

Summer passed, Jesse finally paid the $2500 in full and was relieved to hear that the trial would be postponed until after the first of the year. Working in that dive had drained her, but she was glad to be done with her obligation. She knew she was in good hands; if anyone could get her the minimum sentence, it would be this attorney.

Since she didn't have to work the additional hours, Jesse slid back into working for the Captain's Lounge two or three shifts a week. Her car was old and had gotten even more worn out from all the additional driving, so she was relieved to be working in one location. The blue-collar crowd liked her; she kept them laughing with her bawdy humor.

One afternoon, in the silence between songs, from the stage Jesse had an announcement, "Listen up guys. I want all of you to sign up your wives and girlfriends for a workshop I'll be giving this Saturday..." By this time, the entire bar was silent. "on how to give a blowjob." As if on cue, everyone busted out laughing. Performers often have rituals they go through, Jesse would always walk in the door and announce, "The party's here!"

When asked how she always managed to be happy, she would answer, "I can be miserable, or I can be happy. It's my choice." For the moment, Jesse was learning to accept what she could not change.

Help Arrives

t was a Thursday afternoon at The Captain's. Between sets, Jesse was making her way around the booths and tables saying hello, occasionally touching a shoulder. After hours of invested time, many of the customers were like good friends; she knew more about their lives than their wives.

There was nothing particularly remarkable about the day; Jesse had grown accustomed to the atmosphere of this joint, not much competition, typically, friendly working men grabbing a beer on their way home, or retired, lonely souls looking for a connection. By now, Jesse was a beautiful 47-year-old woman. The intermittent drinking and drugging had not been sufficient to undo the positive effects of 25 years of strenuous exercise. Men were always asking her for a date, most with which she would never be seen in public.

Collin easily stood out with his liquid crystal-blue eyes, curly blond hair, and a wide smile. Jesse took no time in finding a seat beside him after her set. He laughed easily, was generous with his quarters, and beers. He made a point to approach the stage and lay money by her feet, give her a quick eye contact, and walk back to his table.

"Thank you so much for the tips," Jesse said, still winded from the set.

"Yeah, I'm really not that comfortable going up to the stage. I see a lot of guys acting like complete assholes toward the women. The way I see it, you're just trying to make a living like everyone else. I don't try to get more for my dollar just because I'm standing there at the stage," Collin said with unpretentious modesty.

"Well, I appreciate your courtesy as well as the tip."

After that, Jesse returned to sit with him every single set. Collin appeared smitten with her. They had an easy rapport.

"What kind of work do you do?"

"I'm a forklift driver at one of the biggest produce distributors in this area. We even deliver to the White House"

"How did you get into that line of work?"

"I worked for the Keanny brothers back when they started. They got a loan for a straight truck and $2000 dollars. I've been with them pretty much the entire time. Over the last 8 or 10 years they have absorbed every other produce distributor around.

Ah, Jesse thought, nothing sexier than a working man! The more they drank, the harder they laughed. He was generous with his money. Suddenly he whipped his head around looking for a clock, "What time is it; it's so dark in these places you can't tell?"

"It's about 7," Jesse answered.

"Shit, I gotta get home and get some sleep; I start my shift at eleven."

By this time, Jesse was drunk enough that her boundaries were non-existent. "Aww, you don't need any sleep, not with me around," she teased. "I'm off work now, why don't I come home with you."

"I wouldn't get any sleep for sure if you did that!"

Jesse grabbed her bag and headed for the door with Collin in the lead. Outside the club, she asked, "Where's your car?"

Collin pointed to a black, GT convertible Mustang.

"Are you going to give me a ride home?"

"Believe me, I'd like to, but I really have to get some sleep so that I can get up in a couple of hours."

As he was explaining, Jesse was trying to open the passenger door, but it was stuck.

"That door doesn't open from the outside."

Inebriated, she lost her balance as she was leaning in toward the front seat, feet off the ground.

Collin got out of the car and put his arms around her. They kissed lightly, quickly.

"Do you work tomorrow afternoon?"

"I sure do."

"Tomorrow is my weekend, how 'bout if I drop by, maybe you'd like to go out to eat after your shift."

"That would be great! I'll see you then."

Jesse's shift was over by seven, and promptly Collin showed up. Ever the gentleman, he took her dance bag from her, "Let me help you with that."

Before driving off he opened his door and dumped the overflowing ashtray out onto the parking lot, "Sorry about that; you know how us bachelors are. I haven't had a woman passenger for a while."

"Thanks... I never picked up the cigarette habit, but I do like to smoke pot."

Collin smiled, his big-toothed grin animating his face, "I'm glad to hear that," and he whipped out a joint and handed it to her.

418

He took her to a picturesque restaurant near the university. The interior was furnished like a World War I bunker complete with crashed airplanes sticking through the ceiling. The 94th Aero Squadron had a functioning runway adjacent to it for local small aircraft, and excellent food. They stuffed themselves with steak and lobster and drank gin and tonic until last call. What Collin didn't have in education, he made up for by his generosity. He had an easy sense of humor and demanded little from Jesse. It felt familiar, like a sigh of relief when after waiting in the dark on the side of the road, you see the tow truck finally pulling up. Jesse was grateful to have someone young who wanted to be with her, and he worked!

They spent the night with each other. Jesse was underwhelmed but determined to make a try of it. It wasn't a perfect fit, but she felt like she couldn't be picky. He smoked cigarettes; she didn't. The habit disgusted her. He had barely graduated from high school; Jesse had a voracious appetite for knowledge, spending much of her time between the pages of books. Aware of their differences, it did not stop Jesse from trying to create a relationship. Her long-time desperation was suddenly gone, replaced by exuberant energy and many expectations.

Over the next two weeks Collin stopped by daily to hang out, and on his days off he took Jesse on a non-stop tour of the local eating establishments. Jesse learned that Collin had been brought up on a chicken farm in rural Ohio. He had two brothers and two sisters; the youngest brother died at eleven when he was struck by a truck. She learned that his greatest strength was his work ethic. Although Collin didn't have the kind of intellectual depth that comes with reading, he wasn't stupid. Jesse knew she had met someone who would work as hard as she did. These days finding a man who would provide for a woman was rare. So, she closed her eyes to the incompatibilities, and instead enjoyed the attention she was getting, letting Collin provide meals, drinks, and a constant audience.

Jesse was still renting a room from Tanya and her family. The first day of December Jesse unpacked what few Christmas trinkets she possessed and set-up a tiny ceramic village on top of a microwave cabinet she had placed in Tanya's dining room; it was the only intrusion of furniture into the family's space. When she returned home one evening after work, she noticed that her display had been thoughtlessly moved aside and a couple of dishtowels flung over the surface. Jesse felt enraged; she could hear her own thoughts, *I stay out of your way; I never play music, or bring anyone home, and I can't even have the top of my own cabinet?* As she thought about her situation... not even having the financial power to live alone, her anger and resentment intensified. Instead of swallowing her own thoughts, she worked up a good head of steam, descended the stairs ready to give Tanya her due.

"Why did you move my stuff?"

Tanya was caught off-guard and did not register what Jesse was saying. "What are you talking about," she replied sarcastically.

"You are so arrogant and rude. Just because you own this house and I'm renting from you doesn't mean you can treat me and my things like shit," Jesse screamed.

Before Tanya could respond Jesse gathered up the porcelain house and trees, then returned upstairs. Within the hour, Tanya knocked on Jesse's bedroom.

"What do you want?" Jesse asked.

"I want you to leave. I talked to Pete, and you have by January first to find another place to live."

Jesse's faced filled with hot blood; she said nothing and turned her back on Tanya.

Luckily, she was on the schedule for the next day. Jesse was thankful to get out of the house; the atmosphere was thick with silence.

Collin showed up toward the end of Jesse's shift. She began to cry as soon as she got in the car.

"I don't have a place to live now, and I don't have any money; the lawyer took it all. I'm tired, I've been working so hard for so long and I just can't seem to get a break." She was sobbing.

Collin put his arm around her shoulder, "Don't cry; you can stay with me until you get another place."

"You're kidding, really?"

"Yeah, now let's go get something to eat."

Collin had the good taste not to dwell on her emotional meltdown. Just that quickly, like the snap of a thumb and finger, Jesse had been rescued. The crippling apprehension that usually inundated her during unpredictable times like these dissipated like smoke. Accustomed to living without a safety net, yet never comfortable with that uncertainty, Jesse was flooded with gratitude.

It was winter. Summer and autumn had passed quickly for Jesse with the additional dancing and the pressure of having to generate extra money for the lawyer.

Now it seemed she was getting a well-deserved break. Collin enjoyed weed; he was seldom without. This was a plus for Jesse since the buzz from marijuana energized her dancing and made her time on stage easier.

Two weeks before Christmas, Jesse was working the early shift. It was slow and the customers were few, so during her break she went to the lady's bathroom which happened to also be the dancer's dressing room to take a hit off of a pipe she had in her bag. As she inhaled deeply the door opened and in stepped the manager. Jesse had no choice but to exhale.

"Well, what have we here?" Linda asked derisively.

Jesse mumbled, "I'm sorry... it won't happen again." She quickly exited the dressing room to mingle with the crowd that was beginning to grow as guys got off work.

Stepping out into the bar she tried to forget about what had just happened and hoped that she had skated. Two weeks later the manager said that she couldn't use her anymore. Linda was nice enough to wait until Christmas before firing her, so that Jesse was able to make some money before the holiday. It did not diminish her realization that she had no more clubs or bars to work in. Without wanting to explore the seedier clubs or revisit the world of pornography at this stage of the game, she had exhausted the list of establishments that would hire a forty-seven-year-old dancer.

Jesse was now living under Collin's roof, and had seemed uncommitted until she told him what had happened.

"Fuck that urinal. Just don't worry. This will give you a chance to get back in school. You don't need that place!" He was adamant, and with this unaccustomed emotional support suddenly Jesse felt buoyant, almost happy.

Government Loan

hen the approval letter for a federally subsidized loan finally came, Jesse was beyond ecstatic. She figured she would have a degree in Psychology in a year and a half, as long as she could pass the mandatory statistics course. After so many years of spinning her wheels, was it possible that the fruition of her labor would be a ticket out of the smoky bars that she had so stoically tolerated for what amounted to a lifetime?

Suddenly Jesse was thrust full-time back into the demanding role of student. She liked learning, but always thought that the force-feed method took the joy out of it. Regardless, she was ready to finish. She finally had her wish, someone to help her get through school, and she wasn't going to miss the opportunity.

Since she had her sight set on doing therapy for a living, most of her classes were in Psychology, although Algebra, Statistics, and PC 101 were also requirements for graduation. For Jesse the psychology curriculum was like a review. She had read so many psychology books that the material was familiar. Feeling a sense of efficacy, she was confident that she could accomplish her goal of attaining a degree, even after so many years of stop and go. A year and a half full-time, with Collin's help, would be doable.

Living next to the train tracks had seemed inconsequential when she first moved in with Collin, but now that Jesse was in school, she wanted to get a good night's sleep which proved to be impossible with the train blowing its horn every 4 hours. A drunken student had once fallen onto the tracks and was hit by the oncoming train. The city thought the remedy to this problem was to blow the bloody horn throughout the day and night.

"Collin, I can find us a small house for what you're paying here," Jesse said one evening while stroking his back. "I know you don't like to share a bathroom with everyone on this floor. I even put my pretty hand towel near the sink on the back of the toilet. I went back later, and someone had used it to wipe shit from their ass."

After asking Collin repeatedly for a couple of weeks, Jesse became impatient.

"I found a two-bedroom house with a huge garage for $850, plus utilities. Let's go look at it."

Collin was slow to respond, and when he did open his mouth, "Jesse, I'm not sure."

"Fine, I certainly don't want you to do anything that you don't want to do, but I'm not staying here. I can live better than this by myself. I do appreciate all the help you've given me, but I can't stay here. I'm moving with or without you."

"Alright, we'll look at it; it has a garage, right?"

The place was perfect, a mile from the college in a quaint neighborhood, where walking down its streets you would never know that the projects and the inner city were only a half a mile away. The house was minimal and small, but the garage was immense with two stories. It was a garage meant to be lived in, and Jesse was certain Collin would do just that.

Besides driving a fork-lift and drinking, Collin built hover crafts. He spent obscene amounts of money on parts and engines, always fantasizing about selling his design to the military. The trouble was, none of his designs were innovative, nor did they work. At first Jesse had been naively enthusiastic about Collin's potential, not really seeing the true amateur that he was. One thing she knew, he seemed to be quite happy tinkering, and his new garage gave him a reason to be home drinking instead of spending money in the bars.

It wasn't long before Jesse was bored with the relationship. She had just passed her 48th birthday and found herself in the same loveless situation she had endured in the past. At least she was not wrong about Collin's work ethic. He never missed a day no matter how hung-over or ill. The $70,000 a year he pulled in as a forklift operator undoubtedly motivated him. Jesse felt the urge to run away but she sensed that she would be better off finishing her education while someone was around to help. It was a rare opportunity. She could step out on her own again when she could take-care of herself, when she finally had some marketable skills. She would be respected, and brilliant, she ruminated. *With the life I have lived, I'll be able to relate to almost everyone. I will be able to make a living and help people as a therapist.*

Living with an alcoholic presented a whole new set of rules, mostly unspoken. The day before school was to start Cody picked a fight with Jesse. *Why, she asked herself, does he have to start a bunch of crap right when I'm trying to mentally prepare myself for classes?* She ran up the street crying, trying to find somewhere to hang out until Collin passed out, as was his routine. A friend of Jesse's commented, "I'd be happy to find a man like Collin who just worked and came home to do his drinking." Everything is relative.

Jesse settled into a routine; for the most part Collin was low maintenance, except when he reached his toxic level of alcohol. All he required was one meal a day preferably with the focus on meat. He loved steaks of every persuasion. As long as Jesse broiled him a slab and maybe a side of potatoes and veggies, he was happy. He would stuff himself, excuse himself, and go off to sleep for a few hours before he started at 11 p.m. Jesse began to understand how people who were incompatible could live with each other for years. Besides cooking, cleaning, and doing laundry for Collin, Jesse's only goal was to finish school. She studied and got A's, drank with Collin on weekends and holidays, and then immersed herself back into the academic world. The three semesters to complete her bachelor's degree in Psychology flew by, and she found herself in the gymnasium lined up to receive the coveted document. All-together, it had only taken her a total of thirty years. Jesse and Collin celebrated; they ate, drank, and laughed.

She hadn't been basking in the afterglow of her accomplishment for very long before she began worrying that her degree did not have any power. She checked the employment ads; there were no jobs available for a person with a B.A. in Psychology.

Saturday, the University Laundromat was busy. Jesse looked at her watch; she had an hour until this load was dry. Finding an empty seat, she reached out to a young black-haired woman who appeared to be a student from her clothes to the book in her hand.

"Excuse me; can I talk to you? I'm in the middle of a dilemma."

"Sure! Are you ok?"

Jesse blurted out, "I don't know what to do now that I have a Psychology Degree. I want to do counseling, but I don't know how to get there from where I am.

The woman's eyes widened in surprise, "You know, it's kind of amazing that you asked me that. I have a friend who was in the same situation."

Jesse leaned in to hear her every word.

"She enrolled at the University of Maryland, School of Social Work. The graduate program takes two years. After that, all she needed was two years of post-graduate supervision with a Licensed Clinical Social Worker in order to 'hang out her shingle'. With a Licensed Master's Degree in Social Work she can work in the mental health field in any of its areas. I think her specialty is children."

Jesse asked cautiously, "Do you know if a dissertation is required?

"Some graduate programs do require a dissertation, but not this one," she responded confidently.

Jesse felt the 'synchronicity' she had read about; like a miracle or divine intervention, this was the information she needed to take the next step to becoming a therapist!

The Maryland University School of Social Work was right down the road in Baltimore. Jesse wouldn't stop now. She was determined to get into a position where she could support herself in this increasingly demanding society. Social work didn't seem like a glamorous field, but with a master's degree and two years of supervision, she could be a psychotherapist.

Now that she had made up her mind to become a Social Worker, Jesse began the application process, the bane of every person trying to better himself through education. She was required to write a paper answering questions like, why do you want to study Social Work, and what experiences in life led you to your present decision to apply. The school was asking Jesse to persuade them as to why she would be a good candidate.

She had been keeping journals for years, whether mainlining speed or stranded on the highway, a pen was always in her hand. She knew she could construct a sentence and develop coherent ideas from start to finish, having learned from the best authors like Ray Bradbury, Aldous Huxley, Hermann Hesse, and other mutton-chopped tintypes.

One question on the application prompted her to realize that she had no history of community volunteer work that would aptly demonstrate her interest in helping people. The years of impromptu counseling she had done as a topless dancer probably would not impress the judges.

Jesse called the local Suicide Prevention Hotline and made an appointment to be trained as a volunteer suicide prevention counselor. The process involved two weeks of both theory and practical training, most of which took place inside the county police department, a detail Jesse had not foreseen. She felt uncomfortable inside the locked doors of this environment, suffocating and threatening. While heightening her sense of caution, Jesse felt empowered by each session. As she stepped boldly into the belly of the beast, she reminded herself that she was a guest, not an inmate.

The training concluded, and Jesse got her schedule. Day one, apprehension shook her as she parked and locked her car door before entering the run-down building that used to house thriving businesses. New situations unnerved Jesse but in-spite of her fears she stepped forward.

When she gave it thought she could remember the terror she felt on the first day of kindergarten. Jesse's mother gripped her little hand like a vice as she pulled the tiny girl along up the hill to a huge elementary school. Not such an unusual experience, except that her mother had not explained to her what was happening. She simply announced that Jesse would be going to school, proceeded to dress her and out the door they went in the cold Ocean Park fog. Those buried early years, when she did not get an explanation or other gestures of love to instill confidence, were packed-up inside of her and dragged along like luggage, still invisibly influencing her.

Her fears were unfounded since a new counselor was never left alone. She would be given time to learn how to diffuse the *determination* of a would-be suicide. Counselors always had the option of handing-off calls if they felt powerless to continue to avert an action. Jesse volunteered for a four-hour shift once a week to provide suicide counseling, a service she never felt competent to give. This, she added to the now complete graduate school application.

Jesse finally received a response from the university. It read that they would like to offer her a place in the fall curriculum, but that at present, there were no openings.

430

Relieved and disappointed, all her future plans were dependent upon getting the education and licensing to become a therapist. The relationship with Collin had become predictable and strained. What would she do now?

When a local fabric warehouse hired Jesse to work as a cashier, and within a month she was given keys to the store with a promotion to assistant manager, she wondered whether this could possibly turn into a career. Getting strapped to the education system for the next two years accumulating debt wasn't Jesse's first choice, but it seemed like a step forward. Collin had made it clear that he was supplying the roof over their heads and did not have additional money to help her pay for tuition and books. The job was nearly a perfect fit. Jesse had continued sewing through-out her dancing years, sewing costumes to supplement her income. Working around fabric and all the accessories associated with constructing garments was enjoyable.

There were times when Jesse thought that she might be able to be happy and enjoy the constant, if limited, relationship with Collin. If that were true, she could stop her decades-long struggle, scratching after the degrees, and the elusive financial security they might provide.

Since Collin and Jesse worked opposite shifts, their time together was limited. This gave Jesse time to ponder about her present situation. Here she was playing house without any other prospects on the horizon. She didn't know if the school would eventually have a seat for her, or maybe it would never happen. Daily she was confronted with Collin's misery, unleashed upon himself with his compulsive drinking and dedication to keeping his history of pain masked. He had once told her grown son that he knew he couldn't keep a woman because he pissed the bed. Jesse, not understanding Collin's addiction, began to think that all he really needed to gain control over the alcohol was for a woman to believe in him; and how best could she prove this than to marry him. The agreement to get married, and the conversation about it was short as if they were discussing what to have for dinner.

"Well, if we're going to do this, the only place I want it to happen is on top of the Sandia Crest. It's a mountain top just outside of Albuquerque." Jesse said matter-of-factly.

Collin was passive, probably not believing his ears and knowing that Jesse had a habit of changing her mind. "Sure, whatever you want; I can take a couple of days off."

Neither her sons nor friends close to Jesse could figure out why suddenly she decided to marry this man with whom she was largely incompatible. No one knew it was the dress.

A Wedding on Top of the Mountain

esse had been collecting patterns for years, including one for an extravagant Renaissance-like wedding dress. During the hours Jesse worked at the fabric store it was easy for her to fantasize, without her full awareness, of some simple life where she worked a few hours and came home to her loving husband, not that it would have kept her satisfied. One day while she was among the bolts of fabric, standing them up, smoothing the tangled swatches, she noticed a bolt of sea-green, antique-looking brocade, the material for her gown!

From March, when she received the school's letter that they had no room in its program and she asked Collin to marry her, until an hour before leaving Maryland to drive to New Mexico, Jesse worked on the dress. She was still putting the finishing stitches to matching ties and vests for Collin, his teenage son Junior, and Jules, who had been camping on their floor while Collin trained him to be a forklift operator, an opportunity he had jumped at.

Collin bought plane tickets for himself and Junior and flew to New Mexico, while Jesse and Jules drove. Collin didn't want to take any more time off from work than a long weekend, and Jesse wanted to visit friends she hadn't seen in years, so they agreed to meet in Albuquerque. There they would apply for a license, make the drive up to the crest to get married by a Justice-of-the-Peace standing at the top of

433

the 10,876-foot peak. It was a sound plan. Alcohol was waiting in the wings to undo such plans.

Collin and Junior had already touched down, and were hanging out with a Jerry, a friend of Collin's who along with his most recent girlfriend, were snorting cocaine, and beginning to imbibe early. Collin simply asked his son to take a walk while they laid out the lines. Meanwhile, Jesse and Jules rolled into town after driving all night and met up with them at the hotel room. Collin seemed happy to see them as he opened the door.

"Hey babe; how was the drive in that new car? Glad to see you made it ok." Collin was buoyant.

"It was great. Jules drove most of the way."

They kissed lightly, embraced, and Collin introduced everyone else.

Jules and Jesse left after a few minutes, agreeing to meet later after Jesse caught a nap. Then they would navigate up into the Manzano Mountains. Right now, she was impatient to get settled at the house of Lauren, an old friend, who was out of town. She had her key. Although Jules had driven most of the way, it had been nearly impossible to get any real sleep. Collin seemed relieved to see her go; after all, he had a nose full of the white powder. He wasn't concerned about sleep.

Jesse was eager to expose Collin to the southwest lifestyle, and creativity that abounded. She wanted to introduce Collin to her New Mexico friends, the couple who had built a passive solar house, all by hand. Near sunset Collin showed up, and they all piled into the Camaro. Jesse had talked to Alan and Alyssa earlier, so they were expecting them. After getting lost, and having to call to get Alan to escort, Jesse arrived at the overgrown gate posts.

It was nothing like what she remembered. She had left in 1985, and now it was 1997. What had once been a beautiful piece of property within the wilderness was now overgrown with twelve-foot grasses and wild shrubbery. Alan was visibly embarrassed. The inside of the house was even more decrepit. The stench of dog feces, cat urine, old dirty clothes, and an acrid smell of alcohol hit them at the door.

Jesse was cordial though disappointed and proceeded to have a few drinks. Not realizing that Collin had been partying all day and had now hit his toxic level, Jesse tried to engage him, with disastrous results. He lost his temper, grabbed the keys to the car and ushered his son out of the door. Jesse was concerned that he would get lost, especially in his inebriated state. But like Jesse, Collin did what he wanted to do.

Jesse and Jules tried to get comfortable after the drama had passed, but the dogs and cats were noisy, and the putrid odors of the house kept her awake. She could hear Jules snoring. At least he would be rested for tomorrow, her wedding day. She wondered if Collin would call or show up.

Early morning Jesse snuck into her host's bedroom to see if she could get a ride back down to the foothills to her friend's house. Alan slipped out of bed from his wife's side. Giving Jesse and Jules a ride, Alan apologized profusely for the condition of the house. Jesse tried to put him at ease.

Once back at Lauren's house, Jesse called the number of the hotel, and Collin answered.

"Do you think we should do this?" he asked with more sincerity than she expected.

"Look, I know how you are when you've been drinking and on top of that you were doing coke." She answered convincingly. "We don't get like that very often; I don't think it's that serious."

"Ok, what time are we supposed to be on top of the mountain?"

"The justice of the peace will meet us there at 6 this evening."

"Alright, I'll see you then."

Collin dropped off the car and told Jesse that he would catch a ride up to the crest with his friend Rod later in the afternoon.

Jesse thought that if she could just get a nap for a couple of hours, she'd feel revived. But sleep eluded her, and while she was able to rest her eyes, she never lost consciousness. Exhausted physically and emotionally, she was determined to get through what now felt like an ordeal. Her sister who had flown in from California for a work seminar, called to say she would see her on the mountain before the ceremony.

Jules would sleep in until he had to get ready. Jesse envied his ability to sleep anywhere, anytime. She prepared herself, curling her hay-colored hair, and applying her makeup with a little extra intensity, finally stepping into the taffeta and tulle petticoat, and then the aqua brocade gown.

At dusk, with Jules behind the wheel they raced up the back of the Sandia Mountains on a road with hairpin turns until it emptied onto the crest of the mountain. It had been years since she had walked upon this sacred peak.

"Do you remember we came up here to camp when you were a kid?"

"Yeah, it looks about the same." Jules had an excellent memory.

Jesse got out of the car; Collin wasn't in sight.

"Shit, I forgot my bouquet!"

Holding the train of her gown, she walked from the parking lot to where she could stand on the edge of the mountain. Her lungs pumped; her anxiety grew. With the storm front and a sheet of rain heading from the west mesa toward the mountain she was standing on, she wondered if it would reach them before they had a chance to say their vows. Shifting her thoughts to the here and now sunlight above warming the top of her head, she turned to a boy waist level looking up at her.

"Hey lady, why are you dressed like that?"

"I'm getting married," she replied, smiling.

"This is for you," he said as he handed her a wilted bouquet of wildflowers that he had obviously picked himself.

"Wow, thank you so much. They're beautiful!" she answered as she held out her hand to take them.

Jesse and Jules scouted around for a spot near the edge. About that time, Collin walked up with his friends, then Jesse's sister approached, as well as a few other friends. Jesse was surprised to see that so many had shown up. She had been feeling melancholy as she was dressing for her marriage, but now the presence of these few people along with the magnificence of the peak and the land spread like a moonscape as far as eyes could see, had lifted her mood. Life's magic was free, if only one could perceive and appreciate. Jesse was happy to take notice.

Collin turned heads; he looked like a young Robert Plant. He had deliberately kept his hair long for the wedding at Jesse's request. The excesses of the night before hardly registered on his face, and he seemed impatient to get started. The judge easily found the waiting wedding party. With a threatening dark gray curtain of rain as the backdrop, he began by saying that rain was a good omen on one's wedding day. Jesse wanted to believe it.

The ceremony was simple, the Judge genuine in his delivery, but when he began talking about forsaking all others to be only with this one person, she started laughing almost unperceivable, although the photographs that her sister snapped were telling. Not even Jesse could keep her true self from expressing its dismay over her choice for a husband. People marry for the illusion. It is after they are married that people find out who their partners are. Jesse knew that they were not a good fit intellectually, but Collin had a generous nature, and she felt supported in her efforts to escape the bar scene like at no other time in her life. Besides, she told herself that she had invested too much time already, she hated being alone, and she didn't want to get back into the crapshoot of dating.

The approaching storm was reticent, unleashing its torrent only after the pronouncement that they were husband and wife. The ride back down the mountain reminded Jesse of the Mad Toad Ride at Disneyland. She asked Collin to slow down. He ignored her request; he probably needed a drink. Some of the guests were supposed to be following, and Collin had effectively "lost" them. As was Jesse's practice, she bit her tongue and accepted the situation. It wasn't worth another fight. They arrived at her friend's empty house, starving with no money or plans for dinner, so they ordered burgers, with green chile and fries. Not such an elegant wedding dinner but inexpensive, and filling. Jesse's sister said goodnight and left. The newlyweds also said goodbye to each other. Collin and Junior left with Rod in his SUV. Everyone needed to get back to their jobs. Jesse slept like the dead, and then she and Jules left the next day for the drive back to Maryland.

Waiting for Jesse when she returned was grad school with its unrelenting pressure. Although Jesse loved to learn, she had difficulty regimenting herself. She had never been a disciplined student, instead she had relied on her good memory and excellent concentration, which made it easy for her to grasp what was being taught. Her starved intellect was well-fed in the academic environment. During her undergraduate years she had repeatedly volunteered to be a teacher's assistant. It was a strategy she used to give herself an opportunity to be in the company of the professors, like an unofficial apprenticeship.

Jesse continued to suffer from anxiety, but hardly realized it until her classes in mental health helped her to see the symptoms. She took advantage of the ten sessions of counseling offered to every student who enrolled. The counselor helped her identify the ways in which being raised in a toxic atmosphere had handicapped her. Home was a place where she had never been cherished or appreciated and had never been allowed to be genuine. She wondered if, with all her introspection, she would be able to transcend her past which had crippled her so.

While attending school Jesse gravitated toward a group of women her age. Each had a story of how she had gotten to this point. It felt good to be in the presence of women who, like herself, had overcome adversity but had not lost sight of a dream of bettering themselves. They were passionate about the social work field and burned to fulfill an inner desire to make a difference in the lives of those less fortunate. The school was run like most big businesses, to make money. Students functioned under constant pressure, money for parking, money to make endless copies of journal articles that were not provided in a bound book like most required texts, and always another challenge, something different from yesterday. The curriculum spanned psychology, sociology, group work, individual and family counseling, addictions, statistics, and various policy classes, no slight task for Jesse to master.

Students were required to complete two internships, one each year. Her first internship was at an elementary school in South Baltimore bordering destitute ghetto neighborhoods. She and her student partner were assigned the task of getting a disabled child back into school, since her mother seemed powerless to make it happen.

Jesse also had been assigned a second-grade student who had experienced the trauma of watching his mother be threatened by his father with a knife. Now he was six and still acting-out hyper vigilance in the absence of any enemies. She did not feel particularly adept in her role as school social worker, and she was terrified that she would be called upon to handle a situation with a child that was beyond her experience. What she did discover was her natural ability to relate to the adults, and she felt something awaken in her chest. Over and over the stories Jesse heard, especially the women's, reminded her of her own sad and deprived life. Tears stung her eyes more than once while she listened to the children's parents tell of their own unique tragedies. Jesse often experienced overwhelming empathy. She could in fact feel the person's experience as though she were living in her skin. It empowered Jesse to think that she might be able to help her clients help themselves. Her sense of worth deepened as her training took on new dimensions.

The well-known author/psychologist Carl Rogers had established a number of essential principles of counseling if a person wanted to be an effective helper, the first being, *unconditional positive regard*. He theorized that unless the therapist could maintain this non-judgmental openness with his patient, he would be unsuccessful in facilitating change. It wasn't difficult for Jesse to accept her clients. Her own mother had been one of the most mean-spirited, judgmental people in her life. The emotional scars she carried had made her sensitive. Being closed was never one of Jesse's problems, if anything her early emotional impoverishment caused her to be overly receptive to others; her boundaries were poor. As a counselor she was invited into the worlds of her clients. The work was fascinating. But she quickly learned that she could not fix anyone, and she could not, metaphorically, take her clients home with her.

The second internship took her inside the women's prison in Jessup, Maryland. Close by was Baltimore with its 60,000 population of intravenous drug users, inadequate social services delivery system, and a crumbling economy.

Prison social work consisted of facilitating cognitive-behavioral groups that focused on teaching the inmates how to make good decisions and helping the mentally ill and other special needs inmates to come up with viable release plans for transition back into the community. This happened when they were within six months of being released.

It seemed to Jesse that running groups was another aspect of performing. The public speaking part of the work, which ranks high in provoking anxiety, did not bother her. She told herself that if she had danced naked in front of strangers, she could certainly stand up in front of fifteen inmates and teach them the basics of thinking. She liked sharing what she knew. A lifetime of reading and stashing knowledge had left her with a well-spring of knowledge and stories. When she was finished with her internship, she was practically assured a position with the state prison system.

Jesse continued to drink with Collin. Although the frequency of her bacchanalian reveries decreased, she still was a victim to her old patterns more often than she liked. The risky behaviors of her younger years returned during this ill-timed partying, almost derailing her. Jesse knew that she was more prone to depression when she ran alcohol through her system, but she seemed to have forgotten.

Suddenly Jesse stopped attending classes. All she could say to others and herself was "I'm tired." She was turning fifty. It seemed like all her internal cheerleading, and positive narration couldn't keep her from running out of fuel, and while Collin brought home a paycheck, in so many ways he did not contribute to Jesse's well-being.

Feelings of alienation began to eclipse her days and nights. Collin had no interest in the classes she was taking, and was not a reader, so unless she wanted to drink and play DJ for him while he wrenched on his hovercraft, her choices for shared time with him were limited. She knew this when she married him but *had thought* that she could handle it. It was becoming apparent to her that their incompatibilities could not be ignored.

At the same time, Jesse was attached to the comforts and security that Collin provided. She enjoyed the Camaro he had given her, so she would have a dependable ride for school. They ate like royalty, not missing any of the fine cuisine at the local college restaurants. Perhaps his best trait was his worst. He was self-centered which caused him to neglect Jesse. Still, she liked that he gave her freedom from scrutiny.

These were the daily, sometimes hourly, inner conflicts with which Jesse wrestled. Not knowing why after finally getting this close to her dream of degrees and a career, she would sabotage her own progress, everyone around tried to change her mind about dropping out, even Collin. For two weeks she did not attend one class, hand in papers or take tests. Then a band named 3rd Eye Blind began hollering at her from the dashboard speaker, *Can I graduate?!*

Jesse was doing Collin's laundry one evening. Around the outside of the house, she carried the clothes in a basket to the washing machine and dryer in the basement which was only accessible from an outside door. It was inconvenient, going outside and the one thing she hated most about the house. Cold, rainy, muddy, and suddenly she asked herself, *is this what you want, to be dependent on a dude who drinks to oblivion, hasn't read a book in years, and has no interest in sex?* The next day she returned to school to salvage the semester.

Jesse's tolerance for Collin's drunken lifestyle waned. Now that she could see her graduate degree within sight, she felt empowered. Each day on the job gave her a sense of certainty that she had not experienced before, and it fed her dissatisfaction with the relationship.

It reached a peak when Jesse received a phone call from Collin. He had been arrested for driving drunk. He sounded pitiable.

"Will you come and pick me up?"

"Yeah, I'll be there soon." Those were not the words she wanted to say.

Sure, he had supported her while she was a student, but in return she had cleaned, cooked, and fucked. She felt like they were even. In the past few months since the wedding, he had continued to urinate nightly while he slept so rather than ruin a recently purchased mattress, Collin moved into the second smaller bedroom to sleep on a mattress on the floor.

Oddly enough this was Collin's first DUI even though he had been steadily drinking since age 16; so he benefited from a first offender's program requiring him to attend alcohol counseling with a licensed social worker. He controlled his drinking, imbibing only Thursday through Sunday, then Monday and Tuesday he'd dry out for his session on Wednesday, being afraid that they might have a test to be able to detect the alcohol.

During his final session Jesse lied for Collin, saying as little as possible, but still lending substance to the illusion that he had been sober for these last three months. Jesse did not like the complicit role she was forced to play, but she would not bite the hand that was presently feeding her. She would bide her time focusing on becoming a counselor. She realized after stepping out of the Social Worker's office that she could do that work!

Home life resumed its former routine. Collin drank anywhere from eight to a dozen beers daily. Jesse kept him fed, avoided quarrels, and concentrated on finishing graduate school. She would come home with stories about the prison and the inmates where she was doing her internship. Reluctantly he would listen, often shifting to hostility; so, after a while Jesse stopped sharing.

The Women's Prison

he graduated in July, and after months of preliminary background checks, health examinations, mandatory immunizations and urinalyses, Jesse was hired on Jules' birthday October 7th 1998 as a Forensic Social Worker for the women's prison in Jessup just twenty minutes from the house. She would be working in the same environment where she had done her internship giving Jesse a sense of continuity and familiarity. It was hard for her to believe how little anxiety she felt even though this would be her first post-graduate position. She was trained and ready to take on the task of teaching inmates how to make good decisions, how to build belief in themselves, and the other part of the job that she liked less, helping the pre-released inmate create a home plan so she could transition back into the community. Jesse agreed with Nathaniel Branden, the author of 40 books on self-esteem; healthy self-esteem is the foundation of a productive, happy life.

Jesse felt useful, challenged and respected in her paid position as a state Social Worker. The work wasn't routine or boring. Some days she would see inmates to help them with their requests, other days she would facilitate inmate groups, and correct their work. Then she got a call from the office telling her to report to another facility for a urine test. Jesse's heart revved up; she knew she could not pass it.

She had been smoking pot with Collin thinking the testing was finished.

She walked out of the prison, passing through the electric sliding fence to the parking lot. She started her car and headed to the nearest convenience store to buy and consume a gallon of orange juice. Then she parked at a nearby McDonald's and began gulping the juice alternately with a gallon of water. By the time she showed up for the test, the officers were wondering what happened to her.

"Ms. Bell, we were getting ready to call your office," the officer said with a smile as she opened the secured door to the urinalysis unit.

"I am so sorry," Jesse lied, "I misplaced my driver's license and figured you would need it, so I drove all the way home and found it," holding up the errant document with fake bravado.

"Oh, you didn't need it; we can use your DOC (Department of Corrections) badge."

For the next few weeks Jesse lived with the worry that she might be fired for burning the test. The notice never came. After that she always kept a bottle of synthetic urine with her in case she was called for a random test again.

The differences between Jesse and Collin intensified, culminating with Collin picking up a brass glass-topped table and hurling it at her. She threw up her hands trying to stop its trajectory. She suffered a small cut between her fingers during the skirmish that left blood everywhere. Shattered shards of glass covered the kitchen floor. It was obvious that Collin was a miserable soul. He was always talking about his parents and how much better life had been when he wasn't living and working in the city.

Fed-up, Jesse suggested that maybe he would be happier if he went home to the farm in Ohio where his aging mother and father lived. With her encouragement, Collin packed up his belongings onto a utility wagon chained to his Mustang, and left for Northern Ohio, gone within a month's time. Jesse was glad to see him leave for his hometown. But she was afraid for her security, not knowing if she would be able to cover her expenses now that she was alone. She certainly was past the age of taking her clothes off for money.

Jesse contacted the university rental office to post a house to share, hoping to find someone compatible. The first person was an Asian man in his twenties who didn't like that there was no dishwasher. The second was an Asian woman in her fifties who quietly agreed to the rent amount and brought her few possessions the next day. They steamed the carpet where Collin had slept. Jesse had no idea that urine had been soaking through the mattress to the floor while he was using that room.

Jesse observed that Yuriko was self-disciplined in every aspect of her life. She arose every morning at five to study, walked to the college, came home right after school, cooked a small meal, usually of tofu and vegetable soup, drew her bath promptly at nine 'clock to retire by nine thirty. On weekends she would go to the library to study. She was the perfect roommate.

Within the space of a few months, Jesse began to question if she had truly given the marriage a chance. Whether it was the apprehension of taking care of herself, or her feelings of bewilderment at the complexity of modern living, or simply co-dependent behavior, Jesse began to think that she should go up to the farm in Ohio to be with Collin. *She had never lived in that part of the country and it might be a good experience.* She had met Collin's family. They were about as corn bread and bible-belt as could be, although the tragedy of the youngest child's death, the dirt-bike accident that had snuffed out his life at age eleven, had dampened Mom and Dad Jones Christian fervor. Jules, who was living with his girlfriend a few miles north of Jesse, thought she was out of her mind to go back to Collin. Juanita, her friend across the street, was visibly angry with her. None of them figured out that her insecurities, those feelings of impotence and aloneness trumped her past negative experiences with Collin. At least she knew what she was getting into, she justified to herself. She lied to herself, *maybe he will change, maybe he will get better.*

Initially Yuriko was disappointed. She had hoped this situation would be stable until she graduated with her bachelor's degree. However, Jesse had made arrangements with her neighbor Juanita, to rent a room to her. This turned out to be a most fortuitous step, as the two of them became fast friends, and Yuriko benefited because Juanita was the ultimate cook and hostess.

The relationship between Jesse and her supervisor at the prison had degenerated. Ms. Norbuke was jealous of Jesse's ability to connect with her clients. In the short time since she had been hired Jesse had resurrected the re-entry program, the HIV positive pregnant mother's program, this was in addition to her other daily tasks. It did not stop Ms. Norbuke from nit-picking and criticizing her every move. It was the major reason Jesse wanted to run back to "papa" Collin on the farm in Ohio. Jesse did not have much experience dealing with neurotic people in a bureaucratic world.

She was right smack in the belly of the beast. The para-military prison system attracted a variety of self-righteous, power-abusing racists, to fill the roles of correctional officers, nurses, and administrators. In the past Jesse had often run away if things didn't suit her. It seemed like a good strategy now. All her justifications for leaving the prison and moving to Ohio shouted in her mind. She wanted a break from the non-stop pressure, knowing that if she went back with Collin, some of her material worries would be shared. She felt terribly drained. Although she and Collin had been separated for less than six months, Jesse was looking for an escape route from the daily nagging and chastisements she received from her supervisor. She thought, *Really, I came all this way, 2 degrees, a mountain of debt so that I can be abused by a supervisor who does not treat me with respect?* In the end, Jesse could not tolerate Ms. Norbuke's presence, and since they saw each other every day it was inevitable that Jesse would find a way to make a break!

As a licensed clinical social worker Jesse felt optimistic about looking for another position. It was a feeling she had never experienced before, certainly not as an exotic dancer. With her degrees and personality, she figured that wherever she traveled, there would always be openings for her. The field of social work was vast, from working with the homeless and drug addicted to facilitating children's adoptions and reuniting families or providing therapy. Most who graduated with a master's degree in Social Work wanted to be therapists. The field of psychotherapy was quickly being usurped by clinical social workers who could be employed for a fraction of the salary of a clinical psychologist. Jesse imagined herself with a case load of neurotic rich people who with her guidance would step back into their lives with a renewed sense of philanthropy, contentment and joy. She felt that with the obstacles she had conquered in her life, she could help just about anyone.

Jules and Andre filled the U-Haul truck and drove Jesse to the rural town of Wauseon, Ohio where the family farm was. Collin greeted Jesse with affection.

Feeling like she needed a job immediately, Jesse found out the meaning of rural American poverty. This area proved to be a challenge to her patience. The farm was quaint and the town, small. Jesse steadily submitted applications and went on interviews but did not land a job. In the meantime, she was living off of her credit cards, buying both groceries and gas for her and Collin. He had worked a few assembly-line jobs but didn't keep them. This was not Washington, D.C. with its high-paying forklift job Collin had left. Collin's parents let them live rent-free on the top floor of the barn. It had once housed thousands of chickens before being remodeled into two apartments, Mom and Pa lived in the ground floor apartment.

Jesse had squeezed her canopy bed up the narrow stairs to the attic level with its 3 bedrooms, and peaked ceiling. When she first arrived, Jesse flung herself at Collin trying to rekindle some of the romance of their earlier days.

Collin was on his best behavior for about a week and then he began pissing the bed, so Jesse moved upstairs permanently. Even so, Jesse and Collin got along remarkably well as long as she didn't expect too much. They spent many evenings camping out back amongst the seven acres of woods that were still standing in the middle of the planted fields all around. They built a bon fire of harvested dead trees, cranked up the boom box and drank beers. It was fun in a juvenile way. Then as she rode the tractor back to the barn house in the dark, she wondered what she had gotten herself into as Collin stayed back at the campsite passed out in his urine,

Jesse was truly thrilled when she finally got hired on as a MHP or mental health professional at the local hospital only 4 miles away. Traditionally the fifth floor of a hospital is dedicated to the psychiatric ward. Fulton County had an excellent reputation for patient care, and adequate funding that supported a high ratio of staff per patients. She had not worked in a hospital before, so her unease kept her pulse racing, but she was a fast learner and determined to generate money.

At times during the first months, Jesse felt like she was outside of herself going through the motions of becoming proficient, watching herself become one of the mental health team. In this treatment milieu, nurses, social workers, doctors, and secretaries all worked together to provide the needed support for the mentally ill, and emotionally unstable who checked into the 'stress unit' daily. It was in this completely supportive environment that Jesse's confidence as a mental health clinician and her skills expanded. Soon she was running groups, assessing emergency room intakes, and being given praises for her insight and hard work. She even got invited to a local karaoke bar with *the team* and wowed everyone with her dancing. The camaraderie touched Jesse; she felt appreciated. Some of the old psychic wounds were starting to flesh in. But the good feelings disappeared when Jesse mounted the stairs to the barn apartment. There was little joy once she crossed the threshold.

She chastised herself regularly, *how could I have thought that living with him would be alright with me?* Quickly Jesse's hope for a financial surge was extinguished as she realized that although she had been hired full time, when the patient count went down, the manager called-off her staff, as required. Jesse rarely got a full week on her paychecks.

Nine Eleven

esse was in bed sleeping when the telephone rang. It was Collin's mom saying that New York had been hit, that the twin towers were in flames. Collin and Jesse watched the TV screen repeat the footage over and over. From the first viewing, it was apparent that something wasn't right. The way those two buildings fell straight down looked like a controlled demolition, even to the untrained eye. Like those buildings, the relationship between Collin and Jesse imploded with nothing of essence to sustain it.

Six months later Jules loaded his mom's possessions, yet another time, onto a box truck, and drove her back to the metropolitan area. She had been away from her son a total of two years, enough time to appreciate and want to return to the security of being around people who loved her. During that time Jules had established a blossoming relationship with the woman he would marry.

-stern Panhandle

n West Virginia, it took four months for Jesse to find employment. She was hired part-time as a general practitioner psychotherapist at a community mental health clinic. She also picked up twenty hours at the health department in the neighboring state of Maryland as a counselor for inmates at the county detention center. Initially Jesse was hired to do HIV prevention counseling but during sessions it often expanded to general counseling with psycho-social issues pushed to the forefront. In most socio-economically deprived populations, access to help in any form is limited or non-existent. She could feel and understand their need, so overwhelming was the neglect.

The target groups that Jesse worked with were men and women being detained with eighteen months or less on their sentences. She facilitated groups on both the men and women's sides of the jail in addition to providing individual therapy for referred inmates.

In the community, she ran HIV related groups in a room at the health department; the HIV Positive mothers' group had 7 members. She made house calls for follow-up support when deemed necessary. She liked the work. Counseling was a venue in which she could use all of herself, her strange and exotic history, her extensive knowledge of books on metaphysics, and science fiction, and her dichotomous personality, secretively deep and recklessly spontaneous. Her clients liked her, and she began to get a reputation; in jail, word of mouth is highly efficient. Jesse could easily banter with the white, neo-Klan-like officers, turn around and spend forty minutes in a tiny room with a killer, pedophile, drug-dealer, or any variety of sociopathic, yet pathetic emotionally damaged, half-functioning boys-in-men's bodies. These were the cases either waiting for their arraignments and trials or sentenced with eighteen months or less. Her fascination with the lives of her clients never wavered. She listened rapt as suffering humans lined up to tell their stories to Jesse. With each one she saw how the experiences of being abandoned, beaten physically, and terrified psychologically had mutated perfectly ordinary children into confused, fearful, desperate, numb, incommunicative, dangerous, aggressive adults.

One day Jesse's supervisor, Kate, called her into her office.

"Jesse, we've got some money from a grant to offer an esteem building, educational program to the inmates at the detention center; you'd have to go to Baltimore for training. Are you interested?

"Sure; I always like to add to my skills. Kate, don't you think that it's a better use of a Social Worker's time to facilitate groups of people rather than only providing individual therapy?"

"Absolutely, and I'm so happy that you've decided to take on this program!" Kate was ebullient.

Jesse knew that she was making her supervisor and the Health Department look good. She was the worker bee, and she relished the busyness. Finally, she was being challenged, and she arose with a daily renewed sense of

456

purpose, confidence, and resolve to master this new life of hers.

Kate liked Jesse's fearless attitude; she didn't hesitate, she was hungry. Intuitively Jesse knew that a key to her success would be getting as much training as was available and gaining as many diverse experiences in the field of therapy as her employer offered.

The trip to downtown Baltimore would take over an hour. Crawling into the landscape of industrialized America was not her favorite activity; nevertheless, traffic was light and the trip without incident.

After two days of intensive training, Jesse was then expected to head back to her site, the county detention center, screen for appropriate candidates for the group, and have them meet once a week for four months. Jesse laughed to herself, and later explained to Kate, "Whoever designed this program never stepped foot in a jail; there is no way a fifteen-member group is going to stay together for four months in a detention center."

It was true; the detention center was often just a way station for transport to somewhere else. With the limitations in mind Jesse set forth to adapt the program to fit the jail's specific regulations. The agenda included instruction about the great African Goddess Ma'hat, and the fifty directives that formed the moral foundation of the teachings. The matriarchal religion pre-dates most other religions and flourished on the African continent before the appearance of other civilizations. By giving this new perspective to African American inmates it was anticipated by studies done that the program would increase their sense of self-esteem and understanding of basic moral laws.

Designed by the presenter, a well-respected African American professor, he let it slip during the workshop that his daughter's education was going to cost $75,000, but that luckily his fee for designing the program would cover it.

Part of the program introduced African American heroes to the group members. Jesse researched online and printed out short biographies of outstanding Black Americans. Group members were asked to present or read what they had learned about these outstanding Americans. The token white men, those willing to participate, learned about African Americans who had contributed to society too. It was instructive and enlightening for Jesse as well as the men in her group. It dawned on her that her own white middle-class education had not given her an accurate picture of U.S. history. She was learning along with these felons that many modern conveniences that we enjoy and depend upon were invented by African American men; mobile refrigeration for the transportation of perishables, and the movie ticket taker to name two. She saw plainly how history reflects the values of the dominant class, and how those in powerful positions are able to obscure facts and manipulate details for their own purposes; whether to pay tribute and adulate the accomplishments of the 'in-group', the results is always a distortion of the truth.

Her second job as a therapist with the community mental health clinic was a position, she always imagined she would want. As a general practitioner she was required to treat everyone who walked in the door regardless of their problem, diagnosis, or severity. From depression and suicide to personality disorders and addictions, young or old, Jesse did therapy. Of course, she could get supervision, if for any reason she did not feel confident.

Jesse found out that people want to feel better and *get well*, but they are mostly unwilling to change anything to actualize a remedy, not thoughts nor behaviors. Her supervisor said she was experiencing countertransference, an emotional reaction to a client is said to indicate a non-therapeutic attachment. She silently argued that any human would feel frustrated when throwing a drowning-person a lifejacket, and repeatedly watch as the swimmer refuses to take it. Clearly, being a therapist was not as luxurious a career as Hollywood portrayed it. However, she did not lose her fascination and continued refining her counseling abilities with each new person she encountered, each passing year.

Bouncing back and forth between her two part-time positions still did not generate enough money for Jesse to cover all her bills and living expenses. When she was stuck in Ohio without a job, she had begun the unhealthy habit of using a credit card, and now even though she was employed she was still charging gas, food, and her car insurance. Somehow, she continued to believe that as long as she kept plugging away and working hard eventually, she would land a position that would catapult her into the elusive middle class.

She felt encouraged when Dee called, a friend she had met at her first job out of grad school where they were co-facilitating a juvenile sexual offender's group. She was talking about opening a mental health clinic near Washington, D.C. and wanted to use Jesse as a sounding board for her ideas about the direction she wanted to go.

They spoke for a few months and then Jesse didn't hear from her again.

Out-of-the-blue a call came. Dee had recently hired and fired a program manager; it sounded like they were incompatible. Then Dee offered Jesse the position; it paid $50,000. The color of money exploded in Jesse's mind; she thought such an annual figure would solve all her problems. She really wanted the job, but there were a couple of obstacles. First, the clinic was two hours away. Jesse would have to find a place to live close to the clinic, and commute home on weekends. Second, she needed to resign from her two part-time positions.

After calling every possible lead on rooms to rent, her long-time buddy Chaz, a photographer whose specialty was exotic dancers, said, "Why didn't you ask me, I've got an empty room, and I could use some help with a few things around my apartment."

Jesse thanked him profusely and planned to go south to check out the room Chaz was offering rent-free.

She had not seen the rotund free-lancer in a few years. His health had deteriorated from the ravages of diabetes and self-neglect. Jesse entered his apartment and saw him sprawled across a bed he had set up in the living room, complete with chips, telephone, and the remote control. He existed there in his video dominated world occasionally interrupted by food deliveries. With his legs and feet constantly inflamed and in pain, he could not walk far. He wanted Jesse to simply run a few errands for him, pick-up his meds, and empty the trash once a week. There was no discussion of her cooking for him. Chaz's apartment was crawling with cockroaches. Jesse surveyed the empty room.

It needed to be torched, but she would settle for two coats of paint to cover the excretion of the hundreds of roaches that lived under a picture frame so old that it was stuck to the wall. After she described the mess to Jules, he volunteered to do the labor to get the room ready for human habitation.

The situation wasn't perfect, but Jesse's philosophy was *I can tolerate just about anything for a short amount of time*. She told herself, it would not be forever, and she eased her discomfort by focusing on the help she would be providing for her friend. To further complicate the situation, Chaz's eighty-six-year-old father, like a ghost, was living in the adjacent bedroom. Fortunately, the cockroaches colonized in his room instead of hers because of the abundance of leftovers in the trashcan next to the lazy boy chair in which he lived. Regardless, Jesse felt like a miracle had been bestowed on her, a free place to live while she worked in the city, and a chance to move up the income ladder.

Jesse genuinely liked Dee: she thought they would make a great team and looked forward to learning everything about the mental health business from her. Observing them talk, one could see that they shared a strong spiritual bond and respected each other.

It was exactly a month from the time Jesse accepted the position until her first day of work. It took two weekends to scrub and paint. She was so grossed out by the vermin that she even painted the inside of the closet figuring that just the paint odor would be a deterrent. Her professional wardrobe was growing. It was inconvenient to haul her clothes back and forth a hundred miles so she would take a week's worth and reluctantly hang them in the closet. She certainly did not want any cockroaches hitching a ride back home. Chaz owned a fairly new futon and mattress for her to use. She wondered how long it would take her to adjust and actually get a full night's sleep.

Then there was Chaz's kitchen, the vilest galley of the imagination, with roaches living in every crack, nesting in the folds of the broken seal of the refrigerator door and jumping or falling as she opened creaking cupboard doors caked with black excretion. Jesse watched a mouse run the edge of the room, obviously visiting the overflowing trash bin that sat in a corner.

It was heartbreaking when Jesse saw what Chaz had become. He lay like a beached whale, nearly non-ambulatory, day after day, unable to change his situation or the gradual decline of his health. For the months that she and Chaz had talked on the phone, the conversation often revolved around his diabetes and various physical ailments that no doubt resulted from his obesity, and sedentary lifestyle. But all that time she never knew to what degree his body had degenerated until the day she knocked on his door and saw with her eyes.

More than once during her stay she had played out the scenario of her opening the door with the key and finding him dead, although it was not something she dwelled upon. So, with courage and commitment Jesse invested in her goal to become the best program director she could be.

She arrived early for the first day of work, and Dee showed her around the neighborhood (good places to eat lunch), set up her internet account, and continued talking non-stop about the business and her plans. However, the clinic was not open yet and had no clients.

The second week Dee and Jesse kept an appointment with a realtor who showed them a bigger more expensive office space. In its present condition, it would have been a major expense to remodel. Jesse went along and offered her smile and support as Dee did the negotiating.

The third week Jesse traveled to Washington, D.C. to attend seminars on how to apply for the Federal funding most social service agencies depend upon. Some of the application packets were as thick as a phone book. She felt like she was in over her head. Jesse hoped that Dee was not expecting her to suddenly become an expert at procuring grants.

During the fourth week Katrina hit New Orleans, and both Dee and Jesse watched with disbelief at the destruction, and lack of government funding for emergency personnel and services.

Jesse was being paid every two weeks; near the end of the sixth week, the day before payday, Dee looked at Jesse and said, "I don't know how to tell you this, but I don't have the money to pay you."

"You don't have any of it?" Jesse asked with masked hysteria as she felt her stomach turn, her heart pump erratically, and the blood surge to her face.

Gloomily, Dee answered, "I don't know, I'll have to see but I don't think so. I'm really sorry, I feel bad. At least you will qualify for unemployment because you are being laid off. I was really counting on this guy I hired to get us funded."

She was referring to a professional proposal writer to whom she had given $800. Jesse was used to detours and disappointment. It was times like this that her years of practicing non-attachment paid off. It gave her immunity against what would have devastated most others. She knew that getting emotional and upset would not help in any way; it was wasted energy. Instead, she focused on her breathing, located her tote-bag, gave Dee a hug, and left the building.

Chaz was sympathetic. "That woman's insane; I can't believe she did this to you."

Not wanting to play the 'blame game', Jesse changed the subject.

"I'm really sorry I won't be around to help you."

"Well, you couldn't help it. I have felt less stressed out since you've been here. I'm always worried something might happen to me that I can't handle, and then what would happen to my Dad?"

"Talk to social services. You and your dad should be able to get some help."

Jesse cleared out the closet, stripped the futon of the newly purchased bedding, packed her car and said goodbye. The Fates had literally catapulted Jesse out of the situation she had tried to create.

Driving the Capital beltway north toward Jesse's home in West Virginia, she was overcome with relief, broke but glad to be out of the snake pit. Of course, now Jesse was unemployed again. As a dancer, she had rarely experienced the feeling of complete financial helplessness. She could always find another stage to dance upon, another dancer to sell a costume to. Yet now that she had attained her dream of being a college graduate, her ability to generate money still had not improved as promised by the promoters of higher education. She still felt scared. *At least, she mused to herself, I have, not one degree but two; I am well prepared to find a position.*

Within fifteen miles of Jesse's house was a state prison complex with three facilities. She knew that her previous prison work experience would make her an excellent candidate for a state social work position. Maybe then she would finally be able to make a living-wage, an income that respected the life-long effort to get here. It was an extra bonus to get paid for doing work that was meaningful. It's really all she had ever wanted.

There was more than one social work position available in the prison complex. She began by talking to Ann who was the regional supervisor for all three prisons. They established a rapport almost immediately when Jesse quipped during their phone conversation, "I really miss doing groups."

Ann responded, "Good. Have I got groups for you!"

Jesse knew that her own enthusiasm and commitment largely depended upon her supervisor. No one wants to work under a tyrant. It looked like a fit! The process of being accepted into the state employment and prison system would be a long-drawn-out affair. Jesse knew it would test her patience, but having endured a shortage of funds, she saw the prison position as her salvation, her ticket. She was steadfast. First the three-person panel interview, then the extensive background check including fingerprinting, and a session with an intelligence gathering officer for in-depth questioning, and afterwards the wait. It could take up to four months. Ann assured Jesse that she had the job, and for her to be patient until the state, notoriously slow, had processed all the paperwork.

The entire time she was applying, she did not worry about the prospect of being on the inside of a prison among felons again, this time with a male population. She knew she could relate to the inmates having spent enough years living *close* to the streets. Additionally, she was totally comfortable among men, among predators. The years working in the bars and clubs had served and educated her well. Jesse was not intimidated by those who would be her clients. It helped that she had already been a counselor at the men's county detention center.

What elated Jesse the most was, that her profession took her behind the walls doing something that only a fraction of the population could or would consider. Oddly, it was similar to being a topless dancer; her clients were still a bunch of lonely, desperate, confused men, only now she could keep her clothes on, and use what was between her ears to assist them.

When it finally arrived, Jesse ripped open the letter. There it was in black and white; she was being offered the state position starting at $48,000 a year. Now the work began. The learning curve was hard and steep, but nothing graduate school had not prepared her for.

Her training began with the mandatory correctional academy. It was a ten-week course designed for correctional officers, a Para-military school where punctuality and compliance to the rules were strictly enforced. Teamwork was encouraged, the beginning of the camaraderie needed to stay alive. Since the social workers would not be directly involved in physical custody of the inmates, two weeks were shaved off. Jesse did not have to run through the teargas trailer, nor learn how to shackle and transport a prisoner.

She received her completion certificate in the mail because she did not want to drive one more time to the academy. Now she had the rudimentary training to be a forensic social worker in a prison. She was one more step enmeshed in the bureaucratic labyrinth. Her education had given her the mental health training, but school simply gives a person a general education, the real training begins on-site.

The first day that she walked through the metal detectors and placed her transparent plastic purse on the conveyor belt so that it could be x-rayed, she immediately discovered which of her high-heeled shoes had steal shanks supporting the arches as the lights lit up on the monitor. It quickly became her practice to step out of her shoes so that no delay occurred since there was usually a line of employees at the beginning and end of each shift. Ann greeted her at the entrance. She was there to train Jesse for a few days until she was oriented; the gray walls, electric doors, and razor wire topped fences could be intimidating. Jesse would be walking among killers, pedophiles, and the mentally ill, along with less lethal types such as thieves, drug dealers, and scam artists trying to make a quick buck. While working with these men, Jesse began to accumulate a catalogue of stories, and case histories of the inmates she served.

For years, she had felt like her struggle with the physical and emotional abuse at the hand of her mother, the abandonment by her biological father, and the sexual abuse by his substitute, had handicapped her. She thought her suffering had fundamentally ruined her chances for a happy and successful life, maimed and robbed... until she began hearing her clients' stories.

With each horrific tale, Jesse came to understand that on the scale of abuse, what she had suffered was minimal. She began to see how her inability to get past the pain had inadvertently perpetuated it and commanded her in self-destructive patterns. She taught inmates the only thing we can control is our response to life's events, the internal world of our own emotions and belief systems: that we are as limited or free according to our awareness. We are the architects of our lives, the authors of our own books. We decide what the plot will be, and who will be the main characters between the front and back covers of our lives?

Jesse worked to integrate the principles into her own life. She refined her skills. She walked the talk and learned how to be discerning without being judgmental, for she had traveled some of the same streets as these men labeled inmates. Against odds, Jesse had escaped the destiny of the prisoners she instructed. She walked among them as a teacher, and more importantly, as a learner. With each psycho-educational group she facilitated, her appreciation grew for the tenacity of humans in their endeavors to find happiness and construct fruitful lives.

Carol Lynn Jones, MSW

The End

Afterword

first thought about writing this book because of the crazy circumstances I found myself in. No one will ever believe the stuff I have been through; I must write it down.   Later, when I saw from my family tree the names and dates of my Native American ancestors, I thought, wouldn't it be cool if one of my great-great-great grand-parents had left some record of their lives? It was then that I became more determined to tell my story, just to leave a document of my accounting of the more dramatic days of my life.

In a not so user-friendly economy, my pursuit of a stable income distracted me from writing. I found it exceedingly difficult to sustain a writing schedule or to even imagine the materialization of this book knowing how competitive the book industry is. However, with the advent of self-publishing I found the needed motivation to finish this project which started so many years ago.

Everyone has a distinctive story to tell, moments like photographs, events that will never happen again, unique and personal, yet often so universal that all can relate. To tell one's story is to join a long human tradition of passing experiences from one generation to another through story telling. I encourage everyone with the notion to record your experience or your family's, to do it!

Carol Lynn Jones, 2020

About the Author

arol Lynn Jones is the author of *Dancing On The Ledge*. She graduated from the University of Maryland University College with a bachelor's degree in Psychology, and then earned a master's degree in Social Work from the University of Maryland in Baltimore.

After being credentialed as a licensed clinical social worker she worked in a variety of mental health settings, including the Health Department, the Community Mental Health Clinic, the psychiatric floor of a hospital, mobile treatment and in-home counseling for adults and children, the County Detention Center, and two State Correctional facilities.

Before finishing her formal education, Ms. Jones worked 26 years as an exotic dancer performing in clubs around the United States.

She is retired from the Maryland State Correctional system. Ms. Jones continues to offer counseling services and has taught yoga for the local community college. She resides in the West Virginia Panhandle with her married son, his wife and child, and their 3 cats, Foxy, Azula, and Ying.